STANFIELDS' CALIFORNIA

MINING

SIERRA NEVADA

STANHOPE
+
BANK   CANNERY

DEHYDRATOR

CATTLE

CENTRAL VALLEY

+ TUMBLEWEED

OIL

COAST RANGE

LOS ANGELES

Stanfield Harvest

Stanfield Harvest

Richard Martin Stern

WORLD PUBLISHING
TIMES MIRROR
NEW YORK

PUBLISHED BY THE WORLD PUBLISHING COMPANY
PUBLISHED SIMULTANEOUSLY IN CANADA
BY NELSON, FOSTER & SCOTT LTD.
SECOND PRINTING—1972
COPYRIGHT © 1972 BY RICHARD MARTIN STERN
ALL RIGHTS RESERVED
ISBN 0-529-04518-4
LIBRARY OF CONGRESS CATALOG CARD NUMBER: 74-178815
PRINTED IN THE UNITED STATES OF AMERICA
DESIGNED BY JACQUES CHAZAUD

WORLD PUBLISHING
TIMES MIRROR

For D.A.S. with love

Meyer

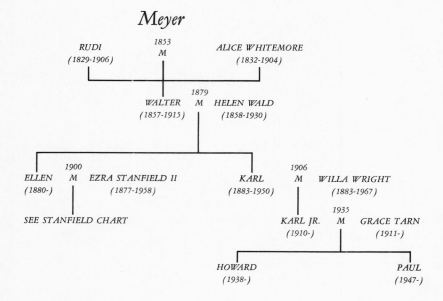

RUDI   1853   ALICE WHITEMORE
(1829-1906)   M   (1832-1904)

WALTER   1879   HELEN WALD
(1857-1915)   M   (1858-1930)

ELLEN   1900   EZRA STANFIELD II   KARL   1906   WILLA WRIGHT
(1880-)   M   (1877-1958)   (1883-1950)   M   (1883-1967)

SEE STANFIELD CHART   KARL JR.   1935   GRACE TARN
                                    (1910-)   M   (1911-)

HOWARD   PAUL
(1938-)   (1947-)

Stanfield

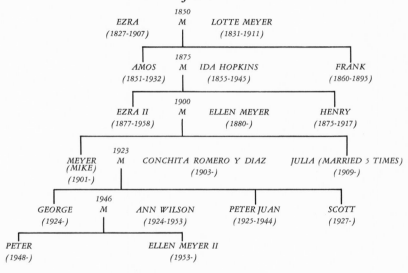

EZRA 1850 M LOTTE MEYER
(1827-1907) (1831-1911)

AMOS 1875 M IDA HOPKINS FRANK
(1851-1932) (1855-1945) (1860-1895)

EZRA II 1900 M ELLEN MEYER HENRY
(1877-1958) (1880-) (1875-1917)

MEYER 1923 M CONCHITA ROMERO Y DIAZ JULIA (MARRIED 5 TIMES)
(MIKE) (1903-) (1909-)
(1901-)

GEORGE 1946 M ANN WILSON PETER JUAN SCOTT
(1924-) (1924-1953) (1925-1944) (1927-)

PETER ELLEN MEYER II
(1948-) (1953-)

Prologue

They were only two in the warm summer evening, and they came by stealth—up from the road beside the sluggish river, through the shadows of the nearby warehouses, into the dehydrator plant itself.

On the dehydrator platform, at the drying tunnel entrances and exits, and in the lofty gloom of the packing shed, night-lights burned, and the odor of dried and drying fruit hung in the air. Beneath each of the eight drying tunnels a twenty-foot gas flame burned with a hollow roar, and in rhythmic accompaniment there was the steady slap-slap of the belts that drove blower fans to spread the heat evenly.

There were only two in the night crew.

The tunnel man sat in the packing shed on two overturned lugboxes with a cup of coffee from his thermos. The long steel hook he used for maneuvering tray-stacked cars into and out of the tunnels lay on the floor beside him. He had checked his temperatures and marked them down only minutes before: all tunnels safely within two degrees of 135. His next pull—one loaded car out of each tunnel, another one in

1

—was not due for an hour. Until then there was nothing to do.

On the platform, the night clean-up man had piled lug-boxes of peach pits five high and gone to get his grab truck to wheel the stack off to the far corner of the platform where the fruit gnats that would swarm before morning would be no more of a nuisance than they had to be.

The younger of the two invaders stopped in deep shadow and indicated that the other was to remain there. Then he launched his reconnaissance and returned in only a few moments, satisfied. He pointed to the packing shed and the platform and held up two fingers. The other man nodded and went on his way.

He was swift and merciless and he used what came to hand—the tunnel man's steel hook. He left the tunnel man slumped face down on the cement floor in a pool of spilled blood and coffee. It is doubtful if the tunnel man ever knew what had struck him.

The night clean-up man, balancing his loaded grab truck, heard a sound and turned his head in time to take a glancing blow over one ear; it was of sufficient force to knock him senseless, and he dropped to the platform in a mess of peach pits.

The younger invader was already at his business, walking quickly along the tunnel heads, throwing the toggle switches that shut down the blowers. The steady slap-slap rhythm died, and only the hollow roar of the flames was left. He waited for his companion, and together they went back the way they had come, through the deep shadows of the warehouses, down to the road beside the sluggish river. The younger man spoke in Spanish, "That will show the sons of whores."

The older man said nothing.

Within the tunnels, with no blower fans to spread the heat, the temperatures began to rise, slowly at first, and then with quickening pace. The wooden trays on the steel cars began to char, and the golden peach halves on the trays blackened and curled and gave off a heavy caramel stench.

In one of the tunnels a flame sprang up. It spread from car to car, tray to tray, gathering force and fury sufficient to

2

reach the tunnel ceiling and transmit heat to the supporting beams which finally buckled and collapsed.

The fire was free then to leap almost joyously into the packing shed where bundles of box-shook, stacks of empty boxes, and piled boxes of curing fruit provided new fuel.

And the gas flames burned on.

Against the black sky the flames were soon visible well into the center of the city of Stanhope.

By then, the two men were long gone.

1

Fire engines arrived first, but not by much, and began pumping their torrents of water. Men's shadows cavorted grotesquely against the flames, and a voice through a bullhorn shouted, "Get that goddam gas shut down!"

Cars arrived and spilled out spectators who jostled and shoved in carnival mood and got in the firemen's way.

A police car arrived, cherry top flashing and siren blasting a path; close behind came an ambulance.

Reluctantly the crowd made way for one stretcher, then a second. The first returned to the ambulance covered with a blanket, the second came back empty.

"One stiff," the ambulance driver said to no one in particular, "and one guy walking around holding his head and talking to himself; cold-cocked is all." He slammed the rear door of the ambulance with unnecessary violence.

There is drama to a fire, but here there was something else, too—a sense of waiting, as in a theater when the curtain has gone up and the play begun but the leading characters have not yet come on stage. Then, at last, they did, and the crowd watched.

It was a bone-white Mercedes 280SL sports coupe, top down. There were two men in it, and neither made a move to get out. The fire chief, bullhorn dangling from his fist, walked over to the car. He spoke to both men, but his eyes were on the older, in the off seat. "We'll find out more when we can get in," he said, "maybe tomorrow after it's cooled down a bit." He paused. "But your tunnel man's dead, Mr. Stanfield, and the clean-up man hasn't any idea what hit him. It looks like the blowers were shut down, and the gas flames were still burning."

Scott Stanfield, the man behind the wheel, said, "Short circuit shutting off the blowers?"

Beside him, his brother George said only, "No." A big man, tall, wide, solid. "The Clydesdale type," Scott had said of him once. "Get yourself two pairs of matched Georges and you've got the ideal team for a London brewery wagon."

The fire chief said, "The insurance people will send somebody to take a look. We'll do all we can, Mr. Stanfield."

A man in civilian clothes came up. He nodded to the fire chief. To the man on the far side of the car, he said, "Ben Walling, Mr. Stanfield. Maybe you remember me. I'm police chief."

"A dead man," George said.

"Yes, sir." Walling had the air of a determined man doing a job for which he had little taste. "I don't like it, Mr. Stanfield, and if that sounds funny, maybe it is. What I mean is, this isn't the first thing happening. We've got Joe Hanson under psychiatric observation . . ."

Scott Stanfield looked at his brother.

"He tried to shoot me," George said. "He missed." Then, "Go on, Chief."

"Now," Walling said, "I've got a body on my hands and somebody walking around who ought to have a murder charge pinned on him."

"Are you trying to blame us?" This was Scott. Closing ranks, he thought, and how ridiculous could he be? But there it was.

5

"No, sir." Walling shook his head. "The last thing I want is any kind of hassle with you, because no matter how it came out, I'd end up with my tit in a wringer." Pause. "But you're here in Stanhope, Mr. Stanfield, when you aren't here all that often, and your father's flying in from Washington tomorrow I hear on the radio, and you've got labor problems with your grapes, and Joe Hanson problems over water; now somebody burns down your dehydrator and kills your tunnel man." He paused again, for breath this time. George Stanfield had not moved. "If you're fighting some kind of undercover war, Mr. Stanfield," Walling said, "why, I want to know about it, because it's my business to handle it, not yours." For the third time he paused. "Okay?"

George nodded briefly. "I'll keep it in mind." Then, to Scott, "Let's go." The Mercedes worked its way through the watching crowd.

* * *

They were three years apart in age and worlds apart in thought and temperament. "I'm the bystander," Scott, the younger at forty-three, had said once, "the observer." Tennis player, professor of history, good liver on almost unlimited funds. "You're the mover."

And George in one of his rare moments of humor had said, "And usually moving in the wrong direction, isn't that what you mean?"

True enough.

Now, driving away from the flames and the crowd and a dead man lying on a covered stretcher in an ambulance, *"Are we fighting an undercover war?"* Scott said. "Is that why you're here in Stanhope?"

"Why are *you* here instead of in Berkeley?" It was difficult to shake George's massive calm.

Scott nodded. Fair enough. "Because our dear mother called me from Washington and asked me to come down—reason one. Reason two—simple decency. The *abuela* is on her way out and the clan gathers."

"Some of it," George said. He was looking straight ahead. "Turn left here." Pause. "Those are your only reasons for coming?"

6

Old George was ponderous, Scott thought, but he was not stupid. And buried somewhere in that massive carcass was an almost feminine sensitivity to mood. "Since you ask, no," Scott said. He was smiling now. "I'm being blackmailed." Without looking he was aware that George had turned to study him, and he was rather pleased. Brownie points for catching old George off-balance. "There is a big-breasted, fat-thighed chick of a graduate student who fancies that I'm the man who knocked her up."

George was looking straight ahead again. "Are you?"

"Maybe."

"And what are you going to do about it?"

"The chick," Scott said, "is determined to have the baby. And she is determined that it will have a name. And she thinks the name is going to be Stanfield." He paused. "It isn't. End of matter." Not quite, he had to admit, or he would still have been in Berkeley where he preferred to be, rather than down here on home territory, in a sense wrapping family security around him. But in due time he would go back and attend to Cathy Strong. "Now," he said, "what's this about Joe Hanson trying to shoot you? Off his rocker?"

George thought about it. "More or less," he said. "some of his wells have gone dry. He thinks our deep wells are the reason."

"Are they?"

"Maybe." Pause. "Turn right here."

Shanty town—one-story buildings, shacks for the most part, wood long unpainted, flaking stucco, corrugated roofs, here and there a garish blue or pink door or window frame, dirt yards, broken fences, scrawled names on walls, graffiti. Stores bore signs in a mixture of Spanish and English: Johnny's Cash and Carry Tienda; La Bodega Bar; Zapatería—Half Soles a Specialty.

During the day it had been hot, air rising shimmering from sidewalk and street. During the day sensible folk who could stayed inside, behind drawn curtains, fans running. Now, in the not uncomfortable warmth of the evening, there were people on the sidewalks. They turned to stare at the white sports car.

A ball rolled into the street, and Scott braked the car

swiftly, smoothly, those tennis reflexes still sound. A small boy came running after the ball, scooped it up and ran back to the sidewalk. People watched the car resume cruising speed. "That," Scott said, "is just what we need—a manslaughter charge for running down a chicano kid." He glanced at George's face. "There's trouble, and you don't think Cleary Ward can handle it, so the chairman of the board drops everything and runs down to home base . . ."

"Slow down," George said. "We turn in here. I want to see Ruben Lucero."

It was beyond the last of the shacks and small stores. Two rows of tall eucalyptus trees marked the road boundaries, and a dirt drive led through a wire fence past a house set well back from the road to a smaller house almost covered by untrimmed vines. "Stop here," George said. He got out and was surprised to find his brother at his shoulder. "You don't have to come."

"Wouldn't miss it for the world. Does he doff his hat to you?"

A single hanging bulb lighted the way to the small house at the rear. Two men blocked the steps—one carried a worn potting spade, the other an axe handle. George said in Spanish, "I wish to speak with Ruben Lucero. My name is Stanfield."

"It is well known." The man with the axe handle spat in the dirt. "But maybe Ruben Lucero does not wish to speak with you."

"Ask him."

"There is no need." Ruben Lucero was standing in the open doorway, a middle-sized man in his early forties in khaki trousers and shirt and work shoes, his dark skin deeply tanned, dark eyes, black hair with no trace of gray, large hands. "Come in, Misters Stanfield."

The small front room of the house was fitted up as an office with rolltop desk, swivel chair, a broken-down plush covered sofa, and against the wall a row of unpainted kitchen chairs. "Sit down," Lucero said, and closed the door.

George remained standing, square and solid. Scott leaned against the wall to watch. "The Stanfield dehydrator is burning," George said. "You have heard?"

"I have heard, and I am sorry." Lucero's voice was deep, vibrant.

"And a man is dead, murdered, did you hear that, too?"

"No, señor." In surprise Lucero slipped into Spanish. "That I did not know." He shook his head sadly. "A man of yours, señor?"

"The man who guards the tunnels at night." George also spoke in Spanish. "His head was broken by a blow. The other man who sweeps and cleans the platform was also beaten unconscious. The blower fans were turned off. The heat rose in the tunnels until the fire began." He was silent.

Old George, Scott had to admit, was impressive.

Lucero said slowly, carefully, in English again, "You believe that I cause this thing?" He shook his head. "I do not. These are not the kind of thing I want." He walked over to his desk chair and sat down heavily. He looked up at George. *"La huelga,* the strike, yes. For higher pay, for better work conditions in the fields, yes. But no violence. Violence bring violence. I know."

George was silent, unmoving.

"When a man," Lucero said as if he had said it before, always with conviction, "can have no pride because he live like an animal and he look at his wife and children and they are animal too, and all he know is to work with his hands, pick grape, pick lettuce, pick tomato, peach, melon, that is all he know to do, and the money is not enough, and the place he work, the place he live is worse, far worse, than the place they keep the pigs on one of your Stanfield farms . . ." He paused and spread his big hands. "If this is his life, without pride, then all he has is anger, and he want to hurt, to burn, to destroy, even to kill. I know." He paused again. "But that is not the way. No matter who say different, that is not the way. It is not our way. You must believe this, Mister Stanfield."

"Maybe you had nothing to do with it directly," George said, "but what about your people? That man outside with the axe handle? The spade?"

Lucero stood up slowly. "They believe I am in danger," he said. He shrugged. "Maybe. Mr. Henry Potter, Mr. Luke Albright, they make the threat. Mr. Joe Hanson, too—he is now in jail." He shrugged again. "Maybe I will go to jail too?

It has happen before." He shook his head, dismissing the thought. "Mr. Stanfield, what I want is contract with you, not violence. I want to negotiate, not have people hurt, killed. Believe me, Mr. Stanfield."

George took his time. From his greater height, his massive bulk, he looked down on Lucero. He said at last, "Maybe." He turned away. Scott followed.

At the foot of the porch steps the man with the axe handle stood squarely in the path. George walked toward him. The man raised the axe handle as in threat. George shook his head gently. "No," he said, and that was all. He walked past, Scott following. The man made no move.

Scott backed the Mercedes out of the drive. "We'll skip town," he said. "I don't enjoy feeling like a Nazi general driving through occupied territory. Do you believe Lucero?"

"What I believe doesn't matter. Somebody did it."

Between the rows of tall eucalyptus the road was straight in their headlights. "It doesn't get to you ever, does it?" Scott said.

George shook his head in denial. "Sometimes."

"When I come down from my ivory tower in Berkeley and tell you that history is against us and others like us, is that what you mean?"

"Something like that."

"A good share of what we have, we stole."

"I've heard that before."

"It's true."

"Maybe it's true," George said. There was still no heat in his voice. "And maybe it isn't. But whether it is or not isn't pertinent today. What would you have us—me—do? Give it all back? To whom? Land to, say, some Anglo like ourselves who took it from a Californian, whose ancestors took it from the Indians, because the king of Spain, who didn't own it, said they could have it in the first place? Does that make sense? Give back the oil properties to the descendants of some poor fool of a wheat farmer who worked himself so deep into debt that great-grandfather Amos Stanfield decided to cut his losses and foreclose? Amos didn't even want the land, he wanted his money, and he'd have turned right around and sold the land if he could have found a buyer. Instead . . ."

"Instead, while he still owned it," Scott said, "they struck oil." He nodded. "In a gruesome sort of way, you may have a point. You——" He was watching the rearview mirror. "Somebody," he said, "is in a big hurry." Headlights were coming up fast behind them, swinging into the left-hand lane to pass.

"Kids," George said. "We used to call it hot rodding." He glanced over at the car which was abreast of them now. Faintly he could make out a single figure hunched over the wheel.

Scott said, "Jesus!" The other car had swerved suddenly toward them. "You damn fool!" He floored the accelerator, and the fuel-injection engine surged with power. They shot ahead, clear. The force of their acceleration pushed them both deep into the bucket seats. "Somebody's gone crazy!" Scott said. He was watching the mirror. The car behind was trying to stay with them and failing.

George said, "Curve ahead." He was watching the speedometer—90, 95, 100, and still climbing. "I said there's a curve! And a canal!"

"I know it," Scott said. "I grew up here too, remember?" Action, competition, tended to steady him. "Hang on." He stood on the brake, shifted down, went into the curve sliding, accelerated out of it; on the straight beside the canal embankment he shifted into top gear again and made the engine howl. Headlights reappeared in the mirror, diminished quickly, and finally disappeared as the car behind slowed, stopped, turned, and went back the way it had come. Scott's foot came off the accelerator. "Go back and try to catch him?"

"No," George said. "Let's call it a night." Pause. "Damn fool, driving like that. Kid ought to be spanked."

Scott was frowning in incredulity. "You think," he said slowly, "you actually think it was accidental?" He glanced at George and shook his head. "It wasn't. Somebody followed us. I saw lights and didn't pay any attention. When we left Lucero's, there they were again." Another pause. "Some-

11

body, brother George, had homicide on his mind. He wanted us off the road into the eucalyptus trees. And he almost got us there." Pause. "Think of the headlines that would have made."

2

Her full name was Ellen Meyer Stanfield II, and she was seventeen years old, George Stanfield's daughter, great-granddaughter and namesake of the old lady in the huge bed upstairs. And now, more or less by default, mistress of the Stanfield home ranch, sneaking like a thief in the night down the long curving eucalyptus-lined drive from the main house to the front gate.

Well, there was no other way for it, given the kind of male contrariness that sometimes seemed to her a Stanfield trademark. Once she had talked about it with her great-grandmother, whom she called Marquesa, and the old lady had shown gentle tolerance. "I sometimes think that from the beginning of time," Marquesa had said, "parents and children have clashed."

"But Pete and Daddy don't just clash," Ellen said. "They don't even speak. Now Pete's gone, and we don't know where."

"He'll come back one day, child. You'll see."

Well, he had come back, if Paul's phone call was to be

believed, and Paul Meyer, her something cousin—how many times removed?—was always to be believed. Paul was twenty-three, and her brother Pete twenty-two; they had been a part of her life for as long as she could remember—longer.

Ellen saw headlights at the end of the drive. Daddy and Uncle Scott, probably, back from wherever they had gone in such a rush from dinner. She stepped behind one of the massive tree trunks and waited; after what seemed a long time the white Mercedes swept past and the night was hers again. At the great main gate she used her key, stepped through, and meticulously closed the gate after her. Over the distant mountains a gibbous moon was rising.

She did not have long to wait. There was the sound of a truck engine, so different from the Mercedes purr, and then a pickup, its headlights dim. It stopped, and a man jumped out, a man she was sure she had never seen before, with a great deal of hair and a beard, a floppy black hat, and some kind of dark glasses that seemed black in the night. For a brief panicky moment she was tempted to turn and run and try to get the big gate open . . .

"Hi, kid." Pete's voice, unmistakable. "Did I scare you?"

From the truck Paul's voice, calm, amused, "He's the wave of the future, or the undertow of the present, or something. Isn't he a beauty?"

"Pete." Her voice was not quite steady. "Such a long time. And no word."

"Who cared?"

"I did." Simple truth.

"You haven't changed." His voice was amused, but gentle. He held the truck door. "Climb in. Let's not be caught hanging around the sacred Stanfield property." He smelled strongly of beer.

Ellen got into the truck to sit warmly close to Paul. "It's your home too, Pete."

"Not a chance." And then, still mocking, "You smell good, like an upright Stanfield should."

Uptight, Ellen thought. It was obvious. "What's happened?"

The black hat waved in negation. "Nothing. Not a single damn thing." Suddenly he smiled, white teeth showing

14

through the black beard. "That's the trouble," he said. "You can't change anything. Paul doesn't know it yet, and neither does his god-who-walks-on-water, Ruben Lucero, but it's true."

Try a new approach, Ellen thought. "We didn't even know where you were all this time."

"Here and there, in and out, over on the coast, down south, back in Santa Fe, Taos, staying out of trouble." There was a warmth in his mind that had nothing to do with the beer he had drunk. But there was disappointment too. Of all the people in the world, he thought, these two, his sister and his cousin, were the ones he knew best, the closest to him, and yet here, now, they were strangers, still living in a world he had abandoned. " 'Float like a butterfly, sting like a bee,' " he said. "Who said that?"

"Cassius Clay." Paul's voice was weary. "Muhammad Ali."

"And look what it got him—busted."

Paul said, "He's on some kind of high." He shrugged. "He's been like this ever since I picked him up half an hour ago."

"Are you drunk, Pete?" Ellen asked.

"On a couple of beers and heady thoughts. Maybe tomorrow will be a better day. It won't, but doesn't hope spring eternal, and all that crap?" The warmth remained, but now the disappointment had changed to loneliness. He leaned forward across Ellen to talk to Paul. "Did they give you that at Davis, too? Or did you spend all your time thinking pure agricultural thoughts, plant hybridization, artificial insemination, and that kind of jazz?"

Ellen said, "Please, Pete." And then, another change of subject, "There were sirens, and it looked like a fire, a big one."

A brief silence. "It was. It is." Paul's voice was suddenly sharp. "The Stanfield dehydrator. A man killed." He looked down at Ellen. "You hadn't heard?"

She shook her head. So that was where Daddy and Uncle Scott had gone. Strangely, tears stung her eyelids; she could not have said why. A man killed, and maybe there were others who had depended on him. Maybe . . .

Pete said, "We kill fifty thousand people every year in automobiles, and how many in Vietnam? But when some jerk tunnel man . . ."

"Knock it off," Paul said. His voice was still sharp. "If you can't talk about something that isn't downbeat, why not be quiet for a while?"

There was silence again. Ellen said, "Where are we going?"

"The idea," Paul answered, "was to just drive around so you could talk with your dear brother, but it seems he's on a bad trip."

"So sober me up, cousin baby. Find a nice secluded ditch and we'll go swimming."

"Ellen too?"

Pete shrugged.

Ellen put her hand on Paul's arm. "I don't mind," she said, "if it will help."

"That's my gallant baby sister. You're outvoted, cousin —two Stanfields to one Meyer."

In the moonlight the water in the irrigation canal gleamed silver, and except for the turbulence where it flowed through a chute and over a drop, its flow was so even that the surface seemed motionless.

Pete kicked off his sandals. "Reminds me of my youth, misspent. Remember the Romero girl? Biggest knockers I ever saw. She and I, skinny-dipping . . ." His trousers came off, and his shirt. Except for the floppy black hat and the dark glasses he was naked. "She didn't know how to swim, but that didn't matter; I wasn't interested in swimming anyway." He started down the sloping cement bank.

Ellen folded her dress neatly and laid it on the ground. She hesitated for only a moment, then took off her brassiere and stepped out of her briefs before she looked around. Pete was already in the water; beneath the dark beard the whiteness of his chest seemed somehow weak, childish.

"Better take off that silly hat and those cheaters," Paul said. His clothes lay in a heap. He looks funny, Ellen thought, with his farmer's tan on face, neck and arms, and all the rest of him, except for the dark pubic area, smoothly muscled but bone-white in the moonlight. He glanced at her nakedness,

16

with approval she thought, and then held out his hand. "Getting in is the tricky bit. It may be a little slippery." His grasp was firm and sure. Together they went down into the water. The current was surprisingly strong.

Pete pulled his hat down firmly on his bushy hair. He swam a few strokes upstream, then made a surface dive and came up laughing, hat and glasses dripping, the drops turning to diamonds as they fell. "Better than that fancy swimming pool at the house, huh, kid?"

"It's lovely." It was. Water and air were almost the same pleasant temperature. The bottom of the canal was smooth sand. Motionless, Ellen felt the flow of the water like a caress, and she was intensely conscious of breasts and groin, those parts of her body normally bikini-covered. She felt no embarrassment, which was probably strange, she thought, but there it was.

She swam a few strokes against the current, dove as Pete had, surfaced. It was odd to be contending always with the flow of the water, like the ocean sometimes when a current set along the coast. Cavorting in the surf, diving under incoming waves, you didn't realize how far from your starting place you had been swept until you came out of the water to a strange stretch of beach.

Pete, hat and glasses still dripping, was saying, "This Romero chick was definitely willing, and I only had a general idea of what to do, but I was sure going to give it a try."

Paul said, "I'm not very interested." He looked at Ellen. "Are you?"

"No."

"She might learn something," Pete said. "It could come in handy. Or maybe she doesn't need any learning. Maybe . . ."

"Why don't you put your head under water and count ten?" Paul said. "Or a hundred?"

Ellen said, "Please, Pete, don't—spoil it."

"Bigger knockers than yours," Pete said, "and the rest of her . . ."

"Goddam it," Paul said, "shut up!"

Pete settled the hat even more firmly. "If that's the way the cookie bounces," he said, "old Pistol Pete will make his

17

own fun. Adios!" He turned and launched himself with the current, swimming hard straight for the chute.

Ellen stared at the glistening flow of water where it entered the cement walls and plunged four feet into white-water turbulence. "Pete!" And then again, "Pete!"

"It's all right," Paul said. He touched her shoulder gently. "Kids do it all the time. You go over the drop to the bottom, and you don't fight it, and the current carries you past that bad part. You'll see." Most times, he added to himself.

"I don't like it," Ellen said. Her tone said: but if you say so. His hand on her shoulder was comforting. She wondered what would happen if he kissed her now, right here in the water, both of them naked. She wished he would, and she hoped he wouldn't.

"Charge!" This from Pete. His white buttocks gleamed briefly in the moonlight. Then he was gone into the drop.

"Like a white-tailed deer," Paul said.

Ellen giggled. "Both of you could use more sun."

"Lady, I'm a working stiff. I can't lie around a gold-plated swimming pool all day." He smiled down at her. "Be nice, though." Pause. "Anything would be nice with you, anything and everything."

"Paul . . ."

"There. See?" He was pointing twenty feet below the drop. The black hat had surfaced. It drifted aimlessly on the strong current, empty.

"Paul! Pete isn't——!"

Paul was already gone, swimming hard, heading for the chute. Ellen saw him raise his head and take a deep breath, his deepest. Then he shot between the cement walls and down into the turbulence.

Ellen scrambled half walking, half swimming across the canal and clawed her way up the cement side. She ran downstream, past the chute and the turbulence. The black hat was already well downstream. She ignored it as she went back down into the water. "Please!" She was whispering. "Please!" She began to move against the current, into the turbulent area. "Oh, please!"

Something caught at her ankle and she almost screamed. Squatting, her head beneath the water, she groped with both hands, found flesh, an arm, held it as tight as she could and heaved toward the surface. She came up gasping, and Paul's breathless voice said, "Good girl. We'll haul him out on the bank." His hands were beneath Pete's shoulders. "Take his legs."

The glasses were gone, and the long dark hair was plastered to Pete's skull and face. Paul knelt, muttering to himself, got the hair out of the way, grabbed Pete's jaw with one hand and his nose with the other, and began to give him mouth-to-mouth respiration. Ellen just stood and watched, her nakedness forgotten. Her mind felt empty, drained.

It did not really take long. Pete stirred. Paul straightened, watching as Pete struggled for air, filled his lungs, rolled over on his side, and began coughing, retching spasms that gradually subsided. For some moments he lay on his side, not moving, breathing audibly. Then he rose weakly on one elbow.

The warmth was gone from his mind, but the sense of loneliness remained. It occurred to him vaguely that in the water's turbulence, as in a nightmare, you could only struggle helplessly, a fly on flypaper or a moth in a spider's web, alone. And what good were all the world's platitudes then? So he was confused. Wasn't everybody? He coughed again and spat into the dirt.

Paul said, "I think the picnic is over." He took Ellen's hand and reached down to give Pete a lift to his feet. "Let's wade back across."

In silence they dressed slowly. Ellen's bra and briefs were sodden, and her dress clung to the bare flesh between. All during the ride home she tried to think of something to say, but Pete was silent, subdued on one side of her, and Paul quietly angry on the other. Conversation was impossible.

At the gates Pete got out. He watched her climb down. From the cab Paul said, "Goodnight." And then, "Sorry."

"So am I," Ellen said. She looked at Pete. "You're all right?"

White teeth showed suddenly in the black beard. "So long, kid. Back to the castle." He got into the truck and closed the door. They drove off.

Ellen let herself through the gate, closed it carefully, and began the long walk up the drive. In the darkness the great eucalyptus trees were shadowy shapes, silent and protective. Pete was outside, she thought, and a phrase came unbidden into her mind: beyond the pale. "Why?" She said it softly aloud, and found no answer.

3

From long habit the great house rose early. Of the family, Ellen, in white shorts, tennis shirt, and tennis shoes, was down first to confer with María, the cook, Consuelo, in charge of the domestic staff outside of the kitchen, and José, the head gardener. She spoke in Spanish.

"The senator," she said, "arrives this morning at the airport at nine o'clock. My grandmother will be with him, and Simpson, the senator's secretary, and Rose, my grandmother's maid."

Consuelo said, "I will have the rooms ready, señorita." Consuelo was thirty years old, plump and pretty, with a husband who tended the family cars and drove for the señora, the old lady upstairs. They had four children. In Consuelo's eyes it was a marvel to behold how capably and well the young señorita managed the household, as the señora had before her—already at seventeen, *la patrona*.

"Flowers for the rooms, José," Ellen said. "The roses my grandmother prefers . . ."

"*Entendido*, understood." José had grown old in the Stanfield gardens, and well before the young señorita's father had even thought of bringing home a bride, José had known which flowers the señorita's grandmother, Señora Conchita Stanfield, preferred in season.

Ellen smiled at the old man. "Of course." She watched his face soften. To María she said, "A roast of beef for dinner." The smile held. It was a small joke between them— always for the senator on the first night, roast of Stanfield beef *au jus.* "First, of course, a salad. Then, with the beef . . ."

"Fresh green beans," María said. She looked at José, who nodded. "And small onions," María said. She choked off the tip of her thumb with the fingers of her other hand to show how small the onions were to be. José nodded again.

"Muy bien." Ellen smiled at them both. "Potatoes, baked, with sour-cream horseradish sauce." She nodded. "For dessert? Melon?" The corners of her eyes crinkled. "Consuelo is thinking of ice cream, no? Very well. Have a gallon of ice cream frozen and well packed." She looked at Consuelo with affection. "The lemon velvet ice cream, is that to your taste?" It was, Ellen knew. *"Bien,"* she said again, and slid down from the old-fashioned white kitchen table where she had perched, swinging bare legs, during the conference. "Juice and coffee now please, María. Señor Scott and I will take breakfast after tennis."

* * *

It seemed to Ellen these last years that there were two Scott Stanfields, and she had often wondered which was the real one. There was the bantering, erudite, handsome, worldly, self-mocking uncle she had always known, of course. But since she had grown to strength and stature sufficient not to match him, but to extend him occasionally on the tennis court, she had discovered the competitive man, too, the ex-intercollegiate champion, nationally ranked, who when points were in danger sometimes put aside his avuncular gentleness and bore down with all of the considerable strength and skill he had in him.

They played three sets this morning, and for the first two Scott played a backcourt game of long ground-stroke rallies, backhand, forehand, deep shots, well placed. "Pretty sharp,

22

youngster," he said as they changed courts after the second set. The score stood at 6-4, 6-3.

"Maybe you're slowing down," Ellen said. "After all, when you're past middle age . . ." She shrugged, smiling.

"That may be it." His voice was light as ever. "Ready?"

Scott served only four times in the first game of the third set, four serves, three volleys. Ellen's return of the fourth service did not reach the net. Love game.

He treated Ellen's service almost brutally, each return a forcing shot behind which he went to net. Once Ellen lobbed over him, driving him back; and once, suddenly angry, she slammed a forehand shot straight down the alley and watched him lunge for it and miss. He smiled at her then. "Good girl," he said. Accolade. But the brutal treatment continued. The final set was 6-0; in six games Ellen had won just three points.

They walked slowly together back to the main house. "Annoyed with me, youngster?" His voice was gentle.

"Not really, I guess." She smiled suddenly. "You make me feel like a little girl."

"And you resent it." He nodded. They walked in silence for a time.

"I don't know if I do or not. Resent it, I mean." Strange, but true. She was thinking of last night, Pete making a fool of himself. As far as that went, maybe all three of them had been making fools of themselves, naked in an irrigation ditch. It seemed a long time ago. She looked at Scott and wondered if he had ever behaved like that.

"Honey," Scott was saying, "I dislike platitudes, but some can't be avoided. Play for keeps. There's no other way."

Ellen thought about it in her own context. She said at last, "Have you? I mean, you weren't just talking about tennis, were you?"

He was looking down at her, unsmiling now, but there was no going back. "I mean," Ellen said, "*you* know, you haven't ever married. Isn't that playing for keeps? I've always thought it was."

Scott was silent for a time. Forty-three years to seventeen —the contrast was unfair. What a ridiculous concept—wasn't he the one who was forever saying that fairness had nothing at all to do with life? But all the advantages of unsullied

23

idealism lay with seventeen, and nothing could change that fact, ever. He smiled down at the girl. "You're right, of course," he said. "And you know why? It's because I've never been able to find a chick my own age like you." He patted her bottom gently. "Fifteen minutes for shower and change, then breakfast. Okay?"

* * *

Cleary Ward parked the big station wagon near the visiting aircraft flight line and left the engine running to keep the air conditioning on. He got out to stand in the already hot sun.

Cleary was thirty, tall, well built in an unspectacular way, with light brown hair in careful casual disarray. His educational background was University of California, Davis campus, and Stanford Business School. He bore no formal title, but in all Stanfield matters here in Stanhope aside from those of the home ranch itself Cleary was George Stanfield's man on the ground. At times like this, a Stanfield clan gathering, it was forcibly impressed on him that he was merely hired help, important only when the important ones were away.

He did not have long to wait. The aircraft, an executive jet, probably half a million dollars' worth of private airplane, he thought, came swiftly into view from the northeast. It circled for its approach, white and sleek and lovely against the distant mountains and the clear blue sky. When it touched down, Cleary glanced at his watch: 0900 on the dot, as predicted.

The Stanfield sons of bitches did whatever they did well, Cleary told himself, whether it was politics, announcing and keeping an arrival schedule, growing crops, finding oil and water where other men could not, making fabulously successful investments in just about anything you could name, from land development to electronic manufacturing to data processing to banking and food packaging, or merely running roughshod over anyone and anything that got in their way. It was something he had better, by God, keep in mind.

He allowed none of these thoughts to show as a car drove up and two men got out. Cleary recognized both—Walt Jones, the younger newspaperman from the local *Stanhope*

Register, and Hanford, the middle-aged man with the down-curved expression from the AP. They headed straight for him.

Hanford said, "Why's old silverlocks coming in?"

"His mother is ill," Cleary said. "She is ninety years old, and it is possibly a terminal illness." Cleary disliked talking to the press; his words tended to come out in stiff quotes-enclosed phrases. Besides, he didn't think Hanford believed him, and for all he knew he was speaking truth.

The taxiing aircraft came to a halt. Promptly the fuselage door opened and steps appeared. "First man out," Hanford said, "will be Simpson, the old man's secretary." He smiled faintly. "Nixon gets off the plane first, but not Mike Stanfield. He's a retired rear admiral in the reserves and he does things the navy way. Senior officer is first aboard, and last off."

Cleary tucked the information away. Sure enough, Simpson was first off, briefcase in hand. A Spanish-American woman in uniform was next. Hanford said, for Walt Jones's benefit, "Rosa, Conchita's maid." He walked forward as another, handsome older woman started down the steps. "There's Conchita." Behind her came the senator, tall, easy, assured, pleasant smile, silver hair and all.

Cleary said, "I have the car over here, Senator." He smiled. "Morning, Mrs. Stanfield, Simpson, Rosa."

The senator nodded. He was looking at Hanford. "Hi, Bill."

"Mike." Hanford nodded to the older woman. "Conchita." Then, "Here on business, Mike?"

"My mother is ill." The senator made a small hand gesture toward the waiting car, and Mrs. Stanfield, Rosa and Simpson turned immediately and walked toward it. "Purely a family affair, Bill."

Hanford said, "Long as I've lived out here, Mike, it still catches me by surprise when things happen straight out of 'Gunsmoke.' Watts I could understand. I'm a city boy, and I've seen riots before. But somebody taking a shot at your son George, somebody killing a man and burning down your dehydrator, barn burnings, fence cuttings, a truck loaded with empty boxes run right up an embankment and into an irrigation canal . . ." He shook his head.

25

Nothing in the senator's face had changed. "Violent times, Bill."

Hanford nodded, accepting defeat. "You'll be in touch with Sacramento?"

"I am frequently in touch with Sacramento," the senator said. He looked at Walt Jones. "I suppose you want a quote, son? You may say that it is always good to be home again." He nodded to them both and walked to the waiting car.

Cleary held the rear door open for him. As he closed it and walked around the car, he heard Hanford say to Walt Jones, "Don't underestimate him. A lot of people have made that mistake and ended up with their noses in the dirt. I've known him a long time, and the silver hair and the sunny smile are just what he wants you to see." Pause. "As far as that goes, don't underestimate any of them. Down at the bottom they're real bastards, and they mean to keep what they've got."

Cleary, behind the wheel, closed his door and any further talk was shut out. With effort he kept his face expressionless.

4

First things first, the senator had always said and believed. He
knocked gently on the door of the upstairs suite his mother
had lived in, sharing and alone, for seventy years. He himself
had been born in the great bed with the hand-carved head-
board brought by sailing vessel around the Horn in the early
1850s. To the uniformed nurse who answered his knock he
said, "I am Mike Stanfield, young lady. When my mother is
up to it, I should like to see her."

"We are having our bath." Implied reprimand. Good
God, the senator thought, did all nurses everywhere talk the
same way? "And then," the nurse said, "we will have our
nap." Teacher speaking to child. It was a mistake.

"Young woman," the senator said, "you might bear in
mind that my concern for your patient is at least as great as
yours. I repeat: when my mother is up to it, I should like to
see her." Pause. "Is that understood?"

Nurse Walters looked displeased.

"I asked a question," the senator said. "I expect an answer." It was his committee hearing-room voice, almost a

purr, accompanied by a particular kind of smile. Cabinet officers, department heads, military men of exalted rank—all had found the combination unnerving. So did Nurse Walters. The bubble of her superiority collapsed.

"Yes, sir," she said. "I mean, yes, Senator, of course."

"Good." The senator patted her shoulder gently, and the smile turned paternal. "I am sure you are taking very good care of her."

He walked down the stairs to the study that had been his father's and that now, when he was in Stanhope, was George's, closed the door and went to seat himself at the heavy desk. Like the bed upstairs, the senator thought, and a good share of the rest of the furniture in the house, it too had been brought by sea from the east to San Francisco and then by wagon down here to Stanhope in the great Central Valley. Ezra Stanfield had sat at it, then his son Amos, and Ezra II, the senator's father, and now George.

Well, the senator could have sat here, if he had chosen; he would have done well at the task of managing the multiplicity of Stanfield interests. He smiled, thinking of that. He could have done it, and he had not. In honesty he had to admit, purely and simply, that he preferred the stage to the producer's office, the limelight and the hurly-burly to contemplative quiet. He was at heart a ham; he had long known it. It amused him that so few people recognized the fact. He picked up one of the two telephones, the private one, and dialed a San Francisco number.

The answering voice—another female in starched white, feeling her own importance?—said, "Dr. Hall's office."

"This," the senator said slowly, distinctly, "is Senator Stanfield."

Hesitation. Then, "Yes, sir."

"I should like to speak with Dr. Hall, if you please. A personal matter of some urgency."

More hesitation. "I'll—see, sir."

In only a few moments a male voice was on the phone. "Mike?"

"Are you alone, Bill?"

28

"I am in my office with the door closed," Bill Hall said. "I left a patient to talk to you. What is it?"

"I want to see you. As soon as possible. Sooner."

There was a pause. "Professionally, or personally?"

"Both."

Another pause. "Look, Mike. You're a United States Senator and a retired rear admiral. There's a place called Bethesda Naval Hospital . . ."

"I said, both professionally and personally."

"I don't get it."

"Someday," the senator said, "I'll give you a chalk talk on it. In the meantime I want to see you. Let's say tonight about eleven, your office."

"Mike . . ."

"I'm asking. I don't recall that I've ever asked before. Your boy graduates from Annapolis this year, doesn't he?"

There was a weary smile in the voice now. "He does. Thanks to you. Eleven o'clock tonight, Mike."

"Just the two of us."

"I already figured that out."

The senator hung up and sat quietly for a little time. He felt tired, almost unable to stir. He knew the meaning of this sense of lassitude, but it had long ago lost its power to frighten him. He roused himself with effort and made his second telephone call, this one to Sacramento where, in the governor's office, no officiousness awaited him. The governor came on immediately. "Mike. Where are you? Washington?"

"I'm in Stanhope. My mother is gravely ill."

"I'm sorry to hear it." Pause. "But there are a couple of Senate votes coming up . . ."

"Bob." That committee-room voice again. "Don't try to tell me how to fill the office of United States Senator."

Pause. "No, of course not. Sorry, Mike."

"I want to talk to you," the senator said. "In private, which means here at the ranch. I'll send my plane for you. Say tomorrow morning, nine o'clock."

Another pause. "I've got quite a bit on my plate, Mike."

"Understood." The senator smiled. "But you also have an eye on the future. You're a bright young man. With help, you can go far."

The governor sighed. "I get the message."

"Stay for lunch," the senator said. "I'll bet you haven't tasted Stanfield beef in a long time."

"I'm drooling," the governor said. There was a smile in his voice. "Shall I bring anyone?"

"This is between us. And maybe George."

"Trouble down there?" The smile was gone from his voice.

"We'll talk tomorrow," the senator said. "About everything. I'll have my plane at the airport at nine."

He hung up again, and the listlessness returned. Busy little cells, he thought, red and white, waging war in the pointless fashion of humans? He did not pretend, nor did he care, to understand the full medical explanations. When a knock came at the door he frowned in mild annoyance. "Come in."

Nurse Walters opened the door. Her attitude was almost deferential. "Your mother would like to see you now, Senator."

The weariness was with him still, but only the paternal smile showed as he got out of the chair. "Thank you, my dear." He walked up the stairs and down the hall to the familiar suite.

In the great bed she seemed quite small. One hand resting on the coverlet was almost translucent. Her eyes, deep set with age, studied the senator quietly. A faint smile lifted her lips. "Are you well, son?" Her voice was slow, but the words were clear.

"I'm fine, mamacita." He bent to kiss the smooth dry cheek, then sat in the chair drawn up to the bedside. "If you're wondering why I'm here," he said, "I can tell you that Washington is hot, miserable this time of year. Some people get spring fever. I get mine in the summer when the *turistas* come to gape."

The old lady smiled. "Did George send for you?"

"No." Truthfully. "My own idea."

"Have you seen him?"

"Not yet," the senator said. "Nor have I seen Scott yet.

George is busy this time of year." Pause. "Correction. He is busy all year."

"As your father was."

"And," the senator said, "as I am not?" He nodded. "George bears the burden, and he bears it well." Credit where credit was due.

"And after George?" The deep-set eyes watched him quietly.

The senator shook his head. "Who knows? Ellen . . ."

"Ellen is a girl, son."

He could smile then and mean it. "You were a girl too, and so were grandmother Ida and great-grandmother Lotte, and they made their presence felt." He shook his head, smiling still. "Women behind the scenes, prompting from the wings . . ."

"Does Conchita prompt you?"

Another smile. "In English, in Spanish, and sometimes in French." Pause. "She came with me, of course. She wants to see you."

"Is there trouble, son?" The question, out of nowhere, hung in the quiet room.

"I don't know how to answer that," the senator said. "There is always trouble, almost everywhere. Hasn't it always been so?"

"Your father's mother," the old lady said in that slow, clear voice, reminiscing now, "her name was Ida, Ida Hopkins, and when she was eight years old she helped her mother bear a baby sister in the potato cellar while a man named Quantrill and his men looted the house above them. That was in Missouri." Her eyes closed briefly. She smiled. "When your grandfather Amos first saw Ida Hopkins she was barefoot." The smile broadened. "Like Ellen today sometimes, but not for the same reason. Ida Hopkins had no shoes. She had worn them out walking from Missouri to California with the wagon." Her eyes closed again. The smile faded.

"You're tired," the senator said. "I'll come back later." He bent again to kiss her cheek.

The eyes opened and the smile returned. "Thank you for coming to see me, Henry. I'll be up and around in a day or so."

31

"Of course you will," the senator said. He walked out and closed the door softly. To Nurse Walters, waiting in the hall, "I think she would like to rest now," he said, and walked on to the rooms that had always been his.

Rosa had already unpacked their things and the luggage had disappeared. Conchita, in the shuttered sitting room, a magazine on her lap, studied her husband's face carefully before she turned off the lamp at her shoulder. "You're tired, Mike."

"A little." He sat down. "She is as good as can be expected." He smiled without amusement. "She called me Henry at the last. He was my uncle, her brother-in-law, killed in France in 1917 in a World War I flying machine."

"Something is wrong, Mike," Conchita said. "Tell me."

"*Nada.*" The senator smiled again and used diversionary tactics. "I'm looking forward to seeing George and Scott. Aren't you?"

"Of course."

The senator stood up. "And God, how I used to hate family gatherings." He smiled suddenly. "Getting old, my dear. In a few months, threescore years and ten." If I make it, he thought, and the odds are pretty poor. "I'm going to have a drink before lunch. Maybe two. Join me?"

5

George Stanfield drove one of the ranch pickup trucks. He wore a khaki shirt, khaki trousers and six-inch lace boots, all of which became him, he always thought, far better than the business clothes required in San Francisco, New York, even Los Angeles, unless you deliberately sought eccentricity. He supposed he was a farm boy at heart, and he knew the concept would cause amusement along Montgomery Street or in the Pacific Union Club.

Beside him in the pickup John Silva sat quiet, waiting to be spoken to.

Here were the vineyards stretching for miles. At intervals roads cut through the rows of vines, and already stacks of empty boxes were set out for the picking. Seedless grapes. Some of them, grown on girdled canes, would be shipped to the eastern premium table market. The rest would in the normal course of things, have been sent through the dehydrator tunnels and dried into raisins to be shipped around the world. The girdled grapes were larger, greener, with less sugar; the others, ripening gold in the sun, would soon sugar up heavily—too soon.

George stopped the truck and they got out to walk among the vines, here and there to pick a small cluster, smell it, taste a single grape. "They're looking good," George said. Maybe too good.

Silva nodded. He was a stocky man, dark-haired, blue-eyed, Valley Portuguese stock. "No rain," he said. "Just sun."

"I'll try to arrange it," George said, and smiled faintly. They walked back to the pickup.

The two men sat for a time, aware of the sun's weight bearing down on the roof of the cab, but neither was conscious of discomfort. As before, Silva waited to be spoken to. George said, "Last night's fire changes things, John. The girdled grapes aren't affected." He left it there, the thought unfinished.

Silva said, "Joe Baca has got a picking crew?"

"He'll have one," George said. It was the old way, dealing with a labor contractor; maybe it was not the best way, George didn't know about that, but it had always worked in the past.

"Ruben Lucero came to see me," Silva said. "Paul Meyer was with him. They asked me to talk with you."

"I saw Lucero last night." Lucero, George could understand. But there had always been Meyers and Stanfields, and Paul Meyer, Karl's son, he could not begin to comprehend. Nor his own son Pete, as far as that went. George thought of himself as a reasonable man and that was the trouble, because other men, like Lucero, Paul Meyer, and Pete, did not see him as reasonable at all; they were utterly, completely, fanatically convinced of their own rectitude. "I saw him after a man was killed," George said, "and the dehydrator burned down."

Silva waved one hand at the broad vineyards, rich and orderly in the bright sun. "I want my grapes to be picked when they are ripe," he said. "I don't want them to be wasted. That is all."

Your grapes, George thought, and smiled gently. Well, in a very important sense they were. Silva lived with these vines 365 days a year, and there was never a time when they were out of his thoughts. They were as much a part of him as if his

34

own seed had fertilized them. "You've done your job," George said. "I'll take it from here."

He drove Silva back to the neat frame house that went with the vineyard job. A pair of sycamore trees flanking the front of the house gave at least an illusion of coolness on this hot day. Silva went inside and came back with two cans of cold beer, and they sat on a bench in the shade for a few minutes of talk.

Silva's oldest boy was at the Davis campus of the University of California. "But he doesn't want to grow things," Silva said. "He wants to go into law, make money. He is—ashamed that his father works with his hands." He looked at George. "I say to him, 'George Stanfield is not ashamed to work with his hands.'" Silva smiled helplessly. "He say that when somebody is as rich as George Stanfield he can do whatever he wants. Is there sense in that?" He shrugged. "I don't know." He paused. "The old Mrs. Stanfield? How is she?"

George shook his head. He finished his beer and absentmindedly crushed the can in his big hands. "She is ninety years old, John."

"She will be missed." Silva pointed overhead. "She told me once that she had these trees planted. She was happy that I take care of them."

"Wherever you look," George said, "there's part of her." Part of all of us, he thought; here among our roots, our dead are buried. He stood up. "Thanks for the beer, John. We'll do what we can." He walked out to the truck. After the shade of the trees his grandmother had had planted, the seat of the cab was uncomfortably hot. He drove back to Stanhope.

You could smell the burned-out dehydrator blocks away — the stench of charred wood and tortured metal, the heavy caramel odor of burned fruit. George parked across the street and walked to the platform.

He knew it well. Summers, as a kid growing up in the great house outside of town, while Scott had played his endless tennis with Peter Juan, the third brother, or swum in the pool or ridden the Stanfield cattle ranges off to the west, George, who played football, had worked long hours at the dehydrator.

"To stay in shape," was the current phrase then. Well,

35

God knew the work had been physical enough — unloading 120 tons of grapes a day with a grab truck, filling in at the spreader, stacking trays, or helping with tunnel pulls when there was nothing else to do. As one of the truck drivers had said, "It makes a man sleep on his own side of the bed at night."

Depression times then, and a book called *The Grapes of Wrath* raised hackles among growers and processors all through the Valley. A pack of lies, they said; things weren't that bad for anybody. Maybe.

A man had come up on the platform one day, just one man out of many, but he remained vivid in memory. He had driven a Model A pickup with tread-bare tires. He wore overalls, faded but clean, and a patched blue shirt, sweat-damp at the armpits; he was perhaps thirty years old.

He had stood for a time, his hands just hanging, looking at the stacked boxes of grapes, watching the dipper man and the crew at the spreader. George, fourteen, mending broken boxes, slowed his work with stripper and box hatchet to listen to the man talk to the platform boss. "You got a full crew, mister?" A twang that was not of California but somewhere to the east, Texas maybe, Oklahoma, even Arkansas.

The platform boss was a college boy, working for the summer. "I'm sorry," he said. "It's a full crew."

"What're you payin', mister?"

"Thirty cents an hour, but it's a full crew."

The man just stood, looking, and you could almost taste the mingled hope, desperation and despair that were in him —and the quiet, helpless rage. "Mister," he said, "I got a wife an' three kids down under the bridge in Hooverville. I'll work for two bits an hour. I'll work for twenty cents an hour. I'll work for anything you'll pay me."

"Sorry. It's a full crew." What else was there to say?

Remembering, George thought: that was then, this is now. He stood quietly at the corner of the platform, looking at the wreckage and thinking of a dead man and of thousands of acres of grapes turning gold in the sun.

Ralph Capadonica came out of the one end of the packing shed which was still intact, picking his way through fallen rubble. Ralph was the dehydrator foreman. His face, hands

36

and clothes were blackened, and his work shoes left sticky fruit tracks on the platform cement. There was a man with him, as dirty as he, a long-nosed little man with sharp ferret eyes. Ralph said, "It's a mess, Mr. Stanfield, and I'm sure sorry."

"Not your fault." George looked at the other man.

"Max Green, Mr. Stanfield," the man said. "Insurance adjuster." His long nose quivered when he spoke. "It wasn't any accident. The blower switches were thrown."

George nodded. And then, finding the implication plain, "If you're thinking it was burned down for the insurance, forget it. It couldn't have happened at a worse time."

Green looked at Capadonica. Ralph said, "We were just finishing the peach run. We start grapes in a week, ten days."

"And grapes don't wait," George said. "If they aren't picked when they're ready, they turn to waterberries or bad raisins on the vine, and if they aren't processed when they're picked, they may mildew. Either way, we stand to lose the cost of a dozen dehydrators." He looked at Ralph. "Have you had somebody here to see what's involved in rebuilding?"

"Yes, sir. Carl Walters is still inside, figuring."

There was little he could do, George thought; if the wheels were turning, he could only give them an extra spin. "Tell him we want a two-stage plan," he said. "Get us back in operation as fast as he can with plywood and baling wire. Then think about the permanent structures." Double work, double cost; it couldn't be helped.

Green's nose quivered in protest.

George turned to him. "It's the way we're going to do it," he said, "because it's the way we have to. When it's finished, we'll send you a bill." Pause. Warning. "Some of the people you insure may find it too much trouble or too much expense to go to court if they disagree with your settlement offer. We won't. Remember that." Then, to Capadonica again, "I'll be here for a day or so. Keep me posted." He jumped down from the platform and walked back to the pickup.

He drove straight to the bank, the Stanhope First National, parked in the spacious lot and went inside. It was a new building, modern in design, air-conditioned, up-to-date, informal. The old bank design George remembered was neoclassical, with impressive columns and high ceilings; the bank's officers had sat on a dais a foot or so above the main floor, protected by a heavy balustrade. Customers were expected to approach in hushed respect, almost genuflecting, when they came to petition for a loan.

Well, times and customs had changed, George thought, but Karl Meyer, moneyman, third cousin once removed, had not. As far as Karl was concerned, you did not have a friend at Stanhope First National, you had a group of sound, efficient, cold-blooded financial professionals willing to do business with you—if your credit and your collateral bore scrutiny. Maybe it was a good thing that Howard, Karl's older son, Stanford, Harvard Business School, modern financial thinking and all, was on hand. But Karl was still boss.

George went straight into Karl's corner office without stopping for secretarial permission. He was aware that Karl considered his lack of formality a form of lese majesty, and he could not have cared less. The Stanfields owned as much of the bank as the Meyers did.

Karl stood up slowly. They shook hands. Karl sat down again, folded his long hands, and looked at George over the tops of his glasses.

George said, "You've heard about the dehydrator fire and the dead man?"

Karl nodded. "An accident?"

"No accident. We'll be rebuilding in a hurry. Carl Walters will be the contractor. He'll send his bills to you."

Karl took off his glasses and looked at them thoughtfully. "A trifle irregular . . ."

"Come off it, Karl." The sharpness of his own voice startled George. He had not realized he was this tight—uptight, as Ellen or Scott would say. And yet, he supposed, there was ample reason—Joe Hanson, last night's fire and murder, that car on the dark tree-lined road, the other things that had been happening recently. He said in a milder voice, "I'll give Cleary Ward authorization to check out the bills before he sends them along to you for payment. Better?"

The glasses were back on Karl's veined nose. He nodded faintly, owlishly. Then, "Have the police any thoughts?"

"They didn't last night. I'll see Walling this morning."

Karl took his time. His conversation consisted largely of silences, and most of his utterances sounded deliberate and weighty. "A good man, George, not a man to be underestimated. The city council hired him from Fresno, and they have given him a free hand. Within reason, of course." The almost inevitable hedge.

Why tell me, George thought. Aloud he said, "I'm glad to hear it."

After a silence Karl said, "I understand your son Pete is back in town."

Nothing showed in George's face. "Is he?"

Again Karl took his time. "Long hair, I am told, a beard, dark glasses, black hat, sandals." He paused, and for a moment the banker façade disappeared. "Do you know what they want, George? Your Pete? My Paul? Carrying a strike sign, following Lucero as if he were a prophet, refusing to live at home, refusing any kind of job or financial aid? Do *you* know?"

"No." What more was there to say? And yet he could not leave it there. "I've tried."

"So have I, George, so have I." The façade was back in place. "A word of warning. Chief Walling is not amused by long hair and radical views. A strict traditionalist, I should say. But, I think, fair."

George stood up. "If you're talking about Pete," he said, "he's of age. He can look out for himself."

Karl shook his head. "You know better than that. If the boy lands in trouble, you won't turn your back on him." Karl too stood up. He held out his long hand for a formal handshake. "Give my regards to the senator when you see him. And to Aunt Ellen." He sat down again and retired into his money thoughts.

Out in the parking lot Juan Potrero, bank attendant, was waiting beside the truck. George shook his hand. *"Qué tal, Juan?"* Even though his visits to Stanhope were rare it was easy to fall back into old familiarities, the *patrón* attitude.

Juan looked pleased. *"Muy bien, gracias."* And then, concern on the dark, lined face. "And the Señora Stanfield?"

"She is old, Juan."

"It happens to all of us."

39

"True." No, not always true; some died young, like his own Ann, only twenty-nine, seventeen years ago, the night Ellen was born. Forget that. Try to forget it.

"A candle for the señora," Juan said. "My wife will see to it."

"*Gracias.* I will tell her." George got into the pickup and drove away with a wave. A candle, he was thinking, and the faith a candle represented. He wondered how it would be to have a faith like that, or any faith at all that did not depend upon himself. It was the kind of speculation Scott would be able to play with ad infinitum; for George facts were the important thing.

He sat in Chief Ben Walling's office and spoke of facts, remembering as he talked what Karl had said of the man. "We will rebuild as fast as we can," George said, and was prepared to explain his reasons because he had supposed the police would want things left as they were until they had completed their investigation. There was no need.

"Understood, Mr. Stanfield." Walling produced a faint smile at George's obvious surprise. "I grew up in the Valley," Walling said. "I know that fruit has to be handled before it spoils." He shook his head. "There's nothing there for us, anyway, Mr. Stanfield. The weapon was probably your tunnel man's hook. It would have been right at hand."

George said, "Fingerprints?"

Walling's smile was gentle. "Not a chance. There rarely is."

"Do you want me to post a reward?"

"No, sir. Not at the moment. For reward money everybody would want in the act, even if they didn't know anything." Walling paused. "A thing like last night," he said slowly, thoughtfully, "nobody gains anything, except that they hurt somebody—you."

"And the dead tunnel man," George said. I don't even know his name, he thought suddenly, and blamed himself that it was so.

"No, sir." Walling was definite. "Harper was incidental. So was the clean-up man. You don't take the trouble to throw eight separate switches located maybe ten feet apart unless that's what you set out to do. Harper and the clean-up man

40

were clobbered so they wouldn't hear the blowers stop and turn them on again. I worked in a dehydrator when I was a kid. You get used to the blower belt rhythm. One blower stops, let alone all eight, and you hear it."

True enough, George thought. His opinion of Walling was on the rise.

"So," Walling said, "somebody sets out to hurt you, the way I see it. Now why would that be, Mr. Stanfield?"

George sat silent, expressionless.

"Joe Hanson," Walling said. "He says he had a specific beef. Two of them. The first is that you drilled deep wells he couldn't afford to drill and stole his water. You didn't drill the wells yourself, of course, but you gave the okay, probably from your office in San Francisco, right?"

"I told them to go ahead," George said.

"And that," Walling said, "is his second beef. Hanson's. You're George Stanfield, Hanson tells the psychiatrist. You say shit, and everybody is supposed to start taking down his pants. That's a quote. You aren't even on the scene, you're in San Francisco, but you nod your head, no more than that, and Hanson's wells go dry." Walling paused. "I'm not trying to excuse him, Mr. Stanfield. I'm just trying to tell you how he thinks. I won't even pretend that I think it's a sane way to think, either."

"Then," George said, "why tell me about it?" His voice was sharp. Because I don't want to hear, he thought; in memory he again watched that man walk onto the platform back in the grapes-of-wrath days, carrying his helpless rage like a cancer in his soul, unable even to find something or somebody to strike out against.

Walling said, "Look, Mr. Stanfield, calm down. Like I told you last night, I treat you with kid gloves or I wish to hell I had. I know that. I don't much like it, but I recognize it, a fact of life. I'm not trying to rub your fur the wrong way. I'm trying to find out who killed your tunnel man and burned down your dehydrator, and why. That's all."

Uptight, George thought, and made himself relax a little. "All right," he said, "what's the connection? Hanson was in custody last night. He couldn't have had anything to do with it."

41

"No, sir, he couldn't. For a fact." Walling leaned back in his chair and took his time. He said at last, "I don't pretend to know about these things, Mr. Stanfield, not like your brother. He was in here this morning telling me about a car trying to run you into the trees last night." He watched George nod faintly, mere acknowledgment. "He," Walling said, "is an educated man. He talks about a climate of violence, and sociological pressures, and cyclical change, that kind of thing."

It sounded like Scott, all right. George said nothing.

"I don't follow all that," Walling said, "but I feel some of it, even if I can't put big theories to it. Kids at colleges are all stirred up, they burn down buildings and break things. Black people riot. Chicanos say they've had the short end of the stick long enough. Everybody and his brother is looking for somebody to blame for something, somebody to take out on whatever they happen not to like. You get that word *establishment* every time you open a paper or turn on the TV. Do you see what I mean, Mr. Stanfield?"

George did, and didn't like it. And yet it was merely what Scott had been saying for a long time, and his son Pete, so he supposed he ought to be used to it by now. "You mean that I, we, are the Establishment, is that it?"

"Yes, sir, that's just what I do mean. Joe Hanson goes for you for his reasons. Last night's thing was for somebody else's reasons. Maybe Ruben Lucero's people, to show you they mean business. Maybe others, like the little man in the bar, looking around for the biggest target they can find. Long-haired kids bust windows of a Bank of America branch, just because it's the Bank of America, the biggest bank in the world. You're the Stanfields; same thing. Even the name of this town . . ."

"I'm aware of it." George stood up. Walling rose with him. George was the taller by three, four inches, and sixty pounds heavier. At the moment he wished it were not so, because the physical disparity seemed to underline what Walling had been saying. "There are people who don't like us," George said. "I'm aware of that too, and there isn't very much I can do about it. But to do something like last night's busi-

42

ness, somebody needed a reason, a big reason . . ." He stopped in surprise. "You don't agree?"

"Like I said, Mr. Stanfield, I don't pretend to be a shrink or even a sociologist, but people who turn their backs on everything, drop out, tune in, turn on, say the hell with everything they've ever been taught, say that the system's no damn good and the only way to change it is to tear it down—those people don't need a reason, Mr. Stanfield. Dirty, long-haired, barefoot kids, especially the ones from good homes, they think anything they do is okay, and if it breaks something, it's better than okay, it's great, groovy, out of sight, it'll show the pigs." He paused. "Cops are pigs, Mr. Stanfield." He paused again. "But so are the people in the Establishment, particularly the ones who run it. You. That's how I see it."

6

Scott Stanfield sat on a straight chair and tried not to show disapproval. It was uphill work. He was a fastidious man, and in light summer trousers, a short-sleeved shirt and polished loafers in this pigsty, he thought, he was both out of place and uncomfortable. Correction. It was not a pigsty; by comparison, pigs were neat and clean. Only man could create filth like this—dirty sheets on the unmade bed, overflowing ashtrays and empty beer cans on chairs and tables, stacks of dirty dishes in the sink, rolls of dirt and dust on the unswept floor, the whole room filled with a sour stench. Pete, his nephew, fitted into the picture with exactitude.

Pete said, "A beer?"

Scott shook his head. "Thanks." He crossed his legs and clasped his hands over one knee—practiced informality, to set students in private conference at ease. "I got your message. Obviously." He paused. "Why me, Pete?"

"Instead of the parent?" Pete's teeth showed white through his black beard. Last night was past, over, almost forgotten—but not quite. He had gone swimming in a canal

44

and almost drowned. So? Maybe it would have been better if he had; the thought had been with him all morning, a nagging, sniggly little thought. "I used to be able to talk to you," he said. "The parent and I were never even on the same wavelength."

It should have been flattering. Strangely, it was not, not in these surroundings. Scott said, "You've taken off in your own direction, haven't you?"

"Instead of conforming, you mean?" Pete walked to the refrigerator, took out a can of beer, and jerked the tab loose. Beer foamed out and spilled on the floor. He ignored it. "You're the one," he said, "who used to laugh at conformity, remember? Little men in little business suits scrabbling for their little jobs, afraid to strike out on their own?"

Had it sounded like that? Scott had always prided himself on liberal, as opposed to conventional, thinking, but was this what it had meant to the young who had listened? Incredible.

"You used to sound," Pete said, "like somebody who could think, not just play back like a tape recorder. The dynamics of change, remember? Well, change is what we need, isn't it?"

"Possibly. Even probably. How do you accomplish it?"

"Look," Pete said, "I heard about Chavez down in Delano, Corky Gonzalez up in Colorado. Tijerina in New Mexico—the pigs have him in jail. Then Lucero right here in my own backyard. So I came back." He drank deep; white foam decorated the black beard. "Paul works with him. I speak Spanish too. I saw him." Painful memory. Ruben Lucero wanted no part of Pete Stanfield.

"The last time I saw Paul," Scott said, "he looked like an ordinary farmhand, not like a freak."

"Whose business is it but mine how I look?"

"Why," Scott said easily, "nobody's business but yours. People can always turn their backs and stay upwind so they can't smell you." He was unable to resist a gesture that included the whole room. "Or this," he said.

"I live the way I like, without a lot of materialistic crap." As last night, the feeling of loneliness was strong, almost overpowering, and the self-assured, easy attitude of the man on the straight chair was affront. "You're really like all the rest

45

of them, aren't you?" Pete said. "You play with ideas in your ivory tower, but nothing ever comes of it."

Scott sat quiet, controlling his temper. He said at last, "What did you want to see me about, Pete?"

Open himself, express his ideas now? No way. "I forget."

Scott waited, but there was no more, and in the end, unable to endure any longer, he stood up. "Do you know what a geek is, Pete? He's the rummy in the cage in a traveling carnival. He gives the rubes a morbid thrill by biting the heads off live chickens. He's gone down about as far as he can go. Maybe he thinks he's free, too."

Nothing changed in Pete's face. "I'll see you around, professor."

Outside the sun was bright, hot. Walking to the car, Scott put on his dark glasses, an automatic gesture. There were three boys standing close, admiring the white Mercedes, one of them kicked the dirt of the street and said, "Hey, man, you on TV or somep'n?"

"Mostly somep'n," Scott said. He got in, started the engine, drove slowly away. For the benefit of the boys he was smiling, but he had rarely felt less like it; annoyed with Pete, with the world, with himself.

So I told him off, he thought, big deal. He needs help, and I give him the back of my hand. Then, strange thought: or maybe I'm the one who needs help. Had that concept been lurking in his mind all along?

He looked at his watch. His father and mother would be at the big house and unpacked by now. Filial duty be damned, he thought; Mike and Conchita can wait, I'll see them at dinner. He shifted down, brought the car around in a tight U-turn, and sent it scudding out of town, Berkeley-bound.

* * *

An hour and a half as the Mercedes rolled; he stopped at a gas station and used the telephone while the attendant filled the tank. As he dialed Scott thought that with the luck that might very well have descended on him, Jenny would be in court instead of in her office, but it was not so. Against the quiet calm of her voice he could picture book-lined walls, solid, comforting furnishings, an atmosphere of competence

46

tempered, because of the woman herself, with compassion and understanding. "I thought you were in Stanhope," she said.

"Until ninety minutes ago, I was, counselor. But I was struck down with a sudden case of the yearns and now I'm here, ten minutes away from you, and ten minutes is too long."

"Scotty . . ."

"I'm asking." Unconsciously echoing his father's words. "I don't recall that I've asked before. Not in this way. Please."

Her voice was still calm, but with a note of concern. "Is something wrong?"

"Yes. No. Out of joint is a better phrase. I'll pick you up. We'll drive. In the hills. I want to talk." Pause. "Shall I say it again? Please."

Indecision was not one of her traits. "Ten minutes," she said, and that was all.

As often as he had seen her, and recently they had been together frequently, each meeting was a fresh experience. There she stood, tall, slender, shapely, auburn hair not quite shoulder length, those turquoise eyes watching him, her lips curved faintly in a smile of greeting. She wore a pale blue dress, uncluttered, even severe in cut. But on her, Scott thought, it was something extraordinary.

He started to get out of the car, but she stopped him. "I'm not helpless, Scotty." She opened the far door and slid in. The door closed with a solid thunk. "You're the pilot," she said, and seemed to relax, letting him choose the pace.

North of the campus, along Spruce Street, and then swinging back from the reservoir and into the park; Scott drove effortlessly, unconsciously, neither fast nor slow, aware that the woman was waiting for him to speak. "Not *déjà vu*," he said at last. "Quite the opposite." He turned to look at her. "If you see what I mean." He shook his head. "Ridiculous. I went to a fire last night. With my brother. There was a dead man. Killed. Then we went to see a man with a mission, a male Joan of Arc with a chicano accent. I intend no mockery." He turned again to look at her.

Her temple was against the headrest, and her eyes

47

watched him steadily. "Go on, Scotty." That quiet, calm voice.

"On the way back to the ranch," Scott said, "somebody tried to kill us. Not ridiculous; unbelievable. But there it was." He paused and smiled, mocking himself. "This morning I played tennis with my niece. She's seventeen, and groping, but already she sees some things plainer than I do. Two hours ago I talked with her brother. He's twenty-two, also groping, although he doesn't think so. But he had some things to say that make me look at myself in a new light." He paused again, and the mocking smile returned. "Tell me, counselor, how does one react to that sudden knowledge?"

"As you have," Jenny said. "With humility." She took her time, studying his face, asking herself how far she wanted to be involved. The answer was clear, and she said at last, "Who was the dead man? Who tried to kill you? What was the fire, and who is the man with a mission?" She paused. "Do you want to tell me, Scotty?"

"That's why I'm here."

She leaned back and closed her eyes then while she listened, and when he was done, "There have to be causes," she said. Her eyes were open again, watching him.

"Of course. We're the target."

She was silent, still watching him.

"Because of what we have," he said, "and because of how we got it . . ." He shook his head.

Jenny said, "I know only part of it." She smiled gently. "The Stanfields came here early, got rich, and have been getting richer ever since."

"The Stanfields," Scott said, "and the Meyers." Was it like this on the psychiatrist's couch, talking without effort as if to yourself, feeling strain and tension flow away? He glanced at Jenny and saw that she understood. "My great-great-grandfather was named Ezra Stanfield. He was a lawyer. He came to San Francisco in 1849; not after gold, after land. He got his first big parcel down in the Valley, what is now Stanhope and the area around it, as his fee for defending the naturalized Californian who held the grant. The charge was murder." He glanced again at Jenny.

"I'm listening." Merely that.

"He lost the case," Scott said. "His client was hanged. I've read what I could find of the trial transcript, and I'd say that either great-great-grandfather Ezra was a rotten lawyer, or he didn't want to win the case. But he got the land anyway."

"Scotty, Scotty. Your great-great-grandfather, a hundred and how many years ago?"

"He was quite a fellow," Scott said. "When California became a state, proving titles was the big thing. There were Indian claims, Spanish claims, Mexican claims, and what could only be called squatter claims, all conflicting. Ezra went into the title field and became an expert. Of course he charged a fee, usually a percentage of the land in dispute." He paused. "Sometimes he ended up owning more of the land than his client."

"The charge," Jenny said, "is still made against the legal profession."

"Ezra's son Amos," Scott said, "my great-grandfather, I knew him vaguely, picked right up where the old man left off. The 1870s were a panic time in California, and Amos, first with Rudi Meyer, his uncle, and then with Walter Meyer, his cousin, made a lot of smart loans to wheat farmers in trouble. The land down south in the Valley where our oil properties are was land Amos foreclosed on. Then there's the water they stole by buying up riverfront property and claiming riparian rights. That's another story . . ."

"And," Jenny said, "you know it well."

"My field is history, California history in particular."

"And did you go into it as an exercise in self-flagellation?" She was smiling, but her steady, watching eyes were troubled.

"Like the man," Scott said, "who goes into psychiatry in order to understand his own mental problems?" He paused. "Maybe." Above all else, he thought, he liked and respected her honesty, her willingness to speak out. "They were plunderers, freebooters," he said. "But they were also builders. They turned that Central Valley from a semi-desert into the richest agricultural area in the country."

Jenny was smiling again, her eyes less troubled. "And you respect them."

"In a way." It was true.

"In their place," Jenny said, "would you have done differently?"

He had asked himself the same question many times, and honesty dictated the answer. "In their place," he said, "in their time, *if* I'd had their nerve and their acumen, I'd have done the same." He smiled suddenly, for the first time that day really meaning it. "So what's all the guilt feeling about?"

"Something like that." She paused, watching him carefully. "Or is there more?"

They had come out of the park and were driving slowly along the Grizzly Peak road. The campus of the university and the city of Berkeley lay beneath them; beyond, the water of the Bay glistened in the sun, the bridges plain, San Francisco rising clean and clear on its storied hills. Scott stopped the car at a turnout, switched off the engine. There was quiet.

"There *is* more," he said. "There is *me*, uninvolved." He searched for analogy. "I played at Forest Hills a few times," he said, "once in the semifinals. I was beaten, and I didn't like that, I never did." Pause. "But the point is that I wouldn't have traded any kind of defeat for a seat in the stands, just being a spectator." He paused again. "And that's what a seventeen-year-old girl and her twenty-two-year-old brother, freak that he's chosen to be, made me see this morning—that I *am* a spectator. I never thought of it that way before." He paused a third time and rubbed his fingers lightly on the smooth surface of the steering wheel. He turned to look at Jenny. "And," he said, "I don't like it one little bit."

7

The senator was on the telephone again when his wife Conchita, summoned, closed the study door behind her. The senator wore an expression of weary amusement. He cupped his hand over the mouthpiece to explain. "Julia," he said, and that was all. Then, into the phone again, "I hear, my dear, and I regret. My plane is not available. It will be in Sacramento picking up the governor . . ."

Conchita watched him pause. His amusement seemed to deepen.

"Who is more important," he said, "my sister, or the governor of California?" Across the room he watched his wife's spreading smile. Into the phone, "Do you know, Julia, I think you have a point. Very well. The plane will be there to pick you up. Los Angeles International Airport at nine tomorrow morning." The smile now was fond. "Have a good flight from Copenhagen. *Hasta luego, querida.*" He hung up. To Conchita he said, "After all, Bob is a young man. He can manage by car."

"Mike," Conchita said. She was shaking her head slowly,

smiling still. "Dear Mike. You all have it, don't you? Total and complete arrogance."

Unperturbed, "And you, my dear?"

"Oh," Conchita said, "I have acquired it." In nearly fifty years of marriage to this vain, unpredictable, stubborn, brilliant, wholly lovable man, she thought, she had acquired many of the Stanfield characteristics. "Julia is where?"

"Paris. Her banker located her by phone with my message." The senator had an actor's talent for miming. His voice became emphatically feminine. "She dropped simply everything and rushed to the telephone to make arrangements."

Conchita could see it—Julia taking command of the situation, any situation. One more question. Important. "Will she be coming alone?"

The senator's smile was paternal now; dear Julia's foibles were easily forgiven. "Alone," he said. "Hans or Tony or Peter, or whichever the last one was, has been sent packing."

"Dios ayude los jovenes aquí," Conchita said. She too was smiling.

* * *

It was late afternoon when George, having left the pickup in the bank parking lot, walked to the shop with the gay banded awning. In the window a single bolt of material striped in cerise, purple, chartreuse, and bronze leaned against and draped over a dark wood and leather chair. A sign in the lower corner of the window read: Clara Wilson—Fabrics. The entry bell tinkled as George walked in.

Clara was there, crisp and fresh in a beige sleeveless dress and white sandals, a plain wedding band her only jewelry. Watching her automatic welcoming smile change to the almost apprehensive expression he remembered so well, George had a fleeting feeling that time had stood still and that what might have been might still be. Nonsense.

"I heard about Ben just this afternoon," he said. It was his management tone, factual, noncommittal. Perhaps that was nonsense, too. "Riverside," he said. "He spun out and crashed?" Was he being brutal? He didn't know. He liked matters spelled out. There were others who did not, he had found, but it was hard to tell in advance. And it came to him all at once that he really did not know this woman even that well—after all these years. It was something of a shock. "And now?" he said. He paused. "I am sorry, Clara. I hope you believe that."

"Thank you." She was poised, balanced, her hands gracefully and comfortingly clasped at waist height, a lesson remembered from childhood ballet and an adolescent charm course. "A long time, George." Pause. "He is in the hospital." Another pause. "From there?" She shook her head faintly. "I don't know."

The air conditioning hummed softly, and the fabrics displayed or stacked in neat bolts on the shelves gave off a faint not unpleasant odor. Feminine rather than masculine, George thought, as different from the odor of tweed and worsted and cheviot in his San Francisco tailor's shop as silk from leather. "Let me buy you a drink," he said. "Somewhere where we can talk."

Hesitation plain. "I'm not sure."

"Tell me why. We're old friends. Were. There is an obligation."

She smiled then, a faint lifting of the corners of her mouth, no more than that, but it brought life to her face which had been unresponsive. "Yours?" she said. "Or mine?"

Always she had been able to reach him, gently goad him. "Both, damn it." He stood large and solid, in this feminine atmosphere totally out of place. "I'm not trying to seduce you. A drink, and talk." He watched her hesitate, and then nod slowly.

Once in Stanhope it would have been a choice of the lounges of the three hotels, with the ghosts of traveling salesmen whispering among the overstuffed furniture, or the single bar and grill. Now it was the Palace or Angelo's or the Grotto Club—soft cocktail music and, if you chose, large dinner menus to study with maîtres d'hôtel named Louis or Frank or Charles available for consultation on food or wine from carefully stocked cellars.

"I liked it better the old way, I think," George said. "When I was here for a few days then it was country, a change from the city. Never mind." He gestured, and a waiter hurried over. George gave their order. He leaned his elbows on the

53

table and faced Clara squarely. "Now," he said, as the waiter hurried off.

Again she could smile. "What am I supposed to say? That I am broken up by Ben's accident?" The smile was suddenly gone. "I am. But not in the way I'm supposed to be, and maybe that's wrong, I guess it is. I'm beginning to think I'm some kind of monster."

"You aren't." Merely that.

Clara shook her head. "No pronouncements, George, please. You don't know me. You never have. Don't look so surprised. It's true. You didn't even know me when I was a child; I was just a kid cousin of Ann's."

"I saw you grow up. All of a sudden." Arguing with himself, with his new sense of inadequacy. The drinks arrived and George waited until he and Clara were alone again. "Damn it, we . . ."

"George. George." She made no move, but her voice held him. "There was a joke we used to giggle at when I was a girl. We thought it was wicked, but it had a point. It ended with the girl saying, 'In Boston, sexual intercourse does not constitute social introduction.' Does that shock you, George?"

In a way it did, just as young Ellen's flippancies sometimes had the power to shock him too. "I'm just a square, Clara." Then, with a touch of the management manner, "Bear that in mind."

"I have. I do. Do you know why I married Ben?"

"I suppose for the usual reasons. He was more your age than I was."

"No." Then, "I married him because you were still married to Ann."

"Ann had been dead ten years."

"The statement stands." Another pause. "Oh, don't think I didn't think about marrying you. I did. You can't know how the—common people look at you Stanfields, you really can't."

"Maybe I'm beginning to learn. A lot of people are trying to teach me." As in the police chief's office that morning, he hadn't realized how uptight he was—this time Ellen's word came naturally to mind. "You . . ."

54

"You're angry," Clara said. She nodded. "Maybe that's good, George, because I'm angry too. Not at you. At myself. At Ben. At everything, because I've made such a mess of it." Pause. "There. It's out. That was why I didn't want to come and have a drink and a heart-to-heart with you." She searched his face. "You still don't understand, do you?"

His anger was gone as quickly as it had come. Always until now, he thought, he had been slow to anger and slow to calm down. Well, that was how things were these days, emotions were swift to surface. The world was changing, and he with it; or maybe the world was changing and he was not changing with it; maybe that was why he was so jumpy. He was, he thought, beginning to philosophize and theorize like Scott. Steady down.

"I'll tell you," Clara said. "I'm not trying to be mysterious." She wore a smile that was turned inwards, self-mockery tinged with self-contempt. "I was thirteen when you married Ann. I caught her wedding bouquet, and that night I cried myself to sleep with it on my pillow. You and Clark Gable, George, and he lost."

It was silly, and it wasn't. Hadn't his own childhood dreams been as real—even more real than reality? Red Grange? Bronko Nagurski? Why not one day George Stanfield, but probably like the legendary Johnny Blood, playing under a *nom de guerre* because of the family? "I didn't know," he said. It sounded weak, even fatuous.

"Of course not." Her smile then was gentle. "I didn't get over it, George." Pause. The smile turned inwards again. "That was why I married Ben instead of you, and if that doesn't make any sense at all, I can't help it, it's the way it was. I told you I made a mess of it."

"And now?" He had not realized before how much he wanted her, and that too was strange because once, only a few years ago, he had thought that he had known her as well as a man can know a woman.

"Now," Clara said, "I am more married to Ben than ever." Pause. "And hating it, but most of all hating me."

* * *

55

She had—face it, Ellen told herself—been waiting all day for Paul's call. Last night was a dim, unpleasant memory, and although she had tried to rationalize it into unimportance she could not forget the picture of Pete on one elbow, retching, uptight, and unable to control himself—there was enough of Pete in Ellen for her to understand this—ranting at the world in general and at those nearest him in particular, an un-grown-up Ajax defying neon lightning—why? Maybe Paul could help explain, but even if he couldn't, she wanted to hear his voice. Now, more than ever.

But the grandparents were here, Mike and Conchita she had been taught to call them from childhood, and Daddy and Uncle Scott. The house had to be run, and now great-aunt Julia was flying in in the morning which meant more arrange-ments because great-aunt Julia, who could call herself Prin-cess if she chose, had very definite ideas concerning almost everything. So the day had been full. Ellen had always under-stood that being busy took your mind off other matters but it wasn't true, it simply wasn't true.

When Consuelo brought word at last that there was a telephone call for her, Ellen flew up the stairs and straight to her own room, there to close the door and shut out the world.

It was Paul. How had she known? Why question cer-tainty? "Hi." His voice was quiet, normal. "You're all right?"

"I'm fine." Understatement of the age—now.

"Sorry about last night." Paul's voice turned grave. "I don't know about Pete. He's flipped. He's always been, you know, like the genie in the bottle, about to pop out in all directions, but he's on some kind of kick now I don't follow."

Never mind Pete. Oh, not really. But at the moment, Pete was unimportant. "How are you?" Ellen said.

"Oh, hell, I'm fine. Ginger-peachy. You know what I feel like? Like the peasant smuggling messages into the castle where the princess with the long golden hair sits up in the tower."

Ellen giggled. The concept was not displeasing. But it did have its drawbacks. "There's always the front gate," she said, "and the front door."

"And run right into your father," Paul said. "No way, baby."

"Daddy . . ." Pause. Then, "Why, Paul?"

"Baby, I don't know." His voice was gentle now. "Believe me, I wish I did. I'd tell you. You do believe that, don't you?"

Hesitantly, "I guess so."

"Look," Paul said, "how I feel and what I do for Ruben has nothing to do with nobility and universal brotherhood of man and all that crap, the slogans and the speeches and the signs in protest marches. And no matter what my father thinks, either, or good old straight brother Howard, I'm not just revolting for the hell of it. I don't want to tear down; I want to build up on what's already there. It's as simple as that, but they can't see it."

He was no spellbinder, her Paul. With him Ellen had heard Ruben Lucero once, talking in Spanish to a group of maybe two hundred *huelgistas,* and she had never forgotten the man's ability to persuade, convince, convert. No, Paul did not have that quality, and yet when he talked, as now, about how he felt, what he believed, his sense of conviction came through loud and clear. "I guess I just don't understand," Ellen said.

He could be harsh, too. "That's crap. The helpless I'm-just-a-witless-female routine doesn't suit you. Pete wears blinders. He always has. But not you." His tone lightened. "Robert Schumann fell in love with his Clara when she was only thirteen. It was pretty much the same with me, but I gave you a couple more years to see how you'd turn out. So you see I know you pretty well."

What could you say to that? "Paul. Daddy isn't an ogre. He hasn't told me not to see you. He . . ."

"Baby." The lightness was gone now; only earnestness remained. "He hasn't told me off, either, and I don't want him to because I don't think he changes his mind very easily, I know he doesn't, and once he decides that cousin or not I'm strictly N.G. for his daughter, that's the ball game."

Ellen smiled suddenly. "Maybe it wouldn't bother you too much." She paused. "Would it?"

"I'll tell you about that some time." Paul was smiling too, she could tell. "The hell of it is," Paul said, "I'm harmless. I

57

don't even want to tear the world apart the way Pete does. All I want is a little change, but I can just see myself selling your father on that. Or mine." Pause. "Never mind. When can I see you?"

Ellen said slowly, almost fearfully, "Paul."

"Right here. Answer my question."

"Paul. Last night, Pete . . ."

"What about him? He looks like a freak and I think his ideas come out of a stick of cannabis, but he's your brother and my cousin and I've known him all my life. What about him?"

"You said he wants to tear the world apart."

"So he says. He thinks the Weathermen have the right idea. I don't." And then, slowly, "What are you getting at?"

Ellen took a deep breath. "Was he with you when the dehydrator caught fire last night? Was he?"

There was a long pause. Then, "You're reaching far out. He talks about violence, but I've never seen him do any. He . . ."

"Was he with you?"

Another pause, longer than the first. "No. Sorry, baby, he wasn't. I picked him up at a bar on the west side, and there were already flames in the sky. But that doesn't mean anything. It . . ." He stopped. "Forget it," he said. "When can I see you?"

She felt almost sick, and she told herself that she was a little fool, but the sick feeling did not go away. "I don't know," she said. "Mike and Conchita are here, and Daddy and Uncle Scott, and Aunt Julia is coming in tomorrow from Europe . . ."

"Goddam it," Paul said, "and it's all on your shoulders, isn't it? Why don't you just cut out and let them . . ." He heard her soft giggle, and he stopped in mid-question. "What's funny?"

"Aren't you the one who's always talking about responsibility?"

The longest pause of all. "You," Paul said, "are the goddamndest chick I've ever known sometimes."

"Unclear syntax," Ellen said. The sick feeling remained, but it was bearable now, tucked away for future suffering. She was smiling into the phone. " 'Ever known sometimes.' Honestly." She glanced at her watch. "I have to go now. Dress for dinner. Family feast." Pause. "I'm glad you called. I was—waiting."

"Were you?" His voice was gentle. "I'm glad I called too. Have fun at the feast. See you."

"Paul. Please." Another deep breath. "See Pete. Find out." Was there more to say? She could think of nothing. "Please," she said again, and hung up.

8

"I suppose," the senator said at dinner, "that my interest in politics began in 1916. That was the year Hiram Johnson first ran for the Senate. I was fifteen." It was a tale told before; Conchita, George, and Scott knew it well, only to Ellen was it new.

"Johnson was finishing his second term as governor of California," the senator said. "He was a Progressive Republican, and Charles Evans Hughes, the Republican candidate for President, didn't consider him a Republican at all. Hughes came out here during the campaign and snubbed Johnson. It was a mistake."

Scott, listening, smiling, let his mind wander pleasantly to thoughts of Jenny Falk.

The senator savored his wine and set the glass down carefully. "Late election night," he said, "a reporter in New York called the Hughes residence and asked to speak to Mr. Hughes. 'The President,' the butler said, 'has retired and cannot be disturbed.' 'Well,' the reporter said, 'the California vote has come in, and you'd better wake him up and tell him he isn't President.' " Pause. Smile. "Hughes had lost California, and the election, by 4000 votes. Johnson was elected to the Senate by a 300,000 majority."

Scott put aside thoughts of Jenny Falk. "Which," he said, "we had a bit to do with."

"True," the senator said. "Father and grandfather contributed to Johnson's campaign. They believed in the man." He watched Scott's slow smile. "There is something amusing in that?" he asked.

"We liked him and believed in him," Scott said, "because he slapped down the Southern Pacific Railroad and broke its political power, so we got lower freight rates."

The senator nodded. "You find that ignoble?"

Ellen looked at her grandmother. Conchita sat smiling, serene. How many times had she listened to the senator in debate, in campaign, on radio and television, at news conferences, in private, as now? They had been married almost fifty years; in that time how well did a woman come to know her man? And, thought Ellen, will I ever find out?

"Not ignoble," Scott said, "but profitable nevertheless."

The senator returned to his wine. In discussion, he had found, as in most of life, timing was everything. One made haste with deliberation—that was a splendid phrase the Supreme Court had come up with—because the considered reply inevitably carried more weight than the snap quip or the thoughtless answer. It was something not a few of his colleagues in the Senate had failed to learn. He set the glass down. "There is a feeling," he said, "widespread in some parts of the political spectrum, that any kind of profit is immoral, illegal, and probably fattening as well. It is a theory I do not subscribe to. Rapacity in the name of profit—yes, that I condemn. Exploitation—that, too, I consider unsavory. But profit, reasonable profit, is not only justifiable, it is mandatory if any enterprise that is not governmental, religious, or charitable is to flourish. I do not support the theory, Scott, that humans are motivated by divine conviction. Even in the Soviet Union there is now some understanding of this. And in Russia the profit motive, as you well know, has been taken from the dung heap where it was thrown in the early days, cleaned up, given a bright new coat of ideological paint, and returned to

61

official status. Father and grandfather supported Hiram Johnson in 1910 when he ran for governor on the basic platform of getting the Southern Pacific out of politics. He succeeded, and we got lower freight rates, true. But the Southern Pacific's rapacity was notorious, and in benefiting only a few it was harming vast numbers; Johnson's actions merely set straight what had long been badly out of balance." The senator smiled. "Some of the press, incidentally, referred to Johnson and his supporters as Bolsheviks. Johnson's people were the liberals of their day, and in supporting them, father and grandfather were taking a position many men of wealth disagreed with."

"We understood," Scott said, "which side our bread was buttered on." He was smiling still, but the old boy had gotten to him and he disliked being put down, particularly in his own field of competence. The trouble was that everything the senator had said about Johnson versus the Southern Pacific was precisely what Scott himself was fond of saying in his lectures. "Knowing which side our bread is buttered on," he said now, "is something the Stanfields have always been good at." He looked at George. "Present company not excepted."

"Why, thank you," George said. It was one of his rare displays of lightness, and if he had tried he would not have been able to explain its cause. The day had been frustrating; he was, he realized, far closer to anger than amusement. "And so," he said, "you can live high on the hog in your ivory tower in the Berkeley hills."

"Antagonizing no one," Scott said. Not true, of course. There was Cathy Strong, and what was he going to do about her? But he had taken the position and he clung to it. "A far cry from a Joe Hanson with a gun, a dehydrator burned down and a man dead . . ." He shook his head.

The senator said, "The governor is coming here in the morning. We'll have several things to talk about."

Here at last he could make a point. "The regime is threatened," Scott said. "Call out the army and the navy and put the bounders in their place. Lese majesty, that's what it is, by God, and up with it we will not put."

In the silence George said, "Somebody been stepping on your corns?"

"No."

"Then there must be a contentious quality in the Berkeley air," the senator said. "Unless it is merely some form of academic itch?"

He looked at his watch and then with fondness at Ellen. "A delicious homecoming dinner, my dear. I thank you. And now if you will excuse me. I have an appointment in the city." He felt suddenly old and weary as he pushed back his chair and stood up, but his smile did not falter. "Pepe will drive me," he told Conchita. "I may be late." He paused. "Goodnight, all." He walked out to the waiting car.

Pepe, Consuelo's husband, was a smooth and careful driver. The senator approved. As a young man, it amused him to recall, like most of his contemporaries he had worshipped speed, not for what it could accomplish in getting one swiftly from place to place, but for itself alone, a bright new symbol of a shiny new world. That he now considered speed unnecessary except in emergency, he supposed was merely one more sign of age, which he did not resent so much as find interesting. Growing old, he had long ago decided, was very much like walking in, say, London; each new year, like each crooked street-turning, opened new vistas for examination.

Once, a journey to San Francisco—which he, like most old Californians thought of merely as the city—had been the most exciting journey in the world, a venture into enchantment. San Francisco was not a city, it was a religion. Broad Market Street with its multiple trolley car lines and the streets coming in at odd angles, the Ferry Building, the flower vendors, the shoeshine stands, the ferries themselves with the smells of the Bay and gulls wheeling overhead, the lurch and the excitement of a cable car, the hush of the Palace Hotel, grand offices where important grown men spoke deferentially to his father or grandfather of matters far beyond a small boy's understanding.

Oh, some of the old magic remained, and would never tarnish, but familiarity and, he knew, change, both in the city and in himself, had robbed the experience of much of its pure joy. And of course, the reason for tonight's visit was scarcely motive for celebration.

Leaning comfortably back in the rear seat, feeling the

sense of lassitude and fighting it, "Consuelo seems fine, Pepe," the senator said in Spanish. "How are the children?"

"Splendid, señor. They will be pleased that you asked about them."

The senator tried and failed to remember how many children there now were in Pepe's family. No matter. However many, there would be more. Zero Population Growth would be a phrase not in Pepe's lexicon. Or Consuelo's. "I am sorry," the senator said, "to have to ask you to drive me this late at night."

"It is nothing, señor."

It was the answer the senator had expected, but it was, he told himself, very much out of step with the times. The four-day work week and time and a half or double time for overtime were far more usual. Strange thought: should he then feel guilty at this display of feudal devotion? After all these years? His thoughts were taking odd directions tonight. He smiled to himself, at himself.

He was punctual at the doctor's office, punctual in all affairs. "The only sensible thing I recall hearing that Louis XVIII ever said," he told the doctor as he was taking off his coat, his tie, and shirt, "is that, 'Punctuality is the politeness of kings.' It is also far more efficient than any form of tardiness. Thank you for obliging me tonight, Bill."

"As you pointed out," the doctor said, "I am indebted to you, Mike." He could talk and work at the same time. "How many people in California are in the same position? No, reverse that, how many are not?" He smiled faintly.

The senator was impassive. "Do you want the political credo, or the personal? That is a whacking great needle, Bill. Must you drain me dry? I endeavor to serve. Is that not the whole justification for a public servant?"

"Do you ever wonder why your blood isn't purple, Mike? And for the record, I am leaving you ample."

"On the other hand," the senator said, "There have been occasions when in small ways I have been able to shape events, and sometimes by shaping them I have even managed to store up Brownie points against future need. That is mere prudence. I see no conflict."

"Do you sleep well?"

64

The senator considered the question. "Is that a profess-sional query, or are you implying that my conscience—? Never mind." He was smiling. "In either case the answer is the same: I close my eyes and sleep. What is done, is done; in the morning we go on to the next matter."

The doctor said, "I have read that in office President Truman was the same."

There was no hesitation. "A very stouthearted little man," the senator said. "We had our differences, but they did nothing to diminish my admiration. The loneliest office in the world, Bill, and some men panic in it. Not he, never he. Are you finished with your impertinences?"

The doctor nodded. "Wait in my office, Mike. There is whiskey and brandy in the cupboard."

Dressed again, the senator went into the office, found a balloon glass and helped himself to Hine cognac. He relaxed in a leather chair and looked at the certificates and diplomas on the paneled walls. There were ways and ways of demon-strating one's position in professional life, he reflected. The walls of his own Senate office, for example, were lined with signed photographs of near-great, great, and even legendary figures he had known, worked with, and sometimes fought in bloody but usually polite engagements. When he was gone, the photographs would remain, and files of correspondence, speeches, press clippings—but what else?

He warmed the glass of cognac carefully in his palms. Now, he decided, he was thinking like a very old man. His face showed nothing when the doctor came in and sat down at the desk. "Very special cognac, Bill. I am flattered." He paused. "Spare me the customary evasions."

The doctor nodded slowly. "You're on oral drug, Mike?"

"Here it is." The senator set down the balloon glass with care, took out his wallet, extracted a prescription form, and passed it across the desk.

The doctor merely glanced at it and nodded again. "For how long, Mike?"

"Almost three years." The senator had picked up the glass again. He sniffed appreciatively and took a small sip, lowered it again to its cradle in his palms. "Chronic myeloge-nous leukemia—I believe that is the term. I was warned that

65

there was no permanent cure, but that remission might last as much as three years."

"That's what the textbooks say." The doctor pushed back his chair and stood up. He walked over to the cupboard and poured a minute amount of cognac for himself. He turned. "Sometimes the textbooks are wrong, Mike."

"But not this time." The senator nodded. "Fatigue, list-lessness . . ."

"And anemia," the doctor said. "You have done your homework well."

" 'Know thyself,' " the senator said. "That applies everywhere. In politics as in war there is another dictum: know thy enemy." Another sip of cognac. In his hands the glass was entirely steady. "Now to practicalities. How long do I have?"

"That I can't tell you, Mike. On TV they do. They are more sure of themselves than I am. I'm sorry."

"I have to force the issue, Bill. Weeks? Months? A year?"

The doctor hesitated. "Important?"

"Very."

The doctor sighed. He was smiling as he shook his head. "Right on the line, Mike? All right. The best I can do. Not a year."

The senator blinked, merely that.

"But," the doctor said, "I'd say more than a few weeks. Maybe a few months, unless there are sudden complications. An educated guess, no more than that."

"November?"

"You're trying to pin me down, Mike. I can't pick a date. It . . ." The doctor stopped. "Specifically, the first Tuesday in November—is that it?"

The senator smiled. "I am glad you're an alert citizen as well as a physician. The first Tuesday in November, yes. Election Day. Will I be alive?"

The doctor shook his head slowly. "Don't tell me you're thinking of running for re-election? You couldn't campaign, Mike. You . . ."

"My term," the senator said, "has two more years to run. The governor's term ends this year. You don't need to know any more than that, Bill. Will I be alive the day after the election?" He studied the doctor's face. He watched the doc-

66

tor's shoulders lift gently and then fall. "Maybe?" the senator said. "And then again maybe not? That's the best you can do?" He smiled then, acknowledging failure. "If that's it, that's it. Now let's talk about more pleasant things while we finish our drinks. Your boy has done well at Annapolis—oh, yes, I have watched him, Bill. After all, I appointed him. He should go far in the service."

9

The chick's name was Benjie, last name unknown and not really important. A swinging chick in bare feet, hip-rider jeans, and a man's blue chambray work shirt with obviously nothing under it but Benjie. She wore octagonal, metal-rimmed blue glasses and carried over one shoulder a fringed leather satchel which was probably the whole of her luggage. Pete liked the go-to-hell look in her eyes. "A thirst?" he said.

She took her time, studying him carefully. She said at last, "You're buying?" She produced a faint, unembarrassed smile. "I'm broke."

"Fair enough," Pete said. "I happen to have some bread. We share."

They sat over beer, sipping slowly, at a small table in the corner of the bar. The jukebox played hard rock that shook the walls, and conversation was as much by lipreading as by sound. "You just made the scene?" Pete said.

Again that smile. "About an hour ago. The guys I was with were going on north. I didn't want to go north. For reasons." Her breasts filled the blue shirt, and when she

68

moved to change position they stirred restlessly. She seemed consciously unaware. "You've been here long?"

"I know my way around," Pete said. And then, "What's up north that turns you off? Family?"

"Name," Benjie said, "rank and serial number. The rest is, you know, classified." She sipped her beer and watched him over the rim of the glass. She set the glass down carefully. "I've heard these Valley towns aren't, you know, very friendly." Pause. "Comment?"

"They stink," Pete said with sudden vehemence. First Paul and Ellen, strangers; then his uncle Scott, refusing to understand, and by his refusal demonstrating the shallowness of what Pete had once considered wisdom. As he had during those few moments of conscious panic in the turbulent water last night, Pete felt lonely and helpless. "They're filled with self-righteous sons of bitches who'll cut off your balls if you disagree with them and then throw you in the bastille and bury the key."

Benjie's smile spread slowly. "One part of that I don't have to worry about." The smile disappeared. "Then why are you here?"

"Like, you know, reasons." Pete was smiling. "Classified reasons. I . . ." He stopped there. The jukebox clamor died suddenly. Pete said very quietly, "How old are you, Benjie? Fuzz just walked in. They'll want ID cards."

Benjie finished her beer. Her hand was completely steady. She wiped her lips with a bent forefinger. "In that case," she said, "if they want to play rough, I may find out what your bastille looks like."

Pete was looking beyond her toward the center of the room. "Let me play it." His voice was very soft and his lips scarcely moved. "You'd better trust me, baby, or you're busted." He looked up then. In a normal voice, "Hi, Joe. Long time."

The policeman was young, tall and wide, with the beginning of a paunch pushing against the short-sleeved blue uniform shirt. He wore a broad black belt with a holstered pistol and six spare cartridges on one side and handcuffs on the other. In his hip pocket he carried a blackjack. He looked at

Pete for a long time in silence. Then, "For Christ's sake, Pete Stanfield."

"Small world," Pete said. "Small town. How's Linda?"

The big man was clearly uncertain. "What're you doing here? And looking like that?" For the first time he was aware of Benjie. "Who's she? Jesus Christ, the pair of you look like real freaks."

Pete said, "A friend of mine, Joe. We're studying life." Pause. "I'll ask again: how's Linda?"

Hesitation. "She's fine." The big man looked down at Benjie. His face wore a policeman's pitiless expression. "You got an ID card? I know how old he is, but you look like jailbait to me."

"Joe." Pete's voice was still quiet, but it had taken on a slight edge. "I told you. She's a friend of mine. We were just leaving." He pushed back his chair and stood up. "Let's go, Benjie." He waited while she rose. Then, "Say hello to Linda for me, Joe." He took Benjie's elbow. They walked across the room, neither slow, nor fast. Pete held the door. The girl walked through.

The policeman said in disgust, "Jesus H. Christ! Barefoot! Even the goddam Mex kids are cleaner than that."

Pete closed the door gently. He let his breath out in a long sigh. "Get moving, Benjie. He might change his mind. He's just the kind of son of a bitch who would." He was aware that his voice was not quite steady. After the event, it was always so. He caught up with Benjie at the first corner. "We turn here. Get the hell out of his sight."

Around another corner, and yet a third. They slowed at last. Pete said, "I guess it's all right now." He was breathing hard. "Pigs," he said.

"You knew him," Benjie said.

"I grew up here. I know a lot of people."

"And your name is Stanfield."

"That," Pete said, "I'm working hard on forgetting."

"Who is Linda?"

"He married her. You ask a lot of questions."

"Sorry about that."

"Oh, hell," Pete said, "it doesn't matter a damn. Joe thought he'd knocked the girl up. Maybe he had."

70

"Or," Benjie said, "maybe you had?"

Pete smiled. "Maybe. But I had the bread and he didn't. I paid for the abortion. So maybe he owed me a little something." He looked at the girl. Her face was only a few inches below his own; a tall girl, well constructed. "You've got a pad?" Pete said.

"No."

"No place at all?"

"I told you, I just made the scene and I'm broke."

"Okay," Pete said. "My pad."

Distantly a siren purred, rose into its banshee scream, slowly died away. Benjie shuddered. "Okay," she said. "Your pad it is."

There were dirty sheets on the unmade bed, dishes stacked in the sink, a littered floor beneath her bare feet. "No place like home," Benjie said. But at least there was a door that closed out the world of fuzz, pigs, people who called her a freak and made her feel like one. She sat down on the straight chair.

Pete said, "Beer? Or grass?"

"That," Benjie said, "is the best offer I've had today. A stick for paradise." She unslung her satchel, dropped it on the floor, leaned back in the chair, and smiled up at Pete. Her breasts thrust against the fabric of the shirt. "I guess I lucked out, didn't I?"

They smoked one joint at a time, exchanging it for long drags, careful retention, slow exhalation. When each stub was too short to hold Pete ground it out carefully in the lid of a coffee tin. "About eight for one," he said. "Diminishing returns, diminishing series, but as the man said, 'Waste not, want not.' " He carefully lighted a fresh joint, handed it to Benjie.

"You quote him too?" She shook her head. "Far out." She took a deep drag, held it carefully. When she exhaled her breath was almost clear. "Somebody I knew once," she said. Her voice had taken on a dreamy quality, matching the relaxation in her mind. "He was always quoting Ben Franklin. Let's sit on the floor. This part looks clean enough."

Cross-legged, companionably close, passing back and forth fresh cigarette, their fourth? Tenth? Who knew? Or

71

cared. "I was supposed to be a boy," Benjie said. "How about that?" She shook her head. "Far out."

"And your name was going to be Benjamin," Pete said. "Right?"

"Right." Another long inhalation, retention, exhalation, "I'm floating free." She was smiling. "But I disappointed them. Him." She shook her head. "Girl babies."

"But," Pete said, "they called you Benjie anyway."

"Right. Square name, Louise. How about that?" She yawned. "Long day." She began to unbutton her shirt.

Pete held the cigarette and watched her. Button after button, looking neither at him nor at herself. When she reached the waistband of her jeans she gave a tug, and the tails of the shirt came free. She undid the last button and shrugged the shirt from her shoulders. She was naked to the waist, her large young breasts jutting free.

She looked down at herself and then at Pete. "The going rate, isn't it? A bang for a bed?" She began to undo her belt.

"Out of sight," Pete said. "Here." He handed her the cigarette, put both hands on her breasts, and began to move them with slow relish. "No rush," he said.

* * *

Once during the night Pete awakened and was aware that Benjie was awake too. He put his hand on her warm belly. "Advance payment for another night?" Benjie said. Then, "Okay. I don't mind."

"Will you answer a question?" Pete said.

"Maybe."

"How old are you?"

"Does it matter? I have all the equipment, don't I?"

"I just want to know."

"Why?"

"I don't know why." Simple truth. His hand moved slowly, caressingly. He felt her body begin to respond. "I don't know why," he said again, "but I want to know."

Her breathing was not quite steady, and the familiar warmth was beginning to spread within her. She moved her hips in slow rhythm. "Okay. You win." Pause. She closed her eyes. "Seventeen. So?"

72

Ellen's age, Pete thought. It came to him with a shock. Ellen and this girl . . .

"You started it," Benjie said, her voice suddenly sharp. "Damn you, you can't stop now!"

Pete bent down to kiss one full breast, and his hand resumed its gentle motions. "Right on," he said.

10

The boy's name was Luther Smith. He was seventeen years old, suffered from acne, and had just finished his junior year at Stanhope High School. He vacillated between fright and defiance in Chief Ben Walling's office.

"I haven't done anything. And I wasn't doing anything that night when your fuzz came along with a big goddam searchlight . . ."

"Sit down, boy," Walling said. "Nobody's charging you with anything. We're after information."

"About what?" Automatic question. Luther sat down. He cracked his knuckles, brushed his hair back from his eyes, and waited, discomfort plain.

"Night before last," Walling said, "you were parked down by the river." He glanced at the paper on his desk. "At 9:02 the patrol car told you to move along."

"With that goddam searchlight," Luther said. The memory still rankled. There was the girl, unzipped and unhooked all the way down and he, Luther, was just getting into scoring territory when all of a sudden there they were spot-lighted in front of God and everybody, no warning at all.

"The searchlight is necessary," Walling said. "I don't want my men approaching parked cars in lonely spots at night without looking first to see who might be in them. You and a girl. All right. No harm done. It could have been something else." Pause. "And it could have been something other than a patrol car closing in on you, too, you and the girl, especially the girl. That's why they told you to move along." Was he getting through? God only knew. This wasn't a bad kid, a tough kid, a cop-hater as they went these days, but even the most tractable kids had learned—been taught—to look at the law as the enemy. "What I want to know," Walling said, "is how long had you and the girl been there before the patrol car showed?" Pause. "Maybe you saw something. How long had you been there?"

"We just got there. We just . . ."

"Not good enough," Walling said. "You're probably a fast man, but it takes even a fast man a little time to get a girl undressed. Zippers and hooks, even if she doesn't object. How long, boy?"

Luther cracked his knuckles again. "Maybe ten minutes."

Walling merely looked at him in silence.

"Well," Luther said, "maybe more." He brushed back his hair.

Walling stood up, walked to the window, and stood there for a few moments, his back to the room. He spoke over his shoulder, man to man. "You parked," he said. "You went through some preliminaries, and then finally got down to what you'd gone there for." He turned back to face the boy. "My guess is that you had one eye on the time, because the girl is—how old?—and probably you had to get her home by a certain hour and you wanted as long as you could to play around. Understood."

Luther cracked his knuckles, crossed and uncrossed his long legs, and without moving his upper body gave the impression that he was writhing in the chair. He said nothing.

"All right," Walling said, and his tone was no longer conversational. "It's important. Or it may be. Important

75

enough so that if I have to, I'll find out who the girl is, talk to her and to her parents, find out what time she left home and where you were going, or supposed to be going——"

"Oh, Jesus!" Luther said. "They'd flip! Karen's only fifteen, and we were only going, you know, to the drive-in, and I had to have her back by ten . . ." His voice ran down. He cracked his knuckles loudly; it sounded like breaking bones. Capitulation. "We got there at a quarter past eight," he said. "I looked at the clock. We had to show first at the drive-in so if anybody, you know, asked, somebody could say they'd seen us." His eyes were wide with misery. "Is that okay?"

Walling leaned against his desk. "Quarter past eight," he said. "You were parked in the trees."

"I didn't want to park in the road. Anybody coming along . . ."

"Exactly," Walling said. He paused. "Did anyone come along?"

Luther brushed back his hair. It promptly fell down again over his forehead. He looked, Walling thought, like a near-sighted sheepdog. Never mind. "Well?"

"One, two cars maybe," Luther said. "I watched the first one, but they didn't see us and I thought we were all right then; I didn't pay much attention to the others that went by." A trace of the defiance returned. "I was busy."

Well, Walling thought, it had been a long shot right from the start, grasping for a straw, no more than that. Still . . . "The others that went by," he said. "Did any of them stop? Until the patrol car?"

"Just a pickup." Pause. "Out on the road. They didn't see us either."

Walling said slowly, carefully, "They?"

"Two guys. Men." Luther paused. "I watched them because they got out of the pickup, and, you know, I didn't know whether they'd seen us at first, and, well, two men, and Karen . . ."

"Two men got out of the pickup," Walling said. "Did they turn the lights off?"

Luther nodded. His knuckles cracked again with a bony sound.

"They didn't walk toward you?"

Luther shook his head. "I was ready to start up the car and cut out if they started toward us. But they didn't." Even in memory there was relief. "They went the other way. Up toward the warehouses, you know, the packing sheds." He hesitated. "Then they came back. They weren't gone long. I watched them again, but all they did was get in the truck and drive off. So it was all right."

Maybe it meant something, maybe nothing. At the moment it was impossible to tell. Walling said, "You got there at a quarter past eight." He watched the boy nod. "How long after that did the pickup stop?"

Luther felt he was already in so deep that the only way to reach safe ground was to swim all the way across. "I'd only kissed her once, maybe twice, and they showed up. I hadn't even touched her. Five minutes. Ten."

"And you were afraid," Walling said, "and I don't blame you. Sensible is the word. So you stopped and watched them." He waited for the boy's nod. "Then they came back, and you stopped again." Another nod. "And they drove off," Walling said, "but you still had time to get down to—details —by 9:02 when the patrol car came by." He paused again. "Say they came at 8:20," he said. "Say they stayed ten minutes and drove away at 8:30. Would that be about right?"

Luther took a deep breath. The far shore seemed nearer all the time. He nodded. "I looked at the car clock. It was 8:30 when they drove off. I had to see, you know, how much time I had. Karen . . ." He shook his head.

"All right," Walling said. "Just one more thing. Did you get a good look at the two men? You watched them pretty close, didn't you? What did they look like?"

Memory was plain, marked indelibly by apprehension. "It was pretty dark, but one of them was big, real big, with long arms. But it was the other one that worried me. A hippie, and I'm not sure about them. He had a beard and a big black hat and dark glasses. He, you know, was scary." One more solid crack of the knuckles. "But they went the other way," Luther said, "so it was okay."

Walling pushed himself away from the desk. "Good for you, Luther. You may have helped us quite a bit." Maybe, maybe not. Too early to tell. "You can go now."

Luther walked out of the room with more swagger than he had shown coming in. In the hallway he stopped, hesitated, turned, and went back to the office doorway. "Hey," he said, "I just remembered something. What the guy with the beard and the black hat said when they came back."

Walling waited. Sometimes, not often enough, but sometimes a break came your way.

"It was in Spanish," Luther said, "and I, well, I don't talk Spanish, but some words I know. He said something about *hijos de putas*. That means sons of whores, son of a bitch, like."

Walling thought about it. "He was chicano?"

To Luther it was evident. "He spoke Spanish. What else would he be?"

* * *

Ben Walling had another visitor that morning—George Stanfield, in tailored summer trousers, polished loafers, and a short-sleeved sport shirt displaying his brawny arms. "I'd like to see Joe Hanson."

Walling thought about it. "Do you mind telling me why, Mr. Stanfield?"

"I want to talk to him." Pause. "Maybe we can work something out about water." He studied Walling. "And what happens," George said, "if I refuse to press charges against him?"

Walling thought about that, too. He said at last, "I could hold him for various things. Assault with a deadly weapon. Disturbing the peace. Discharging a firearm within the city limits." He spread his hands. "But if you want him turned loose, I'd just be clicking my teeth."

"I can't bend the law," George said.

"Maybe not." Walling's smile lacked amusement. "But if you gave it a try, you could sure as hell put a dent in it." He paused. The smile was gone. "Understand me, Mr. Stanfield. I'm a law and order man, and as far as I'm concerned there isn't one set of rules for one man and another set for another, whether they're chicano, hippie, doctor, or bank clerk." He paused again. "On the other hand, some men get better treatment from the law maybe because they can pay for better legal advice, and if that isn't the way it ought to be, there isn't a damn thing I can do about it. Like they say, facts of life."

"And now that you've got that off your chest," George said, "I'd like to see Joe Hanson."

Walling stood up from his desk. "Be my guest, Mr. Stanfield."

Joe Hanson was in his fifties, lean and weathered, with a farmer's tan on hands, forearms, face only halfway up his forehead. He had two days' growth of gray stubble, and he looked at George like an animal glaring from a trap.

"I got nothing to say to you. Son of a bitch steals my water, I got nothing to say to him."

George straddled a straight chair. "You're a damn fool, Joe." Proud and paranoid. How do you talk to a man like that? "Suppose I offered to sell you water, all you need, until the new canal comes?"

Hanson sat down. In his mind he walked carefully all around the question, examining it for booby traps. He said at last, "How much?"

"What it costs me to pump it."

"My water, and you want me to buy it."

"Drill your own deep wells."

"Can't afford it and you know it." Hanson's voice began to rise. "You goddam Stanfields. You own the earth. You sit in your goddam big office up in the city and push a button, and some secretary with big tits makes a telephone call, and that's it. My wells go dry because you've sucked all my water away. If you need spending money, pump a little more oil out of your oil wells, sell a few head of Angus cattle, a few sections of land, stocks, bonds, a building here or there, or maybe some timber or mineral rights." He shook his head. "Not even that. You don't have to sell a goddam thing. Just have your secretary make a telephone call to a city bank, or a bank in LA, or here in Stanhope, or in New York. 'Yes, sir, please, sir, kiss your ass, sir, will a hundred thousand be enough this week? No trouble at all, sir, don't even think about interest, that's for dirt farmers.' Well, I'm a dirt farmer, and with me it's different. I go in the bank and Karl Meyer, he looks at me like something that crawled in out of the sun to die. 'Joe,' he says, 'you're overextended. It wouldn't be sound business practice for me to increase your financial obligations. Sorry about that.' Sorry, shit. Son of a bitch has one glass eye, and you know how you can tell which one it is? It's the one that looks almost human.''

George sat motionless, forearms resting on the chair back.

Hanson said, calmer now, "You don't even have to get mad, do you? Not like ordinary folks. What I say don't matter a damn. It don't even reach you. You've got a wall of glass around you made of money, and you can see out, but only what you want to see, and you can hear, too, but only what sounds good. The rest of us . . .'' He shook his head. "The cotton pickin' rest of us. We've got you leanin' on us from one side, and chicano sons a bitches like Ruben Lucero leanin' from the other side, and the goddam government in Washington sittin' on top of everything just squeezin' the shit out of us, but none of that means a damn to you, does it?'' There were white flecks of spittle at the corners of his mouth. "Now does it?''

"Do you want me to sell you water, Joe? For what it costs me?''

"And what the fuck good does water do me in here?''

George sat up straight, hands on his knees. "Maybe I can do something about that, too. You didn't mean to hit me when you shot, did you, Joe?''

"The hell I didn't. And how I could miss a target big as you are . . .'' Hanson shook his head, and his eyes turned wary again. "What're you doin' this for? Sell me water, get me out of here—why?''

George stood up. He took his time. He said at last, "I don't know. That's the truth. I don't know.'' He walked to the barred door and called for the turnkey. While he waited, "You've had your shot at me, Joe. Don't try it again.''

11

There were cars parked at the Grange Hall. Among them Luke Albright's monster Cadillac Eldorado stood out like a herd bull in a field of calves. Paul Meyer pointed it out as he and Ruben Lucero walked to the building. "Albright has a poor mouth," he said, "but he can afford that."

Lucero's smile was sad, even pitying. "Maybe he have to have it just to show he can afford it," he said. "Your father, or George Stanfield, they do not have to prove something, so I see George Stanfield in pickup truck."

He had a college degree, Paul thought, and yet it was Lucero who had the deeper understanding of what went on in men's minds and hearts. Someone had said that knowledge could be found in books, but not wisdom, and in the year of his association with Lucero Paul had decided that the statement must be true. Lucero's formal education had petered out somewhere in grade school. Who cared whether the child of a fruit tramp family was educated or not? The only important part of him was his fruit-picking hands. Then whence came Lucero's knowledge, deeper than fact, broader than appearance, surer than dogma? A better man than I am—the thought recurred often, strangely enough without pain.

Three men were waiting in one of the small rooms—Luke Albright, Henry Potter, Louis Khasigian. The mere fact of the meeting, Paul thought, was a solid gain. A year ago none of these men, with the possible exception of Louis Khasigian, would have given Lucero and himself the time of day.

"Sit down, gentlemen," Louis Khasigian said. He had large, expressive eyes with girlish lashes. His vineyards were almost as vast as the Stanfields', and he produced his own natural raisins in the largest dry yard in the valley. He was shrewd, emotional in all matters except business, and utterly merciless in any kind of trade. Paul liked him. "It would have been better," Khasigian said, "if Joe Hanson had been able to come, too." He shook his head; his eyes were sad.

Luke Albright, tall, sandy-haired, intense, said, "Everybody's uptight. It's a goddam wonder more people don't go around waving guns." He was looking at Lucero.

Henry Potter said, "And we ought to have somebody to speak for the Stanfields."

Khasigian shook his head again, in negation this time. "Not somebody, Henry, George Stanfield or no one at all." He sighed. "And so we must make do with ourselves." He was looking at Lucero, and his eyes were no longer sad. "The going rate for grape pickers," he said, "is $1.60 an hour . . ."

"And that," Luke Albright said, "is too goddam much."

Paul thought of the Cadillac outside in the parking lot.

"And it is our understanding," Khasigian said, as if there had been no interruption, "that you are asking $1.75 an hour this year, $1.90 next year, and $2.00 the year after, under contract."

Henry Potter watched, listened, and resented Louis Khasigian's lead. The trouble was that Louis sprang from a long line of Armenian rug merchants instead of good sturdy Anglo-American stock, and there was always something exotic and, well, un-American about his attitude. On the other hand, Louis was nobody's fool, you had to give him that.

Lucero was saying, "There are other matters too, Mr.

Khasigian. There is housing, sanitary facilities, medical attention——"

"Jesus H. Jumping Christ," Luke Albright said. "The
world with a nice pink ribbon around it. Everything for you,
but what do we get?"

Lucero's patience, Paul often thought, was the patience
of a saint—if saints existed. Lucero said now, "We offer no-
strike contract, a guarantee supply of labor . . ."

Henry Potter said, "And no more dehydrators burning
down? No more dead men? No more trucks run into canals?"

There was silence. Lucero said slowly, "I am sorry about
these thing. They——"

"That helps the hell of a lot," Luke Albright said. Henry
Potter grunted. Only Louis Khasigian sat silent, attentive.

Lucero looked at them all. He spread his large hands. "I
cannot make different what is done. I can tell you only that we
have not done these thing, that we do not want these thing,
that violence is not our way——"

"And why the hell should we believe that?" Luke Albright said.

"Because," Lucero said gently, "violence hurt us too."
He shook his head. "Violence make you angry."

"You're damn right." Albright again.

"Violence," Lucero said, as if Albright had not spoken,
"bring more violence, police, maybe even soldiers . . ." He
spread his hands again. "We do not want to fight. We want
to pick your grape to make the money to buy the food for our
families."

"Then," Henry Potter said, "why don't you forget this
huelga crap and go to work? Then you'll have pay to buy your
food, and your television sets, and your cars——"

"Henry." Louis Khasigian stirred in his chair. "That is as
fatuous a remark as I am likely to hear. We came here to talk,
not to berate. Maybe the time for change has come. I don't
know. I am not yet convinced of it, but I admit the possibility."

"You and your ideas," Henry said, and Luke Albright
nodded emphatically. "Farmers have always had special problems, and if you don't know it already, then you'd goddam
well better wake up. We——"

83

"In Hawaii, Henry," Khasigian said, "agricultural labor has been organized since 1945, and while I am sure there are occasional minor squabbles, by and large, I understand, everybody is happy. The growers have a dependable labor supply under no-strike contracts, negotiated well in advance. The workers have a guaranteed wage. More prosperous workers can buy more of everything, including food, and they don't have to be supported on relief."

Henry Potter was breathing hard. "And I suppose that's what you think we ought to do? Just roll over and wave our paws in the air and do whatever he . . ." He jerked his thumb in Lucero's direction. ". . . tells us to do? First grapes? Then lettuce, cotton, melons, peaches, every goddam thing that grows? Whose are they, goddam it, his, or ours?"

"I repeat, Henry," Khasigian said, "I am not yet convinced that the time for change has come, but I admit the possibility."

"Well, I don't," Henry said. "I sure as hell don't. Luke?"

"I'll go along," Albright said.

Paul, watching, listening, wondered just what this show of bravado was supposed to demonstrate, let alone accomplish. Once upon a time he had thought that grown men, merely by living to adulthood, had to have acquired a certain amount of intelligence. Not so. There were times, as now, when he had to agree with Pete's assessment of this older generation—that they didn't have heads at all; their necks had just grown round and haired over. And here were Potter and Albright, glaring at the world like monkeys from a cage.

Khasigian sighed. "Shall I be frank, Henry? Luke? Very well. You can posture all you like, but when the decision is made, you'll go along with it, or you'll go under. Even together, you aren't large enough to fight——"

"You?" Henry Potter said. "Think again, friend."

"No," Khasigian said, "not me alone. George Stanfield will make the decision—to negotiate, or not negotiate. And I will go right along with him. Shall I tell you why? Because George is quite aware that his feudal position is threatened not only here in Stanhope with the Stanfield farming and

84

ranching, but in every other direction as well. And so he has to take the larger view. Taxes, government regulations, union power, the sheer weight of population growth, all of these are doing away with the world the Stanfields helped to shape here in California. George knows it. If you don't, then there is no point in my trying to explain. But I will tell you this: I will follow George's lead because I trust his experience, his instincts, and his judgment." He paused. "And you will fall in line, or fall down."

Paul and Lucero walked back to Paul's pickup. Over in the center of the parking lot Luke Albright's Eldorado roared into life and scattered gravel as it whirled away. "Waste of time," Paul said.

"Maybe not." Lucero wore a faint smile. "Patience, *amigo.* Louis Khasigian . . ."

"Oh, he's all right," Paul said. He was smiling too. "He'd cut off your *cojones,* or mine, if it would help him in a business deal, but he sure as hell thinks better than the others. You can talk to him."

"When you make wine," Lucero said, "you must clarify it, make it fine. A little ox blood or white of an egg, you mix with a little wine and pour into the cask. It take time, a week, two week, but in the end, all that has made the wine cloudy will fall to the bottom of the cask, and then you will have clear wine to be bottled." Lucero paused. "Today maybe we have clarify, make clear. Henry Potter, Luke Albright, Joe Hanson if he get out of jail—*nada y nada por nada,* nothing. Louis Khasigian, he is important, but only if he have effect on George Stanfield. George Stanfield, where he go, the others follow." His smile turned brilliant. "Have it not always been so? Your family and the Stanfields?" The smile was quickly gone. Lucero shook his head. "The violence. Bad. George Stanfield cannot be push. That is not the way."

They drove away from the Grange Hall and back to the small house on the edge of shantytown. As on the night of the fire, two men mounted guard. One carried an axe handle. The other, a large, stooped man with abnormally long arms, held the taped handle of a softball bat in one big hand. His name was Julio, and he was mute. Lucero patted Julio's arm as he walked past and up the steps. "I am in your debt, my friend," Lucero said in Spanish. "Always you guard me as if I were important." Julio grinned hugely.

At the doorway to the house Paul said, "You don't need me for a little while?"

"Your time is your own," Lucero said. His voice was gently reproachful. "I am grateful when you give me aid, but I cannot command you."

Paul parked his pickup where yesterday Scott's white Mercedes had attracted attention. He walked up to Pete's shack, knocked, waited briefly, and then opened the door. Inside he looked around in bewilderment—at the neatly made bed, the sink empty of dirty dishes, the clean floor, the emptied ashtrays—and at the barefoot girl in hip-rider jeans and blue chambray work shirt who watched him quietly. "Maybe I've got the wrong place," Paul said. "Pete . . ."

"This is Pete's pad." No embarrassment, no hesitation, only defiance. "I cleaned it up a little is all." She paused. "Is that funny?"

"Funny different," Paul said, "not funny funny." Something was wrong, and he had an idea he was not getting through very well.

"Pete's gone," the girl said. "I didn't ask where. I assume he'll be back, but I don't know when . . ."

"Relax," Paul said. There was silence. He tried a smile. "I don't usually cause a fright reaction. I'm harmless."

The girl's vehemence was startling. "Nobody's harmless. Haven't you learned that yet? Or in your straight world do you still think, you know, that the stork brings babies and, yes, Virginia, there is a Santa Claus?"

Paul said, "Hey. Hey. Easy."

"What do you want with Pete?"

Paul smiled again. "He and I are cousins, kind of, fourth, I think, and once removed, at least that's what I've been told."

"So?"

"And I'm not over thirty," Paul said, "so you don't have to count me out automatically."

"What do you want with Pete?" There was a near-hysterical urgency in her voice.

86

"Talk."

"About what?"

"Not about you," Paul said gently. "There are other subjects."

The girl hesitated. "Somebody sent you?"

"Who?"

"I don't know. Did somebody?"

Paul said, "Maybe you think this dialogue makes sense, but I don't. I don't even know what you're uptight about, and I'm not sure I care. Pete and I grew up together . . ."

"Here? In Stanhope?"

Paul closed the door gently. He took his time. He said at last, "What's happened?"

The girl shook her head in silence.

"Come on, talk up, what's happened? Damn it, do I have to shake it out of you?"

The girl said slowly, "What do you think's happened? They busted him."

"Who? Why?"

"The fuzz, who else?" The girl's voice was scornful. She paused. "Why? Do they need a reason?" And then the words began to tumble over themselves. "I was in the john or they would have busted me too, I know it, but they didn't even know I was here, and I heard them, and Pete didn't say anything, he wouldn't, he just said, 'Okay, if that's how you want it, let's go,' and when I came out of the john they were gone. They didn't—even close the door!"

"Okay," Paul said. "Okay. Easy." He looked around the neat room.

The girl watched him, quieter now.

"What's your name?" Paul said.

"Benjie."

"Okay, Benjie. I'll find out about Pete." He was aware that his attitude was saying plainly that in Stanhope neither the fuzz nor anyone else pushed Stanfields or Meyers around with impunity, and he wondered what Ruben Lucero would think of that. No matter. "You," he said, and looked again around the room. "Is there food?" Strange, paternalistic thought.

Benjie nodded slowly.

87

"Okay," Pete said. "You stay here, right here. I'll be back." He paused. "You hear?"

She was young, younger than he had thought; in this moment it showed in her evident relief that someone had taken charge. Benjie swallowed. She nodded slowly again. "Thanks," she said, and that was all.

12

For the second morning in succession Cleary Ward parked the big station wagon near the visiting aircraft area and left the engine running to keep the air conditioning on.

There was no getting around the fact that he was being used as an errand boy, and he resented it. Consuelo's husband Pepe could just as easily have been sent to meet Julia Stanfield, even if she was the senator's sister, over sixty, Cleary had been at some pains to find out, five times married, no children, a totally useless member of the human community. Cleary was prepared to dislike her on sight.

He watched the sleek white executive jet come up from the south, swing wide toward the distant mountains in its approach pattern, and then swing west again to land neatly and taxi close. The fuselage door opened, steps came down, and Julia Stanfield appeared, smiling like a movie star, probably disappointed, Cleary thought, that there were no cheering throngs to greet her. He met her at the foot of the steps. "I'm . . ." he began.

"You're Cleary Ward," Julia said. Her voice was low-pitched, vibrant. "And it is very sweet of you to take the trouble to meet me. Thank you." She held out her hand. It was warm and strong, and her smile was intimate. On the steps behind her a cute young thing in gray silk waited patiently, a leather jewel case in her hand. Julia spoke over her shoulder in rapid French.

"Oui, madame," the girl said, and walked straight to the waiting car.

The plane's steward came down the steps. "We have a little baggage," he told Cleary without expression, and went to open the belly compartment.

They did indeed have some baggage. Cleary counted twenty-six matching pieces, which he and the steward carried to the wagon and stowed inside and on the roof. Cleary was sweating when he got into the car.

Julia had taken the front seat beside him; the maid was behind, the jewel case on her lap. Julia's smile was friendly as a puppy's greeting. Sixtyish? Cleary thought. With that figure and that face? The air conditioning felt cold on his dampness as he tried to think of small talk. There was no need.

"Such a long time," Julia said. "Since I've been in Stanhope, that is." There was no hint of condescension in her smile. "I was born here. Were you born here, Cleary? May I call you Cleary?"

"Of course." He was flustered, damn it. "I mean, yes, I was, and yes, of course, you may."

"Thank you, Cleary. If I sound a little confused, you'll forgive me, I hope. Josette and I have lost nine hours somewhere between Copenhagen and Los Angeles, and I never understand it." Her smile now was both brilliant and confiding. "I'm very stupid about some things, Cleary. I'm sure you're very clever. George thinks so, and so does my brother. My, how the skyline has changed. What is that tall building?"

"It's the Meyer-Stanfield Building. It was just finished last year." He found himself talking fast to keep up with her grasshopper thoughts.

"I did hear something about it," Julia said. "It cost a great deal, I think. Well, never mind, it is handsome, don't you think, Cleary?"

"I do," Cleary said. "And it is entirely rented and is

returning a handsome profit." He was boasting like a small boy, and about another Stanfield success at that. Damn the woman, anyway, she had him off-balance, and the air conditioning was making him shiver, and that was some kind of perfume she wore that probably cost a bundle, which was maybe why it got to him as solidly as it did. If there was anybody in the car who was confused, it was Cleary Ward.

He groped for his lost aplomb. "A very handsome profit," he said.

Julia smiled fondly. "How clever of George and Karl Meyer. They do understand these things, don't they?"

"Yes, ma'am."

"Cleary." Her fingers touched his forearm gently. "Please. Won't you call me Julia?"

* * *

"Several things on my mind, Bob," the senator said. "First, I'm sorry my plane wasn't available as I promised."

"It's not all that much of a drive," the governor said. They sat in the study, iced coffee at hand. The governor was in his early forties, intelligent enough to be willing to learn, cagey enough never to rush forward eagerly. "You're looking well, Mike."

"Thank you." The senator smiled. The smile disappeared. "Bill Hanford of the AP was waiting when I flew in from Washington," he said. "He mentioned quite a few things that have been going on—culminating, I should say, in the dehydrator fire and the murder that took place the night before. You have heard about those?"

The governor had. In detail. He had 20,000,000 people living in 158,693 square miles as his responsibility, and a constant flow of information into his Sacramento office came to him in digested form each morning. "Do you have any ideas?" the governor said. Watching the senator's bland smile and faint headshake of negation, he thought—teach your grandmother to suck eggs; he's forgotten more about the waiting game than I'll probably ever know. "What do you want from me, Mike?"

"Want?" The senator was still not to be drawn. He shook his head again. "Big subject, Bob. Violent times. The law and

91

order issue. The generation gap. 'Every cliché,' as Churchill once said of an Anthony Eden speech, 'except: Gentlemen will arrange clothing before leaving rest room.' "

The senator paused and sipped his coffee slowly. He was tired this morning, more tired than he cared to admit even to himself. It was one thing to be quite sure that the dark man was looking over your shoulder; it was wholly another to have someone of Bill Hall's quality remove the modifier and leave certainty standing implacable and alone. "How do you see it, Bob?" And then, suddenly annoyed with himself for automatic evasion, "Strike that question. It's too broad for sensible answer." Maybe, he thought, when all doubt—hope?— was gone, you saw matters in a different light. Interesting. "Let me try a few ideas," he said.

The governor worked on his iced coffee and waited. He had no idea what was coming, but of one thing he could be sure—he had not been summoned by cagey Mike Stanfield just to listen to the old boy make small talk.

"The thirties," the senator said. "You don't remember them well, Bob. You were growing up then, and a world war came along to occupy your attention and distort any hindsight you might have attempted." Pause. "I don't know how close we actually were to the revolution some were predicting, but I do know that the violence that was endemic across the country then had a common basis that was just as definite as the virus that caused the 1918 flu epidemic. The common basis was a blend of joblessness, poverty, hunger, frustration, and helplessness." Pause. "The last two nouns are one."

The governor found himself wondering how it might have been to have lived as an adult through those times. He said nothing.

"My question is," the senator said, "does today's violence in the cities, on campuses, here in this Valley, have a similar common basis? If so, what is it? More specifically, how do we deal with it? Frankly, Bob, platitudes out of Washington about law and order are beginning to nauseate me. Sound and fury signifying nothing. You are far closer to what young people call the action." The senator sipped coffee. "Is it organized? I'm not asking for your judgment on the nation as a whole. But is there a connection between trouble on campuses as far apart as Berkeley and San Diego, rioting in Santa Barbara, and murder and arson here in Stanhope?"

"I wish I knew, Mike."

"Are you trying to find out? Quietly? Behind the scenes?"

The governor said, "Law enforcement, except in an emergency when I am appealed to by the executive of a municipality, is a local matter, Mike. You know that."

"Now you're fancy-footing," the senator said. They smiled at one another. "I won't deny that the whose-ox-is-gored principle plays a part, but only a minor part, in my interest. A man is dead, and at precisely the wrong time some valuable property has been destroyed, but the fact that the property belongs to us is incidental rather than vital."

"You want me to interfere, Mike?"

"Interfere? No. But perhaps a little aid . . ."

"Which has not been asked for."

The senator sipped his coffee. There were times when silence exerted its own pressure.

"Stanhope," the governor said, "is proud of its own police force. A man named Walling, brought up from Fresno, is in charge, and he has a reputation . . ." He stopped. "You know him, Mike?"

"Politicians and elephants," the senator said. "Both have, or ought to have, memories to match their aspirations." He smiled suddenly. "Whatever that means. Sometimes an aphorism gets out of hand. But you see what I mean. Walling, given name Ben; yes, I know of him. He may be far more subtle than I believe him to be. I hope he is. But on the record, he dislikes chicanos, nonconformist youth, and other free-thinkers, and he is foursquare for motherhood and against sin. I daresay he will come up with a culprit. I would like to be sure it is the right culprit, that is all."

"Interference, Mike . . ." Again the governor stopped, and watched, waited.

The old man had more to say. "I said I had several things on my mind." He looked at his watch. "Just a few moments more and then we'll have a civilized drink before lunch." Then, with no change of tone, "How would you like to be U.S. Senator, Bob?"

The governor was a good poker player, the senator thought. It was an ability the senator liked to see in a man in public office. The governor's face showed no astonishment. "Senator," he said. He smiled. "You're thinking of retiring, Mike?"

"I am. Perhaps at election time." His tone was still casual, but the senator's eyes watched carefully. "If I resigned, let us say, on the first Tuesday in November, Bob, it would be too late for you to issue writs of election, as the Constitution says, for that general election. And you would still be governor until your successor took office in January. There would be nothing to prevent your resigning your office and being appointed to the last two years of my unfinished term by your lieutenant governor, who would succeed you. There is ample precedent." The senator smiled. "And it is to be hoped that during those two years in the Senate you would be able to consolidate your position, so that at the end of the time election to a full term would follow."

The governor picked up his empty glass, looked at it, and then set it down again; automatic gesture to gain time. He said at last, "But you could resign this month or next instead, couldn't you, Mike? And then there would be ample time to put your unfinished term on the ballot for the November election." He was watching the senator's face carefully. It told him nothing he had not already guessed. "In that event," the governor said, "instead of an easy appointment, I would have to campaign for election in November, wouldn't I? And that would mean not running for re-election as governor." There was no humor in his smile. "And it is possible that, like Goody Knight, I would end up with neither job. Is that what you're saying?"

The senator heaved himself out of his chair. "I didn't say it, but it is quite true, Bob."

The governor too was standing. "And the cost of your waiting until November to resign instead of resigning now, is my interference in this local matter? Is that the *quid pro quo?*"

The senator walked to the door and started to open it. "As I said, a civilized drink before lunch . . ."

"Wait a minute," the governor said. "There has to be a reason, Mike. Why are you even thinking of resigning?"

Nothing changed in the senator's face. "I'm getting old. I get tired these days." True enough, even understated. "I think I've had my days in the sun. Time now to step aside." He shook his head. "Neither yes nor no yet, Bob. Decisions should not be made on an empty stomach." He opened the door. "I think I promised you Stanfield beef?"

* * *

There were six for lunch—the senator and Conchita, the governor, Julia, George, and Ellen. The senator looked around the table. "Where is Scott?"

"He had to go to Berkeley again," Ellen said. In retrospect she was puzzled. "But only after trouncing me on the tennis court." He was working himself up to a confrontation with Cathy Strong, but that Ellen could not know.

Julia said, "He could have gone far." She smiled at everyone.

The senator said, "In tennis?"

"Of course." Was there any doubt? "Wouldn't that have been far better," Julia said, "than just messing about with history books and poking into other people's papers? I hope no one has the gall to poke into mine when I am gone. Although . . ." She paused thoughtfully, and the smile returned. ". . . they might be rather interesting, at that." She turned the smile on the governor. "Did you know that the first governor of California I ever met was right here at this table? I can't remember his name . . ."

"Hiram Johnson." The senator's voice was amused. "It was in March of 1917. He had already been elected senator, but he hadn't gone back to Washington yet." He was aware that the governor looked at him, but he kept his eyes on Julia.

"It can't have been that long ago," Julia said. "Why, I was just a baby then." She looked hard at the senator. "You're exaggerating, Mike. Brothers do. How could I possibly remember that far back?"

"You have always had a superb memory," the senator said. He watched the flattery take hold. "You were just a child," he said then, "but you had memorized Johnson's campaign song, and you sang it for him. He said you ought to go on the stage."

95

"Well," Julia said, and was silent, pleased, remembering now.

The governor said, "Do you remember the song? I have never heard it."

The senator watched, amused.

Ellen said, "I've never heard it, either."

Conchita said, "Campaign songs are a little out of date."

"But that one," the senator said, "was a real swinger. Julia?"

"Oh, dear," Julia said. She looked around the table. "Very well." She began to sing softly in that low, vibrant voice:

> Washington calls to the Golden West,
> "California, be true;
> Send us a man who can stand the test,
> No other one will do."
> From Eureka to San Diego one name leads all the rest.
> "Well done, Hiram Johnson," you'll hear the people say;
> "goodbye, Governor, hello Senator," on Election Day.
> In November, we'll remember your record brave and true,
> And we'll sign your name on the scroll of Fame,
> For we're mighty, mighty proud of you.

The governor, smiling, said, "Bravo." He looked at the senator. The senator was smiling. It was impossible to know what the smile meant.

Ellen said to George, "You haven't said a word, Daddy."

George smiled. "Woolgathering."

The senator said, "Anything new, George?"

George shook his head.

Julia, irrepressible, said, "And what urged you into politics, governor? I know about Mike. He used to make speeches in front of the mirror. Charmed himself, I do believe."

The senator was unperturbed. "Demosthenes had the sea to orate to. All I had was a mirror. I made do with what I had."

"I went with my father to a city council meeting," the governor said. It was obvious he had told the tale before. "A road had been proposed, and my father was trying to have it rerouted because it would take our house." He shook his head sadly. "My father had a petition signed by all the property owners who would be affected, asking that the road be re-routed. He had an opinion from an independent engineering firm recommending another route as better in all ways—from the standpoint of construction, cost, maintenance and use."

The table was silent.

"I watched the councilmen's faces," the governor said, "while my father made his presentation, his plea. They were merely waiting for him to finish. One man was smoking a cigar and reading a magazine. The mayor was drinking Coca-Cola and looking at a secretary with pretty legs."

Ellen looked at her father. George was watching the governor with a strange intensity, and she wondered why, although what the governor was saying was affecting her too, in an unhappy way.

"When my father was finished," the governor said, "the mayor asked if anybody else had anything to say. Nobody did. It had all been said. So they made a motion, seconded it, and took a vote. It was unanimous. The road would go where it was planned. My father had just been wasting his time. I guess we had all known it all along, but somehow we had hoped that what it said in the schoolbooks and in Fourth of July speeches about honesty in government and the democratic process actually would prove out in fact. That time, at least, it didn't, and I watched it." He was silent.

George said, "The reason?"

The governor smiled. "Today there is an enormous shopping center on both sides of that road, one of the first in the area. It was built only a few months after the road was completed, taking our house and the houses of our neighbors." He paused, smiling still without amusement. "Part of the land on which the shopping center was built turned out to be owned by the mayor's brother and four members of the city council. Pure coincidence, of course."

The senator said, " 'Power corrupts.' True, but there is something else—common decency disappears. It is rare at any hearing, except those that are very much in the public eye, that what witnesses have to say is given even ordinary courtesy. Clerks bustle around with papers. Committee members whisper among themselves, or walk out of the room, or

97

don't even bother to show up in the first place." He looked at George. "If members of your boards of directors behaved the same way. . ."

"Words would be spoken," George said, "and if necessary, some resignations arranged. Interruptions . . ." He stopped there.

Consuelo had come softly into the room. She bent over Ellen's shoulder and whispered quietly. Ellen said to the table at large, "Please. I'm sorry. Excuse me." She jumped up from the table and almost ran from the room.

The senator watched George. George shook his head in silence. And then they all looked up as Ellen came back. "Daddy. Daddy, please. The telephone."

George hesitated. He nodded. "My apologies," he said, and pushed back his chair. He followed Ellen down the hall to the study. It was the private telephone that was off the hook. He picked it up and spoke his name.

"Paul Meyer here, sir. I'm sorry to bother you."

George looked at Ellen. She was standing straight and still, her eyes on his face. He said into the phone, "What is it?"

"It's Pete."

"What about him?"

"He's in jail. Chief Walling thinks he may have had something to do with the dehydrator fire. That's crazy, but there it is."

What was it Paul's father, Karl Meyer, had said? If the boy lands in trouble, you won't turn your back on him? Maybe. Maybe not. "Paul."

"Yes, sir?"

"Has he—I mean, did he—?" George stopped, suddenly angry with himself. "Never mind," he said. "I'll come down." He hung up.

Ellen watched him still. "It will be all right, Daddy, won't it?"

"You've seen Pete?" George said. He watched her nod. Accusation crept into his voice. "And you've been seeing Paul?"

"Yes." Still standing straight, but also proud.

George dropped it there and walked to the door. "Apologize for me. Tell them," he said, "that I was called away. An emergency. You don't know what it is." A lie, and he detested lies, but maybe—strange thought—sometimes there was no other way out.

The miners came in Forty-Nine,
The whores in Fifty-One;
And when they got together,
They produced the Native Son.
ANON.

13

It was midafternoon. Outside it was hot; here in this large shuttered room it was pleasantly cool and quiet. From the depths of the immense bed the old lady smiled fondly at Ellen. "Not all of those who came in '49 were miners, child. There were all kinds. Ezra Stanfield was a lawyer. His good friend Dewey Lane had been a gambler on the Mississippi river-boats." Another smile. "But it wasn't polite to ask too many questions. There was a jingle: 'Oh, what was your name in the States?/ Was it Johnson or Thompson or Bates?/ Did you murder your wife/ And run for your life?/ Oh, what was your name in the States?' " The old lady paused for breath. So frail, her skin almost translucent.

"Are you tired, Marquesa?"

One hand gestured faintly, dismissing the question, and the large diamond of the old lady's engagement ring glittered with the movement. "I don't think Dewey Lane murdered his wife," she said, smiling, "but he had shot someone, and he used to say that a change of climate seemed a good idea. He and Ezra Stanfield arrived in San Francisco on the same ship. During the voyage they had become fast friends."

"You knew them," Ellen said. Here was the perpetual wonder—to be able to listen to someone whose knowledge went back to the beginnings. Oh, that wasn't quite true. Rudi and Lotte Meyer and Ezra Stanfield and this Dewey Lane and all the others had come from somewhere, but to Ellen it had always seemed that what had happened before California was as vague and unreal as what they told you had happened in some European castle back in the twelfth century.

"Of course I knew them, child. Sometimes they liked to talk." Another smile. "Just as I like to talk to you."

"I love it." Simple truth.

"I think we like to leave behind some knowledge of ourselves. Perhaps that is the reason." The old lady paused. "Sometimes," she said, "we tell only the good things, but I think the not-so-good ought to be known too. Ezra Stanfield used to say that when he died he expected to be called before the heavenly court to answer for a number of things, so he didn't see much point in trying to conceal them while he was still alive." The hand fluttered again; the diamond glittered. "Don't get the wrong impression, child. He was your three times great-grandfather, and you have a right to be proud of him . . ."

"As I am of you, Marquesa. And of Mike and Conchita. And Daddy. Yes, and Uncle Scott."

The old lady smiled. "I'm glad. And proud." She was silent for a few moments. Then, "You will hear tales about Ezra Stanfield. And Amos. And Rudi Meyer and Walter. All of them. Just remember, child, people should be judged by the standards of their time, not your own. And California in the early days . . ." She paused, smiling. "A phrase I have heard you use. California then was something else. And Ezra Stanfield fitted it."

* * *

101

San Francisco, 1849

He was twenty-two, Boston, Harvard, the law, and in a sense it was this background of strict conventionality that had impelled him to flee, to journey fifteen thousand miles around Cape Horn to see for himself if this new raw land was real.

"And now that you're here," Dewey Lane said, "what are you going to do?" He made a smooth motion with his right hand. A silver dollar appeared, turned edge over edge across his knuckles, and disappeared. "No miner you." It came out "minah"; Dewey's speech bore a faint Southern tinge. He was no older in years, but the time on the riverboats had taught him much. "And I don't see you hanging out a shingle in this tent town. I doubt if there's much law anyway." He had a quick smile, sometimes but not always meaningful.

"I want to look around," Ezra said. "Buy a horse. See some of this country."

"But what are you after, friend? For the better part of seven months I've been trying to study that out."

Ezra smiled. "What are you after?"

"That's dead easy. What I've always had. A little excitement, enough money to support an occasional thirst, now and again female companionship." The quick smile appeared. "I'm not greedy." The silver dollar appeared again, in Dewey's left hand this time. It disappeared like smoke between thumb and forefinger. "Still asking," Dewey said.

"I want roots."

"It appears to me you had roots, deep and solid."

"They weren't mine," Ezra said. "They belonged to the ones who put them down in their own new land." Spoken aloud, the concept sounded pretentious, and he tried to cover it. "I want something new."

Dewey's gesture took in the dismasted ships in the harbor, the tents and canvas houses that climbed the San Francisco hills, the muddy street, the few frame buildings, and the people—miners, Chinese merchants, coolies, Spanish Californians, here and there a gambler almost in a uniform of soft black hat, white shirt, long black coat. "Something new?" Dewey said. "You have it, son. I'll be interested to see what you do with it." He made one more smooth motion so quick it seemed almost illusory. This time, instead of the silver dollar, a small, heavy derringer appeared in his hand. He held it out, butt first. "Take it. I have another. You've practiced with it." During those seemingly endless days aboard ship, something to do. "Maybe it will come in handy. It did for me once." He dropped the derringer in Ezra's hand. "Luck," he said. "Send me a letter some time."

* * *

For Ezra's eastern contemporaries a European grand tour was fashionable. This was an American counterpart. Even the place names were alien: Sacramento, Benecia, Marysville, Atascadero, Yerba Buena, Monterey, San Jose, Tuleburg, Merced, Paso Robles, Santa Maria. And the strange rivers: the Yuba, the Sacramento, the Feather, the Bear, the San Joaquin, Tuolomne, Calaveras. . . .

Ezra saw the coast and the coastal valleys making entrance to the great Central Valley of the San Joaquin. He saw the mountains of the Sierra Nevada towering high above anything he had ever known, and although this was a mild climate when compared to that of New England, during the winter prevailing westerlies heavy with moisture after their journey of thousands of miles across the Pacific deposited on the slopes of the Sierra Nevada the heaviest snowpack he had ever seen, in places 35 feet and even more.

"Freeze the balls off'n a brass monkey, too," one miner told him. And then, with the kind of harmless exaggeration Ezra came to know well, "I recollect a night, no wind blowin', stars near enough to touch, an' me sittin' freezin', teeth chatterin', an' I noticed the flames of my fire weren't jumpin', they weren't movin' at all. Fact. I reached out with a stick and touched them. Them flames was froze solid."

Ezra nodded solemnly. "I'd be interested to hear how you thawed them out."

It was basically a brown land. In the great Central Valley and into the lower coastal mountains the brown was dotted with shiny, frequently dusty, green oaks, in shape and foliage very much like the cork oaks of Iberia. The ground looked too poor to support crops yet grass was everywhere, and one

103

morning after a rare heavy rain the Valley was suddenly green, lush; Ezra made a careful note in his journal. He was not a farmer, but it seemed logical to assume that the difference between the brown of yesterday and the lush greenness of today was caused by only one thing—water. Something to remember.

He stayed at missions. Always the traveler was welcome. At San Fernando Rey de España on El Camino Real in the valley north of Los Angeles he stayed in the Long Building built especially for visitors and saw with interest the agriculture and cattle raising the Franciscans had introduced in what appeared to be the same barren soil of the Central Valley to the north. He spoke to one of the fathers of it.

"You are a farmer, my son?"

"No. I am just interested."

"Most of your countrymen came here only for gold. Not you?"

"No, father. Just to see a new land."

The priest nodded, pleased. "The land will be here when the gold is gone."

"Land like this?" Ezra gestured at the tilled fields.

"With the help of God," the priest said, "and with water, in this land anything is possible."

In a letter to Dewey Lane in San Francisco Ezra wrote of the conversation and added his own comment: "If I were doing it, which is unlikely in the extreme, I would put my faith in the water rather than in the Deity. It seems to me that He has been known to be capricious."

He worked his slow way north again, over the Tehachapi and down into the Central Valley, headed back to what had come to be known as the Mother Lode country. Rivers flowed down from the great mountains on his right, the Sierra, but only as far as the center of the Valley, where they joined the main stream that flowed north to San Francisco Bay. He made a wide-swinging detour west to the foothills of the coast range, and found no water. He also noted this fact in his journal.

Occasional *ranchos,* property grants extending as far as one could see, farther. Lawyerlike, he thought about titles, and decided that if and when California came officially into the Union there was going to be an unholy mess of ownership to untangle. There would be, presumably, aboriginal rights, Spanish rights, and rights under Mexican rule, now rights claimed by those who had flocked here from around the world in search of gold; and the British crown charters for both Maryland and Virginia, if he remembered correctly, at about this same latitude extended to the "western sea," which could only mean the Pacific Ocean, so both the Spanish and the English kings had given to their subjects this land which neither monarch owned in the first place. He made note of this anomaly in his journal, too.

* * *

In the Sierra foothills he almost rode right through a settlement and diggings called Turkey Creek, and often in his long later life he wondered what might have been if he had ridden on. He was never a religious man, but there were times when he wondered if there were indeed forces at work beyond his control, and he disliked the concept.

Turkey Creek was a stage stop. It had a hotel built of unseasoned Ponderosa pine timbers and planks, a post office and general store, and a blacksmith shop with stables and a corral attached. The diggings surrounded the area, and the stream that flowed nearby was perpetually muddy from gold washing. At night cooking fires gleamed in the darkness among the rocks and trees, and from the porch of the hotel you could usually hear a fiddle or a banjo or a jew's harp in melancholy song.

In one of his rare letters back to Boston Ezra wrote of these mining towns: "The essence is impermanence, and the mood is nostalgia. It is not, and for most will never be, home. When the gold is gone, so will the miners be; and they think of only one goal: to strike it rich and go back where they came from. Never were the Argonauts more anxious to see again their own shores."

Tonight on the porch of the Empress Hotel in Turkey Creek over an after-dinner cigar, he met one of the rare exceptions. "Meyer," the young man said. He had a distinct German accent. "Rudi."

"Ezra Stanfield." They shook hands. "I saw you at dinner," Ezra said. To tell the truth, he hadn't paid much attention to the man. "With a young lady." A stunner—golden hair, blue eyes, regal carriage.

"*Mein*—my sister." Only with certain words, cognates, did he stumble in English. "You are here on business, Mr. Stanfield?"

"Just riding through." He had learned that this was the easiest answer. "You?"

In the darkness Meyer's cigar tip glowed briefly. "I am in San Francisco the resident for the eastern firm of Adams and Company Express. We are, I am establishing a network of offices in California to handle gold shipments, and to act in a banking capacity."

From the hotel bar there was a burst of laughter, loud, liquor-laden.

"It is not always easy," Meyer said in his slow, careful way, "for a miner to protect the gold he has labored to dig or wash. And in the end it must be sent to the east to the mint." He nodded toward the bar where there was more laughter, sudden and loud. "Men like those are not miners. Nor are they gentlemen. Yet they have gold to spend which they have not worked for." The cigar glowed again. "It is to protect the wealth of honest men against such as those that we are coming into business in California."

"It sounds reasonable." Pompous was not quite the word for young Rudi Meyer, Ezra thought, but the man's earnest seriousness did amuse him. In this raw rough land where he himself did not fit as well as some, he could guess that Meyer was frequently out of tune. He said, "Have you been out here long?"

There was enough light to see the slow, sad smile. Meyer gestured with his cigar. "We reached those mountains, Mr. Stanfield, but further north and on the other side, in the winter of '46, my sister, our parents and I, part of a larger party." Meyer paused. "In very early spring of '47, my sister and I, with others, reached New Helvetia which you call Sacramento." Again that smile. "The pass through the mountains is named for our party. A dubious honor."

"The Donner party?" Ezra said, and looked at Meyer

106

with new interest. "And you've stayed on, you and your sister."

"This is our home, Mr. Stanfield. Our ties with the old country are buried in the Donner Pass." End of tale. Meyer picked up his lecture as if there had been no interruption. "One day there will be law in California, courts to protect men's property."

Ezra thought back to the *ranchos*, great holdings like Sutter's own being whittled away by miners and others. "And," he said, "the task of settling titles will begin." He could smile. "A barrel of eels will be uncomplicated by comparison."

"You . . ." Meyer began, and stopped while more laughter clamored inside. When it had died again, "You are a lawyer, perhaps?" He watched Ezra's nod. "There will be much work for lawyers, Mr. Stanfield. Perhaps you will stay to attend to some of it."

"Possible." Ezra was beginning to like this solemn young man.

"Land," Meyer said. "There is much land. From Eureka to San Diego. From the towns along the coast, over those mountains behind us, to the desert. And yet . . ." He shook his head. "No land is without limit, and with water . . ."

"You've seen it too?" There was no reason why he should have been surprised, Ezra thought; he had no conceit that his observations were unique, and yet somehow from Rudi Meyer he would not have expected this kind of understanding. He told of seeing the Central Valley turn from brown to green overnight, and he watched Meyer nod in agreement.

"With water," Meyer said, "anything in this land is possible. I have seen it, worthless land . . ."

The laughter sounded again, but this time above it there was a scream, shrill, unmistakable, a woman's voice.

Meyer jumped to his feet and ran for the doorway. Ezra followed. In the hotel lobby they stopped.

A man was standing in the doorway of the bar, a big man, not a miner, wearing heeled boots for riding, and spurs, and a gun at his belt. His broad hat hung down his back from its chin strap around his strong throat. He had Meyer's sister by

107

the arm. Behind him those in the bar watched in sudden silence. "Cute little piece you got here," the man said to Meyer. "Buy her a drink." He had been drinking, but his eyes and his voice were steady.

"*Mein*—my sister," Meyer said. "You will release her, please."

"A Dutchman." The man was smiling suddenly. "Thought so. Where your pantaloons, Dutchman?"

"We are," Meyer said, "we were Swiss. Will you please release my sister?"

"Cute little heifer. Buy her a drink. How about it, honey?"

The regal bearing was justified. The girl slapped him hard. She drew her hand back to slap him again, but he caught her wrist and twisted it, forcing her almost to her knees. Meyer started forward, and the man pushed the girl away roughly and stepped clear of the doorway. He drew his gun from its holster. "I hear tell Dutchmen dance," he said. He fired one shot into the wooden floor close by Meyer's feet. The roar of the gun echoed from the walls. "Dance, Dutchman! Dance!" From the bar there was laughter. The girl screamed.

Ezra said, "Hold it! Let's stop this now." Challenge issued. So be it. There was no other way. The anger he felt was cold, deep, steadying. "Why don't you go back to the bar?" he said.

The big man's attention was on Ezra now, Meyer and the girl ignored. "You dealin' yourself in?" he said. "Why?"

"I could explain it to you," Ezra said, "but you wouldn't even begin to understand. Now go back to the bar."

"Man interferes," the big man said, "he's got to be shown to mind his own business." He was smiling now. "Maybe if I shoot off an ear you'll remember every time you look at it." In the silence he began slowly to raise the gun.

"Don't," Ezra said. It was command rather than plea.

The gun stopped. "Why not?" The man was still smiling. "You think you can stop me? Turn an' run and I'll put the bullet in your ass. Suit yourself." Again the gun began its slow rise.

The flicking wrist movement Dewey Lane had taught him

and made him practice those long months aboard ship—the derringer appeared smoothly, as if by legerdemain. The click of its cocking hammer was plain. Ezra saw the big man's face open wide in surprise, and the low-held gun rose with urgent speed. Ezra pulled the trigger.

The heavy derringer slug caught the big man in the chest and hurled him back against the door frame. He hung there for a long moment while echoes bounced, the gun in his hand almost raised, his face still wide with surprise. Then the gun dropped to the floor, and the man slid down the door jamb and folded into the awful relaxation of a rag doll. In the lobby and the bar there was only silence.

* * *

"And so," Dewey Lane said, "you have joined the lodge." His quick smile appeared. "Welcome." The smile spread. "Eastern tenderfoot kills badman. The story has been in the papers."

"There was no other way," Ezra said. They were sitting at a small table in a corner of the San Francisco barroom. A nearby roulette table and two poker tables made their own quiet occasional talk.

"Unless you're out to force the fight, there never is, friend."

"And I certainly did not mean to kill him." Ezra was trying to reassure himself and knew it. He found the effort contemptible.

Dewey said, unsmiling now, "When you shake that derringer out of your sleeve and pull the trigger you don't know, and neither does anybody else, exactly where the bullet is going. That's not a duelling pistol, son. If you're close enough, you can hit a man with it. You did. It was all you could do." He made a small gesture, dismissing the subject. "This Rudi Meyer. I've heard of him." Again the quick smile. "And his sister, Lotte."

"We traveled together as far as San Jose."

"And now?"

"I've been offered a case," Ezra said. His smile was bitter. "Rather, my sudden notoriety has been offered a case. Defending a man for doing precisely what I did—shooting and killing another man."

Dewey was amused. "And that's not the way it would be in Massachusetts?" He shook his head. "Another world. You said you wanted something new. You have it. Take it."

* * *

Here in the great Central Valley it was hot, and a dry wind out of the west brought dust to grit between his teeth and make rasping sounds as he walked back and forth in front of the jury. Final plea in a losing cause, and Ezra knew it. The knowledge was bitter.

"The dead man's pistol," he said, "has been handled by so many that any evidence it might furnish us now is suspect. It is true that caps are lacking on all six nipples, although the cylinder is fully loaded, but we cannot now know whether caps were never put on the nipples, were put on and removed prior to the shooting, or were removed after the event. That is the pivotal issue of the entire unfortunate affair."

He had tried to find a single friendly face in the jury to speak to. He had failed. He had the feeling that the verdict had long been established and that what he said now, or had said throughout the trial, was without meaning or effect. But all he could do was try. He stopped his pacing and faced the jury squarely. "Did my client somehow manage to remove, or have removed, the caps from the dead man's pistol before their confrontation, as the prosecution maintains? If so, if my client faced the dead man with certain knowledge that the dead man's pistol was unable to fire, then the charge of murder is probably justified.

"But . . ." Ezra's voice rose in emphasis. ". . . but if, as he has testified, and as I myself sincerely believe, my client had no knowledge that he faced anything but a fully operable pistol in the hand of a man who had sworn to kill him, then, gentlemen, you cannot do other than dismiss the murder charge and restore to my client the freedom he richly deserves." Was there anything more to say? He thought not. He walked slowly back to the defense table. "The best I could do," he said quietly as he sat down.

The client's name was Eduardo Bell. Well before the

110

discovery of gold he had become a Mexican citizen and, following custom, had adopted the Spanish variation of his given name. He held a land grant, one of the few in the Central Valley. He was a lean man in middle age, with a drooping yellowish gray moustache and pale blue eyes. "Right from the start," he said, "It weren't no good." There was acceptance in his voice. "The only thing is, I do believe you really tried."

Ezra opened his mouth and shut it again carefully. He made himself hesitate. Then, "I don't believe I understand that." He said it softly. "What else would I do?"

The judge was addressing the jury. Neither man listened. "Bill Wilder brought you," Bell said.

"So?" From the beginning there had been a kind of unreality about the entire affair. It was stronger now. "You weren't exactly in a position to come to San Francisco yourself."

The pale blue eyes watched Ezra's face steadily. "What did he promise you?"

"Wilder?" Ezra shook his head. "We didn't discuss a fee."

"No fee," Bell said, "and you didn't know me from Adam's off ox, so you just come down, two, three days ride, to hold my hand—why?"

He was becoming angry, Ezra told himself, and he had no right to be. Bell was upset and he had every right; his life was at stake and very probably forfeit. Ezra made himself relax. "Call it penance," he said.

Nothing changed in Bell's face. "What does that mean?"

"I killed a man."

"I heard."

"I had never seen him before, but I killed him." Ezra paused. "Maybe I had to. Maybe one day I'll persuade myself of that. But the present point is that nothing was done to me. There were witnesses, and they all testified that he had a gun in his hand and was going to use it on me when I shot him." He paused again. "You killed a man who also had a gun in his hand, and he had sworn to kill you—but you were being tried for your life."

"That's why you came?"

111

Ezra smiled faintly, mocking himself. "Sounds silly, doesn't it?"

"You're a fool, mister," Bell said. "But I'm grateful." He looked up at sudden silence.

One of the jurymen said, "We already got a verdict. We don't need to go no place. He's guilty as hell." There was a murmur of assent from the rest of the jury.

The judge said, "All of you?"

Twelve heads nodded.

"Then that," the judge said, "is that." He looked at Bell and Ezra. "Better stand up," he said.

* * *

They sat in the little cell in what had been the *calabozo,* hence calaboose. "There isn't much I can say," Ezra said. "Maybe there was something I might have done . . ."

"I told you," Bell said, "right from the start it weren't no good. Every man jack on that jury wants me dead. I got land an' they don't like it."

Ezra sat up straight. "You might have told me that before. We might have tried for a change of venue."

Bell shook his head. "Whatever that means, it wouldn't do no good, neither. I shot the son of a bitch, an' half the town saw me do it. An' there weren't no caps on his pistol. That made it murder."

Ezra said quietly, "Did you know that?"

"Hell, no. Like I told you an' told the jury, as far as I knew either I shot him or he was goin' to shoot me. But when I walked up to him afterward an' saw the hammer of his gun down, an' the gun hadn't fired, an' I looked close an' saw that there weren't no caps on the nipples, why I knew right then that I was a dead man too."

Ezra said, "Do you know why there were no caps?"

"Somebody took 'em off."

"Do you know who? Or why?"

Bell studied Ezra's face for a long time in silence. At last he nodded. "Somebody wanted me dead. That's the why. An' I have a damn good idea who." His smile beneath the drooping moustache was bitter. "Fellow named Wilder, Bill Wilder, fellow who hired you. To make it look good."

112

Ezra shook his head. "He didn't hire me. I told you, we didn't even discuss a fee. If I had gotten you off, I would have presented a bill."

"And now?" The blue eyes were steady.

Ezra shook his head again. He said nothing.

"On the house?" Bell said. He smiled with amusement this time. "We'll see." He made a small gesture. "Wilder," he said, "is my cousin. The only kin I've got left." He looked up as the cell door opened. A brown-robed Franciscan priest stood in the entrance. "Come in, father," Bell said, and stood up. Ezra rose with him. "Father García, this here is Ezra Stanfield, my lawyer." Bell hesitated. "I want you to sign something for me, father." He took a folded paper from his shirt pocket and held it out.

The priest opened it, read it, looked first at Bell and then at Ezra. "Do you know what this is, Mr. Stanfield?" His English was musical, but fluent.

Ezra shook his head. "I have no idea." He looked at Bell.

"He don't know, father," Bell said. He hesitated again. "Will you sign it?"

The priest looked once more at the paper. Slowly he nodded. "If it is your wish, Señor Bell."

"Call it my last wish. Man about to be hung gets that, don't he?" Bell gestured toward the small table. "Pen there, an' ink." He looked then at Ezra. "You got a dollar?" He held out his hand. "Let me have it."

Puzzled, Ezra took a dollar from his pocket, dropped it into Bell's palm. The priest returned with the paper. Bell took it. "This here," he said to Ezra, "is a bill of sale for my land grant, the whole goddam ball of wax. It says, 'For one dollar and other valuable consideration,' an' so on, all legal. Father García's a witness nobody's goin' to argue with." He held out the paper. "It's all yours. You busted a gut tryin', an' nobody can't ask for more than that."

"I can't take it," Ezra said.

"I'm askin'." His eyes were steady. "I'll tell you why. That son of a bitch Bill Wilder wants it, an' he framed me to get it. My cousin, my only kin. That's why I'm askin'. Take it. You're man enough to stand up to him an' anybody else who comes along. That's all I ask. That you take it an' keep it and

113

don't let nobody take it away from you." He put the paper in Ezra's hand.

Ezra looked at the paper. He looked at Bell. He looked, at last, at the priest. "What shall I do, father?"

The priest's smile was sad. "The condemned man, Mr. Stanfield, has the right to have his wishes granted, is it not so?"

Ezra took a deep breath. He looked at Bell. Slowly he nodded.

Bell said, "An' that son of a bitch Wilder . . ."

"He won't get it," Ezra said. "I promise you." His voice was solemn. "And neither will anyone else."

* * *

Back in San Francisco again, sitting as before with Dewey Lane. "That is how it went," Ezra said.

Dewey's quick smile was filled with amusement. "There are days," he said, "when it doesn't pay to get out of bed. There are other days when every time you look at your hole card you see an ace. So now you have some land. Do you know how much?"

"I had it surveyed," Ezra said. "The grant read: 'From the white rock to the twisted tree and thence to the bend of the river,' that vague sort of description. If it is mine, and it is, I want a title that will stand examination." He paused. He said slowly, "It's just over two hundred sections."

Dewey shook his head. "Put it in acres. That I know about."

Ezra smiled faintly, disbelieving still. "One hundred and thirty thousand acres."

Dewey whistled softly. He took out a silver dollar and rolled it automatically across his knuckles, made it disappear. "Landed gentry," he said smiling. "I guess it's been your role all along. Now what?"

It seemed to Ezra that he could almost hear the flutter of unseen wings, and the sense of being maneuvered was strong. "It would appear," he said, "that the die has been cast. I made a promise to a man now dead. My land. My home. Care to give me a hand with it?"

Dewey shook his head slowly. He gestured at the roulette

114

table and the poker tables. "This is my home," he said. "But thanks, anyway. I'll come down to see you sometime."

Ezra nodded. He pushed back his chair and stood up. "Anytime."

"One thing," Dewey said, and the quick smile appeared. "Down there all alone, you might get lonesome. You're the marrying kind, son. Better give some thought to a wife."

Ezra was smiling. "I have," he said. "I have indeed. Her name is Lotte Meyer."

14

For the second time that day George Stanfield had visited Chief Walling's office. The second visit was even more unpleasant than the first. "Description from a boy," Walling said, "who has no stake in the matter, but had his reasons for looking close. Floppy black hat, dark glasses, beard . . ." Walling picked up a pencil, looked at it, set it down again. "There aren't that many answering that kind of description in Stanhope, Mr. Stanfield."

Silence was sometimes the best lever. George said nothing.

"Your son denies it, of course," Walling said. He paused. "He speaks Spanish, doesn't he?"

George nodded absently. Mistake. He said sharply, "Why?"

"The boy," Walling said, "heard him say something in Spanish."

"Hardly proof," George said, but it was one more thing. Black hat, dark glasses, beard, sandals—that was Karl Meyer's description of Pete, too. It did not sound very good. "All right," he said, "let's be plain. Where do we stand? I'm a lawyer, but criminal law is not my field. Do I put in a call to the city and get someone down here?"

"Or put in a call to the mayor and the city manager and tell them to haul their asses over here to put me in my place?" Walling pushed back his chair and stood up. He walked to the window and stood there for a few moments, his back to the room. Then he faced George again. "My grandfather," Walling said, "was a doctor, Mr. Stanfield. He was county medical officer down Fresno way."

George was quiet, expressionless.

"They found out," Walling said, "that tuberculosis could be carried in milk, and my grandfather tested all the dairy herds in the area. One of them, the biggest, tested bad. He issued a warning. Nothing. They kept right on selling bad milk for kids to drink. He issued a second warning. He was just beating his gums." Walling leaned against his desk. "So," he said, "he took his horse pistol and went out and shot the herd dead."

George could almost guess what was coming and he didn't like it, but he waited quietly, unmoving.

"Funny," Walling said, "how his private practice fell off after that. And all of a sudden the mortgage was due on his house, and he was a little short of cash. Tough. He lost the house. Other things happened, too, but maybe you see my point."

"I hear what you say," George said. Then, inexorably, "Now maybe you'll answer my question. Where do we stand? On a boy's description of what he saw in the dark you have my son in custody . . ."

"Your son," Walling said. He nodded. He took his time. "I'll level with you, Mr. Stanfield. I'm not sure he's the one we want, so I'll give him to you." Pause. "But I'll keep digging, and if I find that he is the one . . ."

"We'll see about that when we get there," George said. He stood up. "I think you're being fair, Chief."

"Maybe." Walling walked to the door, opened it. "I don't think he'd better leave Stanhope, Mr. Stanfield." He held the door wide. "I'll have him brought out." Pause. A different voice, heavy with irony, "If you don't mind waiting down-stairs."

George ignored the elevator and walked down the stairs. All municipal buildings seemed to smell alike, he thought, and wondered how much of the indefinable odor was fear and lost hope imbedded in the walls. They called one of Manhattan's jails the Tombs. He stood waiting in the lobby of the building.

"Mr. Stanfield." A fresh-faced young man, about Pete's age, probably went to school together. "Walt Jones, Mr. Stanfield. I'm from the *Register*. They're holding Pete?"

"They're releasing him," George said. "There is no story."

"Will he be going back to the ranch, Mr. Stanfield?"

"We haven't discussed it."

"Have you seen him yet?"

Pete appeared then, sandals, beard, as described. No dark glasses and no black hat. "I'm seeing him now," George said. And, he thought, not liking very much what I see. To Pete, "Come along. The car is outside."

The big engine was quiet, the air-conditioning unit hummed softly. George said, "You're coming out to the ranch?"

"No, thanks. Just drop me anywhere." Pete hesitated. "You sprung me. Thanks."

"You're not to leave town."

"Wouldn't dream of it."

George turned his head to look at the boy. Pete was laughing silently. "What's funny?" George said.

"Solidarity. One for all, all for one. Did you give Walling a bad time?"

George said slowly, "Sometimes I don't think you are real."

"Sometimes I'm not too sure either." Pete sounded sincere.

"What are you after?" George said.

"Me."

"What kind of answer is that?"

"If you don't know, I can't explain it."

118

"The phrase," George said, "is probably search for identity. Is that what you're talking about?"

"Do you know who you are?" There was resentment in Pete's voice now. "Or haven't you ever bothered even to try to find out?"

"By sitting crossed-legged contemplating my navel?" Then, quickly, "Never mind. There are more important things."

"Like what?"

"Like, goddam it," George said, "are you the one that boy saw down by the dehydrator? Were you wearing a black hat and dark glasses?" He turned in his seat. "Well?"

"And did I burn the joint down?"

"And," George said, "kill a man in the process?"

Pete said slowly, thoughtfully, "I wonder what you'd do if I said yes. Would you throw me to Walling? Or would you wrap me in the Stanfield security blanket and tell Walling to find somebody else?"

"Are you saying yes?"

"No. But how can you believe me?"

"I can't," George said. There was sadness in his voice, in his mind. "I'm not sure I ever could." Then, "Where do you want to go?"

The white teeth showed. "Would you like to see my pad? See how the other nine-tenths live?" He nodded. "Good idea. Turn right next corner."

They walked together from the car to the little house. Pete threw open the door with a flourish and then shook his head in disappointment at the cleanliness and the order inside. Benjie was there, and she ran to him. "Oh, God, I've been worried! You didn't come and you didn't come and I didn't think you'd ever come!" She stopped and looked at George. "Is he fuzz?" Her voice was doubtful. "He doesn't look like it."

"The honored parent," Pete said. The girl was close, and warm, and suddenly it was good to be missed, to be welcomed. By this much the loneliness was diminished. He looked around the tidy room. "Benjie, baby, you're some-

119

thing else." He put his arm around her shoulders, squeezed gently. And then at last he looked at his father. "A beer?"

George hesitated. They were in another world, he thought, one in which he could only be a stranger. "I think not, thanks. I'll be on my way." What anger he had felt was gone now; sadness had taken its place. "If you want me," he said, "you know how to reach me." He nodded to the girl, and walked out to the car. When he looked back, the door of the little house had closed.

* * *

Scott's house was his own, built to his specifications, perched high in the Berkeley hills, backed up to the park, protected. Part of the house—the library—was two-story, the rest seemed to grow out of the hillside and the great boulders. It extended itself on a cantilevered porch toward San Francisco Bay with an unobstructed view from Vallejo to Hunters Point, the Bay bridges and the Golden Gate center-stage, the city itself rising clean and clear on its storied hills. The scent of eucalyptus was in the air.

Cathy Strong tugged at her short skirt and tried to look comfortable but it was uphill work. For one thing, today the openness of this porch bugged her. Although she had sunbathed nude here with Scott in other, more relaxed times, now, fully clothed, she had the feeling that the entire population of the Bay area could see her and was watching attentively. The second, more important, discomfort was Scott himself, sitting relaxed, easy and assured as if this were just another of their professor-student conferences way back when.

"Drink?" Scott said.

Cathy shook her head.

"Relax." Pause. "I'm not going to eat you alive. Not yet." He had crossed his legs and now he clasped one knee with both hands in the old familiar posture. "What I am going to do, Cathy, luv, is point out a few facts of life. You're trying to blackmail me." He shook his head. "I'm not going to put up with it."

"You had your fun," Cathy said.

He could smile at that. "And you didn't enjoy it? You're

120

a bad liar, Cathy. Maybe I ought to have taped some of your vocal reactions."

She could blush and tug again at the skirt, but she was determined. "Maybe I did enjoy it. But I'm the one who's pregnant, not you. And I'm the one who's going to have the baby. And it's going to have a name . . . ."

"I won't argue with any of that," Scott said. "But the name is not going to be Stanfield. Is that clear?"

She had watched him on the tennis court, and although some of his youthful fire had burned away, she had still been able to recognize the merciless quality that all champions seemed to have. She saw it now, and it both frightened and excited her.

"Shall I tell you some of the counterinsurgencies I can mount, Cathy, and will, if you force me to it?" Nothing changed in his voice or his manner, and the lack of histrionics made the words all the more effective, as Scott well knew. "Private eyes don't just exist in books and on TV," he said. "They are real. They can be hired. They pry. They open up your life and spread it out for microscopic examination . . . ." He left it there, unfinished for emphasis.

The prospect was suddenly terrifying. "You wouldn't do that," Cathy said. "Not to me."

"You're wrong. I would." He paused, watching her carefully. "I don't flatter myself," he said, "that I am the only man who has, in that ridiculous phrase, enjoyed your charms. You have very considerable sexual skills. You didn't learn them from books. If you force me to it, I'll have trained investigators run down every boy you've ever dated, and we'll find out how many have laid you. If there are enough, and I'm confident there are, then we'll brand you a whore, and your paternity claim will go up in smoke."

The only sound was a soft stirring in the nearby leaves. "You son of a bitch." Cathy's voice was trembling.

"This whole thing is your idea," Scott said, "not mine. You're trying to play adventuress, and you aren't up to it." Scott stood up. He looked down at the girl for long pitiless moments. "Now that we know where we stand," he said, "would you like that drink?"

121

She rose slowly, her eyes never leaving Scott's face. "Are you proud of yourself?"

"There is nothing to be either proud or ashamed of, Cathy. In this world you do well to protect yourself from what used to be called blackguards. You're using your body to try to force a marriage merely for money, a name. If that doesn't make you a whore, I don't know what does."

Tears were evident now. Cathy shook her head to clear her vision. "Unbelievable."

"Because I say it aloud? But it's your generation that insists on calling a spade a spade—when you don't call it a fucking shovel."

"We learned it from you, all of you."

"Perhaps," Scott said. "But you would have done well to learn the whole lesson, move *and* countermove." He paused. "When you first came to me with your I'm-pregnant ploy, I offered to pay for an abortion. The offer stands. I'll write you a check right now for five hundred dollars . . ."

"You can take your money and shove it."

Scott nodded. "Suit yourself." He walked to the sliding glass door. "I'll walk you out to your car."

After she had gone he stood again for a long time on the cantilevered porch, staring out at the water of the Bay. Where did responsibility begin, and where end? Nice guys finished last—who had said that? If there was one thing he had learned, from tennis, from his work, from his life, it was that you did everything you set out to do with all that was in you, no easing up, no holding back; you shot the works. And if that made him a son of a bitch like those in the line that had produced him, Ezra, Amos, Ezra II, yes, and Mike, old silverhair himself, why, so be it. Of only one thing was he sure: he had not heard the last of this girl. Maybe he had won a battle, but the war would continue. All right, he could face that, too.

He left the porch, closed and locked the door, and went into the library to the telephone. Jenny was in her office, and her cool calm voice was benison. "I have a large favor to ask, counselor," Scott said. He paused. Was he making the right move? How could he tell? Shoot the works. "Come to Stanhope with me," he said. "I want you to meet the family. I want

122

the family to meet you. I'm going to ask you to marry me, you know."

"Do I know, Scotty?" There was a smile in her voice. "Yes, I guess I do. What I don't know is my answer."

Scott nodded. "Understood. Maybe in Stanhope we'll find out."

15

Paul Meyer stopped his pickup in front of the massive gates, got out and reached through the bars to take the telephone from its box. To the voice that answered he said in Spanish, "Paul Meyer here, Pepe. Señor George Stanfield asked me to come."

"*Sí, señor.*"

The gate lock clicked open and the two wings swung wide. Paul drove through and in the mirror watched the gates close behind him. Somehow they made him think of the jaws of a trap.

A maid he did not know answered the doorbell, bade him wait, then returned quickly, with a smile and a nod, to hold the door wide. Ellen was waiting inside. Her smile was uncertain.

"But you told me to come, baby," Paul said. His voice was light. "You gave me instructions to storm the castle. I'm here."

"To see Daddy."

"This time. Maybe next time it will be just to see you."

Ellen said, "Why can't there be—peace?"

"The way it was when we were younger?" Paul shook his head. "I don't know if the world's changed. I don't really know what it was like eight, ten years ago, even five or six. But the way I look at it has changed, and that part I can't help." He looked past her. George was standing in the hall watching them. "Coming, sir," Paul said. He touched Ellen's arm gently as he walked past.

Into the study, the door closed. "Sit down," George said. He took the chair behind the big desk. "Thank you for coming. We are going to be interrupted a few times, and I apologize for that, but it can't be helped." Pause. "I want to talk to you about Pete."

Paul waited in silence. It passed through his mind that in a year he had learned a great deal from Ruben Lucero: patience, the knowledge that there was a time to speak and a time to listen, appreciation of other men's weaknesses and strengths.

"How did you know Pete was in jail?" George said.

"Benjie told me. Benjie is . . ."

"I've met Benjie in an informal sort of way." The sadness was still in George's mind, but now it was tinged with wry amusement at himself and his inability to enter that other world Pete and the girl inhabited. "I imagine," he said, "that almost everything to do with Benjie is informal."

Paul smiled. It was rare in his experience that this big, solid man, caught up in the immense power he wielded, ever managed to relax to the point of jocularity, and when it happened it was good to see. "Yes, sir," he said. "I think informality is the word for Benjie."

"Had you known her?"

"No, sir. I went to see Pete and found her there alone."

The private telephone on the big desk buzzed quietly. "Excuse me," George said, and picked it up, spoke his name. He listened quietly. "You may tell them," he said without hesitation, "that we do not intend to negotiate. They are in no position to bargain and we are under no obligation to indulge them." He listened again. "No," he said. "That is final." He hung up, and sat looking at Paul for a time in silence. "Fools," he said, "blunder in over their depth, insist that it was none of their fault, and demand that the rest of the world drop whatever it is doing to give them a hand." His smile was bitter. "And when the hand is offered it is rejected because it isn't holding a fistful of extra money." He shook his head. "Never mind." An almost imperceptible pause. Then, "May I ask why you went to see Pete?"

Never for a moment forgetting the point, Paul thought, and was impressed. "Ellen asked me to. It's a—long story." He had gone too far, he told himself; he knew without question what was coming, and wished it were not.

"A story," George said, "I think I would like to hear. I went out against Chief Walling this afternoon with very little ammunition. Next time I want to be better informed." He paused, his eyes steady on Paul's face. "Ellen," he said, "Pete, and you."

"Yes, sir. Pete and I picked her up the night of the fire. Pete wanted to see her." He paused. "So did I." He was braced for a comment. Instead, a question caught him off-balance.

"How was Pete dressed?" George said, and watched the puzzlement in the boy's face. "Was he wearing a beard? Sandals?"

Slowly Paul nodded. "Yes, sir."

"A floppy black hat? Dark glasses?"

Paul nodded again.

"He isn't wearing them now," George said.

"He—lost them." There was no way out other than total obstinate silence. Paul took a deep breath. "He lost them in the canal. He went over the chute and didn't come up, and by the time we—I got him out, the hat and glasses were gone."

George's voice was mild. "Ellen was swimming with you?"

"Yes, sir."

The room was still. "I see," George said, and that was all. The telephone buzzed again. He nodded in apology as he picked it up and spoke into it. Again he listened, silent, immobile. "We have made our offer," he said, "and those are the only terms on which we will bail you out." He listened again. "Lewis," he said, "you are a damned fool. You are caught with your hand in the till, and you probably ought to be facing criminal charges, and you are protesting because we are not going to allow you a profit on the transaction. Suppose I withdraw our offer entirely? Where will you turn then?" A third time he listened briefly. "Very well. Tell Welch to draw up the papers." He hung up and sat unmoving in silence.

Paul watched and waited, and was aware at last that George had no intention of speaking first. "Nothing happened," Paul said, "if that's what you're thinking. We were skinny, but that was all."

Nothing showed in George's face. "You and Pete picked up Ellen here? At what time?"

"A little after ten."

"And how long had you been with Pete?" George paused. "The truth. Chief Walling will check it out if I don't."

"Since 9:30. I met him at a bar. We had a beer and came on out here." Paul paused. "That was the only drink I'd had. Pete . . ." He shook his head. "I don't know."

"And," George said, "Ellen asked you to see him today? Because she had been thinking, wondering where he was before you met him? Were you wondering too?"

Whatever he said seemed to put him and Pete in the wrong. "Look, Mr. Stanfield," Paul said, "Pete's a damn fool sometimes. Maybe I am too. But do you honestly think he'd burn down your dehydrator? That's what you're implying, isn't it?"

"I'm just considering it," George said. "Chief Walling believes it. And someone like Pete—beard, floppy black hat and dark glasses—was seen near the dehydrator at the wrong time." He watched surprise appear in Paul's face and was convinced that it was genuine. "All right," George said. "That's it. Thank you for coming." Dismissal.

Paul got out of his chair. He walked slowly to the door and there he stopped. He looked back at the big man behind the desk, unmoving, unmoved, as on the telephone—pitiless. "Ellen . . ." Paul began.

"Ellen," George said, "is seventeen years old."

"Yes, sir." Paul drew a deep breath, the deepest. "And she's shut up in this mausoleum. Damn it, sir, somebody has to say it. She ought to be outside in the sunlight . . ."

"With you?"

He made himself calm down at least a little. "Yes, sir."

"Swimming naked in canals?"

"I want to marry her. I think I always have. She and I . . ."

"And take her to live with Ruben Lucero? On whatever he pays you? If he pays you?"

Again the room was still, but this time no telephone buzzer broke the silence. "You don't like me," Paul said. "I . . ."

"Aside from faint blood ties," George said, "are there reasons why I should? I appreciate your coming here. I thank you for what you have told me. I am grateful for your telephone call that told me Pete was in jail. But, *like* you? For Ellen?" George shook his head.

Paul hesitated. The words clamored to be spoken. "I think I'm sorry for you, Mr. Stanfield. You're living out of your time. That's why you lost Pete. Maybe you'll lose Ellen the same way."

George waited with the massive patience he had displayed on the telephone. "Anything else?"

"No, sir. I guess I've said it all."

George nodded. "I agree."

He watched the door close and sat motionless. He thought of himself as a reasonable man, and it always came to him as a shock to find that there were those who did not. Oh, for the opinions of most people he could not have cared less, the world was filled with fools and weaklings, and what they thought was unimportant. But, young as they were, for both Ellen and Paul he had a measure of respect; therefore their opinions counted. Respect, there was the word that mattered. Respect and responsibility—without them there was nothing.

He pushed back his chair and stood up. Through the window a movement caught his eye, and he moved the curtain aside to see. Paul was holding the door of his pickup and Ellen was getting into the cab.

George let the curtain fall and turned away. He would not demean himself by interfering. He had made his views plain to Paul, and Ellen was already aware of them. George ex-

pected compliance. Besides, the telephone was ringing again.
He sat down to answer it.

Outside, Paul got into the pickup and closed the door.
"He'll flip," he said. "He just told me off."

Ellen shook her head. Her chin was firm, and she sat very
straight in the hard seat. "As far as the gate," she said. "I
don't care if he sees us." She tucked her arm through Paul's
and moved a little closer.

The long, tree-lined drive to the high fence and the massive gates where Paul stopped the truck and set the hand-
brake. He put his arm around the girl's shoulders and drew
her willingly close. It was a long, urgent kiss, and after a
moment Paul's hand moved up to cup one breast and move
it gently. "Will you come with me?"

"I can't. You know that."

Another kiss, longer than the first. His hand moved
gently on her breast until she raised her own hand to stop it,
but she made no move to take his hand away. "Don't excite
me, please." She paused. "He's lost Pete."

"I told him that."

"And," Ellen said, "he lost mother because of me. Oh,
I know, it wasn't my fault. All I was doing was being born. But
he lost her, anyway." Her eyes were on Paul's face. "Can you
understand? I'm all he has left. That's why I can't go." She
pressed his hand against herself. "Kiss me again." The longest kiss of all.

Ellen moved toward her door, opened it, and stepped
out. She closed the door again and leaned in the window.
"Call me. I'll . . ." She shook her head. "I don't know what,
but we'll think of something. I'll talk to Daddy. I'll . . ." Again
she stopped. Scott's white Mercedes was approaching and
already, on electronic signal, the gates were swinging open.
"Hasta luego," Ellen said. And she added, "Ve con Dios." She
stepped back as the pickup rolled away.

The Mercedes stopped beside her. There was a woman
with Scott, a calm, smiling, stunning woman. Ellen liked her
on sight. "Jenny Falk," Scott said. "My niece, Ellen." They
nodded to one another. "Clamber in," Scott said.

"I'll walk."

129

Scott opened his mouth, but Jenny's hand touched his arm, and she said in her quiet way, "Drive on, Scotty." She smiled again at Ellen as the car moved off.

Ellen started walking, slowly, automatically, almost blindly. It was difficult to see through the tears.

16

Paul drove straight to Pete's house. Pete and Benjie were there, sharing a can of beer. "You," Pete said, "are the hero of the piece, Benjie tells me. *Gracias.*"

Benjie said, "Thank you." Her open enmity was gone. "And I'm sorry for the way I behaved. I was uptight."

"A beer will square everything," Paul said.

He sat on a straight chair, beer can in hand. "First thing," he said, "you'd damn well better shave off that beaver."

"After all the time it took to grow it?" Pete shook his head. "Besides, Benjie likes it. It tickles, and never mind where."

First the father, Paul thought, now the son—Stanfield stubbornness, a commodity never in short supply. "You're going to have to grow up, friend," he said, "and fast, or you'll be right back in the bastille, probably for good."

Benjie said, "But why?" She looked from face to face.

"Walling has a witness," Paul said. "I don't know who it is, but somebody . . ."

"Somebody," Pete said, "saw somebody down by the

dehydrator. I know. The parent told me. And if I shave this thing off, what do you think Walling will think then?"

"He already thinks you're the one," Paul said, "so it won't make any difference in his mind. But what it will do is make it hard for anybody to pick you out of a lineup."

Benjie said, "I don't understand."

Pete shook his head. His face was thoughtful. He said at last, "You may be right. You have the habit." He stood up. "Somewhere I've got a razor. I think." He smiled at Benjie. "Sorry, baby. No more tickle." He started for the bathroom.

"Just one thing," Paul said. He finished his beer, crushed the can automatically, and looked up. "Did you do it, Pete?" His tone was almost casual.

"Cousin baby," Pete said, and the white teeth flashed in the black beard, "would I tell you if I had? Wouldn't that be a pretty dumb thing to do?"

"I'd like to know."

"Tell me why, cousin."

Paul said slowly, "Your father thinks it was our people, and as long as he thinks that, he's going to be hard to get along with." He was thinking of the scene in the study. "He already is."

Pete smiled again. "As a very great man said once," he said, " 'No comment.' "

Benjie said, "Does that mean you did whatever it was?"

"It means nothing," Paul said. His tone was disgusted. "He's a great kidder, our boy. He always has been." He stood up. "But the worst part is that he thinks nothing is ever going to happen to him whatever he does." He was looking straight at Benjie now. "I'll give you some advice, which you probably won't take. Beat it. Cut out. Stay here with him, and you'll only get burned."

"Thanks, cousin." Pete was smiling again. "A real pal."

* * *

Julio was still on guard at Ruben Lucero's house. He stood quietly, big shoulders bent, the softball bat dangling from one hand, a Diego Rivera peasant rooted in the earth. He watched without expression as Paul came up the walk. "Ruben is here?" Paul said.

132

A nod.

"Alone?"

Another nod.

Paul looked around. Julio was alone. "Where is Manuel?"

Julio shrugged and made a small flipping motion with the bat. The gesture said plainly that Manuel was unnecessary. A large, dangerous animal, Julio, more menacing for his silence.

"I think," Paul said, "that maybe you're right." He walked up the porch steps, knocked twice, went inside, and closed the door carefully behind him. "I'm afraid we've got trouble," he said.

Lucero closed the book he was reading and laid it carefully on the desk. Paul Samuelson's textbook on economics, Paul noticed, and again was impressed. Lucero was largely self-taught, and never content; he thirsted for knowledge as some men for their whiskey. In silence he watched Paul sit down.

"I have no proof," Paul said, "only a hunch. But I think it was Pete Stanfield who burned the dehydrator down." He gave his reasons: Walling's belief, George Stanfield's concern, the description, Pete's reactions. "He could be enjoying himself making us think he did it," Paul said, "but somehow I think not. I was with him that night, and he was hopped-up about something."

Lucero was silent for a long time. "He came to see me," he said. "It was not that day. The day before." He shook his head faintly. "I do not trust a man like that. If he do what you say, to his own family, his own father . . ." He shook his head again, sadly this time.

Paul thought of George, solid and secure in his sense of rectitude. "Pete thinks," he said, "no, that isn't right—they *all* think that whatever they choose to do is right." He watched Lucero's smile, and matched it. "The Meyers, too? You're right, of course. It's just that I'm getting a different viewpoint." His smile disappeared. "If Pete did it, he isn't going to admit it, and even if he did admit it, I think his father would still put the blame on us. Damn it!" His voice was suddenly angry. "It isn't fair."

"Fair," Lucero said, "Have nothing to do, *amigo.* Crying fair is to shake your fist at the rain, at God."

133

There were times when the man's strong sense of fatalism was almost too much. "All right then," Paul said, "what do we do?"

"*Esperamos,* we hope. George Stanfield is not stupid; many things, yes, but not that. And Louis Khasigian . . ." Lucero hesitated. "He talked of peace in agriculture in Hawaii, no?"

"And the others, Albright and Potter, told him he was crazy."

"They do not matter," Lucero said. He hesitated again, studying Paul's face carefully. "Are you losing faith? Are you beginning to think maybe it is violence after all that is the only way?" His voice was quiet, grave.

"What I'm thinking," Paul said, "is that we play it straight, keep our cool, rely on sweet reason, but every time anything happens the finger points at us anyway."

"But you tell me," Lucero said, "that Chief Walling looks not at us but at Pete Stanfield."

True enough, but it missed the point. "Walling," Paul said, "isn't a grower, and it's the growers we have to deal with, and maybe to show them we mean business we ought to go out and turn over a few trucks, burn a few barns, dump some grapes in a canal." He smiled then and shook his head. "I don't mean that, Ruben."

"I hope not." But long after Paul had gone, Lucero sat on unmoving, his face troubled, the economics book on the desk, forgotten.

* * *

Julia Stanfield knocked and came into the study. George had the telephone in his hand. He put it down. Uninvited, Julia sat down in the large leather chair. "You are busy, I suppose, George. I think you were born busy, and conscientious. It used to worry Mike."

George liked Julia. She was a butterfly, but he could not have cared less. She was gaiety and light in a world that hungered for both. "I'm a dull boy," he said.

There was tartness in Julia, too. "If you expect argument on that statement," she said, "you are in for disappointment. You ought to be married." She watched George's sudden

134

smile. "After five tries I am an expert on the subject," Julia said. Then she launched her counterattack. "What have you done to that sweet child to bring her stumbling into the house in tears? I mean Ellen, of course."

George thought about it. "I didn't know," he said.

"Then you'd better find out. You're a man of affairs . . ." Julia smiled suddenly, brilliantly. "And I am grateful to you, dear, don't think I am not." The smile disappeared. "But that child is your daughter, and I think your affairs have been more important to you. Mamacita is her *great*-grand-mother . . ."

"She has never had a mother," George said, "as you know."

Julia stood up. "That is exactly what I told you a few moments ago. You ought to be married. All men ought to be married." Julia thought about it. "No, that isn't true, but most of them should, and certainly you." It was as good an exit line as she was likely to find. She swept out of the room. The door closed firmly.

George was smiling as he sat up and reached again for the telephone. He was thinking of Clara Wilson. Maybe Julia had something. He dialed the Khasigian dry yard and got through immediately to Louis. Louis said, "I hear that Joe Hanson has been released through your efforts. Generous, George. The biblical injunction to turn the other cheek?"

"He won't shoot at me again," George said.

Louis gave his soft, musical chuckle, "And now," he said, "to business? You want me to dry grapes for you until your tunnels are back in operation? It is possible. For a price, of course."

"I'll have Cleary Ward come around to see you," George said.

"A sharp young man."

"What does that mean, Louis?"

"Merely an opinion, largely favorable. I knew his mother years ago." There was an almost imperceptible pause. "Her name was Wilder. Did you know that, George?"

He had not, and it meant nothing to him now. He ignored the question. "We'll start picking in a week, Louis, give or take a day or so."

"And how will you pick, George? A labor contractor? Or a contract with Ruben Lucero?"

"I haven't decided yet." That scene with Paul still rankled. "Joe Baca has always taken care of us."

"When you decide," Khasigian said, "I would appreciate it if you would let me know."

George hung up and sat quiet in the big chair. Joe Baca, labor contractor, as against Ruben Lucero, labor leader—why should he even hesitate? Baca had always done the job, and for less money and benefits than Lucero was demanding for his people. Why give Lucero, and Paul Meyer, a foot in the door? Eventually, perhaps, because that was the way the tide seemed to be running, but why now? And why should he himself even bother with the question? Major as the matter might seem here in Stanhope, it was only a very minor piece of Stanfield business, and Cleary Ward could cope. And that led to another thought: why had Louis made a point of mentioning Cleary's mother's maiden name? What difference? Silly questions.

He heaved himself out of his chair, walked to the door, and hesitated before he opened it. The simple, logical approach would be to send a maid to ask Ellen to come down to the study. Suddenly that approach seemed wrong, and he could not have said why. He opened the door almost angrily and walked across the hall toward the stairs. The mountain to Mohammed, he thought, or some such silly business. He did not even pretend to understand females, young or old.

He knocked on the door to Ellen's room. There was a little pause and then the door opened, and Ellen stood solemn and calm, no tears, although her eyes were faintly red. "May I come in?" George said.

She stepped back, held the door wide, closed it gently after him. She walked to a small settee and sat down. She waited.

"Paul, of course," George said. He sat down in an upholstered chair and rested his hands on his knees. "You're seventeen, honey."

Ellen said slowly, carefully, "Great-great-great-grandmother Lotte was fifteen that winter in the Donner Pass. She was not quite nineteen when she married. What difference does age make?"

George thought of Paul's outburst. "Do you feel shut up here in this—mausoleum?"

"Sometimes."

It was not the answer he had expected, and he wondered how to deal with it. He need not have bothered.

"I'm not suffocated, Daddy. I have a car when I want it. I can ride, swim, play tennis, have friends in. You've never put strings on me. Neither has Marquesa." The girl made a small, quick gesture of despair. "I can't explain."

"And," George said, "you're free to go out nights when you want to without telling anybody, as the other night."

"Paul told you about that?" Ellen's eyes were steady, unflinching. "Pete, Paul and I. We drove around a little and then went swimming in a canal. Naked. Did he tell you that? I'm not ashamed of it. Nothing happened, except that Pete almost drowned. What difference does it make? I'm not ashamed of me. Why should I get all uptight just because my brother and a boy I've known all my life, a boy I'm going to marry someday, Daddy, just because they see me without any clothes on?" She was silent for a few moments. "I'm sorry. I didn't mean to yell at you."

"I guess I can stand it," George said.

Ellen smiled faintly. "Sometimes you're sweet, very sweet. I'm not sure other people see it, but you are." She paused. "But you can be a bastard, Daddy, a real bastard. Does that shock you?"

Oddly enough, it didn't. George said, "I don't particularly like to hear you use the word, that's all." He was silent for a little time. The girl waited with patience to match his own.

"Paul and I," George said at last, "are in different worlds, honey."

"I know."

"He told me I was living out of my time, and that was how I lost Pete. He said maybe I'd lose you the same way. Am I going to?"

Without hesitation, "No, Daddy."

137

"Kids," George said, "boys, girls leave home these days. I'm not sure they know why, or what they're after, but they go anyway. There's a girl with Pete now . . ." He shook his head, thinking of Benjie, young, obviously almost shattered by Pete's arrest, defenseless.

"I'm not going to run off," Ellen said. "I told Paul that. I'm not going to because I can't." She made a quick gesture that took in the entire room, the house, the ranch itself and all it represented. "And it isn't because of—all this, either. I think I could just walk out on everything I have here without even, you know, looking back if it meant Paul, however we lived. It isn't that. It's . . ."

"It's Marquesa," George said. He smiled and nodded. "It would break her heart, and she hasn't much time left. I understand. Thank you." He stood up, solid, massive, and looked down at the girl, smiling still. "I guess we don't get through to each other very well, honey. I'm sorry about that." His smile spread. "And you're right—sometimes I am a real bastard."

There was a strange, gentle half-smile on the girl's face. "Only sometimes, Daddy, only sometimes."

17

Scott and Jenny Falk walked together in the cooling evening, past the tennis court, the swimming pool, the gardens, the stables. "It isn't a house," Jenny said. "It's one of those resort hotels. Broadmoor comes to mind." She was smiling.

"It grew," Scott said. "Ezra Stanfield built it for his bride, Lotte. But then they had three sons, and there were always Meyer in-laws, and guests coming down from the city." He shook his head. "They were unbelievable people. When the Southern Pacific put in their Valley line, Ezra and Rudi Meyer together bought a private railway car just for themselves and their guests. They kept it on a siding over in town. It was still around when George and Peter Juan and I were growing up."

"Peter Juan," Jenny said.

"Our middle brother. A year younger than George. He went off to war in 1943. George had to stay home to help mind the store. I was too young. Peter Juan bought it at Omaha Beach. He was nineteen." He looked at his

139

watch. "Better go in. Mike likes a civilized cocktail time before dinner." Scott smiled. "So do I, as far as that goes." He paused. "I want you to know about me, us."

"I'm learning, Scotty."

* * *

The senator poured gin over cracked ice, added vermouth, and expertly twisted a piece of lemon peel over the drink. He picked it up and sniffed it appreciatively. Then, to Jenny, "The martini is apparently a San Francisco invention. Where the idea of a martini on the rocks came from, I have no idea. But I try to move with the times. Your health. It is a pleasure to have you with us."

"I'm afraid I'm intruding on a family gathering."

The senator smiled. "Nonsense. How else would we have a chance to meet you?" He sipped his drink and walked over to sit down in a large chair. He said to George, "The governor was sorry he had to leave before you returned from your—adventure, whatever it was. I trust you coped with the emergency?"

"More or less," George said. There was no point in talking about it now. Pete was out of jail, temporarily at least, and for the moment there was nothing to be done.

Scott said, "What's up? More crises?"

George shook his head. *"Nada."*

"We live," the senator said, "in a time of alarums and excursions. Mamacita would remember when it was not so. I cannot. Pre-1914 . . ." He shook his silver head gently. "Another era. It is hard to imagine how *settled* those times must have been."

"In a good share of the western world," Scott said, "you knew your place and stayed in it."

Jenny was smiling gently. "No upstarts?"

"A few." Scott was smiling too.

The man was in love, Ellen thought, sipping her sherry, watching carefully. She was not sure about the woman. As far as that went, how did you know if and when you were in love? Oh, there were no doubts in her mind about herself and Paul, but that was different; she could not remember when there had not been Paul. He was a part of her. But when a man and

140

a woman, strangers, met and grew to know one another, perhaps began to wonder if the relationship ought to be permanent—how could they be sure, ever?

The senator was saying to George, "I listened to the newscast this evening. Lewis Mattingly's stock brokerage firm was apparently in trouble, but somehow they found new capital, and are expected to survive. You know Lewis, don't you?"

George nodded. He got up and walked to the bar to pour another drink. He held it for a time in thoughtful silence. Then, "We bailed them out," he said. It would probably come out in the press anyway. "Lewis himself is retiring." He walked back to his chair and sat down.

Scott said, "Forced retirement, no doubt?"

"You could put it that way." What point was there in adding that Lewis Mattingly was lucky not to be headed for jail?

"Another power play?" Scott said. He was aware that Jenny was watching him, and he was undecided whether to force the question or let it drop. He chose compromise. "Will you tell us why you thought it worth getting into at all?"

"Because," George said, "there are some thousands of Mattingly customers who would have been badly hurt if the Mattingly roof fell in."

And this, Ellen thought, was a side to her father that she could not remember seeing before—caring enough about faceless people he had never seen to take action on their behalf. She found herself smiling into her sherry, pleased and happy and warm inside.

Scott said, "Humanitarianism? In you?" He paused. Irony replaced scorn. "Or will we make a profit out of the deal?"

"Probably," George said. "And the Mattingly customers will not take a loss." He smiled gently. "So?"

The senator said, "The word is chiaroscuro, I believe, black and white without shades of gray." He was smiling at Jenny. "To the idealist there are only opposites, good-bad, right-wrong, strong-weak. But what absolute moral judgment can be applied here? It seems to me that everyone benefits."

"Except Lewis Mattingly," Scott said.

George nodded, remembering the complaining voice on the telephone. "There is that," he said, and that was all.

Julia swept in, late, of course. "A martini, Scott dear, very cold, very dry, with just a twist of lemon." She looked at the glass in the senator's hand and shivered delicately. "With the ice removed, of course," she said. And then, "This is your friend from Berkeley? How nice." She sat on the sofa where Scott had been. "Lawyer?" she said to Jenny. "How brilliant." She studied Jenny in a friendly way. "And how lovely. Dear, dear. A few years ago I would have been envious. But no longer. No longer. By the way, George . . ." She looked across the room. "Cleary Ward is such a nice boy. We are riding together in the morning. I hope you don't disapprove."

George shook his head, smiling. "Cleary has to look out for himself."

Ellen was watching Conchita, who sat quiet, smiling at the room, letting the conversation swirl around her like smoke. Usually, Ellen had noticed, it was those who talked who drew attention, but Conchita, yes, and in a way Daddy, and now this Jenny Falk, saying little or nothing at all still managed to make their presence felt while Mike and Aunt Julia and Uncle Scott held center stage. Strange.

Scott had mixed and poured the martini, twisted lemon peel over the glass. He carried it to Julia, held it out, and stopped in the movement. He looked at George. "What did you say?" He seemed unaware that Julia had taken the glass from his hand.

George shook his head. "It wasn't that important. Louis Khasigian . . ."

Julia said, "Some of the local names. Honestly."

"I used to know him," Scott said. "What did he say about Cleary?" He listened. "Wilder," he said then. "It means nothing to you?" He looked at the senator. "Or you?" It was obvious that it did not. "It was a man named Wilder," Scott said, "Bill Wilder, William, I suppose, but maybe not, who persuaded Ezra Stanfield to come down here to defend Eduardo Bell on the murder charge in 1850." He smiled. "We all know how that came out. Bell was hanged, and Ezra came out of it with a bill of sale for the entire grant. That was the beginning."

The senator said, almost harshly, "What is your point?"

"Bill Wilder," Scott said, "apparently thought the land should have been his. He and Bell were related, cousins, I seem to remember. He went to court and lost. He came after Ezra with a gun . . ." He paused. "As Joe Hanson came after you, George." He paused again. "But Ezra wasn't home, and Wilder ran into a friend of Ezra's instead, fellow named Dewey Lane, a gambler down from the city. Wilder should have stayed home in bed, under the covers. He was mad enough to wave the gun at Lane, and Lane shot him dead with a sleeve derringer." He smiled again. "Ezra was defense attorney in that trial, too, but that time he won an acquittal." His third pause. "That," he said, "is what the name Wilder means to me."

In the silence, "Such a nice boy, Cleary," Julia said, and smiled at them all.

* * *

Pete had left long, carefully trimmed sideburns, but the rest of the beard was gone, and he had scissored the shaggy mop of hair on the top of his head into a semblance of order. He rubbed his bare chin. "The most naked, lewd object I think I've ever seen," he told Benjie. "It looks like a shaved pubic mound." He paused. "With a difference: my mouth runs across instead of up and down."

Benjie giggled.

"By a process of association," Pete said, "a hunk of verse occurred to me while I was hacking away:

> Our 'Annibal fought in the Pubic Wars,
> 'E planted 'is seed in all of the 'ores
> An' in some of the matrons what opened their doors,
> To see 'im marchin' by."

Benjie giggled again. "I'm going to miss the beard."

Pete sat down. "I've been thinking too, Benjie baby." All lightness was gone from his voice. "Paul is something of a square, but he has a habit of being right. I think you'd better cut out."

Benjie sat quiet, merely watching him.

143

Pete dug into his pocket and pulled out some folded bills. He held them out to Benjie. "Here. This will buy a bus ticket to wherever you want to go."

"I don't want to go anywhere."

"Baby," Pete said, "believe me, it's better. You saw the parent today. Don't let him fool you. He can be a mean son of a bitch, and the fact that I'm his son won't mean a thing, and those lovely knockers of yours won't be any protection either if you're still here with me."

"What are you going to do, Pete? What have you done already?"

"It doesn't matter."

"Then," Benjie said, "at least tell me why."

"You don't want to know."

"Look," Benjie said, "I don't pretend to understand things. I mean, you know, why people do what they do. Even me." She looked down at the folded bills in Pete's hand, and then raised her eyes again to his face. "But I don't want to go anywhere. Not alone. Not any more. And I can't explain that, either." She paused. "Besides, where would I go?"

He disliked the sudden feeling of responsibility and tried to evade it. "You could go home."

Benjie shook her head. "No way. Daddy . . ." She paused. "He might see it, but Mother never would." Her smile was bitter. "What would her friends say?"

Pete thought of Ellen. Same age, goddam it; the old values still nagged. "I bought you a beer," he said. "I brought you here because you didn't have any place else to go." The argument was working itself up in his mind. "Then, you said it yourself, a bang for a bed. Okay." He looked around at the orderliness of the small room. "I owe you something for cleaning the place up."

"You don't owe me anything, Pete. Not a thing."

"Here. Take it." He laid the folded bills on her thigh.

Benjie did not even look at them. She watched Pete steadily. "You haven't told me why," she said.

"I told you you don't want to know."

"I don't mean what you're going to do, or what you've

144

done. I mean why you're doing it. I, you know, try to understand."

Pete shook his head. "You want reasons? Slogans? A
speech?" He shook his head again. "There's too much talk,
too much crap that doesn't mean anything." He was thinking
of Scott sitting in this same room, assured, imperturbable.
And he was remembering too the image he had carried of
Scott: the liberal, the scoffer at convention, best in the best
of all possible worlds. A saber-toothed mouse. "You do
things," Pete said, "because you want to do them." He
shrugged. "You want a beer?"

"Will you tell me one thing, Pete?"

"Maybe."

"Just one." Benjie paused. "Do you want me to go?"

Pete walked slowly over to the refrigerator. He took out
a beer and held it over the sink while he pulled the tab loose.
Loneliness shared—a contradiction in terms but not in fact,
and where did that thought come from? No matter. He turned
away from the sink. Benjie, the folded bills still resting on her
thigh, was watching him quietly, waiting. "That's the hell of
it," Pete said. "I don't want you to go. And I don't want to
take the responsibility for your staying, either."

"I don't mind," Benjie said. She was smiling now. "I'll
take the responsibility." The smile spread. "Okay?"

* * *

In Scott's Mercedes, top down in the warm evening, they
drove around the city of Stanhope, and west on the broad
Valley floor toward the coastal hills. "You've met them now,"
Scott said. "What do you think? Old silverhair?"

"He's sweet, Scotty, and I don't think he misses very
much. Nor does your mother. Ellen is a delight, and your
Aunt Julia is playing a role . . ."

"Written, I'd say, by Oscar Wilde, Noel Coward, and
Clare Boothe, in collaboration." Scott paused. "How about
George?" He glanced at Jenny's face, but it was only a pale
blur in the near-darkness.

Her voice was quiet. "I am one of those thousands,

145

Scotty, who would have been hurt if Mattingly had collapsed. There have been rumors of trouble, and apparently they were true. So maybe I am prejudiced in favor of your brother's— power play."

Scott felt a twinge of jealousy. He made himself smile. "And what do I say to that, counselor?" Out of habit he glanced in the driving mirror as a curve approached. No car followed tonight. "Funny thing," he said, "about Cleary Ward's mother being a Wilder."

"After all this time," Jenny said, "can it be important?"

"Except to a historian, you mean?"

"Scotty, don't." She was silent, thoughtful. "Did the man who was shot have children?"

"A brood. Three, four, I don't know the actual number. They—disappeared. Moved south, I think. It would be hard to trace."

Jenny said, smiling, "And what happened to the man who did the shooting, the gambler?"

"Dewey Lane," Scott said. He shook his head, smiling too. "He was an original. If you can understand a man through the kinds of friends he has, then Ezra Stanfield must have been a more elemental fellow than the family tends to think, because he and Dewey Lane were very close for a very long time, and it's a matter of record that Dewey Lane never stepped aside for anybody. He carried a sawed-off shotgun for a time because there were three, four men who'd said they were going to kill him, not just one. They didn't even try." His smile spread. "You heard what Mike said about the peaceful times pre-1914? Maybe. But not here in California in the early '50s—do I sound like a professor?"

"Like a man who knows his past and admires it. I think I'm beginning to understand you, Scotty."

The moon rose bright over the eastern mountains and seemed to turn the Valley earth to snow. From a bend in the road partway up the western foothills they could look back and see the lights of Stanhope, the scattered lights of the outlying areas, and the steady stream of lights heading both north and south that were the loaded produce trucks on Route 99 running throughout the summer night. "When we were kids," Scott said, "we used to memorize the names of the

146

towns strung along 99. You chanted them: Bakersfield, Delano, Tulare; Hanford, Fresno, Madera; Merced, Turlock, Modesto, Stockton . . ."

"You left out Stanhope."

"We always did. I don't know why." Scott swung the car around. "Enough. Tomorrow's another day." They headed back down the slope.

Jenny's head was relaxed against the padded headrest. The moon was bright, clear, and a single cloud showed silver in the sky. Am I falling in love? she thought; and the answer was—I don't know. Picture Jenny Falk, attorney-at-law, uncertain in the extreme. We can see others' problems and questions so clearly, but we are astigmatic concerning our own. She rolled her head to look at Scott. He caught the movement and smiled. And then the smile was suddenly gone. Jenny sat up. "What's the matter?"

"Ahead." He pointed with his chin, both hands firm on the wheel.

At first it made no understandable picture. On the road ahead there were two lights and moving shapes, but the lights were one above the other at the side of the road instead of horizontal. And the lights of the Mercedes picked out strange rectangular shapes lying on the pavement like scattered tombstones in a field.

And then, all at once, the picture sprang into focus. "Oh, dear," Jenny said. "An accident. A truck overturned . . ."

"No accident," Scott said.

They were closer now, close enough to make out that the scattered tombstones were bales of hay, and that the moving shapes in the glare of the vertical headlights were men, two, three, four men, busy at activity unknown—until a flame appeared, and then a second, and immediately the truck became a giant bonfire throwing flames high into the sky.

Jenny said, "Aren't you going to stop and help?"

"Not with you in the car." Scott's voice was hard, angry. "And not with me, either." He slammed in his clutch, shifted down. "Hang on."

Men were gesturing, and the hay bales were an obstacle course. Scott bore down on the accelerator, took the Mercedes off the road to the left, out on bare dirt, skidding,

147

snarling, into a gentle decline, and then hard right again up the bank and back on the pavement, the burning truck left well behind. No lights followed, and after a mile or so he slowed to normal speed.

Jenny watched his face. "Somebody may be hurt, Scotty."

"I wouldn't doubt it."

Jenny shook her head. Her eyes were troubled. "I don't understand."

"Did you see the color of the truck?" The anger was still in his voice. "It was mustard yellow, a special color. And if you'd been able to read the lettering on the cab door, you would have seen: Stanfield Cattle Company. One of our hay trucks, overturned, burned." He paused. "God knows what happened to the driver."

"But Scotty . . ."

"Counselor, I was not about to throw you to the wolves. Or myself. You wouldn't go blundering around in the middle of an Oakland riot. And you don't mix in something like this either." He turned to face her squarely for a moment. "And if that makes me something less than heroic . . ." He lifted his shoulders and let them drop. "So be it," he said. They drove on in silence.

As they approached the entrance to the ranch he pressed the button beneath the dashboard. The gates swung open and they drove through. He touched the button again, and the gates swung shut. "Times," Scott said, "like now, what I think is that we've reached sanctuary." He shook his head. "And if the peasants are in revolt outside, why, we're still safe in here." He shook his head again. "And I don't like that feeling one single little goddam bit, but I can't shake it. Call it the built-in Marie Antoinette syndrome, can you understand that, counselor?"

* * *

Benjie awakened and for a time could not remember where she was, so she lay quite still and stared up at the darkness and tried to work it out. It was a discipline she set herself, because the first few times it had happened after she had left home, panic had been near and almost overpowering,

148

and once to her shame she had actually screamed out in the night. But unfamiliarity was the norm now, and she liked to think that while at home she had always known *where* she was; now she was beginning to track down her identity. Sometimes the process could be unnerving, but the trick was merely to get through the first few seconds of consciousness without coming apart, and after that it was usually all right. Usually.

This time it did not take long. She remembered the voices of the fuzz while she was in the john, and the other, familiar voice—Pete's of course. But that was yesterday, and he had come back, but where was he now? Because she was alone, very much alone, and moonlight was casting strange shadows into the room.

Naked and frightened she got out of bed and crept to the bathroom, opened the door. It was empty. She went back to the main room, drew the curtains, and turned on a single light. There were her shirt and jeans where she had dropped them. But Pete's clothes were gone. And the folded bills were still on the table where she had put them herself.

She let herself down on the edge of the bed, crossed her arms over her breasts, and huddled into a near-fetal position. What if he had left her? God! She tried not to think of that young, pitiless police pig in the bar that first night, the one Pete had out-maneuvered.

She had heard of these Valley towns and their attitude toward young people like herself. What if she ran into that pig, or others like him? Fuzz only treated straight people gently because they were the ones who paid the taxes and had the local clout. What could she expect? A gang bang? She wouldn't put it past them from what she had heard. Huddled tight, shivering in the warm night, "I'm Benjie. I'm Benjie. I'm Benjie. . . ." She said it softly, insistently. Somehow as a charm it had lost its magic.

At home, the house on Russian Hill, she had had her own room, her own bath, her own telephone, and a small porch for sunning. And on a night like this she had loved to get out of bed and go barefoot out on the little porch to see moonlight catching Coit Tower and the funny little houses on Telegraph Hill, the Embarcadero and the ships, the string of lights that was the Golden Gate Bridge, and the scattered lights of Sausalito and the Marin hills beyond.

Sometimes at night the lights of a freighter would move towards the Gate, on a still night the beat of its engines plain. And she would watch as it steamed beneath the great arch and disappeared into the vast Pacific, bound where? Hawaii? Samoa? Australia? While she, Benjie, stood barefoot on her little sunning porch and watched.

She had pestered. Some of the girls in her class, she said, were spending the summer in Honolulu taking special courses at the university, and why couldn't she?

"You're too young, Benjie. Your father and I have talked about it. Maybe one of the junior year abroad programs . . ."

"But that's after two years of college!" Eternity! Cool it. "You just don't dig, do you?"

"I'm not even sure what the word means, dear. Now let's hear no more about it."

Summers at Carmel, the house in the scented pine trees, the curving beach, the water that was almost but not quite too cold to swim in. Picnics up the Carmel Valley or out on nearby Point Lobos, lunch on the pier in Monterey, the Seventeen Mile Drive. The Big Sur to the south was out-of-bounds, but she knew and had known for two years since she was fifteen and the night with Jimmy whatever-his-name-was down on the sand among the rocks of Pebble Beach, that the Big Sur country was her destination when the time was right, because *B-i-g S-u-r* spelled *F-r-e-e-d-o-m* and that was what it was all about, that was where it was at.

Almost a year now, and she knew the coast from Carmel to San Diego, with looks inland to Indio and the desert scene, and back through San Berdoo, the mountains near L.A., over through the San Fernando Valley to the coast again, Oxnard, Ventura, Santa Barbara, Pismo Beach and inland through Paso Robles, over a pass whose name she didn't remember and down into the Valley itself. But the guys she had come to know were headed north, the Bay area, and that for her would be a bad trip so here she was, and when that very first night she had run into Pete she had known, not just thought,

150

known, way down deep inside, that her luck had changed and she had found something to cling to. Because there was a need in him like there was in her, and two needs could produce that miracle even the straight world understood.

Now, huddled, scared, still whispering her own name meaninglessly over and over, all she could think of was that room of her own, and the bath, the telephone and the little sunning porch, and how dumb could she be? Because she had left all that behind forever, blown that scene, and the ads she had seen that her parents had put in papers up and down the state asking her to come home, saying that everything was all right, OK, groovy—those ads hadn't tempted her a bit. But, dear God! If he *had* gone, and here she was in Fascistville all alone, what was she going to do, what in God's name was she going to do?

The front door opened without warning, and for a moment Benjie thought she was going to scream because it was a stranger, a man she'd never seen before. And then it wasn't, it was Pete, just without the beard and the long hair was all; she'd forgotten that. Her stomach went back down where it belonged, and the warmth that flooded through her was like no relief she had ever felt before, not even yesterday when his father had brought him back from jail. "I was so scared, Pete." Her voice was almost inaudible.

He was smiling. "It's okay, baby. I just didn't want to wake you up."

Benjie stood up. "Don't ever do it again, Pete, please, please."

"Ever is a long time. You and I . . ." He stopped there. He smiled again as his eyes drifted up and down her nakedness. "But you look good to come home to." His eyes were bright and his words came fast as if from inner exaltation. "The hunter comes home and finds his chick ready and waiting. Far out."

It was all right now.

* * *

One more thing of note happened that night. George sat in his upstairs sitting room with a nightcap and found neither

151

interest nor distraction in the accumulated reports that had arrived by messenger that afternoon. But he went through them in his careful dogged way, initialing here, okaying there, penciling terse instructions in the margin, while all the time a part of his mind played truant and found the activity pleasant.

He finished his chores at last, put the papers into the leather attaché case, and fastened the lock. So much for work. He found that his spirits suddenly lightened as he went to the telephone, but then, in sudden annoyance, he realized that he did not know the number. If it was unlisted, he told himself, he was going to be pretty damn sore. It was not, and he repeated it to himself carefully as he dialed.

Four rings, five, six—George looked at his watch. It was almost two o'clock. So? And then Clara's voice, breathless, a trifle fearful, came on the line. "Hello?"

"Hi." Merely that.

Another silence. "George?"

"Who else?" Pause. "I woke you up. Sorry. I wanted to talk." Another pause. He smiled into emptiness at the spectacle of himself. "Not true," he said. "I don't have much to talk about. I just wanted to hear your voice."

Was there hesitation? Concern? "Are you all right?"

"Do you mean: am I drunk? No." There was even a sense of gaiety, of abandon, in his mind now. "In trouble? No more than usual. Am I lonely? Yes. I've begun to realize that I'm always lonely these days, and have been for too long."

"George . . ."

"We used to say that it's my nickel, so you listen. Call it my dime. Inflation." He paused. "Someone told me today that I am a real bastard sometimes. You'd be surprised who it was. Or maybe you wouldn't. *No importa.* But the point is that I'm going to be a real bastard tomorrow." Until this moment he had not realized what action his mind had, without his leave, decided upon. But there it was. "I'm going to see Ben tomorrow, Clara. I'm . . ."

"George. No."

"George. Yes. I don't know what good it will do, but I'm going to give it a try. I wanted you to know that, and I wanted

152

you to know why." Pause. "I'm tired of being lonely, Clara. I want your help." Again that humorless smile at the spectacle of himself as a supplicant. "Correct that. I need you, and your help." Then, gently, "Goodnight." He hung up.

18

Cleary Ward rode a stock saddle. Julia, in jodhpurs and a silk blouse that clung lovingly to her still buoyant breasts, rode a flat saddle and handled curb and snaffle with easy grace. The morning was clear and bright with as yet only a hint of the coming heat.

For a dame her age, Cleary had decided, Julia was a pretty slick chick; as a matter of fact, for face and body she'd do well against females much, much younger. Wasn't it Ben Franklin, after all, who had suggested taking as a mistress an older woman? And Cleary was willing to bet that this one would be out of sight in the rack. Maybe he'd find out. The only thing was that she talked the way those characters talked that Billie Burke played in old flicks on the Late Show, flighty and dumb, jumping around like a grasshopper without any purpose at all.

"It was dear of you," Julia said, "to take the time from your busy schedule to come with me, Cleary. I am simply terrified of riding in the country alone." The last time Julia had felt anything even vaguely approaching terror she had been six years old, and the sounds of the wind in the trees at night had made her think of *things.* "I was thrown rather badly once, and I have been frightened ever since that it might happen again." She had been badly thrown several times hunting, and her only reaction had been to brush herself off, catch her horse, and ride even faster to overtake the leaders. "It is so comforting to have a man to look out for me." Her smile was brilliant.

"Well," Cleary said, and felt a surge of pride.

"You must know this country terribly well," Julia said.

Cleary admitted knowledge.

"I mean," Julia said, "that men always manage to go so many places that women can't go." Smile. "If you see what I mean."

Cleary did. "I've hunted quite a bit through here." He paused. "Dove. Pheasant. You know."

"How exciting. I'm sure you're a splendid shot—is that the word?" On the Scottish grouse moors the opinion was widely held that as a wing shot Julia Stanfield was almost, if not quite, the equal of Harold Macmillan, former Prime Minister and long known as a premier gun.

Cleary admitted that he was pretty fair with a scatter-gun. He felt rather dashing. "Would you like a little run?"

"How exciting." Julia watched Cleary take off the way they did in TV westerns. She followed, touching the snaffle gently when her horse was about to overtake. She anticipated the time when Cleary would rein in, and by the time he stopped she was well behind.

They came to a fence. Julia would have taken it, but Cleary dismounted gallantly, pushed his horse out of the way, and got the gate open. Julia smiled down at him as she rode through. They went on together at a companionable walk.

"You're not married, Cleary? I wonder why." Her tone, if not her words, said clearly that she would have expected women to swarm around Cleary like flies in summertime. "Probably," Julia said, "you just haven't found the girl to— match you, here in Stanhope. I can see how that would be. Do you mind my saying, Cleary, that you have a cosmopolitan manner?"

Cleary did not mind.

"Of course," Julia said, "people have come to California

155

from all over the world, and it is true, isn't it, that the manner one learns at home stays with him?"

"My people," Cleary said, "have been here a long time." He could not resist adding, "As long as yours."

"Really? I had no idea."

"On my mother's side, they were here before the Gold Rush. They held property under Mexico."

"Why, Cleary, how marvelous. And do you have it still?"

"No." He did not even try to keep the bitterness out of his voice. "They lost it. To squatters. A squatter."

"Oh," Julia said, "I am so sorry." She smiled her brilliant smile. "I'm afraid I simply don't understand how these things happen. Maybe I should say that I simply don't understand, period. Do you live in town, Cleary?"

He had an apartment. It wasn't much, but it suited him, living alone and frequently on call to minister to the Stanfield interests.

"I'd love to see it," Julia said. "Will you show it to me, Cleary?"

Cleary swallowed. "Why, sure."

"When?" Pause. "I always like things definite, don't you?"

"Sure. I mean, yes. Whenever you'd like." Jesus, he thought, was this for real? Did she actually mean what he thought she meant? He guessed Ben Franklin had been right on target when he had given as his ultimate reason for choosing an older mistress: ". . . because they are so grateful." "Any time," Cleary said. Just thinking about it he was beginning to get a little horny.

Julia smiled at him. "Would you have time after our ride? I always like to—relax after riding, don't you?"

"You bet," Cleary said. He tried to keep his eyes from those breasts. He hoped they wouldn't sag when the bra came off.

* * *

Naked, Julia's breasts did not sag; they were light and firm and girlish, a triumph of hormone treatment and expensive surgery. By exercise, careful diet, and massage she had kept the rest of her body firm and youthful. By practice she

156

had perfected techniques Cleary had only known about through mention in brochures that occasionally came unsolicited through the mail. Jesus! He lay spent and wondered if it would be protocol to cover himself.

"You're sweet, Cleary." Julia was propped on one elbow. She ran her forefinger in little patterns on the skin of his chest. "And strong," she added. She bent to kiss him lightly. A second time, not so lightly. Her breasts brushed his ribs as she moved her shoulders in subtle rhythm. Her hand moved slowly down his torso.

Jesus, Cleary thought, not again?

"So strong," Julia said. "So very strong. Much man."

Again.

* * *

The man's name was Howard Lang, and Walling had heard of him, but they had not met before. He sat now in Walling's office. "I'm not here to interfere, Chief," Lang said. "It's your bailiwick, and Sacramento knows that." He was quiet and smooth and very, very sure of himself. "But we ask ourselves," he said, "is it strictly a local matter, or are your problems here in Stanhope tied in, say, with a bank burning in Santa Barbara or campus problems at Irvine, that kind of thing?"

Walling said, "They put on pressure, did they?"

"Now, Chief."

"The governor was at the Stanfield ranch yesterday. Today you turn up. You tell me there's no connection?"

Lang smiled, and said nothing.

"Okay," Walling said, "strike the question. The family has muscle, particularly when the senator takes a hand." He paused. "Oh, hell, let's face it—even without the senator they have more leverage than they know what to do with. Okay. You're here, and I'd damn well better cooperate. I get the message. What do you want to know?"

Preliminaries over. Lang was all business now. "That truck burning last night. Could it have been an accident?"

"No." Walling was tempted to leave it there, but there was nothing to be gained by surliness. "No skid marks," he

157

said. "No blown tire. Not enough rise to the shoulder of the road to tip it over. It didn't turn over by itself."

Lang thought about it. "It isn't easy to overturn a truck. How do you figure it?"

"A tow truck was stolen last night," Walling said. "That could be it. Park it across the road with the dome light flashing. The hay truck stops. They clobber the driver, set the hoist hook under the side of the truck frame, up and over she goes. Scatter some hay bales on the road. Tow truck drives off. It looks like an accident, but it isn't. Pour gasoline on the truck." He snapped his fingers to indicate sudden conflagration. "And," he said, "the driver isn't going to tell us anything. He was still in the cab, fried like bacon."

Lang said, "Any ideas?"

"Lots of them, but that's all they are—ideas."

"You've got a Mex here named Lucero," Lang said. "Is he this kind of troublemaker?"

"I don't think so, but that doesn't prove anything. Look," Walling said, "I'm not big on this brotherhood of man crap. We all have to live in this country together, but that doesn't mean I have to like everybody with a Spanish name or a black skin or a hooked nose or slant eyes. But when it comes to pinning a rap on somebody, I try to be color-blind. It's just good sense. That way a charge I've made doesn't suddenly blow up in my face and leave me looking silly. I don't think Lucero has anything to do with what's been happening. But like I said, what I think doesn't prove anything. But I'm not going to put the arm on Lucero just because he's here, and handy, and because he has a Spanish name." He paused. "Stanfield, Sacramento, United States Senator, or not."

"We understand each other," Lang said. He smiled. "But I'd like to talk to Lucero anyway."

"Help yourself." Walling waited until Lang was gone, and then heaved himself out of his chair and left the office. He took an unmarked police car and drove slowly, obeying all traffic lights. He parked in the street outside Pete's little house and looked around.

A crummy neighborhood, he thought, and for the umpteenth time wondered what possessed children of the well-to-do, even of the very wealthy, to turn their backs on comfort

in order to live like this. Those who grew up in these surroundings knocked themselves out trying to escape. Maybe
the others, the Pete Stanfields, came here as some men went
camping in the mountains—knowing that they didn't have to
stay, that whenever they chose they could return to a warm
bed in a warm house with the wind and the rain shut out.
Maybe.

Pete answered the knock at the door, and for a moment
Walling did not recognize him without the beard and the
bushy hair. "Well," Pete said, "the head fuzz. Honored.
Come in." He held the door wide.

Benjie was at the sink. She turned to look at Walling in
silence.

Pete closed the door. "His name is Walling," he said,
"and he's the man. What can I do for you, Chief?"

Walling looked around the small room. It was neater
than he would have guessed, and he wondered how much the
girl had to do with that. He wondered too how old she was,
and what her relationship was with Pete, although he didn't
think he'd have to strain much to figure that out. But morals
were not on his mind at the moment. "You read the papers?"
he said to Pete.

"The Stanhope rag?" Pete shook his head smiling. "And
the city papers aren't any better." Pause. "What am I missing?"

"A Stanfield Cattle Company hay truck was overturned
and burned last night," Walling said. "A man was inside it."

"I heard."

"How did you hear?"

At the sink, without a word, Benjie turned on a cheap
transistor radio. Hard rock music filled the room. She turned
it off again, and the silence was restful. "Answer your question?" Pete said. "We try to keep up with what's happening
here and there."

Walling said, "Do you mind telling me where you were
last night?"

"He was here," Benjie said.

Walling looked at Pete. "You heard the lady," Pete said.
He smiled suddenly. "Tell me, why would I go roaming, when
I have something like that to stay home with?"

159

Walling said, "You shaved your beard."

"It tickled," Benjie said.

He had no leverage, Walling told himself, and from the beginning he had known that the visit was probably futile. But sometimes the urge to see a suspect face to face on his own ground was irresistible, and Walling had long since given up all fear of looking foolish.

"Anything else, Chief?" Pete said.

Walling shook his head. "Not at the moment." He opened the door and went out to his car. He heard the door close behind him, and he wished he could hear what was being said between them now.

Benjie had turned from the sink. She wiped her damp hands on her jeans. Her eyes did not leave Pete's face.

"What's for lunch?" Pete said.

19

George had a healthy man's distaste for hospitals underlain by a feeling that his mere physical presence was an affront to the ailing. As he walked down the corridor toward Ben Wilson's room he thought about what he had said to Clara on the telephone only a few hours ago, and he decided that he had been exact—he was being a real bastard. So be it.

The door was open but George knocked anyway before he walked in. "Hi, Ben." It seemed a ridiculous greeting, but what else was there to say?

Ben's heavy tan had faded, and around the corners of his eyes pain had drawn faint dark lines. But one corner of his mouth was lifted in the old, mocking smirk, and his voice was full and strong. "Georgie boy. What brings you here?" He gestured with one hand toward the visitor's chair. The other hand rested, unmoving, across his chest.

George sat down. "To see you."

"Let me try to guess why." Ben was smiling broadly now. "I owe you money? But I don't, so that can't be it. Let's see. I have something you want to buy? I doubt that very much.

You already have all you can possibly want." He paused. "Or maybe I do have something you want, at that, and its name is Clara. Have you been snuffling around, Georgie?"

It was going to be even worse than he had thought. No matter. "I want to marry her," George said.

"But that would be bigamy! You can't mean it." Ben waggled his head in mock concern. "Certainly you don't intend that."

"Are you having fun, Ben?"

"Great fun," Ben said. All at once the lightness was gone. "I laugh myself sick, lying here looking down at the end of the bed at those lumps, see them? My feet. I tell them to move, and nothing happens. And this . . ." With his right hand he lifted his other arm, released it, watched it fall helplessly. "Hilarious, isn't it?"

"Sorry," George said, and meant it.

"Why, that helps no end, Georgie boy. That makes it all ginger-peachy. And now you want to get Clara back into your bed, is that it? And that helps too. Was this her idea?"

"She told me not to talk to you."

"Big of her. She's turned into some kind of plaster saint, and only a little while ago she told me I was an unpleasant son of a bitch and she wanted no more of me." Ben smiled suddenly. "Can you believe that, Georgie? Sweet docile Clara using bad words like that? But she did."

"Was that before you went to Riverside?" George said.

Ben took his time. "Now, Georgie," he said, "are you trying to play shrink? The psychological bit? I went down to Riverside with an unconscious death wish because dear sweet Clara had spoken harshly to me? Forget it."

George said, "Will you give her a divorce, Ben?"

The smirk reappeared. "Will you make it worth my while? What's it worth to you to have Clara all open and aboveboard? When she wants to be, she's the hell of a lay, and that ought to make the price high, but you know how good she is as well as I do. Finest tits I've ever seen, and that beautiful ass . . ."

"Cut it out, Ben."

"Or what? You'll flex your muscles at me? But it's my

162

wife we're talking about, remember? And if I want to say how good she is in the rack, who are you to object?"

An orderly came into the room. He put a small plastic cup within easy reach on the table beside the bed. It held one large pill. He poured the water glass beside it half full. "Thanks," Ben said. And when the orderly was gone, "My pain-killer," he said to George. "Regular as clockwork." He smiled crookedly. "Where were we? Oh, yes, talking about Clara's beautiful ass. Or are you a tit man, Georgie?"

George stood up. "I'd better go."

"Having temper trouble? You've made my day for me. You're the best therapy I've had. Let me ask one more question." Ben paused for emphasis. "If I offered a divorce, do you think dear sweet Clara would take it? Think about that, George."

George did think about it all the way to his car, and all during the drive back into Stanhope. He went straight to Clara's shop. She watched him come in, and her eyes searched his face. "Bad?" she said.

"Bad."

"I'm sorry you went, George."

"I'm not." He knew now precisely where he stood with Ben. That much at least he had accomplished. Always it was better to have the rules established. "I asked him if he'd give you a divorce," George said.

Clara closed her eyes. She opened them again. "He laughed at you?"

"More or less. And he asked me if I thought you'd take it even if he offered."

"Do you think I would, George?" Her eyes were steady on his face.

"I doubt it." Simple truth.

Clara turned away, walked slowly over to a table, and stood there fingering a bolt of material that lay on display. "I didn't sleep much after your call," she said. She turned to face him then. "Sometimes the night is a good time for thinking." She hesitated. "I told you it was a mess, George. All my fault."

"Clara."

"We had our fling. Maybe that was a mistake. I don't

163

know." She raised her hands and let them fall. "Give me time. I don't know what good time will do, but I can't make any decision now. Can you understand that?"

George drove slowly away from Clara's shop in a rare indecisive mood. He had been away from his city office now for almost four days, and logic if nothing else dictated that he go back to San Francisco and resume control. Logic be damned. Problems in San Francisco were concrete and for a time could be solved by his lawyers, his bankers, his advisers on the scene, or if necessary, by himself, even at this distance. But the problems here in Stanhope were of an entirely different order, and personal on-the-scene attention was mandatory.

How long Marquesa would last he could not say, but he thought not long, and he ought to be on hand when the end came. No real reason. Everyone died alone; dying was the most private of activities. But being on hand was what one did, and although as a rule George cared not a tinker's damn what people thought of his actions, in this instance he did not want any feeling that he had been callous, particularly from Ellen, whose relationship with Marquesa was so close.

He felt a sense of guilt concerning Ellen, his neglect of the girl that Julia had pointed out. But for the life of him he could not see how to mend the situation. He did not have Scott's easy manner, nor Mike's avuncular charm, and that was an end to it—he was what he was. He smiled faintly at that, remembering Ellen's telling him that sometimes he was a real bastard. He rather liked her for it, although he supposed he ought to have been disapproving.

There were the grapes to be picked and processed one way or another—through dehydrator tunnels if the repair work was done in time, otherwise sun-dried in Louis Khasigian's hands. Either way Cleary Ward could cope, but it would be well if George kept an eye on the process.

Last night's truck burning. It was hard to keep down anger when he thought of that. Accidental? Chief Walling thought not, and his assessment sounded right. One more engagement in the continuing underground war against anything that bore the name Stanfield. But why? He had Chief

164

Walling's assessment of that too, and maybe it was right, maybe not.

Pete came to mind, and that girl he was shacked up with. And Paul. Joe Hanson. Ruben Lucero. More reasons to remain on the scene. But the principal reason, of course—face it—was the person he had just left, Clara, and after all this time he was just beginning to realize it.

He resented Ben's cynical talk, but he had to admit that Ben's physical descriptions had evoked memories that were hard to shake, and in retrospect he wondered how he had ever been foolish enough to let Clara marry Ben in the first place. Because, as Clara herself had pointed out, back then he was still married to a dead woman? Possible. He had even taken pride in living alone. Damn fool. No man was an island. No man, no woman. It was, George decided in disgust, his profound thought for the day.

* * *

The main ranch house, shuttered against the heat of the day, seemed quiet, almost deserted. From the direction of the pool George could hear voices and quiet laughter, inviting sounds. He crossed the broad lawn and went around the rose arbor to see.

Scott and Jenny Falk were stretched out side by side in reclining chairs. Ellen lay prone on a sunning mattress near the pool's edge. Scott shaded his eyes with one hand as he looked up. "Join the drones," he said. "Shuck off the cares of the world."

Ellen rolled over and sat up. "Come for a swim, Daddy." Young, slimly rounded, as lovely as his Ann had been, as Clara. . . . George, looking down at her, felt a pang of memory. "Will you, Daddy?"

"Why not?" Set aside the somber thoughts; they would return soon enough. George walked into the pavilion to change into swim trunks.

Behind him he heard Scott say, "Well, what do you know? You've charmed him into relaxation, youngster. He is putty in your hands."

"I wish it were so," Ellen said.

165

George heard no more. He felt a measure of annoyance at Scott, but that was nothing new. He supposed that older brothers usually found younger ones trying at times. Toward Ellen he felt only compassion and that sense of guilt that had been with him since their talk in her room. He ought to have seen to it that she had a mother. Wisdom after the event. Was that what he was trying to arrange now with Clara? He doubted it. He wanted Clara for himself, not for Ellen. Was that selfish? Don't answer that question. He threw a towel over one shoulder and walked out into the sunlight.

Ellen was already in the pool. George tossed his towel on a chair and dove in to join her. They swam, splashed, and came out again into the sun and the warm air. George dried his face and hands, sat down, and stretched out his legs. "Drink, Daddy?" Ellen said. "There's beer and Coke. Or I could send for something else."

George shook his head. "Thanks." Enough relaxation. He was looking at Scott. "What you saw last night . . ." He paused. "You've told Walling?"

"Like a good little citizen."

Jenny said, "He didn't need urging."

"Very little to tell," Scott said. "We didn't tarry at the scene."

Jenny watched George for reaction. "Wise," George said. He was looking beyond the big house to the tops of the tall, cool eucalyptus that lined the drive. Introduced from Australia when? Eighty years ago? But try to picture California without eucalyptus trees. Passing thought. He looked at Scott again and said as casually as he could, "You saw men? You didn't recognize anyone?" He was aware that Ellen watched him closely, but he gave no sign.

"Just shapes," Scott said. "Cavorting in the lights." He studied George's face. "You have ideas?"

"Not even that," George said. Liar; and he disliked lying.

Jenny said, "Could it have been that the men we saw were trying to turn the truck upright, and get the driver out?" Her slim shoulders shivered faintly. She looked from one man to the other.

Scott said, "Doubtful."

"Walling," George said, "is convinced it was no acci-

166

dent." He stood up. "So am I." He smiled at them all. "Chores to do." He went into the pavilion to dress.

When he came out of the men's locker room, Ellen was perched on a bar stool, Coke at hand, waiting for him. Her young face was grave. "You're afraid Pete was there, aren't you, Daddy?"

"I haven't any reason to believe it." Evasion, in some ways worse to his mind than the direct lie; weaseling.

"Paul said Pete had a girl with him." Ellen's voice was entirely calm. "If they're sleeping together, she would know if Pete was with her all night, wouldn't she?"

Did the young really take the facts of sexual life this casually? George supposed that it was a measure of his squareness that he found it hard to believe. He said merely, "Probably."

"But, what?" Her eyes watched him steadily.

"Mightn't she lie? If she cares about him at all?"

The girl was silent, thoughtful. She took an automatic sip of Coke, set the glass down carefully. Slowly she nodded. "I hadn't thought of that. I guess she would." She faced George squarely. "I would if it was Paul." She hesitated. "I think if I had to I'd even lie to you. I never have."

His gesture appeared awkward, strained, he was sure of it. But the temptation to touch her was irresistible, and he put his hand on her bare shoulder, squeezed gently. "Nice to know, honey." He dropped his hand and smiled. "As I said, chores." He started to turn away.

"Don't go, Daddy, please." A soft cry in the night. She watched his face, and waited.

"Honey . . ." He stopped there. "I guess you'd better get me that beer, after all." He was smiling as he pulled out a bar stool and sat down.

Sitting companionably close, Coke and beer in front of them, "What are we going to talk about?" George said.

"Is that how you do it?" Ellen said. "I've never known. I mean, do you, you know, ration your time? 'Speak up. What's on your mind?'—that kind of thing." She was watching him closely.

"I suppose so." He could smile again as he shook his head. "But it doesn't apply to you. Or shouldn't." But he

167

supposed that it always had, and again that sense of guilt was strong. The stereotype, he thought, of the busy man neglecting his family; ridiculous, but there it was.

"Am I like mother, Daddy?" Question out of nowhere.

"You are." He said it slowly. "Sometimes too much like her."

"Pete isn't."

"No," George said, "Pete is very much like his uncle, the one you didn't know." The same attitude of irresponsibility, I-can-get-by-on-charm-alone. Am I still—envious? After all this time?

Ellen said, "Would he have been like Pete, you know, in —revolt like they say?"

"Honey, he was nineteen when he was killed. He'll always be only nineteen. Who knows—?" George stopped. "Maybe it was revolt," he said. "I didn't think about it that way then, but maybe it was. He went off to war with all kinds of ideals . . ."

"And maybe Pete has his ideals, too?"

George thought about it. "Maybe." I'm trying to understand, he thought, and wondered if he ever could. He tried to make it light. "Maybe the trouble is," he said, "that Pete's ideals and mine don't coincide." He stepped down from the stool. "Now I have to go, honey." He stepped forward and kissed her forehead awkwardly. When he stepped back she was watching him with a half-smile.

"Is Mrs. Wilson like mother, Daddy?"

"What in the world . . ." George began. He stopped. "Meaning what?"

"This time," Ellen said, "if you can, are you going to marry her?" Pause, faint but perceptible. "You did have an affair, didn't you? Before she married Mr. Wilson?"

"You were ten years old," George said.

Ellen smiled. "Pete told me all about it."

"Pete would." George started for the door.

"Daddy."

He stopped and turned.

She was smiling still. "Don't be cross." Another pause.

168

"And thanks for talking with me. Can we do it again some time?"

"I think maybe we'd better." Now what, he asked himself, do I think I meant by that? He found no answer.

20

For the senator, any return to Stanhope became a kind of sentimental journey. Pepe drove him into town to the bank where Juan Potrero, with an appropriate flourish, unlocked the chain that closed the parking space after bank hours. The senator and Juan shook hands and walked together to the door of the bank. Juan unlocked that too and held it wide. If it had been within his power, the senator thought as he walked through, Juan would now have given the signal for the band to strike up loud martial music.

Karl Meyer was standing at the desk of one of the vice-presidents. He turned, saw the senator, and came quickly across the floor, bony hand extended. "Welcome, back, Mike."

"Thank you, Karl." The senator smiled at the employees, one and all, and made a special hand wave of greeting to Howard, Karl's son, back by the vault. Karl led the way to his private office, held the door, and closed it as he followed the senator inside.

"You are looking well, Mike."

"I survive."

"More than that, I hope." With his ponderous air you tended to think of Karl as slow, tedious, and perhaps not overly intelligent. You were wrong. Those banker's eyes missed little, and the computer of his mind weighed and stored all manner of information, constantly fed to it from the intelligence network he had established over the years. San Francisco remained the financial center of the west coast. Karl's lines of communication with San Francisco and through the city to the rest of the financial world were both strong and subtle, covering fact, possibility and rumor, large and minute.

The senator sat down in one of the leather chairs. He stretched out his long legs. "George is worried," he said. He and Karl were the older generation. They could speak together without hindrance.

"With reason, I think," Karl said. "Pete was arrested, and released. Chief Walling thinks he may have had a part in the dehydrator fire. Then there was the truck burning last night."

So that was where George had gone in such a hurry from lunch yesterday. Nothing changed in the senator's face. "Symptoms, Karl? Of what. What do your balance sheets show?"

Karl took his time. "Affluence," he said, "and debt. Unemployment. High interest rates, rising costs, frustration. Those at the bottom fighting for more. Those above fighting to hold their place. Washington . . ." He shook his head. "That is your bailiwick, Mike."

"Economists," the senator said, "are a special breed. They rarely agree even on the time of day." He shook the silver head, dismissing economists and their gloomy art. "Are we headed for trouble here, Karl?"

Again the slow contemplation. "Aero-Associates here in town," Karl said, "has a new plant, a new debt, high carrying charges, and a dearth of new contracts. Monday they will lay off one hundred factory workers, and eight engineers and scientists from research and development. Five of those are PhD's, and all of them have been employed in the aerospace field for at least ten years. In Los

171

Angeles County, which is where they might ordinarily go to find new jobs, there are one hundred and twenty thousand unemployed aerospace engineers, technicians, and scientists."

The senator's smile was wry. "I have been hearing a little bit about that from constituents. Let us say more than a little bit. I am doing what I can." He paused. "But right here in Stanhope, Karl. That's where my interest is at the moment." He paused, and smiled. "Your assessment, man. It's a judgment call."

Karl looked over the tops of his glasses. He seemed to relax. He even smiled. "I'm getting old, Mike."

"Why, so am I." The senator was thinking of the other night in the doctor's office. It had never really been out of his mind. "But I'm not ready to get out of the game yet. Are you?"

Karl sat quietly, long hands folded, head cocked as if to the sound of an inaudible voice. He said at last, "The pressures have always been with us, Mike. Nobody knows that better than you. The grape pickers, for example, want higher wages, better working conditions, benefits, and they are in a sense organized now. The growers are caught between rising costs and a decreasing share of the price the consumer pays in the supermarket for their raisins. Joe Hanson comes after George with a gun. Your dehydrator burns. Last night's truck episode. Two men killed." He paused. "We caught one of our tellers with his fingers in the till. He had been with us for five years." He shook his head. "Your Pete going his way. My Paul going his." Karl took off his glasses, looked at them carefully, and put them on again. "I am getting old, Mike, and I am frightened."

They came out of the corner office together and shook hands. Howard Meyer was still down by the vault. "I'll say hello to the boy," the senator said, and saw the flicker of understanding in Karl's face.

"Another, younger judgment?" Karl said. He nodded. "It is wise. I hope that Howard's assessment is more optimistic than mine."

The senator was aware that all eyes watched him as he walked the length of the main floor, tall, erect, confident. He would not have had it otherwise. On his left at the rail he noticed a pretty new secretary, dark brown hair, blue eyes, slim waist, large breasts and a friendly smile. Merely looking at her made him feel better. "Howard, my boy. *Qué tal?*"

"Senator," Howard said. "Fine, thank you, sir." They shook hands.

Come have a drink with me," the senator said. "Unless, that is, the bank will collapse without you."

Howard smiled. He had little of his father's ponderousness. "Hardly, sir."

The Palace was close. "I prefer it to the Grotto anyway," the senator said. "That damned waterfall always makes me think I'd better go pee. I've had your father's state-of-the-world message. It is gloomy. How is yours?"

He was young as bankers went, thirty-two, this Howard Meyer, the senator's third cousin once removed, but impetuosity was not in his makeup. He sipped his drink before he answered. "I'm not selling it short, sir. The world, I mean."

The senator waited. Howard was silent. "Go on," the senator said. "I want to hear your assessment. I told your father it was a judgment call, not cut and dried."

Howard nodded slowly. "My father and I aren't entirely in agreement, sir."

"I'd be surprised if you were."

"Would you?" Howard smiled and nodded again. "Yes, I think you would. Okay. As I see it, we're in a period of adjustment. Everybody wants a piece of the action now. In your day and my father's, I don't think that was so. I think things were pretty settled."

The senator thought back to the total upset of the First World War, the boom and bust of the '20s, the depression of the '30s. Matter of viewpoint, he thought. He said nothing.

"Credit," Howard was saying, "used to be the privilege of a few. Now we live in a credit-card, charge-account economy."

True, the senator thought, the boy had something there.

Howard said, "They say that in Russia there is increased pressure for more consumer goods, better housing, more freedom—because the Russian people know through communications what it is like in the western world." Howard smiled. "We can say the same thing here, can't we, sir? Ruben Lucero's *huelguistas* know what wages are in industry, in construction, and so they want more too. The old way, the rich get richer and the poor get children, doesn't operate very well any more. And that applies to developing nations as well as to depressed areas of our own population."

"For a banker," the senator said, "for a Meyer, you could be accused of radicalism."

"Yes, sir." Howard was smiling. "That's what my father says. But he isn't kidding, and I think, I hope you are."

The senator smiled and sipped his drink. "You're in favor of Ruben Lucero, then? And your brother Paul?"

The boy hesitated. "The first one is easy. I'm in favor of what Ruben Lucero is trying to do—in principle. I don't hold with violence." He paused. "Although, goddam it, sir, sometimes you have to wonder if maybe there isn't something to the idea that without action nothing ever changes. After all, we jump up and down and wave the flag whenever 1776 is mentioned, and that was violence, revolution, treason." Howard paused and smiled. "My father doesn't think much of that comparison, either." He paused again. "But I am not in favor of burning down dehydrators, burning trucks, killing men— above all killing, here or in other countries." He was silent, faintly belligerent.

"That's the first part of the question," the senator said easily. "How about the second?"

Howard seemed to relax. "Do I approve of Paul?" He shook his head. "That's a tough one, sir. He's doing what I couldn't do even if I wanted to. I'm a moneyman. Like my father, like his father, all the way back to Rudi Meyer. Paul is more like you people, Stanfields. He's an agronomist, for one thing. The land and what it can do is his bag. But it doesn't stop there. He's an action boy. He'd shrivel and die behind my desk." Howard paused and smiled. "But he understands a lot more about business than he says he does."

He was proud of his brother, the senator thought, even though his attitude was not wholly approving. Sibling pride was good to see. "But what?" he said.

Howard smiled. "Yes, sir. You put your finger on it. I may

174

approve of what he's trying to do, I think I do, but I think he ought to be going at it from the top, not from the bottom. He ought to be enlightened management, not Ruben Lucero's right-hand boy." He had a long sip of his drink. "One thing, sir. Paul doesn't hold with violence. He's afraid of it, not for itself, I don't think, but because of what it can do beyond itself. A few more things like the dehydrator, last night's truck burning, fence cutting, barn burning, most important, men killed—a few more things like that, and this period of adjustment can turn into an explosion, like Watts, like Oakland, Berkeley." His voice was quiet, grave. "Then we'd be right back in the ooze. That's what scares me, sir."

And so, the senator thought, from two widely separated viewpoints, this boy's and his father's, we arrive at the same conclusion. "Thank you, son," he said.

Out on the sidewalk the senator took out his dark glasses, put them on, and shook hands with Howard. He saw Bill Hanford, the AP man, coming purposefully toward him, and he said, "Better buzz off, boy. I'm about to be inquisited." He was flattered by Howard's quick grin.

Bill Hanford said, "How's your mother, Mike?" There was irony in his voice. Then, "Wrong question. Strike it. Bad taste."

The senator nodded. "I'm glad you appreciate the fact." He began to walk without haste toward the Stanhope courthouse. Hanford fell in step beside him. The senator didn't mind.

"His honor the governor was here yesterday," Hanford said. "Out at your ranch."

"We had lunch," the senator said. "My sister Julia sang Hiram Johnson's 1916 campaign song. For lunch we had . . ."

"And George Stanfield," Hanford said, "went buckety-buckety down to the local bastille, and after a time came back out with young Pete Stanfield, who is one of the beautiful people."

"A misunderstanding," the senator said. Two older women walked by. Both looked at the senator. He smiled pleasantly and nodded.

175

"And today," Hanford said, "Howard Lang drives into town, down from Sacramento. You know Howard, Mike?"

"I may have met him." The senator had not known that the governor had acted. Did that mean that he was accepting the offer of two years as U.S. Senator? Nothing changed in the senator's face or voice. The matter could be looked into in private. "Perhaps Lang is just passing through," the senator said.

"Lang," Hanford said, "doesn't pass through. He rides into town like a hired gun or a private eye on TV, because he's been sent. He's the ferret the governor sends down the hole to flush out the rats, and he stays where he's sent until he's done the job." Hanford paused. "I never like the gunman on TV, Mike, not even when he's supposed to be on the side of the angels. I didn't know you were big for the enforcer idea, either."

The senator said, "You've read about the vigilantes in early California, Bill?"

"I have. And it's my studied opinion that some of them were murdering bastards every bit as bad as the men they picked on."

Where the sun tips the golden Sierra,
Keeps a watch o'er the valley's bloom;
It is there I would be, in the land of the free,
Breathing all Nature's rich perfume.
CALIFORNIA STATE SONG

21

Ellen knocked softly and opened the carved door. The figure in the immense bed did not move, and Ellen started to back out quietly. "Come in, child. I'm awake. Just—thinking."

"I don't want to interrupt."

One hand stirred faintly and the great diamond glittered. "Close the door. Sit down. Be young for me."

It was a strange thing to say, Ellen thought, and she wondered what it meant. She drew a chair up close to the bed.

"Miss Walters," the old lady said, "tells me that a truck was overturned and burned last night. Another man was killed?"

Oh, Nurse Walters said that, did she? Then Ellen was going to have words with Nurse Walters. It did not even occur to her that there was anything incongruous about dressing down a woman old enough to be her mother. As long as Nurse Walters was in this house, Ellen's domain, she would behave herself, period. Upsetting her patient with tales of violence, indeed. "It was probably an accident, Marquesa."

The old lady shook her head. "I don't for a moment

believe it. They say there are cycles of climate, child. Ezra, my Ezra, thought so. I think there are cycles of other things, too. Violence, for one."

"Don't think about it, Marquesa."

The hand moved once more and the diamond glittered. The old lady smiled fondly at the girl. "Violence is a part of life, as much a part as peace and comfort, maybe more. You will learn that, child. Most of us come violently into this world. That is the beginning." She smiled again. "Some of us are fortunate to have large comfortable beds to die in. And family at hand. But some don't."

"Marquesa . . ."

"Ezra's father, Amos, my father-in-law. Let me see. Your great-great-grandfather." The old lady was silent.

Ellen said, "Did something happen to him?"

"To all of us, child. You wonder who arranges these things."

Tumbleweed,
Kern County, 1874

Legend has overridden fact, and in the constant retelling the general hysteria of the day has been forgotten. It would appear that few men like to admit to panic.

By midmorning that early summer day heat from the brown foothills had closed in on the town. A dry wind raised dust devils among the live oaks and drove fine dirt beneath even the tightest doors. Sensible housewives postponed hanging out the wash. By all accounts, everyone felt edgy. And so the weather may have had something to do with what happened.

Luke Watson, telegraph operator in the bank and express office, trotted out of the building and across the street to the hotel bar. He had already told everyone in the express office the news, and besides, Luke had a steady thirst. To Jake Marvin behind the bar, "That son of a bitch has done it again.

Vasquez. Up to Four Corners. Got a thousand dollars from the bank." He forced himself to sip his drink slowly.

Jake was not to be excited. Not yet. "They'll catch him. That Harry Morse." He shook his head. "I wouldn't like to have him after me."

"Up to Tres Pinos," Luke said, "Vasquez and his gang left three dead, an' two unconscious." He paused. "Then over to Kingston, Fresno County, that's too near, they tied up thirty-five men an' took everything in town that wasn't tied down. By God, they ought to call out the army. Hey!" He pointed a long forefinger at the hotel porter, janitor, handyman who was trying to keep up with the incoming dust, uphill work. "You know that Vasquez fellow, huh? He's a Mex, like you."

The porter's name was Juan Baca. "I have heard about heem, señor, but I do not know heem."

"They all know each other," Luke said. "They're all related." He pointed the forefinger again. "What's his first name? I bet you know that."

"Tiburcio, señor," Juan said. "But I do not know heem."

"A murderin' skunk," Luke said. As he finished his drink a small boy trotted in.

"They're callin' for you, Mr. Watson, over at the office. The telegraph is clickin'."

Luke climbed down from his bar stool. It was at times like this that his self-esteem rose. He was the only man for miles around who could handle the telegraph key. He walked back across the street at a dignified pace.

The key was clacking viciously, calling his station. He sat down, tapped out his readiness, picked up a pencil, and waited. The message began to flow, and Luke began to write: VASQUEZ BELIEVED HEADED SOUTH CLOSE OFFICE SOUTHBOUND STAGE. . . . It was at this point that the clacking key went silent.

Luke put down his pencil. He tapped out a query. Another. There was no reply. The next day they found the break in the wire. It is probable but not certain that a piece of wood or a heavy tumbleweed caught in a larger dust devil than most, by one of those freaks that sometimes happen, had caused the break.

179

Luke tore the uncompleted message from his pad, pushed back his chair, and trotted the word over to Tom Willoughby, express station manager. "That's all there is," Luke said. "Line's dead." The implications were beginning to reach him now. "You think the son a bitches cut it?" A kind of siege syndrome was beginning to form.

"How the hell do I know?" Willoughby said. "You're sure it's dead?" He read the incomplete message again.

"It's dead, goddam it," Luke said. "I told you, didn't I? You don't hear them sending, do you?"

"And you can't get through, neither?"

"No, I can't get through. How many times I got to tell you?"

Willoughby read the message yet a third time. He didn't like it even a little bit. "Well," he said, "we'll lock up. The southbound stage ain't due until 12:30, so I don't know what they started to say about that."

"It don't matter," Luke said. He paused. "I'm going over to the hotel. If they're comin' in here . . ." He shook his head, pulled his hat down tighter, and trotted out.

That was the beginning.

* * *

Amos Stanfield was on the southbound stage, at that time running half an hour late, still two and a half hours north of Tumbleweed. Amos was twenty-three, with his father's size and his mother's golden coloring. He worked with his uncle, Rudi Meyer, the active head of the bank Rudi and Ezra Stanfield had established in the town of Stanhope.

There were two other passengers on the stage, a priest and a captain of infantry from the Presidio at San Francisco, bound south for Los Angeles. The captain was lightening the tedium of the journey with periodic jolts of whiskey. They did not improve his manners.

"As far as I'm concerned," said the captain, who came from Ohio, "you can take this whole dirty damn brown country and give it right back to the Mex and the Indians." He paused. "Same thing, really."

The priest, whose name was Alonso-Lopez, smiled gently at Amos. Amos smiled back with effort. During the long

180

morning he had already had quite enough of the captain from Ohio.

"San Francisco's all right," the captain said, "but this . . ." His gesture covered the flat Valley floor and the foothills shimmering in the heat. "What in hell's it good for?"

"This is wheat country, captain," Amos said. "As rich as any you'll find. But then," he added, his face and tone expressionless, "wheat doesn't amount to much. Not to compare with—what do you raise in Ohio, captain?"

The captain suspected, but could not verify, irony. The captain wore a drooping gray moustache. He tugged at it thoughtfully. "How long you been out here in California, boy?"

"I was born here."

"You don't look Mex."

Amos opened his mouth. The priest said quickly, *"Es nada, hijo mío, nada."* It is nothing, my son, nothing.

The captain said, "What's he say?"

"My mother, captain," Amos said deadpan, "came to California from Madrid." Untrue. "That is in Spain." True. "All *madrileños* are blonde." Nonsense. "My father was born in Mexico City." Untrue. "His hair is red." Poppycock. Amos considered adding that all people in Mexico City had either red hair or purple, but decided against it. His expression had not changed.

The priest closed his eyes. The corners of his mouth twitched gently.

"You don't talk like a Mex, neither," the captain said. "I had a colonel in the war. He talked like you, and he came from near Boston."

"I went to college near Boston, captain. Perhaps that explains it."

The captain's thoughts had already veered in another direction. "Los Angeles," he said. "Who the hell ever thought to put a town there? Right in the middle of nowhere? San Diego, Monterey, San Francisco, they make some sense." The captain had learned the value of harbors and transportation by water. "But Los Angeles . . ." He shook his head.

"La Ciudad de Nuestra Señora, La Reina de Los Angeles," the priest said. He smiled. "The City of Our Lady, Queen of the

Angels, captain. You can stand in sunshine, look at the snow on the mountains, and taste the scent of flowers and the salt in the ocean air at the same time. God has smiled on that land. You will see."

At a clip-clopping, running walk on the dusty road, harness jangling, one wheel squeaking rhythmically, the stagecoach body protesting as from age. The pervasive aroma of worn leather and sweat penetrated the dust, along with the captain's alcoholic breath. He dug out yet another pint bottle from his hand luggage, maneuvered out the cork, and had a long pull from its neck. He offered it around.

The priest smiled and shook his head. Amos said, "I'd join you, captain, but I have business to do in Tumbleweed."

"Money business," the captain said. He had a basic mistrust of all civilians, but of some more than others. "San Francisco papers full of money troubles. Bankers' doing, I'll wager."

"At least partly, I am sure," Amos said. His voice was cheerful. "Most people are fools with their money, captain. They try to become rich overnight. They invest in wild schemes, and eventually the bubble breaks. Then we come along to pick up the pieces, and along with the pieces, most of the blame."

The priest said, "I have heard that the wheat farmers are in financial trouble. Is that true, my son?"

Amos nodded. "We, and others like us, have kept them going for—too long."

The captain gestured with the pint bottle. "And now what? You take their land away from them? That it? I've seen it before, back home in Ohio."

"I hope it doesn't come to that," Amos said. "We don't want the land." Oh, some land, yes. In addition to all that Ezra Stanfield already owned, riverfront land was desirable because water was the key that unlocked the wealth of this great Valley. But this land down here, Tumbleweed and beyond, over into the foothills, was poor land almost without water. "All we ask," he said, "is that the money we lent be paid back. Do you find that immoral, captain?"

"Poor bastard farmers," the captain said. "Always get the shit end of the stick. I know. I was raised on a farm." His eyes were not quite in focus on Amos's face. "What you think of that, banker? Raised on a farm. Until we lost it. To bankers."

"Have another drink, captain," Amos said. "It's a long thirsty road yet."

They stopped to change horses at the little town of Four Corners, and the hostler, whose eyes almost stood out on stalks in his excitement, brought them up to date. "Goddlemighty!" the hostler said. "Them murderin' bastards ain't been gone thirty minutes! Stole a thousand dollars! A thousand dollars! Bran' new double eagles from the bank! An' some watches an' rings! Rode into town, tied everybody up . . ."

The captain said loudly, "Who? Goddam it, man, who did it?" Leaning out the window he slapped the flap-covered leather holster at his belt.

Amos decided then and there that if they met trouble and the captain made any move toward his holstered weapon, he, Amos Stanfield, was going to break the captain's arm if he had to before he would see the drunken lout with a gun in his hand. He looked at the priest and saw that their thoughts ran along parallel lines.

"Tiburcio Vasquez!" the hostler said. "That's who! Goddlemighty, with them thievin' bastards around, it ain't safe for man nor boy!" He stepped back from the newly harnessed team. "There you are! Take 'em away!" He spat a stream of tobacco juice into the dust and grinned wickedly up at the driver and guard. "But I wouldn't go none too fast if I was you. You might catch up to them thievin' son a bitches."

They moved out of town at a sedate walk to hold down the dust. Past the last house the driver picked the team up a little, and they resumed their clip-clopping near-trot. The air inside the coach was hot from the brief stop and ripe with the captain's breath.

"Goddam Mex," the captain said. "You can't trust a one of them."

Amos looked at the priest. The priest shook his head faintly. "What have you suffered at the hands of Californios, captain?" His smile spread gently. "Did they, like bankers, foreclose on your property?"

"We took this whole damn country away from them," the captain said. "Marched all the way to Mexico City . . ."

"You, captain?" the priest said. "That was twenty-five years ago."

The captain seemed suddenly an older man. "Yeah, me. I was a pup then." He got out the pint bottle and had a long drink. He wiped his mouth with the back of his hand. "But I wasn't a pup any longer in the Wilderness, an' I stood at Appomattox with a regiment behind me. My regiment. I was a colonel. I hadn't been a pup for a long time. Now . . ." He looked at the bottle, corked it, and dropped it into his valise. "Now I'm back to captain an' right out here in Mex land again." He straightened on the seat. "I hope we catch up with those thieving bastards, that's what I hope."

Amos looked at the priest and said nothing.

They were an hour out of Four Corners, still at their clip-clopping gait, when horsemen overtook them and swept past on both sides of the stage. Amos counted twelve. Each man carried a rifle, and only one bothered to wave. They chattered among themselves and left behind a great cloud of valley dust and a sense of isolation.

"Posse," the captain said. "Civilians. Somebody'll get shot up." He got out his bottle.

The priest said, "Violence begets violence. We never learn."

"I am afraid, father," Amos said, "that this isn't Massachusetts. Not yet."

The priest said, "Massachusetts, New York, Madrid, Rome . . ." He shook his head. "There are men everywhere who choose violence, sometimes because it is easier, sometimes because they believe it is the only way. And then other men feel that they must oppose with more violence, and so on, ad infinitum."

"Turning the other cheek," the captain said, "like it says in the Bible, just gets you two black eyes instead of one." He looked at Amos. "We still running late?"

Amos took out his watch, a fine gold repeater, London-made, a gift from his father on his twenty-first birthday. He opened the case and looked at the time, then bent forward to look out of the window at the flat country, the foothills to the

184

right, the distant mountains rising plain to the left. He knew the Valley well, its landmarks, its scattered ranches and towns. "I'd say almost an hour late," he said as he closed the watch and put it away. "Tumbleweed at perhaps one-thirty."

* * *

In the Tumbleweed Hotel bar there was argument. Word of the incomplete telegraph message had spread, and most of the town's adult males had assembled to try to decide what to do. The wind from the foothills rattled the hotel windows and whistled in the jigsaw trim of the roof. The floor of the bar rasped underfoot with fine hard dust. A dry, thirsty, frightening day. With the telegraph out, the sense of aloneness was almost palpable.

Henry Simpson had closed his butcher shop. He was a big man with large hairy forearms, a beer drinker's belly, and a loud voice. "All right," he said, "goddam it, all right! Let's stop gobblin' like a flock of turkeys an' make up our minds." He gestured to Jake Marvin behind the bar. "I'll have another drink. Beer *an'* whiskey." Thirst was contagious.

Henry tossed off his whiskey. He had a long foamy pull at his beer. "All right," he said. "Like in the army, first things first." He pointed at Luke Watson and Tom Willoughby. "You're sure that telegraph is still dead?"

Willoughby said to Luke, "You don't have to unlock and go inside. Just listen. If it's been fixed, it'll be clacking."

Luke finished his drink. "Give me another, Jake. I'll be right back." He scuttled outside.

Jake Marvin said, "Maybe I ought to close down." He shook his head. "Wouldn't do no good. They'd come in anyway." He sighed. "I'd sure hate to lose that back-bar mirror. All the way from Pittsburgh, P.A."

Willoughby said, "We don't know for sure they're coming. All the message said was they *thought* they was headed south. Hell's fire, they's three, four ways they could be going, maybe straight for the Tehachapi, an' not through here at all."

There was a brief contemplative silence. Henry Simpson shook his head. "Hope for the best," he said, "an' damn well

185

get ready for the worst. That's what my first sergeant used to say. They already been through Four Corners . . ."

Jake Marvin said, "Luke says they got a thousand dollars from the bank. Brand new shiny double eagles, fifty of 'em." Luke had been telling the story in detail to all who would listen.

"Goddam it," Henry said, "it don't matter a fart what they got or how much. I say we got to figger they're comin' through here. All right, what we do?" He paused. "Run for the hills?" He popped his fingers at Jake Marvin and indicated the emptiness of both whiskey glass and beer mug. "Not me," he said. "I got my shop. I got my house, an' the missus an' the kids, an' no goddam Mex robber is drivin' me out. I seen them gray uniforms comin' at Shiloh, an' I didn't run then. I ain't goin' to run now."

Luke Watson came trotting back in. "Still deader'n a doornail. That my drink?" He snatched it up and knocked it back.

Tom Willoughby said, "Well, that almost settles it. If they haven't got it fixed by now, no tellin' when it will be." He took out his railroad watch. "Stage due in a half hour, if she's on time." Stages sometimes carried money, and it did an express station manager no particular good with the company to have a stage robbed in his territory. He hated to think of Vasquez in town when the stage rolled in. He looked at Henry. "What you thinkin'?"

Beyond his declaration, Henry had given the matter no thought at all. Now he tossed back his shot of whiskey and had a long swill of his beer. He wiped foam from his moustache. "Well, hell," he said, "we got guns, ain't we? Let's get 'em. Come back here. Cover every inch of that street. When the murderin' bastards ride in, we give it to 'em!" He paused. He was smiling now. "Show 'em no goddam Mex robber can scare this town." He looked around the assembly. "Well?"

Tom Willoughby said, "Somebody'll get shot."

Henry nodded. "You're damn tootin'. This is white man country, ain't it?"

Juan Baca, in the lobby doorway, listened and liked it not. He had a horse. It was a poor animal, but it could carry him out of town. It did.

Whether he actually met Tiburcio Vasquez and warned him, or not, is a matter for conjecture. But it is a matter of record that Vasquez and nine men by-passed Tumbleweed that day, headed straight for the Tehachapi, rode over it and down into the Los Angeles basin where eventually Vasquez was taken, eventually tried, and quickly hanged.

* * *

With the Four Corners posse ahead of them the stage-coach driver and his guard felt a rising sense of security. The horses lifted to a trot, and the plume of dust behind the stage rolled thick and brown.

Amos said, "You won't have seen it, captain, but when it rains, this Valley turns green overnight." He looked to the priest, who nodded agreement. "One day," Amos said, "men will bring water from the streams that come down from the mountains all the way across the Valley and up and down from Stockton to the Tehachapi."

The priest said, "You have visions, my son."

The captain said, "I still say this whole damn dirty brown land isn't worth the powder and shot to blow it to hell." He paused. "And nobody's going to go to all that trouble, even if it could be done."

"The Romans did it, captain," the priest said. It occurred to him that the Romans were conquerors too. He looked again at Amos. "Vision," he said, "and ambition."

"California, father, is my home."

* * *

Inside the hotel it was hot, and the wind had never for a moment let up. For a time it would murmur in a low note in the railing of the porch, then without warning it would lift its voice in a banshee wail and set the whole building vibrating like a gigantic bass viol. Dust blew in the street outside, and occasionally a tumbleweed would come bouncing along, touching the ground only at long intervals like a jack rabbit with his ears laid back and a coyote not far behind.

They had their guns, rifles mostly, but with a scattering of shotguns. They had long since worked themselves up to anticipatory pitch, maintained it for a time, and were now on

187

the downgrade. Liquor helped, but not enough. Temper and a sense of frustration.

Tom Willoughby said, "I don't think they're comin'. Stands to reason. They'd have been here by now."

Henry had his own doubts, but it had been his idea in the first place, and so he had his responsibilities too. "Mebbe," he said. "An' mebbe your telegraph's workin' again." He had taken charge. He looked at Luke Watson. "Go see."

Luke hesitated. Then slowly he nodded. "Have a drink waitin'," he said. He scuttled out.

Henry said, "The way it was in the army. Settin' an' waitin' when you wasn't walkin' your feet off, mostly in mud." He looked at Willoughby. "You was out here? The war didn't affect you none, did it?" He shook his head. "California was just a name. Gold Rush was over, an' a war to be fought." He aimed for the spitoon and missed. "Trouble was, when it was over, nothin' was quite the same. You'd fought a war an' what'd it get you? You couldn't never get your hands on them responsible. Either they'd skipped the country, or the government protected them." He picked up his shot glass, looked at it, knocked the drink back. "Not like here," he said. "If the thievin' bastards come, we deal with 'em direct, we don't send nice letters back an' forth. We——"

Luke Watson's voice came from the street in a great shout. "They're comin'! They're comin'!" His footsteps sounded on the porch. He burst into the bar, pointing. "The Four Corners road. I seen their dust!" He grabbed his rifle with one hand, his drink with the other. As he drank he looked at Henry and waited.

They all watched Henry. "Windows," Henry said. "Every man at a window. Don't shoot till I say, but by God when you shoot, don't miss." He pointed in turn. "You over there. You there. You . . ."

The wind howling, dropped to its low murmur in the porch railing. A tumbleweed hastened past. And then they heard the sound of trotting hooves, a multitude, and every man looked to his weapon.

"Not till I say," Henry said. "We don't want to give 'em no warning." Like in the lines at Shiloh, he thought, the sergeant steadying them all, because the temptation was to

188

start shooting as soon as you saw something move, when it was still too far away.

The horsemen were in view now, riding at a steady trot right down the main street as if they owned it, each man with a rifle and a determined seat in the saddle. Henry, watching, thought: the son a bitches think they own the world. Well, we'll show them different. They . . . "Hold it!" he said suddenly. "Hold it!" He leaned out of his window for a better view.

All the horsemen had rifles except one, and he rode with his hands behind him, his horse at the lead. And . . . Yes, it was true—there wasn't a Mex among them, not one. No Tiburcio Vasquez. No. . . .

"Them's Four Corners men." Luke Watson's voice, filled with wonder.

Along the row of windows there was a general sighing sound.

Jake Marvin went to the porch door and opened it wide. He watched the men dismount at the rail. They were silent. "Howdy," Jake said. "Welcome to Tumbleweed. Come in. Have a drink." Relief was plain in his voice.

They filed into the bar, twelve men, all with rifles, urging one man ahead. The man's hands were tied behind him, and he said, "You're a pack of goldarned fools, that's what you are, every one of you!"

Henry said, "Who's he?"

"Well," one man said, "I'll tell you." He was a tall, sandy man with a tight grip on his temper. "Vasquez rode into Four Corners." He looked around. "You heard?" He watched all heads nod. "He got a thousand dollars from the bank, double eagles, an' other things, watches, rings. Thievin' son of a bitch. Murderin', too. One man shot, maybe hurt bad, maybe not. Soon's we could we got together and took out after them." He looked at the drink Jake pushed across the bar, nodded, picked it up, and drank it down. "Thanks," he said.

The bound man said, "And these goldarn fools think I had something to do with it." Then, with sudden vehemence, "Goddam it . . ."

The sandy man said, "We never did catch up to Vasquez an' them with him." He paused. "But we did see this one, an'

189

soon's he saw us he turned an' ran like a coyote with his tail on fire." There was silence.

The bound man looked from face to face. "What would you do," he said, "if you saw twelve men with guns coming at you?" Pause. "An' you had money in your saddlebag?" He took a deep breath. "Goddam it," he said, but the fine edge of anger was gone now, and what remained was desperation. "Listen. That's my money! I been savin' it! I owe it to a man, and if I don't pay him . . ."

"A thousand dollars," the sandy man said. "In gold." He paused. "Shiny bran' new double eagles, fifty of them." He was looking at Henry, but he was speaking to them all. "What would you think?"

* * *

Less than a mile outside of Tumbleweed the stage met the twelve Four Corners men. They were riding at a trot, each man looking straight ahead. There was no talking. They spread automatically to ride past the coach. No one waved or even acknowledged the coach's existence.

Amos leaned out of his window to watch their retreating backs. They had flowed together into a group again as effortlessly and as automatically as water flows together in a stream after it passes a rock. Amos pulled his head back in and looked at the priest. "Something's happened," he said. "I can feel it."

"Civilians," the captain said, "with guns. Somebody always gets hurt. Never known it to fail."

The priest closed his eyes. He said nothing.

Dust blew in the main street of Tumbleweed. The street was deserted. The stagecoach stopped at the express office and all three passengers got out to stretch wearily. The driver hauled Amos's bag out of the covered boot. He held it out and then dropped it to the dirt in astonishment. "Goddlemighty!" he said. "Looky there!" He pointed at the barn that housed the smithy.

The bound man was there, his hands still tied behind his back. He was hanging by the neck ten feet above the street from the rope used to hoist hay bales into the loft. His body swung gently in the wind.

190

Amos walked slowly out into the center of the street. He stopped there and stood staring up at the swinging body. The priest came to stand beside him. "Do you know him, my son?"

Amos nodded. He turned to look at Henry Simpson who walked out of the hotel bar to stand on the porch.

"One of them that robbed the bank at Four Corners," he said. "The others got clean away."

Luke Watson came out of the bar. He swayed a little as he tried to stand straight. "Caught him red-handed," he said, and then shook his head. "That ain't right. Gold-handed, that's what he was." He chuckled at his joke.

Henry was still watching Amos closely. "Somethin' on your mind, friend?" he said.

Amos nodded. He had one more look at the swinging body. Then he turned to face the men on the hotel porch. "His name," he said, "is, was, Barnes—Robert Barnes. He was no robber. He was a wheat farmer."

Henry took his time. "Man turned tail an' ran. An' he had a thousand dollars on him, shiny new double eagles, fifty of them."

"I was to meet him here," Amos said. He spoke slowly, trying hard to hold down the anger. "He was to make me a payment against the note my bank holds on his property." He paused. "His payment was to be one thousand dollars."

Henry stood motionless. He blinked. Then he raised his hands and let them fall. He said nothing.

Luke swallowed hard. He swallowed again. He was no longer swaying. He leaned forward and got himself in motion, reached the porch railing, and bent over it to vomit in the street.

Back at the bank in Stanhope, in Rudi Meyer's quiet office, "And so," Amos said, "there it was. The Four Corners bank has the money. And all we can do, as I see it, is take the land."

Rudi thought about it. He nodded slowly. "Land we do not want," he said. "But, what else?"

* * *

The old lady in the immense bed said, "Ten thousand

191

acres, child. Ten years later they found gold in Kern County. The land paid for itself handsomely." She paused. "The year before I was married they brought in the first oil well, the first of many." She gestured faintly, and the great diamond, as if to emphasize her words, glittered like fire.

22

Pepe brought the car to a smooth stop at the curb, got out, and came around to hold the rear door. The senator stepped out and stood for a few moments, expressionless, looking at the little shack. He said in Spanish, "You are sure this is the house, Pepe?"

"*Sí, señor.*"

"*Bueno.*" The senator walked up to the front door, knocked, and waited. He was tired, and he supposed that some rest would be good for him—Bill Hall had said so—but there was too much to be done and too little time in which to do it, and it would not be long before he would begin an eternity of resting. Time enough then.

The door opened, and Benjie looked at the senator, silver hair, pearl gray silk suit, immaculate linen and all, looking cool and fresh even in the Stanhope heat. She looked beyond him to the great car crouching at the curb. "Jesus Christ!" said Benjie.

Nothing changed in the senator's face. "Not at all," he said. "I am Mike Stanfield, my dear. Is my grandson here?"

Pete was. He stood up as the senator entered the little room. "I didn't expect to see you," Pete said.

"Didn't you, boy? Then," the senator said, "you are less perceptive than I might have thought. And," he added, "less polite than you were taught. You might introduce me to your young lady."

Always, Pete thought, the old son of a bitch could put you down with just a word or a gesture. He had almost forgotten that. He made the introduction.

The senator held out his hand. His smile was affability itself. "Benjie. How do you do? It is a pleasure to meet you."

"Please," Benjie said. She took the offered hand, shook it briefly. "I mean," she said, "please sit down." She hesitated. "Maybe you'd like a beer?"

The senator's smile spread. He was not fond of beer, but not for the world would he have disappointed the girl who was obviously trying hard. "Thank you, my dear." He took the straight chair and looked at Pete. "Sit down, boy, and tell me what you have been doing with yourself." Immediately and completely in charge of the situation.

At the refrigerator, opening the beer, pouring it carefully into the least chipped glass, Benjie glanced continually at the two and tried to fit them into one family. There was a certain resemblance. It was, she thought, in the expression around the mouth. But where the senator's was firm, confident, determined, Pete's was, if not weak, unformed and resentful, petulant rather than forceful.

"And when you have had your time of rebellion," the senator was saying, "do you then intend to come out of your playpen into the world of reality?" He was being intentionally brutal.

Pete said, "Maybe my world is more real than yours."

The senator accepted the beer. He smiled at the girl. "Thank you, Benjie. You are most hospitable." Then, to Pete, "It is possible, but the evidence would seem to indicate otherwise." He drank, and nodded at the girl. "Delicious."

Pete made himself sit quiet. It was difficult. First Paul, then Scott, then his father, and now this one, his grandfather, pouring it on; they seemed to come at him from all sides.

194

Well, he had learned some things, and he was not going to allow himself to be drawn.

"You probably expect," the senator said, "that I am going to give you a lecture, boy." He shook his head gently. "I am not. A lecture would be wasted, wouldn't it? Worse, it might even turn into an argument about such clichés as life style and generation gap and lack of communication." He sighed. "Believe me, Pete, I have heard all of that I can stand back in Washington."

Benjie, leaning against the sink, was watching and listening carefully. She had seen this face and heard this voice on TV and been impressed with the poise and the assurance and the obvious self-confidence. Now, seeing the old man in the flesh, she was even more impressed because, by his approach, he had given Pete no opening, no excuse for reaction; he had used guile where he might have been expected to use power, and she could see that Pete was off-balance.

"Perhaps," the senator said, "you thought I would wave the name Stanfield like a banner and appeal to your sense of loyalty." Again the head shake. "I won't, boy. There is nothing in a name that guarantees quality. You have my genes in your makeup, but their pattern is not at all the same. Even if you tried, I don't know if you could be worth the powder to blow you to hell. On your track record, the odds would be against your ever being anything but an also-ran."

Pete said, "Then why did you come?"

"To see you. To meet your young lady. To discharge my own responsibility to my grandson." There was silence. The senator had another pull at the beer. He set the glass down, took out a handkerchief, and wiped his lips. He stood up. "Is there anything you need, Pete?"

Pete too was standing. "Money, you mean?" There was scorn in his voice. "Money isn't . . ."

"I said anything," the senator said. "I don't recall mentioning a price tag."

Pete was silent. Benjie, watching, listening, felt vaguely shamed.

The senator nodded to the girl. "Thank you for your hospitality, Benjie. A painful scene, and I apologize." He held out his hand. "Goodbye, Pete."

Pete hesitated. Then slowly he accepted the hand and shook it briefly. "You don't understand," he said.

The senator nodded. He was at the door, already holding it open. "There are many things I don't understand." He paused. "A pity." He was gone, and the door closed gently.

Pete looked at the girl. For a long time he was silent. Then, "You've met Paul. You've seen the parent. Now this one."

Benjie said nothing.

"Impressive, aren't they?"

"Yes." Benjie hesitated. "I'm not used to being treated like somebody important. Not by somebody who is important in the straight world. He could have put me down. He didn't even try."

Pete nodded slowly. "He's too smart for that. And that's the hell of it. In their own way they're all too damn smart."

* * *

The senator had one more call to make that day. The law offices of Starling, Cluett, Sanchez & Lane were upstairs in the original Stanfield building on the plaza—thick-walled, high-ceilinged rooms with a cool hush and the soft whisper of overhead fans, no air conditioning. Kaye Starling was in, and he came out himself to show the senator into his inner office.

The walls were paneled and lined with well-used law books. The big desk was polished and uncluttered, and the chairs and sofa of soft brown leather were meant for comfort and leisurely talk. Starling closed the door. "A long time, Mike." He was the senator's age, portly, pink-cheeked, unhurried. From a cupboard in the paneled wall he took a cut-glass decanter and two short glasses, and poured a shot into each. *"Salud."*

The senator took his drink to one of the deep chairs. He sniffed appreciatively and sipped. "Still the finest bourbon I've ever tasted," he said. He smiled. "I'd like to take some with me."

"Where are you going, Mike?"

The senator smiled again. "I don't rightly know. Nobody has ever come back to tell about it."

There was silence. Starling sipped his drink, set the glass down. "I won't insult you," he said slowly, "by asking are you sure, or are you joking. I will say I'm sorry to hear it. It won't be the same." He paused. "Does Conchita know? George?"

"No. And," the senator said, "we'll keep it that way. You have my will. You have a power of attorney you can exercise until I'm gone, and then you'll be appointed executor."

"With the bank," Starling said.

The senator nodded. "Are there any bases we've failed to touch, Kaye? Loose ends that could more easily be gathered together now? My papers in Washington are in good shape, I think. You will decide their disposition. There are some . . ." The senator paused, smiled, and sipped again at his drink. "Perhaps some of them ought not to go anywhere except into an incinerator. You will decide that."

"Shall I consult with George?"

The senator thought about it. Was this at least partly why he had come here to talk—to advise, to try to influence events after his death? *Basta,* enough. He said, "I'll leave that to your judgment, Kaye. Geroge lives in the here and now. I am not sure how much interest the past holds for him. Scott, on the other hand, delights in digging into past indiscretions, of which every man worth his salt has a few, and when Scott turns them up he is convinced that he has discovered the whole man. Not true, of course. George tends to make his assessments of the living man himself. I am not at all sure what he would think of some of my correspondence. I've had power, Kaye, and at times I've used it, sometimes perhaps ruthlessly, to achieve what I considered beneficial results. Does that make me a villain? I don't know. 'It matters not who won or lost, but how you played the game.' Aside from the fact that it is bad verse, I think it is ridiculous sentiment. If a game is worth playing, it is worth playing to win. George knows that. None better. When the time comes, he will stand fully accountable, I am sure of it, for his own actions, all of them. But I am not sure that he ought to be placed in a position where he might feel he had to judge mine."

197

Julia, looking younger than ever, inwardly at peace, knocked on the study door and went in. George was at the desk. Julia closed the door carefully. "Nose to the grindstone," she said. She smiled. "I won't keep you long." She perched on a corner of the desk and swung one elegantly tanned bare leg while she helped herself to a cigarette, lighted it from the jade desk lighter, and exhaled with relish. "I rode with Cleary Ward this morning. In some ways he's an—amusing boy."

George had leaned back in his chair to listen. He supposed that in a way they were all a little out of the ordinary, the members of the family. But where each of the others was held in at least partial check—the senator by politics and public opinion, Scott by the guidelines of his discipline, himself by his own built-in squareness—this aunt of his had always considered herself free to fly as high, as far, and as fast as she chose with never a thought to appearances. From swimming naked in Adams House pool as an undergraduate, to driving her own car in the Monte Carlo, to marrying or mating with constant abandon, she had carved a niche for herself as a kind of real-life Auntie Mame, and if you didn't like it, you could lump it. Although if she chose, she could charm you, along with the birds down out of the trees until she had you eating out of her hand. "I hope Cleary still has his—sense of humor," George said.

"A joke, from you." Julia was smiling fondly. "The right woman will do wonders for you, George. Ann would have, but you were both too young." She tapped the cigarette in the ashtray. "Cleary's family once held property here under Mexico. I quote. They lost it to squatters. A squatter."

George said, "The Wilder family?" He nodded. "Probably." He smiled. "Thank you, Julia."

"It was deep, George. Bitter." Julia paused. "Scott told me a tale about a car that followed you from the dehydrator fire and tried to run you into the trees."

George thought about it. He shook his head. "Not Cleary. Not his style."

"You can't be sure. Maybe," Julia said, "I know him deep

down a little better than you do." She produced that brilliant smile. "There are ways and ways, George, to a man's secret thoughts. Cleary resents the Stanfields. I think he hates them. Us."

George smiled. "Even you?"

She was unsmiling now. "Even me. He wants very badly to—dominate me." She stood up then and crushed out the cigarette. "Cocktail time. They were setting out the bar things. There are just Mike and Conchita, Ellen, you and I for dinner. Scott has taken that nice girl of his over to the coast."

George pushed back his chair and stood up. Arm in arm they crossed the room. At the door Julia paused. "Watch Cleary, George."

Empty-headed and flighty she might appear, George thought, but he had long ago learned that she was not. He nodded soberly. "Will do," he said.

23

Howard Lang, the governor's man, drove his own Plymouth Fury with unofficial plates. He parked out in the road and walked along the drive to the small house in the rear. Two men appeared before he reached the porch, and he stopped to confront them.

One was middle-sized, wiry, in his twenties, with black hair in a ducktail cut. He held an axe handle lightly in both hands. "You want something?"

But it was at the other man that Lang looked long and thoughtfully—a big, stooped man with abnormally long arms. His eyes were dark in a dark brown face, and they watched Lang as an animal watches from a cage. He, Lang thought, was the dangerous one. "I want to see Ruben Lucero."

The big man made a quick gesture with his free hand and a popping sound with his tongue. The other man said, "You fuzz?"

"Not really." Lang kept his eyes on both of them, and waited; and as if on cue in the silence the porch door of the house opened and Paul Meyer stepped out.

"Qué pasa?" Paul said, and listened to rapid Spanish from the smaller man. The big man, Julio, made no move. Paul looked at Lang.

"I'm from Sacramento," Lang said. "I was told to come down here and talk to Lucero." Pause. "I do what I'm told." Another pause. "One way or another."

Lucero walked out on the porch past Paul. He stood for a time in silence, expressionless. "Mr. Lang," he said. "I have hear of you. Come in." He turned his back and walked into the house.

In the hot little room, door closed, Paul leaned against the wall, Lucero sat behind his desk, Lang took one of the straight chairs. Lucero had not offered to shake hands, Paul noticed. Lang seemed unaware; his manner was easy and assured, without a hint of belligerence. He smiled easily and often. "Having a little trouble down here, I understand." He looked up at Paul. "You're Paul Meyer? How do. A little out of Meyer-Stanfield territory, aren't you?" Smiling.

Paul shook his head. "Nowhere near as far as it is from here to Sacramento." He was silent for a moment. "Why have they sent a hatchet man? Is somebody frightened?"

"I go where I'm sent," Lang said. "I don't ask why. I try to get cooperation wherever I go." He shrugged. "Sometimes I do. Sometimes I don't. In the end it doesn't matter much one way or the other."

"Tell us what you want," Lucero said. "Then we will see."

Lang took his time. He held up his left hand, fingers spread, and he ticked off points by bending down fingers as he talked. "Three bomb threats in the capitol within the last week. All duds. So far. A courthouse shoot-out. A Southern Pacific freight, mostly refrigerator cars loaded with fruit headed east, derailed near Victorville. A chicano parade turns into a riot. A dehydrator burns down here and a man is dead." He turned down his little finger.

"And," Paul said, "when the San Andreas fault puts on the performance everybody has been predicting, you'll blame us for that, too? And how about the smog in the Los Angeles basin? Aren't we in some way responsible?"

Lang's smile held steady but its quality was changed. "As

201

I said, sometimes I get cooperation and sometimes I don't."

"But," Lucero said, "you have not yet tell us what you want, Mr. Lang."

"He's told us," Paul said. "He told us just by coming down here. We're making waves. We're being told to stop, because if we don't stop, we'll turn out to be part of a Communist conspiracy, a bunch of wild-eyed agitators coming in and stirring up trouble where everything was serene. We may even turn out to be advance men from Mars, about to take over Earth." He paused. "Do you like what you do, Mr. Lang? Don't answer that. Yesterday the governor was at the Stanfield ranch. Today you're here." He thought of the big man in his study, calm and merciless. "Is that how George Stanfield is playing it?"

Lucero said, *"Amigo . . ."*

Paul shook his head. "At times like this I'm ashamed to have been any part of that power structure ever, so help me God I am."

"Well," Lang said, "maybe your father will disown you and settle your worry." Obviously he had researched his project.

"Mr. Lang." Lucero's voice was sharper now. "You still have not tell us what you want." He paused. "Or is it only trouble you are here for?" He gestured warningly at Paul. "Patience. Well, Mr. Lang?"

"Fair enough," Lang said. "I'd just like to have a look at the membership lists of your—what you call your union."

Paul took a deep breath and held it.

Lucero shook his head. "You know more better than that, Mr. Lang."

"Ashamed of your membership?"

Lucero said quietly, "If I give you names, Mr. Lang, then what happen? I will tell you. I have see it before. Juan, he find that his grocery store cannot carry him on credit longer. Pepe, he lose his car to the finance company. Julio, he have a glass of beer, and he end in jail for drunk driving." Lucero's voice deepened, softened. It was his first indication of anger. "The daughter of José, she go to a movie one night an' just smile at a strange man, friendly, an' she is arrest for soliciting. They

202

call her whore." His voice rose now. "I have hear about you, Mr. Lang." Pause. "I spit on what I have hear."

Paul pushed himself away from the wall. "I'd say that the session is ended." He walked to the door and opened it.

Lang stood up. He looked at them both. "As I said, sometimes they cooperate, sometimes they don't." He was unperturbed. "It doesn't really matter in the end." He nodded to each man in turn. "Nice to have met you. I'll know you next time." He walked out down the steps and past Julio's animal glare without even a glance.

Paul closed the door slowly. He felt faintly sick. "Now what?"

Lucero was beyond words, fighting hard for control. His eyes, searching Paul's face, were dark with bitterness and misery. He opened his hands and closed them again helplessly.

"The Establishment," Paul said, "is lowering the boom, is that the way you see it?" He shook his head slowly. "We aren't that important, Ruben, not yet. But George Stanfield is. And the senator. All it takes is a word from them to Sacramento, and we get Lang. Isn't that the whole point?"

Lucero nodded slowly, conquering himself. "When you have ground squirrel in field," he said, "what you do? You go with shovel and plug all holes except one with dirt. Then down that one hole you push cotton balls dipped in something I do not know the name. Then you throw match down the hole, and poof!—explosion—no more ground squirrels. Is that not the way it is?"

Paul nodded. He had seen it done a long time ago and watched in youthful dismay as flattened bodies burst out of the plugged holes.

"We," Lucero said, "are the ground squirrel, what you call annoyance." His voice was normal now, but the bitterness in his eyes remained. "For me," he said, and shrugged, "is not important. Maybe they not even touch me, or you, because somebody might write in the newspaper that we are picked on. But the others, who trust me . . . He shook his head.

Paul said, "Let's go see him. George Stanfield. Lay it on the line. Maybe he . . ."

"Amigo." Lucero wore his faint sad smile of protest. "If I go see him—*comprendes?*—I go with hat in my hand, to beg. Then it is finished, no? We are nothing, *nada y nada por nada,* not even important as Mr. Albright and Mr. Potter who also make loud sound that mean nothing. Do you not see?"

"All right," Paul said, "then Khasigian."

"No. I think here . . ." Lucero touched his chest with a forefinger. ". . . Mr. Khasigian would understand. I have read that his people in Turkey . . ." He shook his head. "He would understand, but only here." Again he touched his chest. "Here . . ." He tapped his temple. ". . . he would see only that we are nothing because we can be hurt, and he think of business, and so he only smile and say he is sorry, but there is nothing to be done."

Paul said slowly, wonderingly, "Is this how it always looks, Ruben?"

The smile again; admission this time rather than protest. "When you look up from underneath? Yes. You are afraid because those above you, George Stanfield, others, they are so big they shut out the sun and no matter where you walk their shadow fall upon you."

"You're not afraid," Paul said. "Not you."

"Oh, yes, *amigo.*" With great dignity. "I am afraid. You are born with fear. You drink fear with the milk of your mother. There is fear around you where you work in orchard, field. Is like smog, but you cannot see it, only feel it; and it burn more than eyes, it burn inside." He paused. "Maybe for black people it is the same. I do not know, but I think so. But I do know how it is for us. I am afraid. It is that I hope I can be more strong than the fear."

"I'll go see him," Paul said. "If that's the kind of stinking dirty way they're playing, then . . ."

"Then what?" Lucero said quietly. "You will tell them? But if they know Mr. Lang and what he do, then you tell them nothing that is new." Pause. "And if they do not know Mr. Lang, then they smile and ask what has he done? Because men who can shut out the sun do not like to know what happen in their shadow."

"I'll still go see him," Paul said. He paused. "Unless you don't want me to?"

Lucero shook his head. "I cannot tell you what to do."

"All you have to do is ask me."

"No. Is your world. Maybe you know better than me."

"That will be a day."

"You think small of yourself," Lucero said. He was smiling again, this time with affection. "You are—how you say it? —the prince. One day you will shut out the sun too, and I will stand in the shadow and look up and try to negotiate contract with you. Maybe then you remember what is like to stand in shadow, and you try to be fair—to yourself, and to us."

* * *

The family was at dinner when Consuelo came in and bent down to whisper to Ellen. Ellen closed her eyes, opened them, looked at George. "Daddy. Please." She pushed back her chair and rose. "Please," she said again.

Julia said, "Well? Don't just sit there, George. If there is a crisis, cope."

Expressionless, George pushed back his chair and stood up. "My apologies," he said, and followed Ellen out into the hallway. "Well?"

"Paul," Ellen said. She took a deep breath. "He's at the gate. He wants to see you."

"About what?"

Ellen shook her head. "I don't know, Daddy. But, please, don't you owe him that?" Another deep breath. "Or if you don't owe him, will you do it for me?"

Or be a bastard again, George thought angrily. He nodded shortly. "Bring him to the study. I'll be in after I've finished my meal." He left Ellen and walked back into the dining room and resumed his place at table without a word. He was aware that Julia glanced at him from time to time, eyebrows raised. George ignored her and made himself eat. The little Cornish game hen was tasteless.

They finished the main course. And dessert. Conchita, wife, mother, customarily silent, said—as she had said how many years ago?—"I think you may be excused now, George." Her smile was gentle. "Whatever it is that demands your attention." As if he were being allowed to go out and play.

They were both in the study, in separate chairs, and Ellen's eyes were red. They jumped up when George walked in and closed the door carefully.

"You'd better beat it," Paul said to Ellen.

Ellen shook her head. In that moment, George thought, she was Ann to the life, tearful as Ann had been sometimes, but standing firm. Had he been a bastard then, too? New thought. "I want to hear," Ellen said.

In the silence George walked around the desk and sat down heavily. "What's on your mind?"

Paul sat down again. He put his hands on his knees and braced himself. "Do you know a man named Lang?" There was a touch of Joe Hanson's belligerence in his voice. Or Lewis Mattingly's. Resentful belligerence.

"I don't particularly like your tone," George said. "But the answer is no."

"He's from Sacramento."

"So?"

"You talked to the governor." Accusation.

"I did," George said. "I was interrupted at that meal too." He paused. "Get to the point."

Ellen was watching Paul. Paul said slowly, "Yesterday the governor was here. Today Lang shows up from Sacramento. Are you saying that's a coincidence?"

It was startling, George thought, to watch them grow up sometimes all at once, between one hour and the next, perhaps even between sentences. It happened in wartime, he had been told, and perhaps that in a sense was what they had here, too. That kind of philosophizing could wait. He said, "I'm saying nothing because I know nothing about your man named Lang. Who is he? What has he done?"

None of them had noticed that the door had opened. The senator walked into the room. He closed the door gently behind him. "I know of a man named Lang," he said. "Perhaps I am partly responsible for his being here. What about him?" He remained standing, dominating the room.

Paul started to rise. The senator's gesture held him in his chair, at a disadvantage. The room was silent. "He came to see Ruben Lucero," Paul said. His voice was low, controlled. "I was there with Ruben. I saw Lang. I heard him." Pause. "A slimy bastard. You . . ." He spoke directly to the senator. ". . . would have him thrown out of your office without hesitation." He turned to George. "You would pick him up and break his back."

"And you?" the senator said.

"We did nothing, because we don't want violence. Can't you see that? Violence is the handle your kind are after. Violence is what gives you the chance to scream for the police, the national guard, call for a state of emergency so anybody you don't like can be busted, tear-gassed, shot." Paul paused, and the room was silent. "So we get Lang," he said. "And sooner or later we get violence in reaction to Lang." He paused again. "And then you have us by the balls." He looked at Ellen. "Sorry, kid, but I'm beginning to believe that gutter language is all they understand."

Ellen was holding her lower lip between her teeth. She shook her head hard and said nothing.

George looked at the senator. The senator said, "I assume that you won't object to a question or two, young man?" The committee-room purr.

"No, sir, I guess not. Even though I know what the questions will be. You see," Paul said, "Ruben Lucero told me what to expect. He went through maybe the third grade, but he understands people like you. The slave gets to understand the overseer." He paused. "Go ahead. What has Lang actually done? Is that the first question?"

Nothing changed in the senator's face. "That is the first question."

"Nothing," Paul said, "except ask to see the membership list. Innocent enough on the surface—is that the second question?"

"You anticipate me admirably," the senator said.

"Innocent on the surface," Paul said. "Agreed. And the third question is probably: what, specifically, do I fear that Lang will do that I am so upset?" He shook his head. "Not being the kind of slimy bastard Lang is, I can't really say, but it will be something, and if that fails, something else, and something else until he gets what he wants—violent reaction."

Lang was the ferret sent down the hole to flush out the

207

rats, Bill Hanford had said. The senator remembered the analogy and thought it apt. "Violent reaction," he said.

"Yes, sir."

"But we have already had violent reaction, have we not? Or don't you consider the things that have happened here violent? Barns burned, a dehydrator burned, a truck overturned and burned, two men dead so far—those are not violent events?"

"They are violent," Paul said, "and we had nothing to do with them. We deplore them as much as you do."

"You have no idea," the senator said, "who could have caused them? Is that what you are saying?"

There was hesitation, faint but perceptible. "No, sir," Paul said. "I have no idea. Neither has Ruben."

The senator took his time. "Let us say," he said at last, "that I believe you, young man. Then all of us are interested together in finding the person or persons responsible, are we not, and in bringing the violence to a stop? 'To insure domestic tranquillity,' is that not our common goal?"

Paul could see what was coming, and he saw no way to avoid it. Admit it, he told himself, you're no match for this wily old devil. "Yes, sir," he said wearily, "that is our common goal." What else was there to say?

"Then why do we not assume," the senator said, "at least until events prove otherwise, that Mr. Lang was sent down here from Sacramento to assist in that common endeavor? Why not that, rather than assume automatically that he is an instrument of the evil Establishment bent on causing more trouble?"

And where was the answer to that? Paul looked at Ellen. There were tears in her eyes, and she shook her head slowly in sympathy. "Ruben had it taped," Paul said. "He told me what I'd run into." He stood up. "Thanks for listening."

"Why," the senator said, "any time, any time at all, young man." He smiled. "I had a talk with your father today, and a very pleasant chat over a drink with your brother Howard."

"Ginger-peachy," Paul said. As he walked out of the study he heard the senator's voice in the quiet room.

"I think a brandy, George? Talking is thirsty work." The door closed.

"Paul." Ellen was there, and she tucked her arm through his as they walked to the front door and down the steps to his pickup. There they stopped and turned to face each other. Ellen rose on tiptoe and slid her arms around his neck.

Her lips were parted, soft and moist, and she thrust her tongue into his mouth, shyly at first, and then with almost vehement passion as she pressed herself tight against him. It was a long kiss, breathless, and when at last it was broken Ellen stepped back.

"Will you meet me tonight?" Her voice was unsteady. "At the gate? Ten o'clock?"

"Baby." Paul said it slowly, helplessly. "We're caught, hung-up, whipsawed, don't you see?"

"I see." She watched him quietly. "But I'm not going to be a bystander any longer."

"Will you come with me?"

She shook her head slowly. "I can't do that. And even if I did, being with you would just give them one more lever." She had grown too, matured beyond measure in just these last few minutes. "But I will meet you, and meet you, and meet you whenever you say. That is a promise."

"And your father?"

"He won't stop me," Ellen said. "That is a promise too." She paused. "Tonight?"

Paul nodded. "I'll be there." He reached for her, but she stepped back, beyond, beyond his grasp.

"If you kissed me again," she said. "I don't think I could stand it." Her smile was as unsteady as her breathing. "Until tonight." She turned and ran up the steps.

* * *

George had come out from behind his desk. He sat now in one of the large chairs, a brandy glass untouched at his elbow. The senator held his glass in both hands, warming the liquor between his palms, savoring its bouquet. "You don't approve of my meddling," the senator said. "I can read your thoughts." He smiled faintly. "I think I could still teach you a thing or two at poker, George."

"I don't doubt it. What kind of man is this Lang?"

"I have heard of him. I have never met him. He is the kind

of man men in positions of great responsibility, men like the governor, frequently have available to use as needed."

George was silent, studying his father, trying to see behind the polished façade. Useless, he thought, he was going to see only what the senator wanted him to see. "And you approve of such men?"

The senator sipped his brandy. "You have lawyers, George, bankers, brokers, managers, men who jump when you snap your fingers, men who gladly run errands and do chores for you."

True enough. "But if it comes to the unpleasant part," George said, "I do it myself." Mattingly's voice on the telephone was still in his mind. He had always liked Lewis Mattingly, he supposed they had called each other friend. But what had to be done had to be done, friend or no friend, and if a small sense of remorse would forever remain, why, that was the price of responsibility. "I don't believe in hatchet men."

The senator smiled. "Admirable. And probably at times onerous." He was silent for a little time. "Do I approve of the Langs of this world? I neither approve nor disapprove. I accept them as a fact of life. Were the vigilantes in the early days decent men driven so far by scoundrels that they had to take the law into their own hands? Or were at least some of them what Bill Hanford called them today, murdering bastards no better than the men they picked on? I don't know, George. That argument has been going on for a long time and will never be settled definitively. But what we all can agree on is that the results of the vigilante activities were a decrease in crime and at least a partial restoration of that 'domestic tranquillity' I mentioned earlier."

George was undecided; there was no point in comment.

The senator said, "I found young Paul's performance tonight rather admirable in its way. He is bursting with idealism, and he runs too fast, perhaps, but I admit that I am impressed." He paused. "He lied, though, when he said he had no idea who might have perpetrated the local outrages. You saw that?"

"I saw it," George said. "And I know why he lied." He paused to taste the bitterness. "He thinks Pete, my son, your

210

grandson, is in this violence up to his ears, and he wouldn't say so."

"I see." The senator's voice was quiet. " 'I will not turn my back on my friend.' I remember another occasion when that was said, and I remember the trouble its saying caused." He put aside that memory. "And do you think Pete is implicated?"

"I don't know," George said heavily. "And I wish I did. Or maybe I don't."

24

The sun was not yet down but the wind had died, and out beyond the lines of breakers the water had taken on a smooth, glassy appearance; the scent of pine trees and salt air was a heady blend.

They had taken off their shoes, and Scott had turned up his trousers. They walked barefoot now in the white sand, behind them the curving point of the Carmel headland, ahead the great green sweep of Pebble Beach, the forest at its boundary dotted with partially hidden houses on the Seventeen Mile Drive.

"There was a song once," Scott said. " 'Come with me where moonbeams/ Light Tahitian skies . . .' Did you ever want to turn your back on everything, lie in the sun forever, lotus-eating?"

That slow, calm smile. "Not," Jenny said, "since about my twelfth birthday. That was when I discovered that my current idol, movie star of course, and I don't even remember his name, was a fickle fellow about to get his fifth divorce, and I decided that I had better settle down to living."

"I am not that fickle a fellow. Would you go with me now?"

"To lotusland?" Jenny shook her head. "My lotusland is here, doing the things I like to do and can do well. I need a sense of satisfaction, Scotty."

"Women's Lib?"

"You know better. Or if you don't, you should." Her tone was gentle, but the words meant what they said. "I am a woman. I want to be treated like a woman except when I'm being a lawyer, and then I want to be treated like a lawyer— without thought of sex."

They walked on slowly, companionably silent. Two young men wearing swim trunks and shiny black rubber frogmen shirts raced across the sand and into the water, threw down their fiber glass boards, jumped on them, and kneeling began to paddle out through the surf. Scott watched, smiling. "Cold, cold," he said. "Oddly enough, a little north of here at Santa Cruz the water is warmer. Warm current sets in." He shook his head, smiling still. "But you have to go south of Santa Barbara for any really good surfing. San Onofre below San Clemente is probably the best."

"You've done that, too? There is so much about you I don't know."

"I think," Scott said slowly, "that I'd like to show you all of it, what there is."

Jenny's face was serious. "Don't pretend to run yourself down, Scotty. You're not a humble man." She paused. "I don't think I'd like you as much if you were."

A ball rolled past them, and a small fluffy dog raced by in pursuit. He caught up with the ball, pounced in a shower of white sand, and came up triumphantly with the thing in his mouth. His tail was up and waving as he trotted back.

Jenny was smiling. "I had a dog once. When I was just a girl. Before college, law school, practice."

"There is a great deal about you that I don't know," Scott said.

Jenny's smile now was pure amusement. "And you are willing to buy a pig in a poke?" The amusement faded. "Why have you never married, Scotty? Or have you, and that is another thing I don't know?"

"Never married." He glanced at the woman. "That bothers you? I'm not queer, if that has passed through your mind."

"I think I'd have known if you were."

One of the surfers had caught a swell. He stopped his furious paddling, hopped to a squatting position, and then rose slowly to full height, feet at a forty-five degree angle to the board's centerline, arms outstretched for balance. He shifted his weight and began to cut across the front of the wave, staying ahead of the white water.

Scott watched critically. "Not bad," he said. And then, in a different tone, "Why have I never married? The easy answer would be that I have never met anyone like you before." He smiled. "That is some of the reason, I think. But there is more, of course. Partly, I think it has been pure selfishness, no one to consult or even to consider when I wanted to go somewhere or do something, plan a house that I wanted, things that ought to be shared."

"Go on," Jenny said. "There is more, isn't there?"

Strangely, he was thinking of Ellen, walking back from the tennis court that first morning at the ranch. Seventeen years old, and she saw deeper than he; she saw through him, sham and all. "Basically," he said, "I guess I've been afraid that someone might get too close, know too much about me. I think it takes more courage than I've ever had to open yourself to someone else."

"I think it also takes a need." Jenny stopped, stooped, picked up a palmful of sand. Walking again, she tilted her hand and watched the grains flow in a trickle, then a torrent, until her palm was empty. She brushed her hands together absently. "I was married once, Scotty. Did you know that?"

"It doesn't matter."

"It didn't work," Jenny said. "I was the one who sued for divorce, but it was he who left me. I wasn't—enough. That hurts. You like to think that you are capable of anything. Oh, you know it isn't true, but it might be. Then when you come right up against total failure you are face to face with your own fallibility, and the whole marvelous illusion is shattered. You are just the same as everybody else, and all along you thought you were something very special."

214

"You are something very special. And your man, who-ever he was, was an unperceptive jerk."

She felt suddenly gay, released. She could laugh aloud and mean it. "Unprofessorial language, Scotty. Do you use the word 'jerk' on the podium?"

"Sometimes worse, far worse." Her change of mood had reached him, lifted his own spirits. "Let's go back, put on our shoes, find a quiet bar and the illusion of privacy. I don't want dogs and boys on surfboards sharing you with me."

They cut straight across the curving beach to the wall where they had left their shoes. They perched and brushed sand from bare feet. "It always sticks," Scott said. "Some of it inevitably gets into my socks, and a grain of sand can feel like a——"

"Mr. Stanfield?" A quiet male voice, quite close.

Scott turned on the wall and looked up. It was a man he did not know. A reporter perhaps from the local paper, al-though how—?

"Mr. Scott Stanfield?"

"That's right," Scott said. "What—?" He stopped there and looked at the paper the man had thrust at him and he had automatically seized. "What the hell is this?" But the man was already walking back up to the street and the center of Car-mel.

Jenny said quietly, "Maybe you'd better let me see that, Scotty. I recognize the technique."

Wordlessly, baffled still, Scott put the paper in her hand, watched her open it and read quickly. Her face was expres-sionless as she refolded the paper and handed it back.

"It would appear, Scotty," she said, "that you are in-volved in a paternity suit."

The mood of gaiety was gone.

* * *

Out of Carmel on the highway headed north and then east there was little traffic. As they began the climb into Pa-checo Pass the only sounds were the muted hum of the Mer-cedes engine and the rush of their passage through the warm night air.

215

"I seem to have blown it, don't I?" Scott said. What he felt was anger, solid and deep, directed at Cathy Strong.

"That depends, Scotty." Jenny's voice was quiet, calm. "I won't pretend that I like it. Another illusion exposed, and that is always painful."

"Did you think I was a celibate?" Anger was protean; it could alter shape and direction with astonishing ease.

"Scotty." Her fingers touched his forearm gently. "One doesn't think, don't you see that? If you had had a wide reputation as a womanizer, that would have been one thing. But you don't."

"No cocksman, he." And then, quickly, "That was unnecessary. Sorry."

"Words don't hurt me, only intentions, actions."

There was silence between them as the night rushed past. They met the first tendrils of fog just short of the summit, and Scott immediately slowed, shifted down to third gear, and lowered his headlight beams.

"It would be," he said. "Aside from summer heat and spring winds calculated to drive you up the wall, this is one of our lovely Valley's more endearing characteristics. It is probably filled to the brim, like a big bowl, with fog so thick you could cut it in slices."

It was. They came over the last rise of the pass and dropped immediately into a sullen, swirling gray mass, clammy on their faces, reflecting headlight beams, allowing glimpses, but only glimpses, of the white line on the road. There were no trees, no sky, and at their new slow pace, no wind of passage. They and the car, dreamlike, were alone in the world.

"What are you going to do, Scotty?" Always afterward, Jenny thought, she would look back to this time as something set aside, out of context, disembodied conversation in a surrealist setting. Perhaps it was just as well.

"I'm going to get us to the ranch, if I can."

"That wasn't what I meant." As you well know, she thought.

He was silent for some time, concentrating on the white line, staying well to the right of it, all senses alert. Safe driving rules implored you to pull over to the side of the road and

216

stop in fog like this. The hell with safe driving rules. "I am going to make Cathy Strong wish she had never been born," Scott said. And probably he would get argument on that, he thought.

He did—subtle argument in the form of Socratic questioning. "Is she pregnant, Scotty? That, of course, can be verified."

"She says she is. I doubt if it's bluff."

"Is it your child?"

"It's possible. It may also belong to any of a number of young studs . . ."

"Do you know that?"

Honesty dictated the answer. "No." Pause. "But the evidence would tend to indicate that she is not without experience." Anger rose again. "In short," he said, "she is very good indeed in the rack." He turned to see the reaction, but Jenny's face was only a pale blur in the darkness and the fog. He was suddenly aware of the dampness on his own face. "Would you like the top up?" he said.

"I like it like this." She took her time. "She is young, Scotty?"

"Old enough to—never mind. Twenty-four, twenty-five. She's a graduate student of mine, and if you say I had no business messing with one of my own students, why, I will have to agree."

"The point is not germane," Jenny said in her calm way. "She spoke to you? What did she ask? Money?"

"Marriage. A name for her child. My name." Pause. "Money is at the bottom of it."

"How do you know, Scotty?"

"Damn it——" He stopped there. Headlights had appeared with unbelievable suddenness. One moment there was only swirling fog, the next the lights were there. The lights drifted past; the car itself was invisible. Gray fog closed in again. "I don't know," Scott said. "I can only surmise."

"That she intended to become pregnant?"

"Yes."

"With all along the intention of blackmailing you into marriage?"

Scott hesitated. It was quite an indictment. "I think so, yes."

"You're an attractive man, Scotty. You must realize that. You are a successful man, a professor at one of the world's great universities. A glamorous man, an athlete. And your name is Stanfield. Isn't it possible that a student might fancy herself in love with you, might even be deeply in love with you? That she might become pregnant without intent? That she might then, and only then, see the strength of her position? Don't be paranoid, Scotty."

This goddam fog, he thought; and yet in a perverse way he was glad of it because it gave him a chance to use his skill and his knowledge in what amounted to a contest. Competition was always welcome. But there was another reason, too, and he was unaware that Jenny shared his feeling of relief in isolation. They could talk as to a stranger unseeing and unseen in the night. Much, much better that way. "Maybe," he said. "But what does that alter? The bitch——"

"Scotty." Jenny's voice had sharpened. "Aren't you angry merely because she had the effrontery to threaten you? You? The mouse challenging the king of beasts?"

"Is that how you see it?"

Again her fingers touched his arm. "You're an honest man. You've shown me that. How do you see it?"

How indeed? Deep in your court, friend, a perfect lob, just inside the baseline. Go back for it. "What difference?" He was merely squirming, scrambling, and he disliked himself for it. "Maybe," he said. And then, "Probably." He felt better. "What I don't see is how she got around to making legal motions. All she has is her salary as a teaching assistant, and what they pay them doesn't run to legal expenses." Was he actually trying to prove to himself that action had not been brought? Ridiculous.

"Some lawyer," Jenny said, "has taken the case on a contingency basis. The legal woods are full of lawyers who would jump at the chance to sue someone named Stanfield. Do you have a lawyer?"

"I have you."

"Scotty . . ." She stopped there, and was silent.

"George has legal eagles in batches," Scott said, "or

218

coveys, however they come. As far as that goes, he's a lawyer himself. He has always handled everything."

"I am beginning to find him quite a person," Jenny said. And then, quickly, "Not in a romantic way. I merely find him admirable, responsible. Will you go to him with this problem?"

"Hell, no." The anger rose again. "Run to big brother because some little chippy—?"

"Why not? It is a family problem, isn't it? That is how the girl's lawyer sees it, I'm sure."

They had reached the flat of the Valley now, and Scott had the odd feeling that they were underwater, driving along the bottom of a vast lake. Somewhere about here—there it was, the left turn; he negotiated it carefully, settled into position by the new white line. The sullen gray fog swirled around them. "Legal blackmail," he said. "We'll pay up to save the family name. Well, damn it, I don't care about the publicity."

"Maybe your brother does." Jenny's voice was patient, reasoning. "Maybe your father and mother do. Maybe Ellen does. You don't exist in a vacuum, Scotty." And then, with gentle insistence, she applied the clincher. "You are involved. You bedded the girl . . ."

"There is a word, straight out of *Moll Flanders*. I . . ." Squirming again, trying to counterattack; all at once he found the spectacle of himself contemptible. "You are right, counselor. Will you take the case?"

Jenny hesitated. "I don't think that would be wise, Scotty. If you don't want to use family counsel, then I will be happy to give you names . . ."

"I want you in my corner. You. Maybe that's unfair, asking the female I hope to marry to defend me in a suit brought by a girl I used to lay—but there it is."

There was a long silence. "Very well, Scotty," Jenny said at last. In the fog her voice was quiet, almost muffled. "I will represent you."

* * *

In Stanhope the fog lay thick, pierced only here and there by a street light or the colorful glow of a neon sign. Even in the center of town there was little traffic, and what cars were on the streets moved at a cautious pace, groping their way as in a blackout.

At the Stanfield Cannery on the east side the parking lot floodlights were scarcely visible, and the parked cars of the night shift were merely dull, dark shapes in the heavy murk. Within the cannery complex itself alley lights mounted above truck height did no more than mark boundaries—their glow did not reach the pavement. Overhead, invisible chimneys poured out smoke to compound the gloom. Odors of steam and heated metal blended with the fog into a kind of vaporized soup.

The man was alone and unseen and he moved quickly, surely, from the parking lot through a side gate, skirting the loading platform and the railroad siding, past the neat row of parked trucks and around the plant maintenance shed to the building that housed the boilers.

He carried a TWA flight bag, and he held it well out from his body as he opened the boiler room door, looked in, and then walked quickly through, closing the door behind him.

Inside it was hot, and the great gas flames that heated the boilers burned with a steady roar. There was light; naked hanging bulbs threw grotesque shadows against the boilers and the walls. The cement floor was stained, and in spots near the corners ancient slime had gathered.

The man set the flight bag down between the two largest boilers. Squatting, he unzipped the bag with care, held open the sides with one hand, with the other made a single thumb and forefinger adjustment to the mechanism inside. Then he pushed the bag into shadow beneath the boilers, hurried to the door, opened it, and stepped out into the fog.

Someone called, "Hey! You! What the hell are you doing?"

The man began to run, bent low, in the darkness and the fog almost invisible. He reached the fence, ran lightly along it to the side gate and through. In the parking lot he was quickly lost among the parked cars. All this time he was counting to himself: *one chimpanzee, two chimpanzee, three chimpanzee . . .*

He crossed the parking lot and reached the street

220

beyond, no longer running but still counting the seconds: *forty-two chimpanzee, forty-three chimpanzee, forty-four chimpan-zee. . . .*

First came the sudden burst of light hideously reflected in the fog. The sound of the explosion followed, like a door closing on a distant closet. At once the cannery whistle began to scream, and a siren burst into its banshee wail.

Unhurried now, the man crossed a weed-grown vacant lot, turned one corner, another, and crossed the street to a parked car. He got in, started the engine, and with dimmed lights drove off into the fog.

* * *

Ellen waited outside the great gates. Her hair and her face were damp from the fog, and from time to time she shivered faintly although it was not really that cold. When she saw headlights she started to move forward, and then, as the gates began to open, she stepped quickly, instinctively, back into the shelter of the far stone pillar. Scott's Mercedes rolled past. The gates closed.

What difference would it have made if Scott and that nice lady friend of his had seen her? She had no answer. What if it had been her father in the car? She could not answer that, either. There were times, she now understood, when you acted first and thought about reasoning later. As this evening leaving the study, following Paul, promising Paul. As now, prepared to fulfill that promise. I would not be afraid if the whole world saw me, she thought, but I'd rather not cause Daddy unnecessary hurt. If that was contradiction, she couldn't help it.

And here came another pair of headlights, the right ones this time; she heard the rattle of Paul's pickup, so different from the Mercedes' purr. She moved forward, had the door open, and was inside the cab almost before the truck had stopped. "Hey," Paul said, "hey."

She was crowded against him. "You're going to have to drive with one hand," she said, "because I want to be held." For protection? Comfort? She neither knew nor cared.

Paul was smiling in the darkness. "Why," he said, "I

221

guess that can be arranged." He put his arm around her and drew her close. It was going to be awkward shifting gears with his left hand, but he thought he could manage. Her hair was damp and fragrant against his chin. "Any place you want to go?"

"Yes." A small voice, muffled.

"Name it."

"Your place. I've never been there."

"It isn't much to see. It . . ." He stopped. "Look," he said. "What *is* this?"

Silence.

Paul shook his head in slow wonderment. Awkwardly he reached across the wheel with his left hand and put the truck in low gear. They drove slowly off into the fog. Ellen's face remained buried in his shoulder.

He was right—his place was not much to see. Living room, bedroom, tiny kitchen, bath, cheaply furnished in bargain store taste. "I like it," Ellen said.

"Then you've lost your marbles." Paul was smiling. "Beer? Or I think there's sherry." He made a sudden sharp gesture. "A lie. I know damn well there's sherry. I've had a bottle, unopened, for the better part of a year." Admission. "I hoped some day you'd come here."

"I'm here." Her smile was unsteady. "I don't want a drink. Not yet."

"Look," Paul said. "Ellie. Damn it."

She stood motionless. Her eyes, fixed on his, were somehow so open that he could see deep into her thoughts. She said nothing. The room seemed very still.

"What am I going to do with you?" Paul said. "A precocious chick, stubborn as a Stanfield . . ." He shook his head. "Baby," he said in a different, solemn tone, "baby. I'm trying to be sensible. For both of us. You're not helping. You're . . ."

"Stop trying," Ellen said. She drew a deep, unsteady breath. All her life, she thought, she would remember this moment. "I don't want to be sensible any more."

222

25

George sat again in Chief Walling's office. Howard Lang was there too. It was morning, bright and clear, the fog long since burned off. "For a wonder," Walling said, "nobody was hurt this time. The plant maintenance man saw the door to the boiler building open and somebody came out, but that was all he could see because the door closed again and in that fog . . ." Walling spread his hands.

George nodded shortly. He said nothing.

Walling said, "The maintenance man yelled and tried to run after whoever it was because nobody has any business in the boiler building, but he didn't have a chance to catch him. He was going back to see if everything was all right, when she blew. A few seconds earlier and he might have gone up with it."

Lang was attentive, George noticed, and so far silent. Paul Meyer had called him a slimy bastard; George had nothing yet on which to base judgment. The man did have an air of assurance, but that was all. George said, "It is established that it wasn't a boiler explosion?"

"Beyond doubt." This was Lang, quiet, positive. "There are a couple of army demolition experts poking around there now. They've found enough pieces to know that it was a bomb with a timing mechanism. Dynamite, probably, and there's plenty of that available."

Walling said, "There's also some pieces of material. We're having it looked at." He folded his hands on his desk. "Any ideas, Mr. Stanfield?"

George shook his head slowly. He looked at Lang.

"I've only been here a day," Lang said. "Maybe I have a few ideas, but no more than that." He sat quite still, making none of the small gestures most men make when they talk. "One thing I can say," he said. "These things are always for a purpose. It isn't just somebody playing games. And usually you don't have to look too far to see what that purpose is." Still no movement, no gesture, no change of expression. "You're having labor troubles, Mr. Stanfield?"

George began to see now what Paul Meyer had felt. The man was slick, smooth, maybe slimy wasn't the word, but bastard wasn't far off. "No labor troubles," George said.

Walling said, "Wait a minute, Mr. Stanfield. How about Lucero and his people, the *huelguistas*?"

"I repeat," George said, "no labor trouble. I haven't decided yet whether to deal with Lucero or not. Until I do we have nothing to argue about."

Lang said, "These things that have been happening could be attempts to make your decision for you."

The man's mind was made up, George thought. If he could hang the blame on Lucero, he would, and never mind if he stretched a few facts in the doing. "It could be," George said, "but if it is, they're going about it in precisely the wrong way. And I haven't found Lucero stupid."

Lang smiled easily. "You can't always tell about these people, Mr. Stanfield. They're hotheaded. They . . ."

"By *they*," George said, "you mean Mexican-Americans?"

Walling opened his mouth. He closed it again in silence. "That's what I mean," Lang said. "They're emotional.

They . . ." He stopped there. He watched George carefully and waited.

"You are treading pretty heavily," George said. "My mother's maiden name was Conchita Romero y Díaz. Call me half-chicano if you like, but don't try to tell me how *they* think. Lucero is not stupid. I won't try to answer for his people."

"Or for your son, Mr. Stanfield?" Walling said.

George merely looked at him.

"That hippie he's living with," Walling said, "says he was with her all night, night before last when the truck was burned. Maybe. Maybe not. I can't argue with her, yet. Last night . . ." He shrugged.

George said, "Have you asked about last night?"

"No."

"Maybe we'd better," Lang said.

George stood up. "I will." He nodded to both men and walked out.

Walling looked at Lang. Lang smiled. "You win some," he said, "and you lose some. It's the percentage that counts."

Walling looked at the ceiling for a little time in silence. Then, "Fellow I knew in the army," he said, "used to be a hunting guide in Alaska. You know those big brown bears they have there, go up to maybe 1,500 pounds? Well, he told me that you never, *never* shoot at one unless you're above him, never on level ground no matter what kind of gun you've got, because however much lead you put into him he'll get to you." He paused. "I figure going up against the Stanfields is just about the same. Before I choose one of them, him particularly, or the senator, I'm going to be damn sure I'm on high ground with lots of firepower. You better do the same."

Lang smiled again. "Oh, I will," he said. "I will. Where does this son of his live?"

* * *

For the second time George stood in the living room of Pete's house feeling very much like an outsider. He was glad to see that Pete had shaved off the beard and done something

225

about his mop of hair, but the long sideburns made their own declaration and nothing, really, was changed. "I'll bet," Pete said, "that I know why you're here. Did I blow up your cannery last night?"

Nothing showed in George's face. He stood tall and solid, immovable, studying the boy, seeing the weakness, the bravado, the facile charm, and the basic stubbornness more clearly than ever before.

Benjie watched both men in silence.

"What are you thinking?" Pete said. "All the clichés? All the questions? Where did we go wrong? Why am I like me, and not like you? That kind of thing?"

"More or less," George said.

"Well," Pete said, "I'll tell you why. It all boils down to four words: we never did communicate. We use the same words, but we don't talk the same language. I've heard you talk about loyalty." Pete shook his head. "To a friend? And what does it mean to you? Lewis Mattingly—it's in the newspapers. Friend of yours, but now he's finished, wiped out, and who did it. His good friend George Stanfield. With him for a friend, you don't need enemies."

Benjie said, "Pete."

George made a gentle movement with one hand to silence her. "Go on," he said to Pete.

"I could go on indefinitely," Pete said, "but what's the use? I'm talking about color to the blind. All you see is money, power. You've already got too much, but you want more. Why? So Julia can buy herself another prince to play with, or maybe a grand duke this time if there are any left? So you can add another line to your listing in *Who's Who*? What about the really important things? Like love? Like peace? Things that are relevant?" He shook his head. "You're on a bad trip, all of you. You've got to be shown, and talk won't do it."

There was a long silence. George said, "There is a man named Lang in town. From Sacramento. Paul Meyer can tell you about him. Maybe you'll listen to Paul. I will say only that *if* you had something to do with the dehydrator fire or the truck burning or last night's explosion at the cannery, any or all of them, then you'd better leave town, go as far away as you can, and stay there. If you need money, I'll give it to you."

Pause. "And if," George said, "by your criteria, offer of help from me is just one more proof of my moral bankruptcy, then I'm afraid there's nothing I can do to alter your opinion." Another pause. "'You know how to reach me." He nodded to Benjie. "I hope you don't get hurt, young lady. The bystander frequently does." He walked out and closed the door gently.

Benjie said, "He's trying to understand. That's more than most of them do."

Pete shook his head. He was disappointed at the mildness of his father's reaction. "He's just trying to keep the name out of the papers."

George walked out to his car. He started to get in and then saw the parked Plymouth with Lang beneath the wheel. He closed his car door and walked over. "I've already talked to him," George said.

Lang smiled and nodded. His self-assurance was infuriating.

"I've heard you described," George said, "as a slimy bastard. Would you care to comment?"

Lang's smile altered a trifle. "I have no quarrel with you. Yet."

George nodded. "Let me know when you do."

"I go where I'm sent, Mr. Stanfield. I do what I'm told. I'm usually successful. One way or another."

"This time," George said, "make sure it's a legitimate way." He turned and walked back to his car before the temptation to violence became too strong.

He drove away slowly, without conscious destination, merely impelled into motion by unfamiliar restiveness. He was aware that Scott had often compared him to a Clydesdale dray horse, large, powerful, docile in the extreme, and the concept had amused him. But did the Clydesdale sometimes shy inwardly like a frightened racehorse, want desperately to roll his eyes, lay back his ears, and kick down the sides of his stall, to rear and scream like a mad thing—and find himself trapped within his own large, calm image, unable to stoop to such foolishness?

"We never did communicate," Pete had said. "We use the same words, but we don't speak the same language."

227

Then there could be no understanding ever; it was the story of the Tower of Babel all over again.

Oh, you could discount what Pete said because of his youth and his obvious anger, but could you ignore it entirely? George thought not. He supposed that it was rare indeed, and perhaps not even healthy, when a child fulfilled exactly all of his parents' hopes and expectations, but what was it that caused a child to reject *all* parental values, to label an entire way of life totally false?

You could understand the duckling hatching in the clutch of hen eggs and, to the consternation of the hen, immediately heading for water. But the hen had not produced the duckling, and there was the difference. I sired Pete, George thought, just as I sired Ellen, but where is the kinship between us? He wondered if it would have made a difference if Ann had lived. Futile speculation for a usually pragmatic man.

The gay striped awning caught his eye, and he wondered if his subconscious had directed him here. And there was a parking space immediately in front of Clara's shop. He maneuvered the car into it, put a nickel in the parking meter, and walked into the shop.

Clara was with a customer. George sat down on a too-small chair and began to leaf through a copy of *House & Garden*. There were fine color photographs of houses and rooms and gardens. To George, all the rooms looked antiseptic and unlived-in, and he wondered if they would have a hospital corridor smell. The women and men pictured in the gardens showed not a single dirty fingernail or sweat stain. Presumably the flowers were planted, watered, mulched, fertilized, thinned, and eventually picked by some sort of remote control. He closed the magazine and tossed it on the table.

Clara said, "Not feeling *House & Garden* today, George?" The customer was gone. Clara smiled down at him. "Not quite your style," she said.

He stood up, smiling ruefully at the spectacle of himself in these surroundings. "I'm not quite sure any more what my style is," he said. "Can you close up, come drive with me?"

"Where, George?"

"Just around." And then, "No. That's wrong. I want to

228

see mountains. Isn't that where questions are traditionally asked, and answered?"

* * *

Lang looked at the girl who answered his knock. Hip-rider jeans, man's blue work shirt, big breasts, no bra, probably no underpants, maybe eighteen, but he doubted it—he filed the information away in his memory bank. "Stanfield?" he said.

Benjie stepped back and held the door open. Lang walked in smiling. He looked around the little room, at the man sitting in the chair.

"I'm Pete Stanfield," Pete said. He had a can of beer in his hand. "And you're a man named Lang from Sacramento?" He appeared totally at ease.

Lang nodded, still smiling.

"Sit down," Pete said. "Beer? No? What's on your mind?"

Lang sat down and settled himself in his neat way. "Things have been happening," he said. "I'm interested in finding out why." That brief scene outside with George Stanfield rankled. He had heard of the Stanfields, of course, and always in an abstract way he had resented them merely because they *were;* now it was a personal sort of rancor. His smile seemed friendly. "That explosion last night, for example," he said.

"At the cannery," Pete said. "I heard about it. A bomb?"

Benjie had retreated to the sink as to sanctuary. She stood there now, watching quietly, feeling a deep unease.

Lang nodded. "A bomb."

"One of the wonders of our civilization," Pete said. "Anybody can find out how to make a bomb. They put out pamphlets. Did you know that? It's a how-to culture we have. All you have to do is read the right instruction booklet. We get more and more gadgets, and less and less of the things that really matter." He paused and drank thoughtfully. Then, wiping his lips, "Civilization not only carries the seeds of its own destruction, it provides the means as well. How neat a package can you make?"

229

Lang's smile was appreciative, without amusement. "Food for thought." He paused. "You wouldn't have any idea who might have done it? No? Foolish question, really."

Pete studied the top of his beer can. He looked up at last. "You've talked to Paul Meyer?" He watched Lang's nod. "And Ruben Lucero who-walks-on-water?"

"I've seen them both."

Oh, no! Benjie thought. And then, why, Pete? Why are you pointing at them, whoever Ruben Lucero is? Paul is the one who got you out of jail. He. . . .

"They're out to give the parent a bad time," Pete said. "You know?"

Lang said slowly, carefully, "He says no."

Pete smiled. He drank deep, wiped his lips with his bent forefinger. At the sink Benjie watched and waited in near-horror. First Paul and a man named Lucero, now his father. Pete said, "What would you say if you were in the parent's shoes, maybe almost ready to lower the boom on Lucero and company. Would you say they were annoying bastards, or would you say they were nice fellows and you can't imagine how or why when the roof falls in on them?"

Benjie said, almost breathing the words, "Pete! Don't, please! That isn't true what you're saying!"

"Purely hypothetical," Pete said. He smiled easily, still watching Lang.

Lang stood up. "More food for thought," he said. He stood for a few silent moments looking down at Pete. "Thank you for your time," he said at last. "I expect I'll be seeing you again."

"I'm counting on it," Pete said.

Benjie waited until the door was closed. Then she walked slowly to the window and watched Lang get into his car and drive away. She turned to look at Pete. "Why?" she said. "You deliberately sent him after Paul. Your cousin. Your friend."

Pete stood up. The beer can was empty. He tossed it into the trash. He turned slowly. "I don't have any friends." Shared loneliness—the phrase echoed in his mind. "Neither do you," he said.

Benjie closed her eyes.

"There's only me," Pete said, "just as there's only you.

230

It's something you have to learn. You won't find it in books."

Benjie's eyes were open again. "I never knew that," she said, and turned quickly away, walked to the bathroom, closed the door. There was the sound of running water.

Pete took another beer from the refrigerator, opened it carefully, and drank deep. He had resented his father's visit, but maybe it had been for the best because it had laid the groundwork for this little talk with Lang. He had a sense of luck running with him.

The bathroom door opened, and Benjie asked a question. Pete turned and looked at her blankly. "All I said," Benjie said, "was that I can't find that flight bag. You know, the TWA one?"

Pete said, "Going somewhere?"

Benjie shook her head. Her eyes were red, but her voice was firm enough, if puzzled. "I took it to market yesterday, you know? And when I got back the door was open." She shrugged. "You were here, and you opened the door?"

"I remember," Pete said. "So?"

"It isn't anything to get uptight about," Benjie said. "It's just that I can't find the bag, and I think the door key you gave me may be in it, that's all."

26

Ellen came out of the shower, dried herself, and carefully studied her reflection in the mirror. No change that she could see, which was hardly possible. She was simply not the same person she had been; how could she be? Yesterday I was a virgin, she thought, today I am a . . . She didn't know any word for a nonvirgin; maybe there wasn't one, and that was strange too.

She went into her dressing room. Bikini briefs, bra, cut-off jeans, short-sleeved blouse. Familiarity. Not only was *she* unchanged, *nothing* was changed. Incredible. Nor had the experience itself been what she had expected. Not really.

She had expected it to hurt; that was what happened the first time in books she had read. It hadn't hurt at all. But neither had it driven her wild with pleasure, the other extreme that was supposed to happen.

Oh, all that preceded it, the kisses and the fondling and the feeling of naked intimacy, these had aroused her as she had never been aroused before. But the actual act was something of an anticlimax after all she had read and heard and thought, and she would have given a great deal to be able to talk frankly and explicitly with someone with more experience, to find out if she was unusual. Her great-aunt Julia came to mind, and that made her giggle. She could just see herself exchanging intimate chatter with Julia.

She skipped down the stairs and out to the kichen to discuss menus with María. On the way it occurred to her that one thing had happened as it was supposed to—she felt a sense of happiness that was almost too much to contain. She wondered if anyone would notice.

María did, and gave no sign. Consuelo did, and smiled gently. Julia, home after another refreshing bout with Cleary Ward, looked at Ellen's happy face and recognized the symptoms immediately. "It might be well," she said, "if you didn't glow quite so obviously, dear. Your father might wonder what you've been up to." She paused, smiling. "Or down to."

Ellen blushed. She could feel it.

Julia patted her arm gently. "How lovely to be young," she said. "Don't let it slip away from you too soon."

* * *

George and Clara were into the mountains now, the heat and the dust of the Valley behind them. The air, perceptibly cooler, was scented with evergreens—red fir and sugar pine. By a tumbling stream they saw the dark blue spikes of monkshood, at the side of the road magenta fireweed, in an occasional open meadow, orchid-to-red patches of shooting stars and the vivid blue of wild iris.

They came at last to the stand of big trees, and George stopped the car. They got out and walked slowly into the almost cathedral hush of the giant Sequoias to look up through the lofty, lacy branches to the clear blue of the sky. "Technically," George said, "these aren't redwoods. Sequoia is the generic term: these are big trees, and the others that grow over near the coast are the redwoods. Only these two species left." He was smiling. "It makes you think—that something as big as this . . ." He pointed to the nearest tree, twenty-five feet in diameter, rising over 200 feet, ". . . can die out, become extinct. Makes me, anyway, feel pretty insignificant."

It was a side of him Clara had never seen before. "You come here often," she said with sudden certainty.

"Here or over in Muir Woods, the redwoods near the city." George smiled suddenly. "Or, for that matter, just out to the coast, Seal Rocks, to watch the swells march in after traveling—how far?—five thousand miles and more, to break on that particular spot. . . ."

"I didn't know you were a religious man, George."

"I'm not, certainly not in any kind of formal sense. Mike and Conchita go to church. It's good politics. Nobody else in the family does. I guess we never saw any reason for it." He looked down at her. "Does that bother you?"

Clara shook her head, smiling. "I went to Sunday school when I was a little girl. I learned to make paste. I ate it. That's as far as religion went with me."

"Peter Juan and I," George said, "packed in from a place called Rock Creek on the other side of the Sierra, over Mono Pass at about 9,000 feet into the Fourth Recess. We camped there for almost a week, fishing. There are twelve- and thirteen-thousand-foot mountains all around you. A trickle of water drops down a thousand-foot sheer cliff into the lake that feeds a stream running through the meadow. At night the only sounds are that trickle of water and occasional small pieces of rock breaking off the cliff and falling into the lake. At that altitude, seven, eight thousand feet, and with no city lights to blind you, the stars look close enough to touch, and you look at the Milky Way and think of a hundred billion stars in it, and our sun only a medium-sized star among them, and you think that all that is just one galaxy out of billions of galaxies in the universe, and you find it hard to believe that we, mankind, sitting on this little planet have all the answers, or even some of them." He smiled suddenly. "Peter Juan was eighteen, I was nineteen. In that week we saw only one person, a sheepherder with his flock. He went off and we never saw him or the sheep again. The next year Peter Juan went off to war. I stayed home. He didn't come back. My Pete is

234

named for him. I used to think they were pretty much alike. Now I don't know. No point to all this. No pattern."

"I think," Clara said, "that there is a great deal of point. You're troubled, George. About what?"

George spread his hands, let them fall. "Ann and I," he said, "spent six weeks one winter skiing in Austria up above Innsbruck in a little village called Igls. There is a wind called the Föhn that occasionally blows over the mountains from Bavaria. There's a barometric change that comes with the Föhn, and it affects almost everybody, some, of course, more than others. In Innsbruck they set up Föhn clinics, dispensing tranquilizers, I suppose. They postpone all surgical operations except emergencies until the wind stops. While the wind is blowing everybody to some extent is uptight. You have the feeling that you don't know what's going to happen next, but it is going to be bad. You want to look in all directions at once as if, say, you were suddenly caught on foot in the traffic at the Place de la Concorde at rush hour. You begin to comprehend paranoia, the feeling that the world is coming at you from all sides." He shook his head.

Clara said, "Is that how it is now?"

"That's how it is," George said. "I'm not usually a nervous man, but there's a kind of Föhn blowing and driving some people into madness, and the hell of it is that they don't see that it is madness."

"Pete?"

"Among others," George said. He hesitated. "I was up early this morning. Five o'clock. Work to do, reports to read. I was just going into my study when Ellen came into the house. She had apparently been out all night. She didn't see me. She wasn't seeing much of anything. There were stars in her eyes." He looked at Clara. "What would you think?"

Clara said slowly, "Probably the same thing you do." She paused. "But I don't happen to think that the world is going to hell, George, or that the young people, like lemmings, are trying to exterminate themselves. Maybe some are, but not Ellen. If she spent last night in somebody's bed, it wasn't just for a cheap thrill, because she doesn't hold herself cheap. She is a great deal like Ann, George, and from somebody, proba-

235

bly that dear old lady she calls Marquesa, she has gotten a set of values that are every bit as sound as Ann's were. And from you, yes, you, even if you have neglected her disgracefully, she has learned what the word responsibility means."

George watched her in silence. Much woman, he was thinking, very much woman, perceptive and understanding beyond expectation, compassionate.

"Personally," Clara said, "unless she gets pregnant, and I think she's too sensible for that, I don't see that sex is going to do her any harm. Physically, she's a grown woman, George, and that means that she has appetites as well as values, and she'll balance the two out for herself." She smiled suddenly, brilliantly. "And she is you, Stanfield, with all the stubbornness, yes, and the arrogance, that goes with it. She will do her own thing regardless, but I don't think you have to worry that it will be a bad thing."

George smiled faintly. He breathed deep of the cool, forest-scented air, and looked with approval at the woman facing him. "You give me hope," he said. "Thank you, Clara."

* * *

The lab man sat impatiently in Chief Walling's office while Walling read the typed reports. Walling set them down at last. "Those are the facts," he said. "Now for the guesswork. You've identified the pieces of material as one of the synthetics. What's it used for?"

It was this kind of questioning, the lab man thought, that made him wish he had never gone in for police work. The cops themselves were always ready to guess at things, and he was not; he wanted demonstrable evidence before he ventured any opinion. He evaded as best he could. "It has many applications. It is one of the more versatile synthetics, you see, and . . ."

"Henry," the chief said, "I don't want a lecture. I want an intelligent guess about what use this synthetic could have been put to that would somehow logically bring it into that boiler building to be blown up." Walling smiled. "I'll take a wild guess myself. Was the bomb carried in this synthetic material? Wrapped in it, say?"

Henry thought about it. He shook his head. "I don't see

236

why. If you're going to carry the bomb in something, why not a suitcase, or something like that?" Damn it, despite himself he was guessing after all. It was a way Walling had of conning you. . . .

"I asked a question, Henry," Walling said. "Is this synthetic ever used for luggage?"

Henry thought about that. As a matter of fact, it was. He said so. "It's what they make most of those flight bags out of," he said. "You know, the ones with the airline's name on the side that they give away to passengers?"

Walling did know. "Would one of those bags be large enough?"

The worst of it was that there was a kind of excitement that was generated once you started guessing, and it was hard to maintain a technician's proper detachment. "The army fellows said it could be about so big," Henry said. He measured with his hands. "A flight bag would be big enough for that." He paused. "And the way that material was scattered all around the place, that's just how it could have been, too. Maybe he just left the bomb inside the bag."

Walling thought about it. It sounded possible. It sounded interesting, too, because would any of Ruben Lucero's people be likely to have a flight bag in the first place? It would bear looking into. "Now," Walling said, "you said you had something else?"

Henry took out an envelope, opened it and shook a blackened piece of flat metal on the desk. "The army fellows found this over in a corner. It had to be pretty close to the center of the blast, they figure, because of what the heat did to it."

Walling looked at the piece of metal and shook his head. "What is it? What makes it important?"

Henry was on safe ground here—no guesswork required. "It is, it was a key, a door key to a Yale lock." He paused. "The only lock anywhere around that boiler house is a padlock, nothing to do with this."

Walling poked at the tortured metal with his forefinger. It was something out of place, and anything out of place could be of interest. "Could somebody identify it? A locksmith? Make one, say, that would fit the lock this one used to fit?"

Henry thought it possible.

"Then let's get it done. Maybe we'll find the right door. I know a couple I can try for a start."

When Henry had gone back to his lab Walling pulled out his lower desk drawer and, leaning back, stretched his legs out on it. He stared at the far wall; it was as if, relaxing, he could project his thoughts against that wall as a ball is bounced against a backboard, and have them come back to him sometimes strengthened, sometimes altered.

Lang. Walling disliked the man and all that he had heard about him. He was a hunter of other men, and while at times that kind of activity was necessary, and Walling himself would join the chase if he had to, some of his sympathy always remained with the fugitive and, unlike Lang, he took no pleasure in the hunt.

Lang would dearly love to nail Ruben Lucero's hide to the barn wall. That had been evident from the start, and the reason was not hard to find. Walling did not pretend much knowledge of politics or politicians, and he supposed that the governor in Sacramento, with all the problems of this busting-at-the-seams state of California on his hands, was no worse and possibly no better than those who had gone before him.

But the governor in his speeches and interviews did seem to give the impression that *he* knew best, and that if things were going to change at all they were going to change *his* way, and so a relative upstart like Ruben Lucero, rocking the boat and causing unhappiness for important people, needed to be shown the light. Enter Lang.

But after that scene with George Stanfield this morning, Walling thought, Lang had unquestionably added Pete Stanfield to his list, and while Walling had to admit that he wouldn't object to seeing a Stanfield nose rubbed in the dirt, he was going to be damn good and sure that it was done legitimately or not at all. He would keep a sharp eye on Lang. And Pete Stanfield. And hope for the best. Amen.

* * *

Julia drove herself into town in one of the ranch automobiles wearing a crisp turquoise linen dress and matching sandals, the cost of which by government standards would have supported a family of four in relative comfort for a month.

238

She parked in the bank parking lot, shook hands and stood chatting for a few moments with Juan Potrero, then went inside to see Karl Meyer.

They were almost of an age, third cousins, each from his own way of life looking at the other with friendly, amused contempt. They sat in Karl's inner office. "You are looking your usual lovely self, Julia," Karl said. "Unchanged from the photographs of your last marriage—or was it the one before?" Irony in Karl seemed as out of place as belligerence in a jackrabbit.

Julia smiled easily. "Age has improved you too, Karl. You have mellowed like fine old vinegar." The smile spread to its full brilliance. "And now that we have the compliments out of the way, I want to talk business. Not," she added, "that I know anything about business or can even understand it."

Karl folded his hands and waited. Julia's helplessness was one of the family's more lovable myths.

"How much autonomy does Cleary Ward have?" Julia said.

Karl considered the question and its implications. "Have you spoken to George about this?"

"I'm speaking to you."

"Julia. You should know that I cannot discuss——"

"*Merde!*" Pause. "For your information, that is a French word. . . ."

"I know what it means." Karl looked faintly shocked. There was, there always had been, in Julia this ability to descend into coarseness without turning a single immaculate hair.

"Can Cleary, for example," Julia said, "sign checks on his own against the Stanfield Cattle Company, the Stanfield Land Company, the Valley Oil Company? Does he collect and handle the rent for office space in the Meyer-Stanfield building? Does he handle the accounts and the payroll for the ranch? How much freedom does he have?"

Karl took off his glasses, looked at them, put them back on again. "Cleary Ward," he said, "is a fine young man, Julia. He is a Stanford Business School graduate with a degree also from the University of California, Davis campus. . . ." He stopped there. "Have I said something amusing?"

239

"Perhaps I know Cleary a little better than you do, Karl."

"How can you? I've known him all his life while you have been gallivanting around Europe and other places."

"There is a kind of circuit-rider righteousness to you," Julia said. "You'd have made a good Bible banger. Did you know Cleary's mother?"

"I did. Her name was Helen Wilder before she married Joe Ward. Joe Ward had great energy and poor judgment. A losing combination. His schemes always failed. The Wilders . . ."

"Are a family with a long memory," Julia said. She explained. "Cleary has been carefully conditioned. You may believe that. I know Cleary far better than you ever could." She paused, smiling now in genuine amusement. "Karl, you're blushing!"

Karl shook his head. He drew a deep breath and let it out in a sigh. "You are unbelievable." He was silent for a few moments. "What, specifically, do you suspect Cleary of doing?"

"That's simple. Dipping into the till, getting back some of what he considers his own."

"I can't believe it."

"And," Julia said, "my guess is that you're going to find it a hard trail to follow. He didn't go to business school for nothing." She stood up. Karl rose automatically. "I'll leave you with it," Julia said. "I don't think George even needs to know until you turn up solid evidence."

"You are very sure of yourself, Julia. But then, you have always been." Karl sighed. "I will have it looked into."

"By someone who knows what he's doing."

Karl smiled wearily, and nodded. "By Howard," he said. He shook his head once more, in sadness this time. "One more distressing thing in a distressful world," he said.

"That," Julia said, "is how the cookie sometimes bounces."

She waved to young Howard on her way out, paused in the lobby to put on her dark glasses, and walked unhurried into the sunlight. To Juan Potrero she said, "It will be all right if I leave the car here for a few minutes?"

240

Juan's smile and nod said that forever would be dandy, and he himself would guard the car with his life.

"You're sweet," Julia said, and walked on.

She enjoyed walking in Stanhope. The heat did not bother her, and she found the town itself interesting. Too many Europeans and even some visitors from the eastern seaboard saw in these California towns only the obvious, the Karen's Kandy Kitchens, the Big Boy Hamburger stands, the enormous used car lots where Honest John and Crazy Pete tried to give cars away but their wives wouldn't let them, the monster discount houses featuring TV sets and gaudy furniture. They saw row upon row of identical development houses cheek-by-jowl, all with picture windows facing other picture windows, each displaying a large table lamp with the shade still wrapped in cellophane. They saw traffic jams and dust and smog, and more freeways under construction to carry more cars into bigger and better chain collisions. They saw the lurid paperback displays in drugstore windows, the skin flick movie houses and the bowling alleys complete with bars and nurseries. They saw automobiles, automobiles, automobiles.

Oh, these things were all part of the scene—Julia would have been the last to deny it. Nor would she even have tried to defend the garish, the impermanent, the childish, the simply stupid: the land laid waste by uncontrolled placer mining, the lovely beaches ruined by sewage or by oil, houses built in canyons where brush fires were inevitable, or on fill dumped without consideration into dry washes, natural courses for cloudburst run-off. You could not condone the horrendous tangle of freeways in Los Angeles, or the smog that sometimes filled the basin from Santa Monica to the Cajon Pass and spread south to Long Beach and San Pedro. It was a mess, and there were those who for years had been saying that the whole Sodom-Gomorrah complex would slide into the sea one fine day when the San Andreas fault really stirred itself—and good riddance.

But for Julia, walking unhurried on the streets of Stanhope, a sense of the land was in her being, and the vitality that in a hundred and twenty years had done horrible and some-

241

times marvelous things was all around her. Behind the gim-
crackery and the ballyhoo the vitality remained, as deep and
as limitless as the ocean that rolled halfway around the world
to fling its breakers on the thousand-mile California shore.
This was the part that could not be explained. This was what
her European or eastern friends could never comprehend.
This was home.

She reached the plaza, smiled in approval at the World
War I memorial column to the men of Stanhope who had
fallen in France, her uncle Henry among them, and crossed
the street to the original Stanfield Building. Upstairs in the
cool, high-ceilinged office she gave her name to the recep-
tionist, and immediately Kaye Starling came out to lead her
into his private office.

"Prettier than ever, Julia. I don't know how you do it."
They sat in facing leather chairs. "Once . . ." Kaye shook his
head, smiling.

"Once," Julia said, "I thought you were going to ask me
to marry you. I waited, but you didn't."

"How could I have? You were Julia Stanfield. I was a
young country bumpkin lawyer." His smile was rueful. "I
didn't relish being laughed at."

"The hilarious thing is," Julia said, "that I wouldn't have
laughed." Her smile appeared, brilliant, untinged with regret.
"On the other hand, I would have made you a wretched wife."
She dismissed the past with a finger flick. "I want a favor Kaye.
I want to know if George has given Cleary Ward a power of
attorney, and don't, please, tell me to ask George. I have
warned him about Cleary, but he doesn't take me seriously."

"Will you tell me why, Julia?"

She told him the tale. "It came out quite by accident that
Cleary was a Wilder, and Scott knew the story."

"And you take it seriously?"

"I don't want to shock you, Kaye, but let's say that my
knowledge of Cleary Ward is—substantial, and yes, I take it
very seriously." She paused. "I have already asked Karl Meyer
to have Cleary's financial dealings looked into. He has
agreed."

Kaye thought about it. Slowly he nodded. "Cleary has a

242

limited power of attorney. He is free to dispose of certain properties as he sees fit."

"And who can rescind that power of attorney?"

"George."

Julia sighed. "I was afraid of that. George is a lamb." She smiled. "But he is stubborn." The smile spread. "As we all are, aren't we, Kaye?" She glanced at her watch, and looked up smiling still. "You may take me to lunch, unless you already have an engagement."

Kaye got to his feet. "If I had, I would gladly break it, Julia."

27

It was nothing, the senator told Conchita, a simple case of sniffles which two aspirin tablets, his evening quota of cocktails and a good night's sleep would attend to. And tomorrow he was going to Sacramento, a few things to attend to, and in the afternoon he was flying south to San Pedro to find out firsthand about Ecuador's heckling of the tuna boats fishing in the Humboldt current well out beyond the twelve-mile territorial limit the U.S. recognized as sovereign Ecuadorian territory.

"In the inelegant vernacular," the senator said, "I have been sitting on my duff here at the ranch too long." He sneezed. "A devoted servant of the people, he," he said.

"I will miss you," Conchita said.

The senator looked at her sharply.

"I always do, Mike." She was smiling. "When the time comes, I hope I go first."

"Nonsense."

"I mean it. If you are left alone, you'll find a hundred things to interest you, even in what you will call retirement.

I can see you, writing letters, making telephone calls, summoning people and telling them what ought to be done, righting wrongs, quite possibly writing your memoirs . . ."

"Woman," the senator said, "stop talking poppycock."

"But if I am the one who is left," Conchita said, as if he had not spoken, "what then? Can you see me interfering in George's or Scott's affairs? Ellen's? Flitting here and there like Julia?" She shook her head. "You are my life, Mike. For almost fifty years, you have been. I can't even think of life without you."

The senator sneezed again. "I'll take those aspirin now," he said, "if it will get you off this gloom kick."

* * *

Benjie had seen weirdos before, lots of them, but these were something else. They were all Spanish-American, for one thing, and while she had carefully schooled herself away from Wasp prejudice or sense of superiority, she was not really comfortable with chicano types, especially when they were speaking Spanish, which she did not understand. Pete, of course, chattered away without effort.

They all had long black hair and sideburns and wispy beards, except one. And all except one wore black berets and dark, dark glasses. When they looked at her the glasses gleamed and the faces showed no expression. So many Che Guevaras. All but one.

He was older, maybe in his forties, a big solid man with heavy shoulders and abnormally long arms. He carried a softball bat in one hand when he came in, and he stood it carefully against the wall by the door, handy, before he even looked around. And the first thing he looked at was Benjie.

She had been looked at before, many times. From the time her body began to change from the straight lines of childhood she had known what it was to be studied by boys and men. And sometimes, as now, she could read as plainly as if it had been written on their foreheads what some boys or men were thinking. Sometimes that kind of look was pleasurable, flattering. But not this time. This time that kind of look made her stomach writhe as if she had cramps, and she wanted to fold her arms over her breasts in protection, wish-

245

ing for almost the first time since she had left home that she were wearing a bra, one of those real heavy ones that just made you look lumpy.

The man, Pete called him Julio, did not speak, and that somehow made it worse. He listened to the Spanish chatter and seemed to understand, while from time to time he turned his head to look at Benjie, a direct stare that stripped her bare and left her cringing inside and trying hard not to show it. Once, while his eyes drifted over her body, his tongue came out and moved ceaselessly sideways, back and forth, moistening his smiling lips, and his thoughts punished her brutally. She would have left the room, but there was no place to go except into the bathroom, and that she could not bring herself to do. She remained, and endured.

Finally they left, Julio last. Softball bat in one big hand, he paused in the doorway for an ultimate naked appraisal. Then, smiling, he made an animal noise deep in his throat and waved the bat to Pete in a gesture of farewell.

"*Hasta luego,* Julio," Pete said, and closed the door. He looked at Benjie. "He thinks you're out of sight."

"God!" Benjie said. She closed her eyes, opened them again. "He undressed me . . ."

"I didn't know you minded that." Pete was smiling.

"It depends who's doing it." She was silent for a moment, shaking off the memory. Then, "What were you talking about, Pete?"

"Things."

She watched him quietly.

"Name," Pete said, "rank and serial number, remember? All other information is classified." He paused. "Believe me," he said, "it's better that way. Okay?"

"Okay," Benjie said. "I guess." She shook her head slowly. "I'm uptight, Pete. I'm confused."

"Aren't we all?" Pete was smiling again.

"I used to think," Benjie said, "I knew exactly what I wanted. Now I don't know. I'm walking around in little circles in my mind, you know? When I first left home, I wanted to try everything, pot, acid, booze, sex with guys, with other girls, it was all a groove, experience, and that was what it was all about, wasn't it? Now I don't know what I want. I just know

246

some things I don't want." And then, with no change of tone, "There's ham and some of that cheese. Is a sandwich okay for lunch?" She watched him nod silently. "I'll fix it," Benjie said, and turned away.

Pete said, "Hey," and waited until she had turned slowly back to face him. "Uptight," he said. "Confused. Work that over for me."

Benjie raised her hands slowly and let them fall. "You're doing something," she said. "I hope it isn't what I think it is, but it's something. It makes you alive. Sometimes it gets you way up—I can see that and feel it. Sometimes it gets you uptight. I can feel that too. But it's something you think is worth doing, or you wouldn't be doing it, and that's what makes the difference." She paused. "And I don't even—relate to it. I'm outside." Another pause. "I've never felt like this before, you know, useless."

"You aren't useless." His voice was almost harsh.

"I know," Benjie said. "I'm a good lay." She shook her head. "But that isn't enough. I'll fix those sandwiches."

She was at the sink spreading mustard on bread when Pete came up behind her. He put his arms around her, his hands on her breasts, and held her with gentle pressure while he kissed the back of her neck. "How would you like to leave here? With me?"

Her hands stopped their motions. She stood quiet, almost tense. "Where, Pete?"

"You name it."

Benjie waggled her head in negation. "If you mean it," she said, "make it real. Please."

"You know New Mexico? Santa Fe?"

Benjie closed her eyes. "Tell me about it."

"Seven thousand feet high," Pete said. "Twelve-thousand-foot mountains right behind it. The clearest air you'll find. Oh, it's cold in winter, and in summer the sun is hot, but not like here. The sun goes down and it's cool at night. Adobe houses. They look funny at first. Miles of open land, nothing but piñon and juniper and jackrabbits. Fenced land now, most of it, but there's some still left."

"Groovy," Benjie said. Her eyes were still closed. "But are there, you know, jobs?"

"We can cut it. They need guys who are bilingual in a lot of spots. Spanish is one thing we got as kids that was relevant." He paused. "No big deal, no riches, no apartment like on Nob Hill, no Mercedes, just a pickup, used at that."

Benjie moved her head in protest. "Do you think it matters to me?" Her gesture took in the entire room. "No more than this. A fire in winter to keep us warm. Some food. You know. What else?"

Pete was smiling. "A pioneer-type woman."

"Sometimes I wish I had been." Benjie looked down at his hands holding her. "I'm strong, Pete. I could do whatever had to be done. Then maybe I could feel—meaningful." She turned to face him. Her eyes were solemn but filled with hope, the eyes of a child on Christmas morning. "You mean it, Pete? You're not just kidding?"

Pete smiled. "Cross my heart and hope to die. On my honor as a waiting-list Brownie. For real. One more week and we cut out."

Benjie took her time because to question seemed churlish, but inevitably the words had to be spoken. "Why wait, Pete? Why not now, tonight? By bus as far as the money you tried to give me will take us, then start hitching?"

"A week," Pete said. "Maybe a couple of days less, but not now." He smiled again. "And don't ask me why. Okay?"

Benjie closed her eyes and swallowed with effort. She opened her eyes again. Slowly she nodded. "Okay," she said.

California isn't a State of the Union;
it's a state of mind.

ANON.

28

Nurse Walters opened the door to Ellen's knock. She hesitated and then stepped back and held the door wide. The dressing down this minx had given her two days ago still rankled, and she had told herself that she was going to have more words with the child if only to restore her own sense of importance; but she knew now, and the knowledge was painful, that she was afraid to go up against this young, clear-eyed, fearless brat who had minced no words in making her point.

"You are expected to take care of Mrs. Stanfield," Ellen had said, and raised her hand in a sharp gesture. "I am speaking. You listen." She did not even raise her voice. "There will be no more tales of violence told to her. Is that understood?"

And Nurse Walters, furious, had said, "I know my job, young lady. I will carry it out as I see fit."

"You are wrong," Ellen said quite calmly and with complete assurance. "As long as you are in this house you will behave as I expect you to behave. Make up your mind right here and now." She pointed to the wall phone. "Shall I call the doctor and tell him we wish another nurse?" She was not

249

a seventeen-year-old girl speaking to an older woman. She was mistress of this considerable ménage, laying down the rules for the hired help. "Well?"

There remained a spark of defiance. It flared briefly. "You wouldn't dare," Nurse Walters said.

Ellen looked at her steadily. "Try me," she said, and that was all.

Now, in the open doorway, "I will sit with her for a while," Ellen said. Nurse Walters hesitated, nodded, and stalked out into the hall. The door closed quietly.

Ellen walked to the bed. There was movement. "Are you awake, Marquesa?"

One hand moved and the great diamond flashed. "I have been hoping you would come, child. But you are busy. I know. The house does not run itself."

Ellen bent to kiss the dry cheek and then drew a chair up to the bedside. "I'm in love, Marquesa," she said. She was smiling happily, probably foolishly, she thought, and could not have cared less. "Oh, I've known it for a long time, forever, but not like this."

"Paul?"

"Of course. There's never been anyone else."

"I am happy for you, child."

"Daddy thinks I'm too young to know what I want. What do you think, Marquesa?" And then, in case the old lady's memory was for the moment unsure, "I'm seventeen."

Marquesa smiled fondly. "A lovely age. Too young? You are the only one who can know that, child. When I was fifteen, I thought I was in love. Maybe I was."

"With great-grandfather Ezra?"

The old lady smiled again. "With his uncle. Frank. Amos's youngest brother. He was twenty years older than I was. Thirty-five. He was in charge of the lumbering operations up north, in Humboldt County." The smile spread again in memory. "He was tall and strong and his face was always tanned, and he seemed to bring the strength of the redwoods themselves with him whenever he came down to Stanhope."

Ellen thought of Paul. "Was he in love with you, Marquesa? Did you—talk about it?"

"Once." Again the smile. "I wanted him to take me back

to Eureka." She paused. "Oh, dear, what a family tempest that would have caused."

"What happened, Marquesa?"

The old lady hesitated. There was no smile now. "It was a very long time ago, child."

* * *

Humboldt, 1895

Frank Stanfield went alone, north to San Francisco by train and then aboard a Stanfield lumber steam schooner out through the Golden Gate and north again around Cape Mendocino. The climax of the journey was the ferocious crossing of the Humboldt Bar where, once the ship was committed, there was no turning back. They came at last, recurrent miracle, safe into Humboldt Bay itself.

The firm ground of the town of Eureka rocked gently beneath Frank's feet, and his thoughts were still going in several directions at once as he carried his own bag, stretching his legs toward the Stanfield Lumber Company offices. The Carson mansion on the hill dominated the scene. Frank smiled at it. Maybe one day he would build one like it—for his bride.

He was a big, solid, brown-haired man; at thirty-five, there was a touch of gray at his temples. That little vixen, Ellen Meyer, first cousin once removed, fifteen years old and behaving as if she were thirty, had teased him about that gray the last time he had seen her. "Now let me see." She had put her square young chin in both hands and stared. "Does it make you look distinguished, or merely old?"

"Snippet, you ought to be spanked."

"Why," Ellen said, "I wouldn't mind, if you would do it."

"You're shameless."

"Why do you have to go back to Eureka, Frank?"

"Because there are things to be attended to. Things you wouldn't understand." Pause. A boyish smile set crookedly in

251

his tanned face. "Or maybe you would, at that. You're a precocious little beast."

Ellen sat up straight and stuck out her tongue. "Beast yourself." She was silent for a few moments while her hands idly pleated her skirt. She said at last, "Take me with you, Frank." She raised her hand to stop comment. "I mean it. I'm not a child any longer."

His one big hand covered both of hers. "Yes, you are. You're a sweet child, but you're still a child."

"Do you know how old Juliet was? She and Romeo?"

He was smiling gently. "This isn't Italy, and it isn't a play. Can you think of the uproar if you and I skipped off together?"

"I wouldn't care. Would you?"

Frank said slowly, "It might almost be worth it. Almost."

"Lots of girls are married at fifteen. Well, some anyway." Pause. "I know, there's almost always a reason. They have to be married. All right, suppose we had to be?"

"Precociouser and precociouser. Do you know what you're suggesting?"

"That you make me pregnant. Then they couldn't say no. Does that shock you? Why should it? It happens all the time, doesn't it?"

"But people don't talk about it."

"We aren't people, Frank. You're you, and I'm—me, and why should it make a difference whether I'm fifteen or twenty-five? Would you take me with you then?"

His hands squeezed hers. His smile was gentle. "You wouldn't have to ask me, snippet. I'd be on my knees asking you."

"Well, then."

He shook his head and smiled. "I'll miss you, snippet."

Resentment disappeared like smoke. "Will you, Frank? Because I'll miss you. Here." She had read of such things. Her hands untying her blue hair ribbon were not quite steady. She held it out with sudden shyness. "Will you take it?"

He took it. "And treasure it," he said. He bent then and kissed her quickly. He did not look back as he walked away, tall, broad, solid, confident.

In San Francisco, Ellen's ribbon tucked away in an inside

pocket, Frank saw his father in the Montgomery Street office. Ezra was sixty-eight, tall, straight, decisive. They sat in leather chairs. Sounds of horse-drawn traffic reached them from the street below.

"You may have some trouble," Ezra said. "You know the history—ten years ago all Chinese were driven out of Humboldt County. I won't discuss the merits; at this point discussion means nothing. Their absence is a fact. Title to some of the area you are logging is clouded—there are Chinese claims, and others, and there may be litigation. In the meantime, I want you to continue logging. If eventually there are judgments against us, we will deal with them. But to stop now would be folly."

Frank thought about it. "Yes, sir. But where's the trouble?"

Ezra smiled. Dewey Lane would have recognized the smile; the Stanfield ears were laid back and the Stanfield heels dug in. "Since our title is at question, there may be others who will think to move in. There is a man named Marley, from Maine, with eastern money behind him. . . ."

"I've met him," Frank said. "He likes to handle his dealings in person, sometimes with his boots, sometimes with an axe." He paused. "I'll talk to Marley, sir. If I have to, in the language he understands best. We'll keep on logging until you tell us to stop."

* * *

Frank had not particularly liked the Eureka area when he first came here; this last hundred miles of California coastline was too different in climate, perhaps, from the Central Valley with its clear bright heat. Here it was wet, rainy, given to lush green growth.

But from the start Frank had liked the work out in the giant redwoods. There was a sense of mastery, of man over nature. The trees to be felled, some of them over twenty feet in diameter and as much as three hundred feet high, were selected with care. The topper, or high rigger, with climbing irons and rope, saw and axe hanging from his belt, worked his way up the giant to lop off its crown and reduce the danger of splitting the entire tree when it fell; as the crown broke free

253

and fell crashing to the forest floor, the topper rode the sway-ing trunk like a topmast hand in a heavy gale.

There was the unbelievable accuracy of the axe, and saw-men who, to minimize damage to smaller growth, brought the great trees down to the shout of "Timberrr!," precisely on the line they had chosen. One day Frank watched two men on a bet fell a topped redwood with such accuracy that the trunk drove clear into the ground a six-foot stake that had been set fifty paces from the base of the tree.

There was the swamping out of the limbs and the sawing of the great trunk into maneuverable lengths; then these sec-tions were attached to heavy cable, sometimes as much as five miles of it, run out in a great loop from a bull donkey engine set in concrete. Where it was necessary to drag the trunk section at a new angle because of forest growth or terrain, the heavy cable was slackened and passed through a new block set in a standing redwood. The area within this angle was called the bend of the line, and no one ventured into it when tension was again applied.

When the tree section had reached the bull donkey, teams of oxen were hitched to it, and the ox driver ran up and down alongside the team, talking to the animals, swearing at them, poking with his goad, his voice rising and the beasts crouching in their harness until, at his final shout, they heaved together and, as Frank's first woods boss told him, "If what they're hitched to has two ends, it's going to move."

The oxen hauled the giant sections over corduroy road to water deep enough to float them to the sawmill pond. At places where the road climbed, however slightly, grease spread with heavy brushes helped ease the drag; and at down-grades, buckets of sand were kept ready to help slow the monster if necessary. Once in Frank's experience the sand had not been enough. The ox driver had jumped and scram-bled out of the way but the oxen could not, and the twenty-foot diameter trunk section caught them and passed over them, grinding the animals into bloody mash without even slowing.

It was a man's world, and a strong man could glory in it. And when work was done there was payday and a bout with the Eureka waterfront saloons and brothels, or, if your tastes ran to less social activities, there was the mountainous back-country itself, largely untouched.

There was stream fishing—the Klamath River, the Trinity, the Mad, the Eel. There was hunting—deer, elk, bear, cougar, ducks in the salt marshes of the bay, geese, wild turkey in the woods. You could sail in the bay, or bathe in the Maine-cold water of the ocean. And perhaps best of all, on a winter's night in front of a roaring fire you could listen to a howling gale sweeping in from the west and thank your lucky stars that you were not trying to cross the Humboldt Bar in it.

* * *

Young Eddie Small was alone in the Stanfield Lumber Company office when Frank came in. He jumped up. "Gee, I'm glad to see you, Mr. Stanfield." Eddie had red hair and freckles and excitement to match. "I'd a gone down to meet you at the wharf, but they told me to stay in the office. They're all gone out to the camp, Mr. Stanfield. They wouldn't let me go."

Frank set down his bag. "What's happened, Eddie?"

It came out in a rush. "Sven Ericson's in the hospital. He's hurt bad, Mr. Stanfield. Mr. Marley, he got him down an' put the boots to him. He's all broke up inside. They say it was a fair fight, but nobody seen it an' how could it a been a fair fight when Mr. Marley ain't even marked up? With Sven?"

Sven was the Stanfield woods boss, large and healthy, and quite able to take care of himself. But apparently he hadn't. So here it was, Frank thought, sooner than he had expected. Maybe sooner was better. "Is Marley out at the camp?" he said. He watched Eddie's bright head bob. "Go tell the sheriff I want him," Frank said, "while I get out of these city clothes."

He was dressed in woods clothes, jeans, calked boots, flannel shirt, when Eddie came back, breathless, the sheriff with him. Frank said, "Well, Dan? What about Sven and Marley?"

The sheriff was uneasy. "They say it was a fair fight."

"Marley not even scratched? You know Sven."

255

The sheriff was stubborn, too. "All I know is what they tell me."

"And what does Sven say?"

"Sven ain't talkin'. He's still unconscious. Maybe he'll never talk."

"Then," Frank said, "it's murder."

"Not if it was a fair fight."

They were getting nowhere. "All right," Frank said. "I'm going out to the camp. You want to come along?"

The sheriff thought about it. Slowly he shook his head. "I don't reckon. Can't see I'm needed."

"You know, Dan," Frank said, "I rather thought you'd say that." He paused. "We'll talk more about this later. A lot more." He looked at the boy. "You mind the office, Eddie." He walked out.

It was an hour-and-a-half drive in the buckboard over backcountry dirt road, jouncing, jostling, the horse maintaining a steady shambling trot. The day was bright and clear, warm for this part of the country. Dark firs climbed the hills into the distance, and lush green grass grew up to the road and between the wheel tracks. Here and there Frank saw clumps of wild strawberries and larger bushes of wild blackberries heavy with fruit; at the edge of the woods ferns stood out against the dark trunks.

The firs stopped abruptly and the road wound into logged-over redwoods, the gigantic stumps like pustules on the land. Frank had never found the stumps ugly before. Strange. From them shoots had sprung as if the dismembered giants strove vainly for life, and never before had he found this somehow sad, either. Ferns had moved in, and the magenta spikes of fireweed, nature trying to fill the vacuum men had made. What in the world had started his thoughts in this direction?

When he had changed clothes and automatically gone through his pockets he had come across the blue hair ribbon, smiled at it as at a piece of foolishness, and then, on impulse, rolled it into a small wad and tucked it into the breast pocket of his shirt. He took it out and looked at it now. Ellen, strange, intense child-woman; he had watched her grow from babyhood and never really thought of her before as anything but a baby cousin. Suddenly now, for no reason that he could fathom, he found himself wondering what she would think of this land, and instantly he knew.

She would love the salt taste of the ocean air and the mountains rising green. She would love the trees. She would delight in the wild flowers he could show her—the wild iris, purple larkspur, shy wild violets, roses in the sun, and near the many streams, watercress and the odd-shaped stems and leaves of miner's lettuce. She would love the animals—squirrels, rabbits, the fearless, friendly skunks, deer sometimes seen and elk, occasional porcupines, beavers at their dams and otters frolicking. She would love it all because it was her nature—somehow he understood this—to see and to love the good things wherever she was as long as she was happy. And happiness to her would be simply being with the one she loved.

He put the ribbon away again. He was approaching the camp, driving still through logged-over desolation. Ellen, he thought, would weep if she saw this. He put Ellen out of his mind as he drove into camp.

The buildings were temporary, frame and canvas. There was the cook tent and the long tables where the lumberjacks tucked away unbelievable quantities of solid food. Frank had seen harvest crews at table down in the Central Valley, but until he saw a logging camp at mealtime he had never really seen eating. The first camp cook he had known had been philosophical about it. "Man," he said, "has got to have somethin' to keep his belly away from his backbone." He had added, "I do hate to see a hungry man. They get mean."

Nearby, but at a safe distance in the event of explosion or cable break, the stationary bull donkey engine chuffed and whuffed as it labored to drag in its enormous load of redwood trunk sections.

And over there, talking to two men from the office and one lumberjack, Frank saw, was Marley, who was not a hungry man, but was more than sufficiently mean. Frank got down from the buckboard feeling an anger that was deep and strong. He walked over to the woodpile and picked up the double-bitted axe that was used for splitting firewood. "Marley," he said, and moved toward the group.

257

Marley turned. He was a big, heavy man, with a belly that looked soft and was not. He looked at Frank, and he looked at the axe in Frank's hand. "Somethin' you want?" His voice was faintly nasal, with a Yankee twang.

"Several things," Frank said. "First among them is your absence."

Marley looked thoughtful. "Askin' me to leave?"

"Telling you." Frank raised the axe easily with his right hand. "I just got off the ship. I just heard about Sven Ericson. There are some things I want to find out. Then you and I will have a talk. However you want it." He paused. "Right now, I'm giving you until I count to five to get out of this camp. One . . . two . . . three. . . ."

Marley's eyes were on the axe. Then he looked at Frank's face.

". . . four. . . ."

Marley turned and walked away.

In the silence Frank looked around at the office men. "You're not being paid for standing out here talking," he said. "Back to town." Then to the lumberjack, whose name was Joe Turner, "I want to talk to you, Joe." He walked to the buckboard. Turner followed.

Frank handed him the axe. "Do you know anything about the fight?"

Turner shook his head. He was a hammered-down heavyweight, born in this northern country, raised in and near lumber camps, woods-wise, shrewd. "Sven had an argument with Marley. We heard shoutin'. Got here in time to see Marley puttin' the boots to him. Sven tried to grab his foot. Missed. Looked like a fair fight."

"Marley isn't marked," Frank said.

Turner shot a stream of tobacco juice ten feet into a pile of rocks. "Noticed that myself," he said. "Wondered some." He looked at Frank. "Sven always figgered he was bull of the woods. Maybe he crowded his luck too far."

Dead end, Frank thought. He had known that Sven was not particularly popular. On the other hand, running a logging camp was not like running for public office—popularity was not the goal. "You take over, Joe."

Turner hesitated.

"It means," Frank said, "an extra fifty dollars a month."

Turner thought about it. He launched another stream of tobacco juice. He said at last, "That's all right. That's fine. But . . ."

"I'll take care of Marley," Frank said. "You just run this camp."

Turner ran his tongue inside his lower lip. He nodded. "You're the boss," he said.

Frank climbed into the buckboard. He picked up the reins. "What was Marley talking about?" He made the question as casual as he could.

Turner shrugged. "Said this wasn't Stanfield land. Said we'd all end up workin' for him."

"He's wrong," Frank said. "Keep the logs coming." He shook the reins and drove off.

On the way back to town he detoured to stop at the sawmill. The mill pond was filled with floating redwood, the huge bandsaw was shrieking, and the taste of redwood sawdust filled the air. Frank went into the foreman's little office and closed the door to block out some of the noise.

Tom Handy was at his desk, laboring over paperwork. They shook hands, and Frank perched on the corner of the desk. "All quiet here?" He smiled suddenly at the ineptness of the question; even through the closed door the shriek of the saw was plain. "No trouble?" he said.

Handy shook his head. He leaned back in his chair. "I heard about Sven," he said. "Marley comes around here, I got a peavey that's just about his size."

Frank smiled. There was an independent quality to men raised in this big country that was frequently lacking in city men, particularly the easterners he had known. He supposed there was a reason for it. He had heard it said that only the brave and the strong reached California back before the railroad; the weak did not survive the journey and the fainthearted didn't set out in the first place. Natural selection at work. "Joe Turner is running the camp," he said. "Keep him busy. I'll be in town if you want me." He stood down from the desk.

Handy said, "There's money behind Marley, I hear tell."

Frank nodded. "There is. We'll let them take care of that

259

down in the city. Trees and lumber are our part." He paused. His smile was wicked. "And Marley is my part," he said.

Back into town and straight to the hospital. Boots had scarred the floors, and the windows always seemed to have a fine film of salt deposit from the ocean air, but the hospital itself, inured to the emergencies of logging accidents, was calm and efficient.

Sven Ericson was not allowed visitors. His condition was critical. Perhaps Dr. Hopper was free to see Mr. Stanfield. Dr. Hopper was—white coat, short gray spade beard and moustache, steel-rimmed pince-nez on a black cord. "I don't suppose," Dr. Hopper said, "that there is a particle of use in pointing out that men are alleged to be above wild beasts."

Frank agreed that there was no use at all.

"Ericson," the doctor said, "has taken unbelievable punishment. Internal injuries. . . ." He spread his hands. "How extensive we cannot tell yet. Concussion. Probable skull fracture, although there is no depressed area."

"Where?" Frank said. He watched the doctor touch the back of his head. So that was it, Frank thought, that was why Marley was unmarked. His face showed nothing, but the deep anger started up again. "What's your forecast?" he said.

"Indeterminate. Tomorrow, the next day, we may know better."

Frank drove the buckboard back to the office and had Eddie Small take it to the stable. There was work on his desk, but it could wait. He closed the door of his inner office and settled down to write a comprehensive report for his father, facts and observations. When it was done he sealed it, addressed the envelope, and summoned Eddie to deliver it in person to the captain of the steam schooner that had brought him from San Francisco only hours before. "Tell him," Frank said, "that I want it delivered, by hand, as soon as he docks." The schooner would not sail for a day or two, but the alternative was the telegraph, and this report was for Ezra Stanfield's eyes only. There was nothing more to be done. Frank settled down to the backlog of work.

He dined alone at a restaurant. He had many friends in town, both male and female, but for some reason that night he craved solitude. In the chill evening, with fog rolling in

260

across the bay and creeping up the streets from the waterfront, Frank walked, without destination, letting his thoughts run as they chose.

He thought of the doctor's remark that men were allegedly above wild beasts. Not necessarily so. Men were capable of savagery and violence almost beyond comprehension. He was himself; he had long known this. And what made some men's actions even more reprehensible was that frequently they were the result of considered malice, rather than, as with beasts, the result of hunger or fear or the blind killing rage of a weasel in a hen house. Sven Ericson had been deliberately brutalized. As a warning? A challenge? Time would tell. Marley was not through.

Frank thought of the land itself, now in dispute. Perhaps it was tainted. First the Indians who lived here were massacred. Then, only ten years before, all of the Chinese in Humboldt County were driven out, their property forfeit. And the violence persisted.

Perhaps it was always so in new, raw lands before law and order and tranquillity could be established. But how then explain the periodic outbreaks and upheavals that still plagued European countries after all these centuries?

He was supposed to be an educated man, but he had no answers to these questions; it would take someone wiser than he to unlock the riddle. A woman, perhaps, with the kind of intuitive wisdom women sometimes seemed to have. Ellen. He smiled at the thought, and was conscious of the little wad of hair ribbon in the inside pocket of his coat, tucked there again when he had changed from his rough working clothes.

He was being foolish, he knew, but he wished that she were here, to look at, to talk to, to listen to. More than that? Intimacy? Absurd, of course, that a fifteen-year-old snippet should creep so persistently into his thoughts. Or was it? For Ellen, as for his own mother, Lotte, ordinary rules did not apply. His mother had been only Ellen's age that dreadful winter in Donner Pass, and she had come through it unscarred, unafraid, ready to face a new life in a new land with only her brother Rudi, himself no more than seventeen, for guide and strength and counsel—until

261

Ezra Stanfield showed up that night in Turkey Creek with a derringer in his sleeve. Violence again, with no rational beginning, no end.

He passed a saloon; voices and laughter reached out through the swinging doors, and on impulse he turned and walked in. Instantly all sound stopped; he looked around for the reason, and found it. Marley was sitting at a table with three men, a local lawyer, the local banker and Sheriff Dan Hodges.

Frank walked over to the bar and ordered whiskey. He stood sipping it slowly while conversations started up again but in subdued tones. He finished his drink, tossed two bits on the bar, and turned to face Marley's table. He did not raise his voice, but with the first word all other conversation stopped. "Ericson," he said, "has a skull fracture. Back here." He patted the back of his head. "Is that your style, bully boy? From the back? With a rock or a club? And then the boots?"

The large room was quite still. Marley said in his faintly nasal Yankee twang, "Be you askin' to find out?"

Frank was smiling, but the anger was hard to control. He shook his head. "Not right now." He paused. "But when I do, I'll watch my back." He left it there. The immediate buzz of talk reached through the swinging doors into the fog as he walked out.

A fire was laid in the grate of his study at home. He touched a match to it and stood for a time idly watching it flare, catch, settle down to steady warming flame. He turned away at last and walked to his desk, lighted the lamp, and sat down to write the first letter he had ever written Ellen.

Snippet:
You said something the other day that struck me, and has remained in my mind ever since. You said that we were not people, you and I. Perhaps you are right. I hope you are. Because I don't think I like people. Individuals, yes; people, no. People have plundered this land. I saw it today for the first time, looking through your eyes, or imagining that I was. Oh, individuals have directed the people in their plundering; we cannot escape that responsibility. I have said, "Cut there, and there and there," and trees that took a thousand years to grow, two thousand,

262

came crashing down, and something was gone that can never be replaced, and we are all the poorer for the loss.

I will continue to do it. I will even fight for the right to do it. Why? I do not know. But tonight for the first time I question our feeling that we can do what we please, for profit, in the name of progress. Do I sound as if I have lost my mind? But I think you will understand. I hope so.
Yrs,
Frank.

He addressed the envelope simply Miss Ellen Meyer, Stanhope, California, sealed the letter, and left it on the desk. He went off to bed feeling unaccountably easier, relieved, as if loose ends had been neatly tied up, nothing left dangling.

Dressed in logging clothes, he called the next morning on the lawyer who had been in the saloon with Marley. The lawyer's name was Perkins, middle-aged, solid, folksy.

"There may be litigation down in the city," Frank said. "My advice to you is to leave it there."

Perkins smiled. "Well, now, Mr. Stanfield," he said, "it's a kind of local matter, you see. Land the heathen Chinese went off an' left is right here, as you well know . . ."

"If you don't leave it alone," Frank said, "it won't be a local matter."

Perkins thought about it. "I'm not right sure I follow you."

"I think you do. It's eastern money behind Marley. But your ties are with San Francisco, not New York or Boston." And in San Francisco, Ezra Stanfield and Rudi Meyer could exert leverage—there was no need to spell that out.

Perkins said, "Are you threatening me, young man?"

"Just think about it," Frank said, "and I'm sure you'll decide that it's better to let them fight it out down in the city."

He went next to the banker named Boggs who had also been at the table. "We maintain a sizable account," Frank said. "Putting it all together, the logging operation, the saw-mill, the ships, we are probably one of your larger customers."

Boggs nodded slowly. His eyes were wary.

"Perhaps you would like to keep it that way?" Frank

263

paused, waited. There was only silence. "I would like an answer," he said.

Boggs said, "I don't—ah—like threats, Mr. Stanfield."

"Then don't put yourself in a position," Frank said, "where you are asking for them. Do you want to keep our accounts? Do you want to continue to act as correspondent bank for banks in San Francisco? Or do you want to pull in your horns and revert to what you were when you started, a purely local operation with almost no large depositors and no business sent to you from the city?" He paused and then applied the clincher. "If I close out our accounts, there will be questions. And no doubt some of the firms we do business with will close out their accounts too. A run on a small-town bank is easily begun, but it is very difficult to stop."

"Mr. Stanfield, what you are threatening . . ." Boggs stopped there. His face had lost color, and his breathing was not quite steady.

"Go on," Frank said. "Or shall I make the protest for you? Marley is a respectable businessman, and you reserve the right to do business with anyone you choose? But he isn't a respectable businessman. He is a bully, and my woods boss may die because of him. And he represents eastern capital trying to force their way into the lumber business in California, and we are going to fight them. But in the city, not here. And your freedom to do business with anyone you choose is Hobson's choice: you may take any horse in the stable—as long as it is the one nearest the door. That means us. Stanfield. Is that clear?"

Boggs's face was white now. His hands were trembling. He swallowed hard.

"Bankers," Frank said, "aren't supposed to be talked to like this, are they? No doubt it takes getting accustomed to." He walked to the door. There, his hand on the knob, he paused, turned. "I am sending a full report to the city. That means to my father. He will wait to hear from me what action I would like him to take." He paused. "California is our home. We staked out our claims. We will fight to hold them. Remember that." He walked out.

His last call that morning was on the sheriff. He did not bother to sit down. "What I have to say won't take long, Dan.

264

I have talked to Perkins and to Boggs. I believe they have seen the light, but you may want to ask them for yourself. Marley is leaving Humboldt County. He may not know it yet, but he will find out. As a matter of fact, I am willing to wager that he is leaving California. Permanently. You may tell him that if you like." Pause. "That will leave you alone, Dan, very much alone. Think about it." He paused again. "You may tell Marley too that if he wants to see me, I will be out at the camp."

Once again he drove the buckboard, without haste, over the backcountry dirt road. It was another rare, clear, warm day, and it seemed to him that he was seeing everything in preternaturally bright colors: the blue sky with scattered fluffy white clouds, the dark fir-covered hills and mountains, the green grass in the open meadows, the berry bushes, the ferns. Once he caught a movement in the trees, quickly gone; deer most likely, buck or doe he could not tell. He was glad that wildlife remained despite man's encroachments.

When he came into the logged-over area, he looked again at the huge stumps as he had looked at them yesterday—with Ellen's eyes. The letter he had written her still lay on his desk. He had seen it this morning and wondered if he was actually going to send it. Things looked different in daylight. And yet his view of this plundered land was unchanged.

Perhaps at bottom—sudden thought—his new unhappiness with the desolation logging had caused sprang from his childhood in the Central Valley. What he was accustomed to there was the kind of activity that used the land but did not plunder it, that year after year planted and then harvested, a continuing process. It was different here.

Here, as he had said in his letter to Ellen, when one of these giants was felled, that was an end to it. In Germany and in Austria, as he had seen, for a thousand years, they had tended their evergreen forests, fir, pine, larch and spruce, harvesting trees and then planting seedlings to replace them. But it was futile even to try to replace a redwood; on the rings of one of these giant stumps you could count back to the year Christ was born and still not be back to the tree's beginning. And so eventually, inevitably, the giants would disappear. Was there a word for the massacre of an entire species?

But there was no stopping. The trees were there. They

265

could be logged and sawed into planks or timbers, split into shakes, sold for profit, therefore it would be done. Why on this beautiful morning were his thoughts taking this gloomy turn? He was beginning to wonder if the hair ribbon, resting again in his shirt pocket like some potent talisman, was affecting his entire life. He was smiling at the concept as he drove into the camp.

He tied the horse and walked over to put his head into the cook shack. "Where will I find Joe?"

The cook pointed with his cleaver. "They're settin' a new block out yonder. Quarter, maybe half mile."

It was pleasant walking in the logged-over area. With the great trees gone the sunlight was warm on his shoulders and head; underfoot the hundreds of years' accumulation of redwood needles were a spongy carpet.

He passed the steam donkey, panting quietly now, the heavy cable at rest. He waved at the operator and walked on.

They had pretty well logged-over the area within efficient distance of the camp. Time soon to move to a new location. Maybe the bull donkey could be left where it was, because to move it meant tearing up its concrete foundation and, more important, laying a new corduroy road to water. Something to think about—always something to think about.

He came at last to Joe Turner and a crew fixing a new block to a standing redwood, thereby altering the angle of the cable's motion. In the distance he could see the huge trunk section that was the cause of the change, twenty feet through at the butt, forty, maybe fifty feet long, chained to the cable like a gigantic slave being dragged through the woods. He was still seeing the world through Ellen's eyes.

He stood for a time watching the men at their work. They moved with the unhurried sureness of skilled workmen, respect for the job implicit in every motion: respect for the weight and strength and downright irascibility of the big cable, respect for the enormous load it would carry through this new block; constant respect for, and awareness of, the multitude of accidents waiting to happen whenever man ventured into the redwoods with his axe and his saw and his intent to plunder.

He sensed rather than heard movement behind him, and

266

he reacted instantly, ducking and dodging away. The blow which would have landed on his head struck him instead in the broad of his back, still with sufficient force to drive him stumbling to his knees.

He made no attempt to stop the fall. Instead he launched himself in a twisting, rolling dive, at the end of which he came to his feet and crouching, turned. Marley was coming at him in a bent rush, arms spread and fingers hooked, a catch-as-catch-can brawler, dangerous as a bear.

Frank feinted to his left, moved quickly to his right, had his feet planted for power, and landed the first punch of the fight, a thunderous left hook that slowed but did not stop Marley. Frank crossed his right hand, landed again, and hooked once more, to the body this time, then felt the power of those clutching arms and hooked fingers as Marley caught him.

This was no boxing match—no referee would step in with instructions. This was survival, pure and simple, as Sven Ericson had found out. Frank made no attempt to resist the power of those grabbing hands. He let them haul him in and even accelerated the process by lunging forward, head down, smashing his skull into Marley's face with an audible cartilage-crunching sound. The hands loosened momentarily, and Frank jumped back, free, had his quick look, then moved forward again.

Marley's nose was smashed, and blood was running from a cut over one eye. He shook his head to clear his vision, but the grasping hands were uncertain, and Frank landed three big punches, left, right, left just above the swell of Marley's belly, before the hands even located him, and then their grasp was unsure. He jumped back away from them, then moved back in.

Distantly, he heard a blast from a whistle, repeated. He gave it no heed. He was busy, in close now, his head against Marley's shoulder, feet widespread for leverage; with both fists and the full power of his shoulders, body, and legs he pounded at the belly, ignoring the hands which were weaker now, and weaker, and at last totally ineffectual.

Frank stepped back then. Marley was still on his feet, his face a bloody mask, shoulders slumped and hands hanging, swaying like a redwood about to fall. Frank stepped in again, merciless, and drove punches, left, right, left into the mutilated face, their power holding the man erect until his knees buckled and he began to go down, and still the punches continued until at last the body was on the ground.

Frank stood erect, his breath coming in great painful gasps. He was hurt; he had not realized before that he had taken blows, but it had to have been because his ribs were bruised as if they were cracked, and the side of his neck was already beginning to stiffen. But he was on his feet, and Marley was not, and would not be for some time—and that was all that mattered. Or was it?

What, actually, had he accomplished? His thoughts were picking up again their astigmatic quality of today. He and Marley, like two bull elks in rut, but without even the elks' physiological excuse. He stood over Marley, looking down at the havoc he had wrought, and found himself without a sense of triumph. With nothing. Emptiness.

He was vaguely aware that voices were shouting at him, and that the laboring sounds of the bull donkey had resumed. He looked around in bewilderment, remembering now the two whistle blasts, signal for power on the cable. There was the standing redwood with the new block fixed. Here where he was standing was the bend of the line, no-man's land. Here——

It happened too fast for sight. The sound was as of the thrumming of a giant bowstring. The new block, caught between the force of the steam engine set in concrete and the weight of the redwood trunk section the cable was dragging, failed in its fastening and pulled loose. The cable, released, shot across the clearing at chest height. Frank neither saw nor heard. Standing motionless, his arms hanging at his sides, he was severed into four pieces as cleanly as by a gigantic cleaver. When the cable at last came to rest, a blue hair ribbon was firmly caught within its strands.

The Stanfield schooner fought its way out over the Humboldt Bar three days later. It bore Frank's report to his father, the only letter he ever wrote to Ellen, and his dismembered body in a shiny coffin beginning its journey back to Stanhope.

* * *

In the great, cool, dim room there was silence. Ellen closed her eyes. She opened them again. "I am so sorry, Marquesa, so terribly sorry."

The old lady in the bed waggled her head gently. "You must try never to regret what might have been, child. The past that did not happen is as hidden from us as the future we cannot yet see." She was smiling fondly. "A long time ago, as I said. And my life with Ezra was very happy. It was probably for the best." And then, almost whispering, to herself, not to the girl, "But sometimes I still wonder."

"You are tired, Marquesa. I'll call Nurse Walters."

One hand stirred. The diamond flashed. "What is real to you now, child, at seventeen, is just as real as it will be at forty. Believe that."

Ellen stood up. She bent again to kiss her great-grandmother's cheek. "I do," she said.

29

The telephone call she had been waiting for all day did not come until Ellen had bathed, dressed for dinner, and come downstairs to oversee cocktail and dinner arrangements. Consuelo answered the call on the wall phone in the pantry and came smiling into the kitchen. "For you, señorita."

María watched, expressionless.

"I will take it in the study," Ellen said with what she hoped was apparent unconcern, and knew that it was transparent. It was hard not to run; and she made herself close the study door gently, an exercise in self-discipline. When she picked up the phone and spoke into it she heard the immediate click as Consuelo hung up the extension. Bless Consuelo.

"Hi." Paul's voice, of course.

"I've been waiting for you to call," Ellen said. And if that was not recommended behavior for a young female, so be it. Marquesa's tale of herself at fifteen was still strong in Ellen's mind.

"I almost didn't." Pause. "You know why?" Another

270

pause. "Because I was afraid that you might feel differ-ently. . . ."

"I don't." And then, almost fearfully, "Do you?"

"That," Paul said, and relief was plain in his voice, "will be a day." There was silence. It was obvious that Paul had not planned the conversation beyond this point.

Ellen said, "Tonight?"

"Baby." Mild protest. "I don't want to get you in bad with your father, the family."

What a family tempest it would have caused if Frank Stanfield had taken Marquesa, aged fifteen, back to Eureka with him. But maybe then Frank would not have been killed. Family tempest be damned. "I don't care," Ellen said. "I——" She stopped as the study door opened. George walked in, saw her with the phone in hand, and hesitated.

In the phone Paul's voice said, "What is it, baby?"

"Nothing." Ellen's voice was firm, determined, and sud-denly over-loud. "Tonight. At the gate. Ten o'clock. Okay?"

There was a smile in Paul's voice. "If you say so."

Ellen hung up the phone. She watched George close the door and cross the room slowly. He stopped only a little distance from her, tall, broad, solid as Frank Stanfield must have been. From his great height he watched her quietly. "Paul?"

"Yes, Daddy,"

"All night again?" He watched her eyes widen in sur-prise; and then a faint blush began, rising out of the neck of her dress, bringing a glow to her cheeks. "I saw you come in, honey," George said. "I had come down here early to work."

"I—didn't see you."

"There were stars in your eyes. I don't think you saw anything."

Ellen's eyes closed. She opened them again. "I don't care what you say, Daddy."

"I haven't said anything yet." He walked slowly around the big desk and sank wearily into his chair. Ellen turned to face him and stood quietly, waiting. "I am not as glib as some," George said, "but ordinarily I don't have trouble thinking what to say. This time I do."

271

"Do you want me to help you?" Ellen said. She took a deep breath, thinking again of Marquesa, aged fifteen. "All right. Do I love Paul? Yes, Daddy, I do. Am I ashamed of—spending the night with him? No, Daddy, I'm not. I'm proud. Does that make me—bad? I don't think so. Everybody says that parents wonder, and worry, and are afraid to ask so they never know about their kids. I don't know if you wonder or not, and you don't have to ask, I'll tell you anyway. Paul is the only one, and last night was the first time. I don't want you to think I'm a little hot pants, just anybody's lay."

"Thank you for that," George said. Clara had said that Ellen had her standards—apparently Clara was right. If he and Clara had not had their talk in the big tree grove, would he now have felt outrage instead of near-relief? He spread his big hands and let them fall. "They say," he said, "that all parents are baffled these days. I don't know if that's true or not, honey. I think I would have been baffled by you in any time. The only difference is that thirty years ago I suppose I would have made a speech and laid down the law and told you you were going to hell in a hand basket. Now I don't know what to say."

"You're trying, aren't you, Daddy? Thank you for that."

George nodded slowly. "I'm trying, honey. Sometimes I feel as if I'm groping around in a strange room in the dark, barking my shins on furniture I can't see, or stepping on fragile things that have no business being on the floor. I can't talk to Pete without losing my temper. To your Paul I'm the bastard you say I am sometimes to you. You've deliberately challenged me, haven't you? Tonight at the gate at ten o'clock. You're daring me to be there, and I am not generally thought of as a man who will take a dare." He shook his head slowly.

There was a great similarity, Ellen thought, between the picture she had built of Frank Stanfield and Daddy; she could not imagine either of them avoiding what had to be done, ever. She supposed that merely meant that they accepted responsibility. Well, in his way, Paul did too, as Pete did not. Did she? She hoped so. She was, she told herself, that square. She said now, "Are you going to be at the gate, Daddy?"

"I don't know, honey."

272

Ellen nodded. "But you'll do what you think is right, won't you? Even if it hurts?" She shook her head. Then, in a different voice, "You were wrong, Daddy. When I said I wouldn't leave here with Paul because I couldn't, it wasn't because of Marquesa. Or only partly because of her."

George watched her, frowning.

"It was mostly because of you," Ellen said. "You see, I try to do what I think is right too."

* * *

In the late afternoon, drinks at hand, Scott and Jenny sat on the cantilevered gallery overlooking San Francisco Bay. Here and there lights had come on, small candles flickering in distant windows. The setting sun backlighted the city's hills and skyline.

Scott said, "Do I get a report?" He tried to keep his voice unconcerned. "You saw him, Cathy's shyster? A slimy little man? Walk-up office? Raymond Chandler type character?"

"You're not like that really, Scotty," Jenny said. "At least I hope you aren't. I don't find cynicism attractive."

He had said the same to Pete, hadn't he? Well? Taking a sharp honest look at himself, Scott was not sure he liked what he saw. "I withdraw the questions." He paused. "But you can't expect me to like the situation."

"Scotty. Scotty." She was shaking her head gently. "If you want me to represent you, then try to relax with me. You don't have to play a part, any part. Not the worldly rake, not the outraged academic, not the rich paranoid. You aren't really any of these. Relax and assume that I have a certain amount of—worldly knowledge too, that I understand perfectly well how you got into this . . ."

"Tell me, counselor." He was behaving badly, and he knew it, but some imp of the perverse pushed him on. "Explain it to me."

Jenny looked at him steadily in her calm way. Nothing changed in her voice. "There is an aphorism," she said. "It is considered in some circles an axiom. It is that a stiff prick has no conscience." From her, the vulgarism was all the more shocking. She watched him quietly. "Does that explanation satisfy you, Scotty?"

273

There was silence. Somewhere distantly a ship blew three short blasts on its whistle; they echoed across the water and up to this lofty, isolated place. Scott said slowly, "That signal means: 'My engines are in reverse.' " He looked at Jenny. His voice was quiet, shamed. "Maybe I'd better reverse mine." He hesitated. "Sorry, counselor." He smiled apologetically. "May we start over?"

Slowly, "Thank you, Scotty." There was approval in her eyes. She made a small gesture of dismissal. "I saw Cathy Strong's lawyer, yes. His name is Judson Brown. He wears his hair long, but his fingernails are clean, and he does not leer. He is probably twenty-five years old, and I think the word is —dedicated."

Scott was silent, looking out over the Bay. The lights were coming on on the bridges now; their reflections shimmered in the water.

"He took your course in California history," Jenny said. "He made a point of telling me. He said he had great admiration for you."

"But now," Scott said, "that I have feet of clay, I am a son of a bitch, is that it?"

"You are trying to sound like one." Jenny waited, but there was no comment. It was not easy for him; she appreciated that. On the other hand, she thought, it is not easy for me, either. "I don't know what he thinks of you," she said. "It doesn't matter. His concern is for his client. Properly so."

"I offered to pay for her abortion."

"Isn't that a confession of guilt, Scotty? At least of conscience?" There was no answer. She had expected none. Jenny went on. "I wanted to know what they were asking. The girl wants marriage. With you."

Scott picked up his drink. He drained it. "What does young, dedicated Judson Brown figure to get out of that? Does he think that if I married her I'd immediately give her a big fat bank account? Because I wouldn't. I——"

Jenny's voice cut across his, silencing it. "I don't think that young, dedicated Judson Brown figures to get anything under any circumstances, Scotty. His is what is called a store-front operation. I imagine he has another practice, probably with an established firm, that supports him." In the gathering

274

darkness she watched his face. "You are skeptical? Then you are the one who is being unworldly. These practices, like free medical clinics, are part of today. You said it yourself. Cathy has no money. She needs legal advice. Where else, logically, would she turn? I should have seen it, but I didn't. I thought, as you did, that some ambulance chaser was hoping to fatten himself on Stanfield money. Not so."

Scott sat quiet, silent. A darting, twisting shape flitted into his view and he watched it idly. A bat, he thought, emitting his inaudible beeps, catching their reflections and finding his way unerringly, even through the tall eucalyptus foliage, avoiding obstacles that could cripple him, closing in on his prey, a tiny creature attuned to his environment. Could man in his pride say the same? He turned to look at Jenny. "What do you want me to do?"

She shook her head. "What do you want to do? It is your decision. If you had thought from the beginning that Cathy was nothing but a young roundheel, I don't think you would ever have bothered with her. A man like you doesn't need to stoop to basement bargains." Her voice was still quiet in the evening air. "I think there must have been some measure of affection, too. I hope there was. I hope she was not just a warm young body." Her silence made it plain that a question had been asked.

Scott spoke to the darkness. "You've made your point, counselor. I enjoyed her. I basked in her obvious—admiration, if it wasn't infatuation. Guilty as charged."

Jenny said, "Does pregnancy suddenly turn her into a monster?" She paused. "It is too easy to apply a rule of absolute, Scotty, to say that she is either a fool or a knave— a fool if she is pregnant without intending it, a knave if the intent was there. But one of the things I have always admired about you is that you are not like too many academics; you are not dogmatic, simplistic, trapped in thinking that has become ritualized. You haven't yet been caught up in a sense of your own infallibility. Don't be now, please."

In the darkness, as in the fog on the road down from Pacheco Pass, Scott had the feeling of isolation, or was the word privilege? Of being able to speak his thoughts without embarrassment or a sense of disclosure. "You're quite a

275

female," he said. "If I had known you, there wouldn't have been a Cathy."

"Maybe." Her voice was toneless.

He frowned. "What does that mean?"

"Maybe," Jenny said slowly, "Cathy was, is, a catharsis. Maybe you needed her, Scotty."

He thought about it, smiling. "And now I can put aside my childish toys? Strike the question." The smile was gone. "Would you have me marry her?"

"I—can't answer that, Scotty. Do you know the saying that a lawyer who pleads his own case has a fool for a client? It is true; and the reason is that when the matter is too close to home, you substitute emotion for reason."

Scott said gently, "Am I too close to home? Is that what you're saying?"

"You are." Jenny's voice was not quite steady, her calm shaken at last. "And all because of that wretched girl!"

"Bless Cathy." Scott was smiling as he got out of his chair and in the darkness moved toward her.

* * *

Clara Wilson walked down the hospital corridor as to the whipping post. Ben's door was open. She knocked gently and walked in. He lay on his back, one hand behind his head, the other resting helplessly at his side. His eyes were open, and as soon as he saw her the wicked smile appeared.

"Dear, dear Clara, little helpmate." His voice was light, its tone false. "You are looking ravishing tonight, a woman fulfilled. Are you a woman fulfilled?"

It was going to be bad. "I brought you some books, Ben," she said. "There's a new Rex Stout, and a Ross MacDonald, and I don't think you've read the Hillary Waugh." She laid the books on the bedside table within easy reach.

"Thank you." Then, as she started to move back toward the visitor's chair, "No kiss?" His smile mocked her.

Clara hesitated. She moved to the bedside and bent to kiss his cheek, but he turned his head and with his single good hand pulled her down until their lips met. It was a long moment before he released her. "That's more wifely," he said.

Clara sat down. She wanted to open her purse, take out

276

her handkerchief and scrub at her lips, but she refused to give him that satisfaction. She sat erect, silent.

"Gossip of the outside world," Ben said. "Specifically, gossip concerning you and Georgie. How is the romance going?"

"Ben . . ."

"Have you seen him?"

It was no use, she thought. She was here. She could do no other than answer his questions. Evasion would only make her feel guilty, furtive—more guilty, more furtive. "Yes," she said. "We drove today up into the mountains, and walked in a redwood grove." Then, remembering, "Big trees," she said, "not redwoods. I didn't know that before. Did you? Redwoods grow near the coast."

"Fascinating. What else did you do, you and Georgie?"

"We talked."

"About me?"

Clara shook her head. "You were not mentioned." But you were there, she thought, every moment you were there.

"I wonder why." Ben was smiling broadly. "And then what?"

"We drove back here. That is all there was, Ben."

"Do you mean to say," Ben said, "that he hasn't laid you yet?"

"Ben. Please." All she had to do, she told herself, was stand up and walk out, and she knew that she could not. Why? She had no answer, only wild surmise. Maybe unconsciously, she thought, I am deliberately submitting myself to this torment as punishment for failing him as a wife, maybe I am basically masochistic, maybe, maybe, maybe.

"Tears?" Ben said. "But why?" He paused. His voice altered. "Aren't you going to call me an unpleasant son of a bitch and tell me you don't want any more of me, the way you did the day I went to Riverside?"

The tears were flowing freely now, running down the sides of her nose, tasting salt in her mouth. She could not stop them, so she tried to ignore them. "I'm—sorry I said that, Ben."

"Why apologize? You meant it, didn't you? Didn't you?"

"Ben, you . . ." She stopped and caught her lower lip between her teeth. She shook her head helplessly.

"Do you want a laugh?" Ben said. "Georgie even thought I deliberately cracked up at Riverside because of you. Isn't that hilarious? The death-wish bit."

Clara closed her eyes. The tears burned and stung. She opened her eyes again and sat quiet, enduring.

"But the fact of the matter," Ben said, "is that I was jilted the day we were married." The mocking tone was gone. He was unsmiling now. "Worse than jilted, lover—I wasn't even there. Do you remember that night in the hotel in Carmel?" He paused. "Speak up, goddam it. Do you remember?"

Clara nodded. "I remember."

"You really poured it on that night," Ben said. "You were the sexiest, most wonderful thing in the world, and I thought, 'Jesus, and all of this is mine!' " He was silent, watching her.

"I was yours, Ben."

"That's crap, and you know it. I wasn't the guy in bed with you. It was Georgie, Georgie Stanfield, the son of a bitch. Did you know that I decided once to kill him? Fact."

Clara wet her lips with her tongue. She shook her head. "Ben . . ."

"I've been waiting quite a while to say this," Ben said. "You might have the decency to hear me out. You didn't marry me, you married him. It took me a little while to see that, but then it was plain as could be."

"Ben, I promise you, I never once . . ."

"You never once cheated on me? Is that what you were going to say?" He smiled in helpless anger and waggled his head on the pillow. "A lie, Clara baby, a big fat lie. It was my body you went to bed with, but it was Georgie in your mind."

Clara opened her purse and took out her handkerchief. She wiped her eyes. The tears had stopped. I have no more tears, she thought; I am shamed beyond them.

"I grew up in the shadow of Stanfields," Ben said. "Scott, Peter Juan, and the big one, Georgie. There wasn't any place I could go without being smothered by Stanfields. Anything I had, they had more of; anything I could do, they could do better without even trying." He waggled his head again. "I wasn't even in the same ballpark with them; it was like competing with Superman." His voice was quiet now. "Then I made the big score. You." The room was silent while he watched her. "You're the only thing that kept me in Stanhope. You. Because I had you, I could sneer at Georgie." Another long pause. "Only I didn't have you after all. He did." He made a quick, short gesture with his good hand. "I'm no shrink, but maybe I did spin out on purpose. Who knows? I was an unpleasant son of a bitch and you wanted no more of me." He was silent.

Clara sat quite still. She had no words; her mind was numb. Later, she knew, she would think back on this scene with pain; right now she was beyond pain, in a world of unreality and desolation where a wind seemed to blow through tumbled wreckage with a soundless howl. She tried, but she could not take her eyes from the man in the bed.

He was smiling again, and the mocking tone had returned. "So I decided to kill Georgie, lover. But I found I was afraid even to try. What do you think of that? I was afraid that no matter what I used, pistol, rifle, shotgun, the son of a bitch would get to me and take me with him. Superman. And I didn't want to die. Not then."

Clara opened her mouth, but no sound came out.

Ben said, "You aren't very sparkling company, so why don't you cut out? I'll send for you if I want you again."

She stood up automatically, tried to think of something to say, and found nothing.

"Leave me your purse mirror," Ben said.

Clara hesitated. Then, slowly, obediently, she opened her purse, took out the mirror, and handed it to him.

"You're wondering why?" Ben said. "Simple. I want to admire my big white shiny teeth. Close the door when you go out."

At the door she stopped and turned. "Goodbye, Ben."

"A smashing exit line." He watched her walk out. The door closed.

He lay for a few moments, motionless, staring at the closed door, the mirror in his hand. Then with deliberation he reached out to open the topmost book and tuck the mirror into its pages, let the cover fall. Painfully he lifted himself on his one good arm and rested on his elbow. He stared at the shapes of his legs and feet beneath the coverlet. "All right, you sons of bitches," he said, "move! Goddam it, move!"

Nothing happened.

Ben closed his eyes. He breathed deeply in and out, in his mind counting each breath until he had reached ten. Then he opened his eyes again. "Now, you fuckers, move, move, move!"

He strained with his good arm, his torso, his will. Tendons in his neck stood out like cords, and the skin of his face took on a flush that deepened into the purple of near-apoplexy; a vein bunched on his forehead, and his breathing turned to labored panting. He was sweating.

And nothing happened. The shapes beneath the coverlet were motionless, unfeeling.

He sank back against the pillow, eyes closed, feeling the pounding of his heart and the ache within his lungs from the exertion. He waited until the signs had abated, and then he roused himself once again, this time with his one sound hand he lifted the other arm and, holding it erect, stared at it for long moments, dreading the test.

"It's up to you, you bastard." His voice was a whisper. He took a deep breath and strained until it seemed that the obedient muscles would tear. Then, at last, he released the upheld arm. It fell to his side, bounced helplessly on the coverlet, and lay still, a dead thing. So there it was.

He turned his head slowly to look at the clock on the bedside table. Five minutes to the hour. Five minutes to wait. He closed his eyes and lay quiet until the gentle knock came at the door.

The orderly came in with the small plastic dish and a single pill. He set them on the bedside table and his eyes caught the books. "Rex Stout," he said. "His new one? Wow. Can I borrow it, huh?" He reached for it.

"Leave it alone," Ben said sharply. The extended hand withdrew. "I haven't read it myself," Ben said in a different tone. "When I'm finished . . ." He made himself smile. ". . . then okay." He watched the orderly smile and nod and turn away. "Close the door," Ben said. "I feel like a nap."

"Okay, Mr. Wilson." The door closed softly.

Ben waited for a few moments, almost expecting the door

to open again. It did not. Why should it? Who the hell cared about Ben Wilson? Bitter thought. Who the hell, when it came right down to it, cared about anybody except himself? Bolder thought, somehow satisfying. "So here we go." He said it aloud. "We're off to see the Wizard."

He opened the Rex Stout book and took out the small mirror. For a time he looked at its back without expression and then turned it to show his own reflection. "Silly bastard," he said.

He cupped the mirror in his hand and brought it down hard on the bedside table. It shattered, and three tiny spots of blood appeared on his palm. He licked them absently while he studied the shards. One was long enough and sharp enough to do the trick. He looked at the clock as he picked the shard up. He could count on three hours before someone came into the room. It would be enough. At least, he hoped so. He goddam well didn't want to botch the job the way most did when they didn't really want to die, just to make an impression.

Ben turned back the coverlet and pulled up the short hospital gown. The things they taught you in the army, he thought, as he probed in his groin with his middle finger. The leg was without sensation, but somewhere about here—yes, there it was, the big femoral artery, pulsing away at its job of carrying freshly oxygenated blood—how about that phrase so long remembered?—from lungs and heart as if it still mattered. Well, in a large sense, perhaps the largest sense, it did matter. It was release.

With the sharp point of the glass shard he began to dig into the unfeeling flesh. It was easier than he had expected. Smiling, he lay back at last and drew the coverlet up to his chest. A red stain appeared almost immediately. It spread fast.

30

From the window they could see three of the big stumpy-bowed tuna boats at the San Pedro wharves. The senator was quite familiar with them. They were expensive, efficient, self-contained vessels, radio- and radar-equipped, capable of staying at sea for weeks at a time; hunting the tuna fish, catching them, processing them aboard, and refrigerating them against the long voyage home.

Off the coast of Ecuador 3,500 miles to the south, the cold Humboldt current rose from the depths, carrying sea life in prodigious quantity to the teeming surface. Here in the richest tuna fishing area in the world, the Ecuadorian government had seen fit to extend its claim to territorial waters far beyond the twelve-mile limit the United States recognized.

The big brawny man in the leather chair, Harry Wall, said, "Oh, the little bastards are nice enough, but their gunboats mean business. I don't want anybody hurt, so standing orders to my captains are to do what they're told. When a gunboat tells them to heave to, they get in touch with me by radio. I pass the word along and eventually I guess somebody hears about it in Washington, we pay a fine, or the U.S. does, and the boat is allowed to go." He was leaning back in his chair looking at the senator. "Does that seem to you like the way to do it, Mike?"

"No," the senator said. His cold was no better, but he was the only one who noticed it. It had frequently amused him that of all the common ailments that beset mankind, two of the most miserable, the common cold and the common hang-over, rarely aroused sympathy. "It is the hell of a way to run a railroad, Harry," the senator said, "but so far nobody has come up with a solution."

"Twelve miles," Harry said. "That's what we recognize as their territorial water. Up off Alaska, that's how far out we make the Russians stay. But down there off Ecuador we fish a hundred miles offshore, Mike, a hundred and fifty, and here comes a goddam gunboat and says my captain has to follow him into port. You know what I'd like to do?"

"Yes," the senator said. "You'd like to have the navy send a cruiser down there, or an aircraft carrier, and the next gun-boat that came out to bother your tuna boats would be told to haul his ass back inside his twelve-mile limit and stay there. Or else."

Harry was smiling. "You read my mind. Now I'll read yours. You're going to tell me that isn't how it's done these days."

The senator sighed. "Exactly. And whether that is good or bad, I'm not sure I am qualified to say, Harry; it is a fact of life, to be accepted."

"And has it gotten us anyplace, this be-nice-to-everybody attitude?" Harry waved one heavy hand. "Oh, I know you're doing what you can, Mike. The OAS, our embassy protesting, people in Washington speaking harshly to their ambassador, talking about cutting aid, that kind of thing. But what I'm asking is have we really gotten anyplace?"

"Or," the senator said, smiling, "should we start tossing a few hydrogen bombs around just to show people we mean business?" He shook his head. "I would be a larger damn fool than I think myself, Harry, if I believed that I could give you an accurate assessment of the long-range profits and losses of our foreign policies of the last twenty-five years. That assessment will have to wait on the future." He paused, smiling again. "No matter how many candidates at election time claim to have the answers." He was more tired than he had realized, speaking like this in a less than decisive way. He smiled again. "I'm getting old, Harry."

"Aren't we all?"

"But I promise you," the senator said, "that State and Commerce and the White House itself will hear your side of the story. Even though they already know it, a little push isn't going to do any harm." He heaved himself out of his chair, and for a moment the room seemed to tilt.

"You okay, Mike?" Harry was on his feet, concern in his voice. One big hand grasped the senator's elbow and held it firmly.

"All right, Harry." The room was steady again. "Just dizzy for a moment."

Harry said, "Where are you staying up in L.A.?"

"I'm not." The senator had just this moment made the decision. "I'm going back to Stanhope." He smiled. "Car right outside, with driver. My plane at the airport, if the pilot is there . . ."

"I'll see that he is," Harry said. He paused. His hand had not loosened its grip. "You're sure, Mike? Maybe check into a hospital, just overnight, get some rest? You don't look very good."

"I am going to Stanhope, Harry." It was the committee hearing-room voice. "I am going home."

In the rear seat of the rented limousine the senator leaned back and closed his eyes. His thoughts, he found, insisted on springing about, settling down briefly, finding new stimulus, and jumping off in a totally different direction. Annoying.

Tuna fish. He had never particularly liked tuna fish, and he could hardly imagine a less likely source of friction between sovereign nations. Except perhaps ears, human ears; what was that fellow's name—Jenkins?—who claimed the Spanish had cut his ear off down in the West Indies back in the eighteenth century, and England declared war? Or was he thinking of Van Gogh's ear, cut off for his mistress? Why?

284

Somewhere the linkage between cause and effect was lacking, as in a bad play.

He opened his eyes to stop this thought-jumping. They were on a freeway now, traffic flowing all around them. If the automobile was the modern deity, then Southern California was its principal shrine. What were the statistics? More automobiles registered in Los Angeles County than in New York State? Ridiculous, but there it was. Jake Javits would never believe it. Fantasyland, Disneyland—the senator had heard all of Southern California referred to as Disneyland. It was not true, except in certain limited ways, but he could remember when the concept would never even have come to mind.

At the wheel, not turning his head, the uniformed driver said, "Are you all right, sir?" He was watching in the driving mirror. "I can get off this freeway, go back to Pedro . . ."

"Young man," the senator said, "we are driving to the airport."

"Yes, sir. Of course, sir."

Southern California, the senator thought, which meant principally Los Angeles, although San Diego and Long Beach were centers on their own now. But not too long ago, Los Angeles was it, period, and not much at that. The senator remembered it well, dozing in the bright sun.

Now it was a never-never land made real, and largely by the faith, courage, and downright gall of a single group of men who believed that Los Angeles could be made into a metropolis. Sartori, Chandler, O'Melveny, Phillips, Hellman, Robinson, Cass, Chaffey—these were some of the names that ran through the senator's mind. And some of their accomplishments—the downtown Biltmore Hotel, the Coliseum, the Olympic Games in 1932, the All Year Club, the push to attract people and business to Los Angeles, Los Angeles, Los Angeles . . . ballyhoo.

Personally, the senator disliked Southern California. In privacy with Conchita he had tried to analyze his dislike and found it difficult. "I do not hold with the usual criticisms," he said, "the traffic, the smog, the alleged isolationist attitude, the movie-worship, the constant fad trends, although this last comes closest to the heart of my dislike."

"The sense of impermanence?" Conchita said.

The senator smiled fondly. "Perceptive, as always. Yes. The sense of impermanence. I am not opposed to change; in this world of ours the only real constant is change. But my feeling about Los Angeles is that change exists there merely for its own sake, that there is a planned obsolescence built into everything Los Angeles does, which is not true, of course —merely a feeling I have." The senator paused, smiling. "I almost expect to fly into Los Angeles one fine day and find that the whole stage set of a city has been packed up and moved to some other unlikely semi-desert location and is again playing to standing room only."

"And yet," Conchita said, "in almost twenty-two years you have represented it as if you loved it."

The driver of the limousine said, "Were you speaking to me, sir?"

Had he been talking to himself? No matter. "No," he said, and closed his eyes. Silently now, he answered Conchita's implied question. "Buried deep in all of us," he said, "there is a sense of chauvinism that is too often overlooked or disclaimed. I admit mine. I can quite understand Lee's feeling that he was a Virginian first, and an American second. Los Angeles is part of California, and I am, and have always been, a Californian." He smiled again. "O. Henry wrote once that, 'Californians are a race of people; they are not merely inhabitants of a state.' It is true. Six months after they have moved here from Dubuque or Amarillo or Worcester, Mass. new settlers have already contracted the disease of California-itis, the feeling that they now live in a blessed land. I know no other part of this country of ours where the same is true." He paused, smiling again. "Maybe Texas, but I don't think so."

The senator's airplane steward was waiting at the airport. The senator got slowly out of the rear seat, watched the ground tilt gently, and waited for it to steady itself. He took out his notecase and handed a five-dollar tip to the limousine driver. "Thank you, young man."

The driver said, "Thank you, sir." He hesitated. "Is there anything—?" He stopped and looked helplessly at the steward.

The steward shook his head faintly. "The plane is right this way, Senator," he said.

Once they were airborne, and the senator comfortable with a pillow at his head, the steward went forward into the flight compartment. To the pilot, he said, "You'd better call the Stanhope tower and have them phone the ranch. The senator's ill. He's talking to himself."

"What's he saying?"

"All I caught was one phrase," the steward said. " 'Going home.' "

* * *

The blackened piece of flat metal lay on Walling's desk, beside it a shiny new Yale key. He looked at them both, and then at Henry, the lab man. "You're sure these are the same?"

The lab man was on safe, sound ground here. He nodded decisively. "Same technique we use to bring out the serial number of a firearm when it's been filed off. The number's forged, it's in the grain of the metal. Acid will bring it up."

Walling nodded. He dropped both the distorted key and the new one into an envelope, tucked it away in his pocket as he stood up. "One thing, Henry," he said. "No word about this to anybody." He was thinking of Howard Lang. "That clear?" Rhetorical question. He walked out.

He drove straight to the house where Ruben Lucero lived. Julio, bat in hand, glared at him but made no move to stop him. Walling went up the few steps and knocked on the door. There was a barrel lock above the doorknob, he noticed, but it showed no trade name.

Paul Meyer opened the door and stepped back. Lucero, seated, stood up slowly. He made a small bow. His eyes were wary. He said nothing.

"Just a couple of questions," Walling said. "Do you own a flight bag? One of those bags, so big, the airlines sell or give away?"

Lucero looked puzzled. "Airlines, *señor*? But what have I to do with airlines?" He spread his hands. "When I travel . . ." He smiled suddenly; his teeth were very white. "I walk, I ride in pickup truck, sometimes I ride bus." He shook

287

his head, smiling still. "Airplane? No. I have never been in airplane."

Paul said, "What about a flight bag? I have—I used to have a couple. I don't have one now."

"What happened to them?"

Paul shrugged. "Ask at my father's house. They're probably still there. So?"

It rang true, Walling thought. As he had guessed from the start, this was an unlikely place to have produced a flight bag. He took out the envelope and shook the shiny new key into the palm of his hand. "You won't mind," he said, "if I try this in your lock?"

"Whatever you wish," Lucero said.

Walling bent to look at the lock. The trademark was plain —Schlage. He straightened and dropped the key back into the envelope. "New lock?" he said. "They're expensive."

Lucero smiled sadly. "It is Paul who had it put in the door. Almost a year ago."

"What was there," Paul said, "was an old-fashioned lock, the kind you could pick with a bent wire. We wanted a little security." He looked straight at Walling. "Is there something sinister about that?"

A chip on his shoulder, Walling thought, nor was he sure he could blame him. "Nothing sinister," he said. "Sorry to have bothered you." He felt Julio's eyes following him all the way out to his car.

His next stop was Pete Stanfield's house. Benjie answered the door, and what was in her face as she looked at Walling could have been fear, but there was no way of telling. Behind her Pete's voice said, "Come in, Chief. I've been expecting you."

Walling walked in slowly. "And why would that be?" he said.

"Now, Chief." Pete was smiling. "Anything happens, you think of me, right? You, and a lot of others? The parent. The Lang cat. Even Ruben Lucero who-walks-on-water."

Benjie drew a deep breath but she said nothing.

"A beer, Chief?" Pete said.

Walling shook his head. He kept his voice carefully uninflected. "You have one of those flight bags from an airline?"

288

Benjie drew another deep breath, and again was silent.

Pete said, "I did have. But Benjie baby . . ." He looked at the girl. "Tell him."

A third deep breath, but the girl's voice was steady enough. "I lost it. I took it to market and, you know, set it down while I looked at some fruit and things, and, you know, I guess somebody walked off with it." She spread her hands.

Maybe, Walling thought, maybe not; who was to tell? He got out the envelope, and from it took the shiny new Yale key. "Mind if I try this in your lock?"

Pete's smile was weary now. "Help yourself."

The key did not fit; it would not even slide into the lock. So that, Walling thought, was that. He dropped the key back into the envelope. He was a patient man, and he never expected success to come easily. "Sorry to bother you."

Pete waved his hand in a careless gesture of dismissal. But it was at Benjie that Walling looked long and carefully. She was uptight, that was plain. Why? "Anything wrong?" Walling said to the girl.

She shook her head, maybe a little too vigorously.

"How old are you, Benjie?"

Pete said, "Oh, come on!"

Benjie said, "I'm twenty-one." Her eyes were steady.

"ID card?"

"Sorry," Benjie said. "I don't carry one. On principle."

Pete said, "You could look at her teeth. That's how they tell horses' ages."

"Benjie isn't a very common name for a girl," Walling said. "I can have newspaper personal ads checked in the likely places—Monterey, Laguna, San Francisco, Santa Barbara." He paused. "Do you want me to do that, Benjie? Maybe your folks have been trying to locate you?"

"Why don't you spend your time," Pete said suddenly, angrily, "taking care of the things that matter? Killings, robberies, burglaries, drunk drivings, that kind of thing, instead of busting people for smoking pot, or making sure that everybody carries a *carte d'identité*?" There was disgust in his voice. "Don't bother to explain. I know the answer. The fuzz work for the Establishment, and the Establishment always gets its priorities ass-backward."

He was working himself up to a pitch, Walling thought. Intentionally? A distraction? Walling said nothing.

"There are how many people in this town," Pete said, "who need help? Who need food? Medical attention? Better housing? But instead the town pays you a good salary to spend your time threatening people like Benjie. Does that make sense?"

Walling said, unperturbed, "Do your folks know where you are, Benjie?"

Benjie was silent, defiant.

"I have a daughter," Walling said. "She's seventeen. If she took off, I think her mother and I would . . ." He shook his head. "I don't know what we'd do."

"If she takes off," Pete said, "it will be your own damn fault."

Walling looked at him for a long time in silence. He said at last, "Maybe. But that wouldn't make us feel any better." He walked out and closed the door softly behind him.

Benjie stood quite still, staring at the closed door. Then, without turning her head, "Did you change the lock, Pete?" The question hung, unanswered. Benjie turned to face him. "Did you? Because if you did . . ."

"If I did, Benjie baby," Pete said, "it's my business."

"I lied about the flight bag," Benjie said. "There are lots of flight bags, and maybe it didn't mean anything. But the key . . ."

"Like I said, my business."

The room was still. "Pete," Benjie said, "please. Let's go away. Right now. Let's just walk out and get on a bus and go as far as we can and then start hitching. Please."

Pete shook his head. He walked to the refrigerator, took out a beer, opened it, and drank deep. He wiped the foam from his lips. "I told you. Just a few days."

Benjie closed her eyes. She opened them again almost fearfully. "What are you going to do, Pete?"

He was smiling. "Chicks," he said, "ought to be seen, not heard. Oh, yes, and felt. They're good for that, too."

31

The Stanhope County district attorney said, "This is in no sense an official investigation, Mrs. Wilson, but when a violent death occurs, it is my obligation to look into the facts concerning it." They were sitting in the hospital administrator's office. Beneath the window the air conditioner hummed softly. The world seemed shut out. "Your husband had only one visitor today. It was you."

It was all unreal. Clara could close her eyes and see Ben smiling at her from the pillow as he tore her apart bit by bit, a sadistic small boy tearing the wings from a butterfly. And now they said he was dead. "A violent death?" The phrase had reached her at last. "I don't understand."

"Don't you, Mrs. Wilson? But I think you do. He, Ben . . ." The district attorney stopped there, and for the first time Clara remembered that he and Ben once were close friends, golfing buddies, poker-playing buddies. Were? Had been.

There was a commotion in the outer office. And then the door flew open and George walked in. "Hello, Clara."

He looked at the district attorney. "Star Chamber proceedings, Will?" His voice was cold.

"A private conversation," the district attorney said.

"Not any longer." George sat down on the sofa beside Clara. "Officially," he said to the district attorney, "Mrs. Wilson is entitled to legal counsel. I am here to supply it." He paused. "If unofficially you think you can eject me, Will, you're welcome to try."

The district attorney walked to the door and closed it firmly. He went back to lean against the desk. "You didn't like Ben either," he said.

George nodded. "That is correct. I thought he was a louse. His death doesn't change my opinion."

"And what do you know about his death?"

"Only," George said, "that it is on the local radio that he died quite suddenly here at the hospital. I have no idea how, or why."

"He bled to death from a stab wound."

Clara drew in her breath with a hissing sound.

"You're a very tactful fellow," George said. He covered both of Clara's hands with one of his own and squeezed gently. "Are you charging Mrs. Wilson with homicide?"

"I am conducting," the district attorney said, "or I was conducting, an informal investigation."

"Then get on with it," George said.

The air conditioner hummed on. The district attorney walked to the window and stood for a few moments facing the outer darkness, his back to the room. Then he returned to the desk. His face showed nothing. "You were Ben's only caller today," he said to Clara. "That has been verified by the floor nurse. What was the purpose of your call?"

"He was my husband. Isn't that enough reason?"

"Considering how you felt about each other, no."

"Your opinion, Will," George said. "It carries no weight."

Clara said, "I brought him some books to read. Mysteries. He likes them. Liked them." The sense of unreality was strong.

"What else did you bring him?"

Clara shook her head. "Nothing."

292

"Think again."

"The lady has answered your question," George said.

"Falsely," the district attorney said. He was looking straight at Clara. "Pieces of a purse mirror were found on the table beside his bed. Now where do you suppose he got the mirror?"

Clara took a deep unsteady breath. "I gave it to him. He asked me for it as I was leaving. I—forgot all about it."

George's hands squeezed hers. George said gently, "Did he say why he wanted it?"

Clara said slowly, "He said he wanted to admire his shiny white teeth. It was the—kind of thing he used to say."

George was watching the district attorney. "It was a piece of the mirror that killed him? How?"

"The big artery in his groin," the district attorney said. "He could have done it himself. His legs were anesthetized, the doctor tells me." He paused. "Or he could have had help."

"Oh, God," Clara said.

"He left no note," the district attorney said. "Suicides usually do." He paused. "But if he had help, there wouldn't have been much point to a note, would there? He could say whatever he had to say."

Clara's voice was scarcely audible. "He had already said it."

"That's enough," George said, and his hand squeezed hers sharply. "Let's get a little order into this," he told the district attorney. "The floor nurse saw Mrs. Wilson go to his room? Did she see her leave?"

"Nobody saw her leave. The orderly went into the room with medicine, but whether Mrs. Wilson had already come and gone, or not yet arrived, nobody can say."

George remembered the orderly coming in with the pill in the plastic container during his own visit. "Ben was all right when the orderly went in?"

"As usual. Three hours later he was dead."

"Let's get the orderly down here," George said. He watched the district attorney hesitate, nod shortly, and turn away to leave the office.

Clara said, "Oh, God, George! I didn't know! I didn't

think!" She shook her head remembering. "He—stripped me bare, George, and threw filth at me. He said that you and I . . ." She stopped.

"Easy," George said.

"I didn't even think when he asked me for the mirror. All I wanted to do was go."

"Did he say anything when you left?"

Clara nodded. She was holding her lower lip between her teeth. She took a deep breath. "I said, 'Goodbye, Ben.' And he said, 'Smashing exit line.' That was all. Can you—?"

"I can hear him saying it," George said. "All right. Let's see what the orderly has to say."

The orderly was uncomfortable in the presence of the district attorney. He spoke too fast. "I went in with his pill. He was okay, as okay as ever. He was kind of touchy, but they all are sometimes."

George said, "Did you see Mrs. Wilson?"

"I sure didn't. Maybe she came in later."

"Or maybe she had already left," George said.

"I sure don't know," the orderly said.

George was silent, thoughtful. They all watched him. He said at last, remembering how it had been, "You brought his pill in that little plastic cup and set it down on the table?"

The orderly nodded.

"You do it," George said, "every so many hours, is that right?"

"Every three hours."

"Was he asleep?" George said. "Did you wake him up, disturb him?"

"He was awake, just lying there."

The district attorney said, "I fail to see . . ."

"This isn't a courtroom," George said. "I'll take some leeway in my questions." He paused. Then, again to the orderly, "Were you supposed to do anything else than bring the pill? Bathe him? Straighten his bed? Disturb him in any way?"

"I told you. Just the pill on the table like every three hours. That was how I found him, when I went in with another pill the next time."

"Slow down," George said. "I'm interested only in the

last time you saw him alive. You said he was touchy. About what? Did you do anything different?"

"All I did," the orderly said, "was pick up the book, and he like to took my head off."

The district attorney opened his mouth and closed it again in silence.

George said gently, "Book. What book was that?"

"The new Rex Stout he had with two others there on the table. I asked him if I could borrow it. I like Rex Stout." He paused. "That's all, but he got on me for it."

There was only the sound of the air conditioner. George looked at Clara. "What mysteries did you bring?"

"The Rex Stout," Clara said tonelessly, "a Ross Mac-Donald and the new Hillary Waugh."

So there it was. George looked at the district attorney and saw that he too understood, but just for the record he spelled it out anyway. "The books were there when the orderly went in. That means Mrs. Wilson had already been there and left them. There is no other explanation. And Ben was all right, touchy, but all right. What happened had to be later, and Mrs. Wilson was long gone. Satisfied?" He waited for no answer. "Let's go, Clara." He felt no sense of triumph, only what Clara herself had implied—a sense of uncleanliness.

He had taken the first ranch vehicle that was handy, a pickup. It stood by itself in the parking lot. He said to Clara, "You drove your own car?"

"They sent a police car for me." Her voice was dull, lifeless.

"They would," George said, and held the door of the pickup for her. He got in too, but did not start the engine. The cab smelled of hay. No matter. It was a cleaner smell than the stench that was in his mind. He could not have said exactly what words had been spoken between them in Ben's hospital room, but he had known Ben, and he saw the effect of the words on Clara, and he could guess how the scene had gone. Only how many hours ago he and Clara had been up in the clean, fresh fragrance of the big trees? Now this.

Clara said, "Do you think he meant it to look—the way they saw it? As if I had had something to do with it?"

Yes, George thought, I do. "I can't say, Clara."

"Did he hate me that much?" Then, slowly, "Yes, I think he did. He didn't need to leave a note. He had said everything that could be said. More. He——"

"Listen to me, Clara." George's voice was commanding. He gripped the wheel hard with both hands and fought to keep the anger down. "Ben was under drugs and in pain. He probably knew, not guessed, knew he would never get out of bed again, that he would just lie there and wither away, and he couldn't face it. I don't think I could, either. He was bitter because it had happened to him. He took it out on you . . ."

Clara's hand was gentle on his arm. Clara's voice now was quiet, controlled. "A fine try, George. Thank you. But, you see, some of the things he said were true, and those are the ones that hurt and will keep on hurting. I told you I made a mess of it, didn't I? Well, I did for sure." She paused. "Take me home now, George, please. Unless you have an engagement of some kind?"

Automatically he looked at his watch. Five minutes of ten. Ellen and Paul at the gate—he had the feeling that that decision had been made for him. "No engagement," he said, and started the truck engine.

"I'd like it," Clara said, "if you would stay a little while with me. Just talk, George. I'm being selfish. I don't want to be alone."

"As long as you want."

* * *

It was Julia who took the telephone call about the senator from the Stanhope Airport tower. She listened without expression, jotted down the ETA, and said quietly, "Thank you. We will cope." She hung up and sat back to consider the situation.

George was gone. In an emergency, she thought, George was the one who came to mind first, the solid man always willing to accept responsibility. But something on the radio news had sent him hurrying out of the house. So, in his absence, you accepted responsibility yourself, simple as that. As we have not often accepted responsibility, she thought, Mike and I, our generation—copped out, as they would say it today. We left it to father and Mamacita, and then to George, and even Ellen, the solid ones, while we attracted attention and sometimes took the bows, on stage. As she reached for the Stanhope telephone book she wondered if she ought to feel regret that she at least had played no vital role. She felt no regret.

Kaye Starling was at home. "Kaye, luv," Julia said, "Mike is flying in from Los Angeles, and the steward says he is ill, quite ill." A thought struck her. "Do you know about this, Kaye?"

"What do you want me to do, Julia?" Merely that.

Give him marks for keeping anything he might know to himself. "A doctor," Julia said, "and, I think, an ambulance." And then, with deep certainty, "He'll want to come here, not the hospital, whatever is wrong."

There was protest. "Julia . . ."

"I am telling you, Kaye, I am not asking or suggesting. He will want to come here. In the end, if it is the end, we all do." There was silence on the phone. "Do you hear me?" Julia said.

"The castle on the hill," Kaye said, "the seat of power . . ."

"Wrong, Kaye." Julia paused. "The word is home." She hung up.

Conchita, of course, would have to be told. And Ellen? Yes, Ellen too—Ellen was mistress of the house. Julia walked out of the study and down to the small library where Conchita sat with her needlework (another petit-point for Brooks Brothers to make into a waistcoat for Mike? He loved their flamboyance). On the record player at low volume Heifitz played the Bruch concerto.

Julia said, "Mike is flying in, Chita." She watched the sudden smile appear. "He's ill." The smile froze. "We don't know if it's serious or not, but I've called Kaye Starling to have a doctor and an ambulance meet the plane."

Conchita poked her needle carefully into the fabric, bundled the work, and tucked it into her bag. Her movements were careful, controlled. She said at last, "You will bring him here, of course." It was a statement, no question.

"I have told Kaye."

Conchita stood up. "Will you drive me to the airport?"

"No. Please." Ellen was standing in the doorway. She looked at both women. "Let me. I'll tell Consuelo. I won't be a minute." She was gone. The tall clock in the front hall showed three minutes of ten as she went through to give instructions to Consuelo and out to the garage to take a car. Pepe, of course, could drive, but this was a family matter.

She picked Conchita and Julia up at the front steps. Both women got in back. Ellen drove out the long curving drive, touched the switch beneath the dash, and watched the great gates open. She drove through and stopped. Paul's pickup was there, and when he saw Ellen he jumped out and trotted over.

"We're going to the airport," Ellen said. "The senator's coming in. He's ill." She had not realized how uptight she was. "I'm sorry . . ."

"Move over," Paul said, and opened the door. He slid in beneath the wheel. They pulled smoothly away as the gates closed. "You go," Paul said, "I go." He patted her knee gently. "Simple as that."

* * *

The runway lights were on, and they could watch the sleek jet slide down its path to touchdown, lose speed, and then, turning, taxi to the visiting aircraft area where the ambulance waited. The fuselage door opened, and the steps came down immediately. The doctor trotted up them and disappeared.

Julia stood beside Conchita. "Give him a moment," Julia said.

Conchita merely nodded.

It was little more than a moment. The steward appeared in the fuselage doorway and beckoned, and the ambulance men came forward with their stretcher, then they too disappeared inside.

Conchita and Julia moved to the foot of the steps. Paul stood off with Ellen, his hand in hers. "It doesn't look very good, kid," Paul said.

"I know." Strangely, Ellen was thinking of Frank Stanfield after the fight, standing erect, tall, strong, triumphant—when the block pulled loose and the released cable flew across the clearing.

Standing now, watching the scene beneath the lights, the two women, the sleek silent jet, now the stretcher beginning to emerge from the fuselage doorway, she remembered what Marquesa had said about Frank, that he always seemed to bring the strength of the great redwoods with him when he came to Stanhope. Well, they all did—Daddy, Mike, yes, even Scott with that curious, usually hidden spirit of combat that was in him. And watching something so strong now fallen, as the figure on the stretcher was, brought her close to tears. She gripped Paul's hand for comfort.

The senator on the stretcher was an old man. In a matter of hours his cheeks had sunk and the flesh around his chin had turned flabby, his eyes seemed to have receded into his skull, his breathing was labored. He looked up at Conchita and tried to smile, but the result was mere grimace. She bent to kiss his cheek and then, her hand on his shoulder, walked beside the stretcher to the ambulance.

The doctor said, "The hospital . . ."

"No." This was Conchita and Julia together. Julia added, "The ranch."

The doctor was young, sure of himself. "Madam," he said, "I cannot allow sentiment to get in the way. At the hospital he will have care that cannot be provided at home."

The senator stirred feebly and raised one hand in protest.

Ellen said softly, "Oh, Paul!"

"It's okay, kid." He dropped her hand and walked forward. "Doctor." His voice was clear and commanding. "The patient wants to go home. The family wants him home." He paused. "Home is where he is going." He looked at the ambulance attendants. "Get moving." He looked then at Conchita. "You want to ride with him?" He nodded. He spoke again to the doctor. "Are you coming?"

The doctor hesitated. The stretcher was already in the ambulance. "Under the circumstances," he said, "I seem to have no choice."

Paul driving Julia and Ellen led the way, opened the gates

299

with the dashboard switch, swirled on up the long curving drive. Ellen opened her door, jumped out. "Don't go," she said. "Please."

And Julia, smiling faintly, said, "I think the least we owe you is a drink. Come in, young Paul." She smiled again. "You're a different breed of cat from your father. Interesting."

* * *

In the sitting room of the senator's suite the doctor spoke on the telephone to Dr. William Hall in San Francisco. "I think pneumonia, Doctor, but it seems to have come on so quickly from merely a mild head cold . . ." He was silent, listening. He said slowly at last, "I see. Thank you, Doctor." And then, "Of course. I will call her." Expressionless, he walked into the bedroom.

Conchita came out to the phone. Bill Hall said, "I've told your Dr. Ross all I can, Conchita, and I am sure he will do what is necessary. But if you want me to come down now, tonight . . ." He left the sentence unfinished.

"Would it help, Bill?" Her voice was calm. "Will anything help?" She paused. "Don't answer that. I think I know. I think I have known, and pretended that I didn't, for some time. I am going to miss him, Bill."

"When he goes, we all will, Conchita. But don't give up yet."

Conchita hung up. The medical ritual, she thought— never admit that death is at hand. She walked to the wall telephone that rang down in the servants' quarters. To Consuelo she said in Spanish, "Send Señorita Ellen to me, please."

She sat down to wait. There was nothing she could do. Nurse Walters was helping the doctor with oxygen, injections, all of the ministrations that in the end would do no good. Yet the attempt had to be made—convention demanded it. But did humanity?

She looked up as Ellen came into the room, so young, so fresh, unspoiled, not yet touched by life's realities. Conchita was unaware that she spoke in Spanish. "Find your father, child, and telephone your Uncle Scott in Berkeley."

Was there anyone else who should know? Conchita thought not. Mike's death would be important news; there would be eulogies in the Senate, statements to the press, messages of condolence flowing in from members of Congress, Cabinet officers, the President, from names she would not even know whose lives Mike's influence had touched. But Mike's dying was a family affair; outsiders could share only his memory.

She smiled at Ellen. This time she spoke in English. "And thank Paul for me, dear." She had no tears. They would come later.

32

They were there again, the chicanos in their black berets and even at night, their dark glasses. And Julio was with them, from time to time eyeing Benjie, undressing her, making her crawl inside.

The talk was in Spanish, and although Benjie knew nothing of the language, the one word that recurred, *agua*, had meaning for anyone who lived in the west. *Agua* meant water —as in *agua caliente*, hot water, *agua fría*, cold water. *Agua*, water, and what in the world could that mean to these weirdos? Sitting quietly in a corner of the room Benjie tried to concentrate on this question and ignore Julio. It was not wholly possible, but even a little success helped.

They left at last, Julio, as before following all the others after a final careful look that stripped Benjie naked.

"*Hasta jueves*," Pete said, smiling, and closed the door. "Baby, how about a joint—or six or seven?"

They sat on the floor, cross-legged, companionably close, passing the hand-rolled cigarette back and forth. Pete's smile never faded. "You're flying," Benjie said. "Tell me why." And then, "Why were you talking so much about water?"

Pete's smile held, but its quality had suddenly changed. "Were we?"

"That's the only word I know in Spanish," Benjie said, "except maybe *adios* means goodbye." She accepted the cigarette, inhaled deeply, held the breath; her exhalation was almost clear. "What about water, Pete?"

"Water, baby, is a thing." He was smiling, and his tone was light, teasing. At times like this Benjie never knew whether to take him seriously or not. "Oceans of water," Pete said. "Lakes of water. Rivers of water. It's, you know, important. Important to have, to steal, to sell."

"Steal water, Pete? I don't understand." She had another long drag from the cigarette. She was, she thought, beginning to float. It was a lovely feeling.

"Lots of ways to do it," Pete said. "Dam a stream, divert it, suck it dry. Or buy up riverfront land, miles of it, and claim what they call riparian rights. Drill wells deeper than your neighbor's, and if you pump enough to lower the water table, his wells go dry." He paused for a long drag. Then, smiling, "We've gone the route, baby, we've done it all, put it all together. We've robbed this Valley blind. Oh, when we've taken all the water we could use, then we've let the other poor bastards have some too, but always, always we came first."

Benjie said dreamily, "In the city we didn't think much about water."

"Wrong, baby, dead wrong. If there's one place that's uptight about water, still, after all this time, maybe not everybody, but the ones who think about it, it's the city, San Francisco. You don't know your history, baby. Why do you think there're all those reservoirs scattered around? It's because of 1906."

Benjie was smiling happily. "That was the earthquake."

"Right. But it was the fire that did the damage. The water mains were broken by the quake and the only way they could stop the fire was by dynamite, because they had no water." Pete carefully crushed out the cigarette end. He lit another and inhaled deeply. "I'd like to have seen it. Blam! Blam! Buildings going up, falling down. Old Rudi Meyer was there.

He was seventy-seven, and he was up in the city on business with a fellow named Giannini, money business, what else? He had enough, more than enough, but he was after more, throwing in with Giannini's Bank of Italy, and did that ever pay off!" He stopped. "What was I talking about?"

Benjie took the cigarette. She giggled. "I don't know. Does it matter?"

Pete waved one hand in a broad gesture of dismissal. "You said I was flying. Didn't you say that? Well, baby, you are right. Flying is the word."

"I'm flying too, Pete."

* * *

Ellen walked down the stairs to the study. Paul was there. He stood up. "I'd better be on my way."

"No. Please." She walked straight to him and buried her face against his shoulder. She felt his arms close around her, strong arms, protective. But Frank Stanfield had been strong, too, and Mike. Would even Daddy's strength disappear one day? Would Paul's? Ridiculous questions, because the answer to each had to be yes, and she had known it all along, hadn't she? But never before this moment had she felt it—there was the difference.

Marquesa was going, she had accepted that. Now Mike, to whose voice everyone had always listened, to whose wishes and beliefs even presidents had attended carefully, to whom, when summoned, a governor would drop whatever he was doing to come running. Finished now. The world would never again be quite the same. As it had never again been quite the same, or even vaguely the same, for Lotte and Rudi Meyer, fifteen and seventeen, orphaned that winter in Donner Pass; for Ezra Stanfield, twenty-two, stepping aboard that sailing vessel in Boston to see California for himself.

"You okay?" Paul's voice was soft, gentle. He kissed the top of her head.

Ellen leaned back to look up. She nodded and managed a smile. "Okay," she said. "But don't go. Please." If the world was changed, then you went to meet its new conditions— wasn't that what Marquesa had sometimes seemed to say? "Try not to regret, child, what might have been," she had said. Wasn't that the same as saying, "Live your life in such a way that you won't ever have to look back and regret what might have been?" To Paul now she said, "I have to make some telephone calls. Then I want you to do something with me. Okay?"

"Whatever you say," Paul said.

Ellen went to the big desk and sat down. Scott first, she thought, because he had to come from Berkeley. She dialed his number and waited while it rang and rang. Be there, she thought, *please* be there. She was just about to hang up when Scott's voice, not very friendly, said, "Yes?"

Ellen wondered what he might have been doing, and decided that probably she could guess. "This is Ellen," she said. "Conchita asked me to call you. Mike is ill, very ill. Conchita wants you to come."

"He was fine yesterday," Scott said. "What's the trouble?"

Ellen took a deep breath. "Nobody has said it aloud," she said, "but he is going to die."

There was silence. Then, "Youngster . . ."

"I'm not a youngster any more," Ellen said with sudden decision. "And I am telling you that your father is dying and your mother wants you to come home. I can't make it any plainer than that." Everything was changed. So be it.

There was more silence. "I'm on my way," Scott said. "Thank you for calling, youngs——" He stopped. "What shall I call you after all this time?" All at once there was a smile in his voice. "Thank you, Ellen," he said, and hung up.

Now Daddy, Ellen thought, and wondered where to begin. He hadn't said where he was going in such a hurry. She looked at Paul. "I don't know where Daddy is."

"I can guess. It's been on the radio. Ben Wilson died."

More death. Ellen closed her eyes. And maybe a new beginning for Daddy? Hopeful thought. Then death was not always an end? She had never tried to sort things like this out before. Maybe that was what being a child meant—you took things for granted and assumed they would never change. And then all at once a curtain was lifted and you saw the impermanence, and accepted it.

She found Clara Wilson's number in the phonebook.

There was a penciled check mark beside it, and she smiled at that as she dialed the number. Clara's voice was quiet, subdued. "Hello?"

"This is Ellen Stanfield, Mrs. Wilson, and I'm sorry to bother you, but is Daddy there? It is important."

George's voice came on immediately. "Yes?"

Ellen told him straight out, and this time there was no hesitation, as she had known there would not be. Not with Daddy. "I'll be right there," he said, and hung up.

Paul was watching. Ellen put the phone gently in its cradle. "That's all the telephoning," she said, suddenly shy.

"And what is it you wanted me to do with you?"

"Don't laugh. Please."

"I'm not even close to laughing."

Ellen pushed back the desk chair and stood up. "I want you to come with me."

"Where?" And then quickly, "Never mind. Wherever you say."

She was standing a little distance from him, looking up into his face. She said, "It is real, isn't it? You and me?"

"What do you think?" He was smiling. Slowly the smile faded. "That isn't good enough, is it? All right. It is real. We both know it." He spread his hands helplessly. "I don't know how to make it plainer than that. You're the one I want. Now. For all time. Just you." He was silent.

She took her time, savoring the moment. She guessed she was smiling, or maybe glowing was the word. "That's good enough," she said. She took his hand. "Come with me."

Up the stairs, down the long hall. "Wait here," Ellen said. She knocked gently on the door, opened it, and stepped inside. A lamp burned on the bedside table, and she could see the old lady's eyes open. "Marquesa?"

"Come in, child."

"I have someone with me, Marquesa. May I bring him in too?"

"Paul, of course," the old lady said. She was smiling. "Bring him in, child."

They stood together beside the bed, hand in hand, awaiting judgment, while the old lady studied their faces. "She is very young, Paul."

306

"Does that matter, Aunt Ellen?"

"Ask her."

"No," Ellen said. "It doesn't matter, Marquesa. You told me so yourself."

"Only if you know it, child."

"I know it." Her voice was steady and strong.

The old lady took her time. Her eyes studied Ellen's face again. At last she nodded. "I think you do." She looked then at Paul. "You will be good to her."

"A promise."

"And you, child, will be good to him. Women forget that sometimes."

"I won't forget, Marquesa. That is a promise, too."

The old lady brought her hands together. They rested quietly on the coverlet for a few moments. Then slowly she drew the great diamond from her finger and held it out to Paul.

Ellen said, "Marquesa."

"Take it," the old lady said to Paul. "Give it to her. Remember your promises."

Paul took the ring slowly. He shook his head. He looked at Ellen.

Slowly she raised her left hand. He took the hand and slipped the ring on her finger. Ellen looked down at the old lady. "Marquesa . . ."

"I am tired," the old lady said. She was smiling. "Kiss me, child."

Ellen bent to her cheek. "Marquesa . . ." she said again.

"Bless you," the old lady said. She closed her eyes.

In the hall Ellen closed the door softly. She stood for a little time, unmoving. Slowly she raised her left hand, looked at the diamond, and then looked up at Paul.

"It isn't from me," Paul said. "I couldn't afford it. Probably not ever."

Ellen was smiling now and shaking her head gently. "Wrong," she said. "It is from you. Marquesa gave it to you, and you gave it to me. Unless . . ." Her smile was suddenly sparkling ". . . you want to take it back?"

"No way." He put his arm around her. It was hard not to skip as they walked to the stairs and started down. "It's going to look pretty funny," Paul said, "when you're on your hands and knees trying to keep our dirt floor polished."

"I'll manage."

And she would, too, Paul thought. But damn it, her father had seen it right—he, Paul, had no business even thinking of taking her out of this house, this luxury, into what he could offer. He had gone to help Lucero with his eyes open. That was one thing. But it was something entirely different to drag Ellen into squalor as well.

The front door opened as they reached the bottom step. George walked in. He looked at them both and then slowly, automatically, closed the door.

Ellen said, "Daddy, Paul . . ."

Julia walked out of the small library. She said, "Paul was good enough to drive us to meet Mike's plane, George. He was also forceful enough to have Mike brought here where he wanted to be and where Conchita wanted him, rather than to the hospital where the doctor wanted him taken."

George's face was expressionless. "Thank you, Paul," he said.

Ellen said, "There is something else, Daddy." She was standing straight, proud. She held out her left hand. The great diamond glittered. "I took Paul to see Marquesa," Ellen said. "She . . ." She stopped and gathered herself. Tears were close, and she could not have said why. "Marquesa said I was very young."

"You are," George said.

"Paul," Ellen said, "asked Marquesa if that mattered, and she said to ask me. It doesn't matter, Daddy. I'm me, and what I feel now isn't going to change."

Julia said, "And Mamacita agreed?"

Ellen nodded. "She made Paul promise to be good to me, and she made me promise to be good to him. It is something, she said, that women sometimes forget."

"Amen," Julia said. "Mamacita does not pull her punches."

George was looking at the diamond. "And she gave you that ring?"

Paul said, "She gave it to me, sir. She told me to give it to Ellen. I did."

There was silence. George said slowly, "We'll talk about this later." He started for the stairs.

Julia's voice stopped him. "You don't usually walk around a decision, George."

"This time," George said, "I am." He went up the stairs two at a time.

San Francisco, 1906

It was a land of riches, and a land of poverty, a land of myths and shattered dreams. For some, California was merely an adventure, for others a gamble, for many a land to visit, to exploit if possible, and then to abandon. But to the hardy few who remained, and built, it was the Promised Land, and their devotion to it never wavered.

Scott Stanfield: *A History of California.*

The telegram sent April 17 merely said that Rudi Meyer was delayed in the city for a few days. The letter that followed, also written April 17, reached Walter Meyer at the bank in Stanhope the morning of April 19.

My dear son: I have today spoken at length with young Amadeo Giannini and informed him of our intent to purchase 100 shares of the new stock offering in the Bank of Italy at par value of $105. This purchase will increase our stock holdings and those of your uncle Ezra in the Bank of Italy to 300 shares.

Young Amadeo is a man of charm and of vision, and your uncle Ezra and I are agreed that he should go far. His visions are bold, but I remind myself that it is a young man's world, and that ours is still a young, growing land, and where else might bold visions be better served?

And yet we do have our sometimes slavish devotion to the past. For example, when the price of whiskey in the Palace Hotel bar was reduced from 25¢ to 15¢ there was outcry. Men accustomed from San Francisco's earliest days to viewing a two-bit piece as the smallest coin to be counted were insulted when a dime was pushed across the bar in change. Let us never cling that hard to tradition.

As I said in my wire, I will be delayed a few days. It is a distressing matter, and I can only hope that I can bring it to a somewhat satisfactory conclusion; I know your uncle Ezra would wish me to try.

I heard only by chance today that his old friend Dewey Lane has been in hospital. There was what I believe is called an embolism, and it was necessary to amputate one leg. Dewey is, and has always been, a proud man, and in recent years, I think I may say, something of an anachronism as well. I know that your uncle Ezra has offered loans, employment, permanent residence in Stanhope; Dewey has refused them all.

Old friends are rare, and to be treasured. I shall see Dewey tomorrow, and I shall try to persuade him to come with me back to Stanhope at least for a period of convalescence. If he agrees, and is fit to travel, it is possible that we shall arrive before this letter. But if Dewey must on doctor's orders wait a few days, then I shall remain here, staying at the Palace, until he is able to be moved.

On the lighter note, the Metropolitan Opera Company of New York is in town, and the Italian tenor Caruso has taken a suite here at the Palace. I find him quite pleased with himself, but it is said that he sings well.

Until later, then,

Your father,

Rudi Meyer.

Rudi dined well on the Palace Hotel's superb cuisine that Tuesday evening, considered attending the Metropolitan Opera's performance of *Carmen*, Caruso singing the lead, or Victor Herbert's *Babes in Toyland* playing at the Columbia Theatre on Powell Street, or Richard Harding Davis's *The Dictator*, with young John Barrymore. He decided against them all in favor of a full night's sleep.

He was seventy-six years old, still in good if not robust health, after sixty years thoroughly attuned and devoted to this adopted land. Oh, a faint trace of the German accent remained, but almost no memories of the old life in the old country; it was as if the winter in the Donner Pass had been a turning beyond which there was no looking back. His past began on this side of the Sierra Nevada; he and California had

310

grown up together. Rudi slept well that night in what Californians boasted was the finest hotel in the world.

He awakened just after dawn to the insane ringing of church bells and a sense of being at sea in a violent storm. A deep rumbling rose from the street as he half clambered and half fell from his bed. There was enough light to see his watch on the bedside table, and he caught it as it was about to slide off to the floor. It read: 5:13.

In the hotel corridors he could hear voices, some lifted in screams. He began to dress himself as quickly as he could.

* * *

Within minutes crowds had gathered in the streets. Some people were dressed, some still in night clothes. They had experienced earthquakes before, but none like this. They stood quiet, stunned.

The original tremor had lasted, building in intensity, for only forty seconds. It was followed by a ten-second pause, as if the earth gathered itself for another, more violent effort. The second tremor, of increased force, lasted twenty-five seconds.

In less than a minute and a half, the huge $6 million city hall at Larkin and McAllister near Market lay in ruins. South of Market four hotels, the Valencia, Brunswick, Denver and Cosmopolitan, had collapsed, and no one knew how many were already dead or trapped in the wreckage. Throughout the city frame houses built on fill tumbled into debris. In the wholesale district north of Market Street brick buildings collapsed, and their wreckage filled the streets. Virtually every chimney in the city was down, and fifty fires—a hundred, two hundred, no one knew—blossomed as walls and exposed structure began to burn.

What the city had yet to learn was that the quake had ruptured the water mains, and for the next three days fires would have to be fought with whatever was at hand—water from cisterns or the Bay, shovels, dynamite.

* * *

The Palace Hotel seemed safe enough as Rudi came out on Market Street, but in the area south of Market smoke was

311

already climbing into the sky, and a fine ash was falling. The Southern Pacific Railroad yards at Fourth and Townsend lay in that direction, and the fine private railroad car Rudi and Ezra shared stood waiting on a siding. Rudi gave it only brief thought as he watched a fire engine tear past, its great brass boiler gleaming, its four horses jangling their harness as they galloped.

There were no cable cars running, and a cab seemed out of the question. Very well, he would locate Dewey Lane on foot. Rudi began to walk.

Central Hospital had collapsed at the first shock. There was as yet no fire, and rescuers were probing the wreckage, freeing nurses, patients, doctors, who stumbled, dazed, out of the debris. Astonishingly, the amount of injury was slight, and already the staff had begun to set up a temporary hospital in Mechanics' Pavilion across the street. Rudi made his inquiries there.

There were no hospital records. "They're over there," a nurse told him, and gestured to the collapsed building across the street. "And we're busy."

"I appreciate that, young lady, but I am trying to find an old friend who needs help." Rudi smiled, a grandfather smile. "He is as old as I am." He seemed very helpless. "His name is Dewey Lane."

Luck at first try. Dewey had made his presence felt. Irrepressible, full of tales of the old days, flirting outrageously with the nurses, from a wheelchair entertaining an entire ward of children with sleight-of-hand tricks—oh, even on this morning of chaos the nurse remembered Dewey well. "He left. One day, two days, three days ago. I don't know. I'm all —confused. He left. On crutches, of course."

"Thank you, my dear."

And where would Dewey have gone? To his own rooms? To sit and feel sorry for himself? Rudi thought not, but he knew no other place to look.

It was a long, weary walk, past Nob Hill, up the flank of Russian Hill, pausing for breath from time to time, turning to look back at the city. South of Market now most of the buildings were gone or going; there was no clear sky to be seen. Along Market Street itself, the Emporium, Holbrook, Merrill

312

and Stetson's, the Hearst Building, and the eighteen-story Call Building were already gutted, and although Rudi could not make out details, it looked as if the entire city, his city, the city he had watched grow from nothing, was beyond help; sad, bitter thought.

Dewey was not in his rooms. Along the sidewalk furniture was piled, and personal possessions, clothing, toys. One woman sat in the midst of her belongings saying monotonously, "I'm not hurt, but what do I do? I'm not hurt, but what do I do?"

Dewey's landlady-housekeeper said, "He wouldn't stay here. Not him. One leg and all, when there is excitement to be had . . ." She shook her head. " 'Mrs. McNeal,' he said, 'ye'll manage. I know it. And I'll only be a burden to you here.' And off he goes, tipping his hat, riding high on somebody's cart." She studied Rudi. "Ye'll try to find him, sir?"

"I'll try." He turned to look again at the smoke rolling up from the burning city. An old man, he thought; no, two old men stumbling around in this chaos. He looked again at the landlady. "Have you suggestions?"

"Only one." Mrs. McNeal's mouth was disapproving, but her eyes were fond. "He has always said that the finest whiskey in town was to be had at the St. Francis Hotel." She hesitated. "Ye'll know it, sir? On Post at Powell?"

"I know it." Rudi smiled wearily. "Thank you, Mrs. McNeal."

* * *

The fires had not yet reached Union Square and the St. Francis Hotel was untouched, but the smell of smoke was strong, and ash fell like mist. Rudi made his way inside to the bar. A familiar voice was saying, "I have heard that there is $40 million in coin and bullion in the mint's vaults. I have also heard that the figure is closer to $200 million. Take your pick, gentlemen. Isn't it lovely to think about?"

"Hello, Dewey," Rudi said. He sat down wearily. "I've been looking for you."

Dewey's quick smile was gentle. "Mr. Rudi Meyer, banker, oil man, financier—I believe entrepreneur is the word. A whiskey for Mr. Meyer." Then, to Rudi alone, "I might have expected Ezra . . ."

"Ezra and Lotte are in Europe," Rudi said. "They plan —they planned to see spring in Switzerland and in the Tyrol, to spend a little time in Vienna . . ." He shook his head. He was very tired. "When Ezra learns of—this he will hurry back. It is his home too."

Dewey set a glass of whiskey in front of Rudi. "And in the meantime," he said, and his voice matched the smile, "you are trying to look out for me. For Ezra." There was no mockery in his tone. "Thank you."

Rudi said, "I do not know about trains, the station . . ."

"At last report," someone said, "the fire had not reached Townsend."

"Why, then," Dewey said, "let us be on our way." He saw the fatigue in Rudi's face. "If you are rested enough." Again the quick smile. "There is no point in staying here. By city council orders all bars must close at noon." He stood up and tucked crutches beneath his arms. One trouser leg, the right, was neatly pinned up above the knee. He looked around the bar, smiling still. That was how they would always remember him. "I think our advanced age, gentlemen, entitles us to a sensible retreat. I wish you all luck." He swung out on his crutches. Rudi followed slowly.

It was Dewey who saw the cart clattering up Powell from the direction of Market, and who swung out into the street and forced the driver either to halt or run down a one-legged man. "Goddam it," the driver said. "Out of my way!"

"Why," Dewey said cheerfully, "all we are asking, friend, is a ride for two old men. Up you go, Rudi. Now give me a hand. There. Drive on, cousin. In adversity all men are kin."

"I," the driver said, "will be goddamned. You've got your goddam nerve."

"It is about all I have left, cousin," Dewey said. He looked back toward Market Street. The smoke rose in billows blotting out the sun and the sky. "I should think that East Street would be our best bet," he said to the driver, and got grudging agreement.

"The goddam fire's moving north. It's crossed Market. I'm trying to swing around it, like you said, for the waterfront." He turned around on his seat to look at the two men. "Where you dudes headed?"

"Fourth and Townsend," Rudi said. "The Southern Pacific yards."

"Where, I reckon," the driver said, "you got yourself a nice private railroad car just sittin' waitin' for you." He was beginning to be amused.

Rudi looked at Dewey. Dewey's quick smile threatened to break into laughter. "You just guessed it, cousin," he said.

They were sitting on a heavy canvas which covered the cart's load. Dewey poked at lumps beneath the canvas. They were hard, angular, boxes he guessed, and wondered what they contained.

"That," the driver said, "is none of your goddam business."

Dewey's serenity was unshaken. "I was just asking out of curiosity. On a day like this there are many strange loads. Did you know, for example, that two tellers from the Anglo California Bank pushed a wheelbarrow loaded with $1 million in negotiable securities down Market Street to the Ferry Building? It is safe in Oakland now."

Rudi, weary still, said slowly, "And young Amadeo Giannini has driven the Bank of Italy's liquid assets to San Mateo for safety. Covered with crates of oranges as camouflage." He shook his head. "I heard that while I was searching for you."

The driver said, "Every light-fingered mother's son is looking to see what they can pick up." The skirt of his coat swung wide in a sudden breeze, and Dewey could see that there was a pistol tucked in the waistband of the driver's trousers.

"And so," Dewey said, "you are driving an unidentified cartload to the waterfront, and are prepared for contingencies on the way." He nodded approvingly.

"I told you," the driver said, "goddam it, that my load was none of your goddam business."

"We are not inquiring." This was Rudi, and there was authority in his voice.

"But you're getting nosy," the driver said, "and . . ."

Rudi said sharply, "If you used your wits instead of your temper, you would see that my friend and I benefit rather than menace you."

"What he means, cousin," Dewey said, "is that we are far better camouflage than crates of oranges." His voice had lost some of its lightness. "Think on it."

They were approaching East Street when they heard the first explosion. They had turned off Powell, crossed Columbus, and were staying as far south as they could on their way to East Street. The explosion came from their right, in the area south of Market. "It will be dynamite," Dewey said. "If they are to stop the fire, they will have to level a swathe of buildings in its way." He looked at Rudi.

Rudi closed his eyes briefly. His city. "I could weep," he said.

Dewey took his time. "I see it as the turn of the card," he said at last. "There is the difference between us." One of the differences, he thought, but left those words unsaid. "There is a street-corner prophet in Union Square telling everybody who will listen that this is the Lord's retribution, Sodom and Gomorrah all over again." He watched Rudi's face. "Do you believe that?"

"No."

"Neither do I. And yet—" Strange thought. "—sometimes things do seem to be planned." The quick smile. "Because I was in a hurry, I caught the first ship I could find on the east coast back in '49."

The driver whistled softly. "You was here then? Jesus Christ!"

"I was here, cousin. And my friend had come before me." Dewey smiled again. "And because I caught that particular ship, I met Ezra and taught him what he knew that came in handy that night in Turkey Creek." He spread his hands. "Was that planned?"

Rudi sighed. "I do not know. Lotte and I—we had come seven thousand miles, by ship, by wagon, on foot, just as Ezra had come fifteen thousand miles around the Horn—for the three of us to meet that night, as you say, in Turkey Creek." He shook his head, remembering.

The driver said, "What happened at Turkey Creek?"

316

"Now, cousin," Dewey said, "you are the nosy one. What happened is ancient history." He cocked his head at the sound of more explosions.

The smoke around them was thicker now. "Christ," the driver said, "if the waterfront's on fire, we're up shit creek."

"We can swim, cousin."

"Not with what you're sittin' on. All I want to do is get to Pier 13, foot of Vallejo. And then——Oh, Jesus Christ! Somebody's talked. Jump, you gents! We're going to have some trouble."

Dewey craned his neck to see over the driver's shoulder. Four men blocked the street, holding rifles. The smoke swirled around them.

"Jump, goddam it!" the driver said. "I got to whip up this horse! Jump!"

Rudi looked at Dewey. Dewey was smiling. "Now, cousin," he said, "we joined forces. We are on your side. Whip up the beast." His right hand disappeared beneath his coat. It emerged carrying a short-barreled revolver. "Lie flat, Rudi," he said. His voice was calm, and the smile remained. "Ezra would never speak to me again if I let anything happen to you. On, cousin!"

The horse broke into a trot, a shambling gallop. The cart swayed and teetered, and as Dewey watched, the four men drew two to each side of the street, rifles lifted. The driver had his pistol in one hand, the reins in the other. "Son a bitches," he said. "Light-fingered mother fuckin' son a bitches." He fired once. Two rifles responded immediately.

"Those on the left are yours," Dewey said. "I will take care of the others." He held his fire.

One of the men on the right lifted his rifle, sighted, fired, a snap shot. Rudi heard it buzz angrily overhead. The cart swayed, the horse's hooves clattered on the pavement, the smoke swirled around them. Dewey fired once. He fired a second time. Rifles answered him, and Rudi lost track of time and events.

And then they were through, clattering on into the smoke, and Rudi raised his head to look back.

317

Two men lay on the pavement. A third, on Dewey's side, struggled to raise his rifle and did, and managed to get off a last shot before he pitched forward on his face.

"Jesus!" the driver said. "It was close. An' look, the smoke's clearin'! There's the Bay!" He turned to look back. "Oh, Christ!" he said.

Rudi was on his knees, crouched over Dewey. Dewey was smiling. The hand that still held the pistol was relaxed. A great red stain was spreading on the white shirt beneath his waistcoat, and still the smile remained.

Rudi said, "He is hurt. Badly. We will find a doctor."

Dewey's head waggled gently. "Better this way." The smile even spread. "Never wanted to be old. A cripple. Much better." He held out the pistol, butt end first. "Take it. Once before a gun of mine brought somebody luck." The smile faded, returned. "Say hello to Ezra. Tell him I—did the—best —I could."

* * *

They loaded the heavy boxes beneath the canvas into one of Tom Crowley's launches at Pier 13 at the foot of Vallejo Street. The driver told the launchman, "Mr. Crocker says just go out in the Bay an' sit there. Never mind what's in the boxes."

The launchman looked at Dewey's body lifted back into the cart. "Don't want to know," he said, and cast off.

Rudi said, "I will pay you well if you will drive my friend and me to Fourth and Townsend." He paused. "There is a private car. I will take my friend home with me."

The driver shook his head. "No pay." His voice was harsh. He looked down at Dewey's body. "For cousins, it's on the house."

318

33

Benjie awakened alone and, as before, lay still for a few moments staring up into the darkness, trying to orient herself. She and Pete, stoned. She remembered that, and if she had not, the lingering, pervasive odor of marihuana would have been enough to remind her.

They said that pot didn't leave you with a hangover the way alcohol did, and that was true enough as far as it went; but like most things that were said so positively about pot, it wouldn't bear strict examination. Her mind felt fuzzy, unclear, unsure; and her body was tired, but maybe that wasn't from the joints they had smoked, but from what had come after. She had never found Pete so fierce and yet gentle, so overwhelmingly possessive in his lovemaking. She had said it of him herself—he was flying, buoyed up and bubbling with some inner excitement that communicated itself to her and lifted her to a level of frenzy she had not achieved before.

She stretched herself now and smiled up into the darkness. Out of sight, she thought. And it was probably no wonder that she was tired. But where was Pete?

She got out of bed, drew the curtains, and turned on the light. There were her clothes, jeans and shirt; Pete's were gone. Naked, she sat on the bed wishing she were not alone, but feeling none of the panic she had felt that other time. Pete was gone, Pete would return—it was as simple as that.

Oh, she wished he would stop what he was doing, defying his father and the Establishment, the system; not even in her mind would she put stronger words to it than that. But as he had told her it was his business, not hers; and so through uninvolvement her innocence remained intact. Maybe that was what they called rationalizing, but Benjie didn't care. That was the way it was.

When she and Pete left Stanhope, rode the bus as far as the money would take them and then hitched the rest of the way, all of this would drop behind like the burned-out first stage of one of those moon shots she had watched on TV. And maybe, like the first-stage booster, all that had happened here in Stanhope would somehow disappear, burn up or atomize or just plain fade away in the happiness of the new life.

Her father had been fond of saying that you could never walk away from yourself, leave your past behind. Benjie supposed it was something Ben Franklin had said once, but it was B.S. anyway. She had left her San Francisco-Russian Hill-vacations-at-Carmel past behind, hadn't she? Well? And she was older now, more mature, so leaving Stanhope behind, out of sight, out of mind, would be even easier. She crossed her arms over her breasts and hugged herself. It was going to be groovy. Santa Fe with Pete. . . .

She heard the key in the lock, and she jumped up from the bed, smiling. The door opened, but the man who came quickly through was not Pete—it was Julio. Under one arm, carried negligently, he held a stout wooden box. He set it down and closed the door with a quickness that was surprising. He looked at her, and he was smiling.

Benjie screamed. She tried to cover her nakedness with her hands, which was futile, and then she turned and tried to run into the bathroom, which was worse.

Julio caught her from behind and spun her around as if she were a toy. Somehow with one hand he had managed to catch both of hers behind her back, and he held them in a punishing grasp. He dug the fingers of his other hand into the muscles of her cheeks and covered her mouth with his own.

She tried to struggle, but he was much too strong, far stronger than Pete even in frenzy. She tried to bite his lips which were bruising hers, and found that those strong fingers held her jaws paralyzed. She tried to scream. All that came out was a muffled, bubbling sound that matched the noises deep in Julio's throat.

And then all at once he released her head. Still holding her hands imprisoned he stepped back and, with a quickness she would not have believed possible, struck her twice with his clenched fist. The first blow, to her belly, drove all breath from her lungs. The second, to her jaw, brought instant unconsciousness. . . .

She struggled up out of blackness into a kind of nightmare, neither conscious nor oblivious, sentient, but disbelieving, swirling in darkness that was shot through with light, trying to scream and incapable of a sound, trying to struggle and unable to move the weight that covered her.

Pete had gone mad—somehow this thought appeared and then dropped off into nothingness. But what was happening to her did not stop.

Hands were hurting her breasts, crushing them. *Why was Pete so brutal?*

Her legs were being forced apart, and she was helpless. *Why, Pete, why?*

A man drove into her with bruising force, thrusting, punishing. *Pete! Pete, you're hurting me! Please! Please! Dear God! Please! I can't stand it!*

She blacked out.

When she came to this second time she was alone again, on the bed, bewildered, hurt. It was a painful effort to raise herself and look down at her body. There were blotches on her breasts already turning darkly red, purple with suffused blood. There was a large bruise on her belly where the fist had pounded her. And there was blood on her thighs; when she rolled over she saw the red stains on the sheet.

She struggled up to a sitting position and sat helpless, her mind at last fully awake, remembering. She was unaware that she was crying; the salt taste was without meaning. She

321

began to whisper to herself the old magic incantation: "I'm Benjie, I'm Benjie, I'm Benjie . . ." The magic was gone.

How long she sat there, she had no idea. At last her young strength returned, and with it an overpowering sense of nausea. She got to her feet, lurched into the bathroom, and dropped to her knees to vomit into the toilet.

* * *

Pete came back at last, as she had known he would. He too carried a stout wooden box, twin to the other, and he set it down with care. Then he looked at Benjie. "Up, dressed, at night?" His voice was light, too light.

He couldn't help seeing the bruise on her jaw, Benjie thought, but he ignored it. It would do no good to show him the bruises on her breasts, either, or the large bruise on her belly. And the bruises in her mind were not for display. "You sent him," she said.

"Now, baby. Don't give me riddles."

Benjie said, "He brought that." One hand behind her back, she pointed with the other at the first box. "He had a key, so you sent him." She had tried to find another explanation; there was none.

"Benjie, baby, I couldn't carry both boxes. And they came from different places." He walked toward her slowly.

"Don't touch me."

"Now, baby."

"I mean it," Benjie said. She brought her hidden hand into view. It held the kitchen carving knife. "Touch me," she said, "and I will kill you, Pete." Her voice was quiet, emotionless; her mind, for the moment, drained of feeling. "I've never been raped before," she said. "I've always given it for free if a guy I liked wanted it enough. But now I know what the word rape means. It isn't something I'll forget."

Pete said, "Benjie, baby, believe me. If I'd thought that . . ."

"You knew," Benjie said. She glanced at the two boxes. "You sent him here with that box of dynamite." She was looking steadily at Pete now. "And you knew there was dynamite in his mind too. I won't ask you why, because I think I know. You need him for whatever you're going to do. And I

322

was the price you paid him. Are the others coming too? Maybe a gang bang?"

Pete lifted his hands and let them fall. He spoke patiently. "You've got it all wrong. I wouldn't do a thing like that to you. I told you . . ."

"You've told me lots of things. I believed them. I even believed I was grown up, mature, that I understood how it was, and how it was going to be." She shook her head slowly. "You're sick. It shows now. You don't know it, but you are— sick, sick, sick."

Her leather satchel was on the table. She slung it over one shoulder and walked to the door. Pete watched her in silence. He seemed bewildered. With one hand on the door-knob, Benjie paused. "Goodbye, Pete."

Pete shook his head in sullen silence.

"I'm sorry for you," Benjie said.

And suddenly there was anger in his face, beyond control. "Don't bother, damn you!"

Benjie nodded with a calmness she did not feel. She tucked the knife into her satchel. "All right. I won't." She opened the door and walked out into the night. As in a dream.

It was cold. Overhead, dimly, stars dotted the black sky; but here at ground level a light mist had gathered, and its chill penetrated Benjie's shirt and jeans. Her bruised breasts ached, and as she walked, her thighs tortured the painful tenderness of the pubic area. Never mind that; the real hurt was in her mind, in her soul. "I'm Benjie," she whispered, and then added a new corollary: "And Benjie is a fool." She walked steadily, her bare feet making little sound on the pavement.

There was a phone booth near the market where she had shopped. The directory hung from a chain and some of its pages were torn, but thank God, the page she wanted was intact. She repeated to herself Paul Meyer's telephone number and address.

She had no money. Except for the kitchen knife, she was leaving Pete as she had come to him. Correction, she thought as she began to walk again, I am leaving a part of myself behind. And inevitably the new concept followed: Is it always so? Do you always leave something of yourself wherever you

323

go, wherever you stay? Was that what her father had meant, that you could never really walk away because always a part of you stayed? "I'm Benjie, and Benjie is a fool." This was the new, sobering incantation, cautionary rather than comforting.

She knocked and knocked, and Paul came to the door at last, opened it only a crack. "Please," Benjie said, and saw him hesitate, nod, and step back. She walked in and the door closed after her.

Paul was in his shorts. "I'll put on some pants . . ."

"It doesn't matter." She stood silent. Now that she was here, she had no idea why she had come. Except, she thought, that she had no other place to go. "I'm sorry," she said.

"What's happened, Benjie?"

"Nothing." She shook her head. "Everything." She was silent again, waiting to be told what to do.

Paul touched her arm gently. Benjie stiffened, and then made herself relax. "Sit down," Paul said. He smiled at her. "I'll feel better in pants. Only a moment."

He came back into the room zipping the fly of his jeans, buckling his belt. He had not bothered with a shirt. "A beer, Benjie? Coffee?" He watched her shake her head. "All right," he said, and grabbed a chair, swung it up to face hers. When he sat down their knees were almost touching. "Now, tell," he said. "All of it." He smiled again. "Not like the first time we met; don't make me pull it out of you one tooth at a time."

Benjie opened her mouth, but no sound came out.

"Yes," Paul said. He was nodding understandingly as he reached into his pocket for a handkerchief. "I think tears will help. Go to it." He put the handkerchief in her hand and sat back in his chair. "Take your time," he said.

The tears stopped at last. Benjie wiped her eyes, blew her nose, and took a deep breath. The words came slowly at first, but then, caught up in their own flow, they began to quicken until they almost tumbled over one another.

Paul listened in silence, and when at last the words ran down, "Are you all right, Benjie?" he said. "Physically, I mean?"

Benjie unbuttoned her shirt; the action was without coquetry. She held it wide. The purple bruises on her breasts stood out against the creamy flesh.

324

"I believe you," Paul said. He stood up. "Hang on a minute." He disappeared into the bedroom, came back with a tube of ointment. "This may help." He sat down again. "A couple of questions, okay?"

Benjie nodded. She had dropped her satchel to the floor. She shucked off her shirt and began to rub ointment into the flesh of her bruised breasts and belly. "Okay," she said.

"Dynamite," Paul said. "You're sure?"

Benjie nodded again. Merely touching herself was painful, and she didn't know if the ointment would help or not, but he had given it to her and he was trying to comfort her and that was what mattered. "The lid was loose," she said, "and I looked. I don't know why. I was waiting for Pete because I had to talk to him, can you see that? And I guess I just had to have something to do. Little rolls of heavy waxy paper, packed in sawdust, and besides, it said what it was on the outside of the box." She stopped rubbing her breasts. The ointment was beginning to ease the pain. She wondered if she rubbed some in her crotch it would help there too. She asked Paul.

"I don't know," he said, "but I'm sure it won't hurt. Can you wait a minute?"

"Sure." For this man, anything. The dreamlike feeling was strong. "I'm Benjie," she said, "and Benjie is a fool." Somehow it seemed important to say it to him.

"I don't think so." His voice was gentle. "Put your shirt on." He watched her hands obey. "Maybe a little mixed-up," he said, "but not a fool. You're how old, Benjie?" She told him. Ellen's age, he thought—God! Never mind that now. "Do you know what the dynamite is for?" he said.

Benjie shook her head. "They were there today. Julio . . ." It was the first time she had used his name, and she watched Paul's face set.

"Describe Julio," Paul said. He listened. He nodded. His face was grim. "It figures." He made himself relax, and said gently, "How are your breasts?"

"Much better," Benjie said. "Thank you." He had helped her; she tried to help him. "They talked, but I

325

don't dig Spanish, and all I got was *agua.* They said it over and over again." She was silent, hopeful that it would mean something to him.

"Nothing else you caught?" Paul said.

She shook her head. "I'm sorry. When they left, Julio was the last one, and Pete said asta, or something, that's all."

Paul bent forward. He took both of her hands in his. "Now try to remember, Benjie. The word he said is *hasta,* h-a-s-t-a, it means *until* in Spanish. Until when? What was the next word? Was it *luego?*" He hoped it was not; *luego* meant merely *then, hasta luego,* a common enough form of goodbye. "Was that the next word, Benjie?"

She shook her head. "It began with a *w*, like in, you know, *what.*"

Paul squeezed her hands gently. "Good girl. An aspirate. That means a *j* in Spanish. Can you remember how the rest sounded at all?"

Benjie concentrated. Then slowly, "It reminded me of *whey.* You know, like in the nursery rime, curds and whey?" Her breasts and the bruise on her belly were much more comfortable, but the painful tenderness between her legs was torment. Never mind. If she could help this man who had taken her in without question, without disapproval, who made her feel like somebody and not just a female body to be used, then she didn't care about pain; in this dream it could wait. "Does that help?"

Paul said slowly, carefully, "Was it *jueves? Hasta jueves?* Is that what Pete said?"

Benjie could smile. "That's it. What does it mean?"

Paul stood up. "It means, 'Until Thursday.' " He paused. "Day after tomorrow." He walked across the room, turned, walked back. *"Agua,"* he said, "and *hasta jueves.* Maybe . . ."

Benjie was standing. "Please. May I use your bathroom? I think maybe I'm bleeding." She walked into the bedroom.

Paul watched her go. Seventeen, he thought. Jesus. But there was nothing he could do about that at the moment. He looked at his watch. Well after midnight. So *jueves,* Thursday, was tomorrow, not the day after. Well, there was nothing he could do about the late hour. He walked to the phone, sat down, and began to dial.

A sleepy voice with a Spanish lilt answered. Paul said, "Señor George Stanfield, *por favor.*"

"But, señor, the hour . . ."

"I am aware of it." Paul spoke commandingly in Spanish. "The matter is urgent. I am Paul Meyer. Awaken Señor Stanfield and tell him I must speak to him."

Long hesitation. Then, *"Si, señor."*

Benjie came back into the room. She had been crying again. "It hurts," she said, "but I think the stuff helps."

"I think we'd better get you to a doctor," Paul said. And then, into the phone, "Sorry, sir. I have to talk to you. It can't wait." He anticipated the inevitable question. "It's not about Ellen. It's about Pete." He paused. "I either have to talk to you, or to the police."

* * *

Benjie sat quiet in the pickup truck. The mist was thicker now; the headlights threw back a blurred reflection. Paul drove slowly, and it was as if they moved in a dead world, alone. "It's much better now," Benjie said. "Please. I don't want to go to the hospital. I don't have to, do I?"

A child crying out in the night, Paul thought, and felt a surge of paternal affection. "Whatever you say," he said, and turned out of town toward the Stanfield ranch.

"You aren't a girl," Benjie said, "so you don't know. They poke at you, and it's, like, I guess degrading; you're, you know, like something on display. That's why I don't want to go to the hospital. I'll be all right. I'll be fine." She touched Paul's arm gently. "You're a nice, sweet guy, you know that?"

Paul was smiling. He said nothing.

"It's like," Benjie said, "you know, everything is changed, all at once, do you know what I mean? I'm not sure myself." The dreamlike quality remained. "What I mean is," she said, "that wearing no bra, and my boobs bouncing when I walked, that was a groove, it made guys look at me, guys like Pete, and that was great. I felt like something special." She paused. "I guess I was just asking for it, wasn't I? You know, throwing it around like one of those go-go dancers. You've seen them?"

"I've seen them," Paul said. The girl was trying to unwind, he thought, and the least he could do was listen even though his mind was on other more urgent matters.

"Do they," Benjie said, "you know, give you a charge?"

"Not much."

"No," Benjie said. "I guess maybe I see that now. Only the wrong guys, you know, really get a charge." She folded her arms suddenly over her bruised breasts. It was not from pain; the action was instinctive. "Do you have a girl?"

"Yes. Pete's sister." Paul smiled. "She's just your age."

Benjie said slowly, "But I guess she's a lot different." And then, "Where're we going?"

"To see her father."

Benjie thought about it. "Does she live at home? Your girl?"

"Yes."

"I used to live at home." Pause. "That's a pretty silly thing to say, isn't it? I guess everybody lives at home, for a while, anyway. Most people." She closed her eyes and hugged herself painfully tight to hold down a scream that suddenly tried to escape from her throat. She breathed deep. She said at last, "Why is everything all screwed up? Everything?"

"I don't know the answer, Benjie."

There was a long silence. The mist swirled in the headlights and they were alone. Unreal. Benjie said, "Louise. My name. How about that?" Her short laugh was without amusement. "Little starched dresses and patent leather shoes with little white socks, can you see it? Me? Little girl parties with nice little boys. The Fleishhacker Zoo. Muir Woods. The Fine Arts Palace, remember that? With ducks and swans in the pool?" She paused. "But they tore it down. Why? Just part of the general fuck-up?"

The headlights picked out the great gates of the ranch. Paul set the hand brake and got out to use the telephone. He got back into the cab and closed the door. Benjie said, "God, is this it?" Watching the gates swing slowly open she shook her head. "Pete told me about it. And you. All one family, really, aren't you? You know, I'd heard about the Stanfields and the Meyers even before I blew the home scene. Like the Huntingtons and the Crockers, like that, or the Rockefellers in the east, only you've been here since the beginning." She looked through the rear window and watched the gates swing shut. "It's like a, you know, castle kind of thing, isn't it?"

"It is," Paul said. "Like the castle on the hill, safe behind its walls and its moat." He paused. "While the peasants are dancing in the streets, and looting the village shops, and getting ready to storm the gates."

* * *

Consuelo answered the door. She looked at Benjie and said not a word as she led them to the study. George was waiting behind the desk. He stood up when he saw Benjie and nodded acknowledgment, then sat down again. Paul waited until the door was closed.

"She came to me," he said. "She was raped tonight. Sit down, Benjie." His voice was gentle. Then, to George, in a different, harder tone, "The man who raped her brought a box of dynamite to Pete's house. Pete came in later with another box."

The study was quiet. George sat large and solid behind the desk, his face showing nothing. "Go on."

"Damn it," Paul said, "am I getting through to you at all?"

"You are. I said go on. I'm listening."

Paul nodded. "Okay. I'm uptight. I admit it." He was silent for a moment. "There was a meeting at Pete's place this evening. Last evening. They spoke Spanish and Benjie doesn't, but she heard two things—*agua* was repeated many times and when they left Pete said, *'Hasta jueves.'* "

"Thursday," George said. "Day after—no. It's tomorrow now, isn't it? That's why you couldn't wait." He nodded. He looked at Benjie. "There's a doctor upstairs," he said. His tone was not unfriendly. "We'll have him look at you, Benjie, and see if you need medical attention."

"I'm okay. I'm fine."

"We'll have him check you anyway," George said. He looked at Paul. "Consuelo's in the kitchen. Tell her to bring Ellen down here." And when Paul was gone, "I'm going to ask you a question, Benjie. I want you to answer it with the truth."

He was almost frightening, this big, solid man who expected his commands to be obeyed. Anyone like that had to

329

have power that was awesome to throw around as he wanted, and that was frightening too. Benjie moistened her lips with her tongue. "Okay," she said.

"It's simply this, Benjie," George said. "You're blowing the whistle on Pete because of what happened to you. That's understandable. But what I want to know is are you telling the truth? Was there dynamite? Or did you make that up? Now is the time to say."

She hadn't thought of it as blowing the whistle on Pete, but of course, that was exactly what it was. Finking, and never in her life had she ever finked on anybody. She sat silent, in torment.

"Did you make it up?" George said.

Wrong question; the girl sat mute, miserable.

Paul was at the door, and he saw and understood. He walked to the girl and laid his hand on her shoulder. She looked up at him. "You cop out on Pete, Benjie, or you cop out on the rest of the world because that's what he's doing."

"You're his friend." But Pete himself had said that he had no friends.

"I was. But when he turns into a mad dog, I'll do whatever I have to to stop him. Two men dead already, probably because of Pete. Two cases of dynamite can kill a lot more. If there really was dynamite. Was there, Benjie?"

Benjie closed her eyes. When she opened them again tears spilled out and ran down the sides of her nose. "I promise you," she said. "Like I said, I looked, and—why would I make it up?" She looked at George, and with sudden movements almost ripped open her shirt to bare her blotched breasts. "Isn't this—enough? Why would I have to make up something else?"

· There was silence. George said gently, "I apologize, Benjie."

Ellen stood in the doorway. She wore a robe, and her hair was tousled from sleep. She looked at them all. "This is Benjie," George said. "My daughter Ellen."

Benjie's fingers were clumsy on the buttons of her shirt. She looked around at Ellen and nodded. "Hi." Unreal, it was all unreal.

"Take Benjie upstairs," George said to Ellen. "I want

Doctor Ross to look her over, and if anything is necessary, see that Benjie has it. If the doctor says she is all right, then I think Benjie could use some sleep, with perhaps a sedative. Mention that to the doctor too."

Benjie stood up. She looked at Paul and then again at George. "I'm okay," she said, "but thanks." The tears had stopped. "To both of you." Still unreal.

Ellen said, "We'll take care of it, Daddy." She smiled at Paul. The diamond glittered on her finger as she turned away.

George sat quiet behind the desk. "Close the door," he said to Paul, and gestured toward one of the leather chairs. "You said either me or the police. Why me?"

"If you don't know," Paul said, "I sure as hell doubt if I can explain." He was unaware that he had dropped the 'sir'; he was speaking as to an equal.

"Try me," George said.

Paul took a deep breath. "Okay. If I go to the police all I'm doing is what you said Benjie was doing—blowing the whistle on Pete. I'm willing to do it, but I want to get as much mileage out of it as I can. Is that plain enough?"

"Plain enough," George said.

"I'm doing something else, too," Paul said. "I'm blowing the whistle on one of our own men. Julio, the big one with the softball bat, is the one who raped Benjie and brought the first case of dynamite. You haven't believed us all along. Maybe you will now. None of what's happened has had anything to do with Ruben, or with me. I wanted you to see that, understand it. That's why I came to you."

"Am I important," George said, "because of Ellen?"

"Of course you are." Paul's voice rose; he controlled it. "You're also important because you're George Stanfield, and what Louis Khasigian said to Henry Potter and Luke Albright is exactly right. You fight us, Ruben, me, and they'll all fall right in with you. But you go with us, sign a contract, and they'll have to go along whether they like it or not."

George thought about it. Slowly he nodded. "That's good enough." He pushed back his chair and stood up. "I'm going to see Pete. Are you coming?"

34

The little house was dark, and there was no answer to George's knocking. "Stand back," George said, and raised his foot to kick twice, hard, with his heel. The door flew open. They walked inside and turned on the light.

The house was empty. "No Pete," George said. "No dynamite. If the girl is telling the truth . . ."

"Are you so used to lies and trickery," Paul said, "that you find it everywhere, in everybody?" Then, quickly, "Never mind. Let's find a telephone." He led the way back out to his pickup.

They drove to the phone booth near the market. George said, "You want to phone whom?"

"Ruben." Never mind the hour; time was running out.

"Why Lucero?"

"Come with me and you can listen."

Ruben answered the telephone on only the second ring. His voice was clear, alert. To Paul's apology for the hour, *"No importa. Qué pasa?"*

In Spanish, "Julio, Ruben. Is he there?"

"A moment." Ruben was back almost immediately. "He is not here. Juan has not see him. Why, Paul? What has happen?"

Paul spoke quickly, succinctly. "Now both Pete and Julio are gone. With the dynamite. Where would they go?"

There was a pause. Then, slowly, "You are tell me, Paul, are you not, that they are in the *barrio*?"

"Where else?"

Ruben's sigh was audible. His voice was sad. "I think yes." He paused. "Who know about this, Paul?"

"George Stanfield. He is here with me. The father of Pete, Ruben."

"Understood." The words came slowly, reluctantly. "Tell Mr. Stanfield for me, Paul, that we will try to find his son. And Julio. And the dynamite."

"I will tell him." Paul paused. "They talked about water, Ruben. What would that mean?"

He could almost see the shrug, the spread hands, the Latin grimace. "Who knows?" Ruben said. "Perhaps to dynamite a well? The wells of Mr. Stanfield? This I cannot say. But, Paul . . ." The voice paused for emphasis. ". . . it is you who know better the mind of Pete. He is one of you."

Paul hung up. He turned to look at George. "You heard?"

"One of us," George said. He nodded. "He *was* one of us." He walked slowly to the pickup and got in. "Let's go," he said.

"Where?"

"The police," George said. "Where else?"

* * *

They sat in Chief Walling's office and watched the sky lighten and the ground mist begin to dissipate. A uniformed sergeant appeared in the open doorway. "He's on his way," he said. "Maybe ten minutes." He paused. "Coffee while you're waiting?" He watched them both nod, and as he turned away he wondered what it was that was important enough to get them out of bed this time of night and to get the Chief out of his plush and downy as well.

Paul said, "You're going to tell him all of it?"

"What would you do?" George watched him steadily, one generation studying the next.

"I don't know." Then, truthfully, "I'm glad it isn't my decision."

George nodded. "But you came to me."

"I told you why."

"The point is," George said, "that you made a decision. You didn't walk away from it."

"That," Paul said, "doesn't make me some kind of hero."

"No," George said, remembering Ellen's accusation of him, "to some people it makes you some kind of bastard." He did not express his own view.

Paul stared out of the window. The upper edge of the sun peeked over the distant mountains, turning the sky to gold. "Where the sun tips the golden Sierra. . . ." The lines of the state song came unbidden to mind. Sometime, unnoticed, coffee had arrived in paper cups. It was bitter. Still watching the sunrise, "So I'm a bastard," Paul said, "a rat fink." He looked at George. "What else could I do?"

George shrugged. "You will probably spend the rest of your life trying to answer questions like that." He looked up as Walling walked in. "We have some problems for you," George said.

* * *

Howard Meyer sat in his father's inner office at the bank. He had a yellow legal pad in front of him but most of its penciled information was also in his head. "Cleary Ward has been neat," he said, "and not too greedy. Unless there was reason to look into his total activities from here in Stanhope, on the ground, I think he could have gone on for some time, maybe indefinitely. Audit from the city would show nothing out of line."

So helpless, flighty Julia had been right, Karl thought. He folded his long hands on the desk. "How has he done it?"

"One of the ways," Howard said, "is by dummy companies. Easy enough and no reason for the city auditors to look twice. Cleary checks and certifies all deliveries of raw fruit and vegetables to the dehydrator and the cannery. He has control of the weight slips for the Stanfield trucks. John Silva out at

334

the vineyards, for example, has no way of knowing whether he sent two hundred tons of grapes to the dehydrator in a given period, or one hundred and eighty tons or maybe one hundred and ninety. The loads aren't weighed until the loaded trucks go on the scales in town. And John doesn't see checks from the dehydrator written to a company that doesn't exist paying for Stanfield grapes that have been credited to their account. And to the city auditors everything balances." Howard smiled suddenly. "It shows what a business school education can do for you."

It was not a matter for amusement, Karl thought, but let it go. "Are there other ways he has been helping himself?"

"Kickbacks. The easy way, and the hard one to prove, but I don't think there is much doubt. All supplies for the dehydrator and the cannery, tires, gas, oil, repairs for all the trucks, new heavy equipment from time to time, everything for the Angus herd, labor contracts for pickers, supplies for the ranch; he buys all those. And he handles rents in the big building . . ." Howard shrugged. "He has ample scope."

"And have you located any of this—loot?"

"Some of it. Those fake company bank accounts are active, but they never show a large balance for long. But Cleary has accounts with two stockbrokers here in town and at least two more in the city, and I think we'll be able to show that the money passing through the fake company accounts eventually goes into stocks and bonds in one of Cleary's portfolios. I think he has done very well for himself."

Karl took off his glasses, looked at them, put them back on again. "So it would appear," he said.

"Do we bring him in, confront him with it?"

Karl shook his head. "It is George's affair. We will let him decide what to do."

* * *

Benjie had slept heavily, and she awakened now with the old sense of unfamiliarity and the brief time of near-panic while she tried to remember where she was. Memory returned like a bad dream and she threw back the covers and looked down at herself for verification. It was true—there were the bruises on her breasts and belly, and the sick feeling grew

335

again in her mind. She closed her eyes. The dreamlike quality was gone.

From the doorway Ellen said, "You're awake?" She stood quietly, expressionless. "Maybe a hot bath would help."

"I'm okay." Benjie's eyes were open now. She looked around, seeking a diversion. "This is a nice room."

"When he was a little boy," Ellen said, "it was Pete's."

"No kidding."

"It's been changed since then."

Benjie nodded and managed a faint smile.

"You liked Pete," Ellen said. A statement, no question.

"He was good to me," Benjie said. She smiled bitterly. "Isn't that a laugh? On TV, in the flicks, some stupid chick is always saying that the guy was good to her. No matter what he does, that's what they say, 'He was good to me.' " There was a dam inside her, she thought, and it was going to break, and she was going to come apart, dissolve into little pieces like a sand castle on the beach when the tide came in. "But he *was* good to me!" She heard her voice rising, and she tried to control it, and failed. "And I—finked—on him!" The last words were almost a scream, and the dam had burst.

And then Ellen, if that was her name, was holding her together, holding her tight, and maybe she wasn't going to dissolve after all. As from a great distance she heard Ellen's voice saying, "It's all right. It's all right."

It wasn't, and Benjie doubted if it would ever be again, but it was sheer relief just to be able to let herself go in great sobs that let some of the sickness out of her mind. It seemed to burst out in great yellow-greenish gobs, like sour vomit.

* * *

In Walling's office, the sun long since up, George was saying, "We have no proof." He was watching Walling's face. "Or do we?"

Walling opened his desk drawer. He took out the envelope and shook the shiny key and the blackened piece of metal out on his blotter. He touched the blackened metal. "This was at the scene of the boiler explosion," he said. "This . . ." He picked up the new key. ". . . was made to the same serial number." He looked at Paul. "You've seen it. It

336

didn't fit your lock. It didn't fit your son's lock, either, Mr. Stanfield, but we asked around a little and found a junk shop where a fellow had traded in one Yale barrel lock for another. The key fits the one that was traded in, and the description of the fellow who traded it fits your son."

George sat solid and expressionless. "All right," he said. "We have proof of a sort." In one way it was unhappy news, in another, it was relief.

Walling said to Paul. "This Julio. Is he the big, long-armed character with the softball bat out at Lucero's house?"

Paul nodded. He was thinking of the sadness in Ruben's voice, understanding it. "That's the one."

"He," Walling said, "fits the description that boy Luther Smith gave of the second man the night of the dehydrator fire." He looked up. Howard Lang stood in the doorway, quiet, expressionless, assured.

"A private discussion?" Lang said. "Or can anyone get in?" He looked from George to Paul. "You've joined forces? You don't mind if I ask why?"

George said easily, "I told you there were no differences between us." The man was dangerous, he thought, and the way to handle him was not by sheer power, but by smoothness. Oh, if it came to the real crunch, George had no doubt that he could take care of Lang, but one of the secrets of wielding great power successfully was not to waste it in messy little gutter fights.

"I've been asking around," Lang said, "and that wasn't quite the way I heard it. Your son Pete, for example, has a different view."

Paul glanced at George. George's face showed nothing.

"And two growers named Potter and Albright," Lang said, "don't think that Ruben Lucero is quite the man in the white hat some people make him out to be. They think truck burnings and dynamite explosions would be just about his speed."

"Luke Albright and Henry Potter," George said slowly, distinctly, "couldn't pour piss out of a boot if the instructions were printed on the heel." His voice was cold. He turned to look at Walling. "I think we'll get along. There isn't any more we can tell you." He went off on the false trail. "The girl was

337

raped. There's no doubt about it. I had Dr. Ross examine her, and I'm sure he'll cooperate." He stood up. Paul rose with him.

Walling said, "Thanks for coming in. I do appreciate it." His hand covered the piece of blackened metal and the key. When Lang turned to watch the two men walk out, Walling slipped both articles into his desk drawer. "You're up early," he said to Lang. His tone was bland.

Lang took his time. "So are you."

"Rape," Walling said, "is a major crime."

Lang walked over to a chair and sat down. He crossed his legs comfortably. "I went to young Stanfield's house," he said. "There's nobody there. And somebody had broken the door in."

"Is that right? I'll have a patrolman take a look."

"And two cases of dynamite were stolen last night from two different State Highway Department projects. A watchman was clobbered, but the description he managed to give fits young Stanfield."

"I thought," Walling said, "that he was a pretty ordinary looking fellow. Put him in a lineup and he'd be hard to pick out."

Lang said slowly, "You aren't very helpful, or friendly. Why?" His voice had not risen, his expression was unchanged.

Walling pushed back his chair and walked to the window to stand looking out at the distant mountains. "Where're you from, Lang?"

"What difference does it make? I'm here. I work here. For the state of California."

Walling turned around. "But you're a carpetbagger, with a carpetbagger's ideas. I'll tell you why I'm not very helpful, or very friendly. It's because you're trying to hang all that's happened on somebody, either Lucero or Stanfield."

"And," Lang said, "what are you trying to do?"

"I'm trying to find out who did it, and put a stop to it. I'm not trying to crucify anybody."

Lang stood up. He was smiling. "Same thing."

Walling shook his head. "Like I said, a carpetbagger with carpetbagger ideas. We outgrew lynch mobs some time ago."

338

* * *

At the gates of the ranch Paul stopped the pickup. George got out. He stood uncertain for a moment. Then, "You'd better come in and have some breakfast." He walked to the gate, put his key in the electronic lock, and held it until the gates swung wide. He followed the pickup through and closed the gates again. They did not speak all the way to the main house.

Julia met them in the hall. "Scott's having breakfast. Conchita is upstairs. Mike . . ." She shook her head. "This is one he can't campaign his way out of." She paused. Her voice changed. "Does that sound flippant?"

Paul was silent, watching, feeling very much out of place.

George said gently, "Not flippant at all, and Mike would be the first to agree." It was a compassionate side of the big man Paul had not seen before. "What does the doctor say?"

"It's the pneumonia that's killing him." Julia's voice was toneless. "But it was the other that—destroyed his resistance." She paused. "He's been dying of leukemia for a long time. Did you know that?"

George shook his head. He said slowly, "I will bet that Conchita didn't know it either."

Julia nodded. "We keep our troubles to ourselves, don't we? But I'm not sure that is the best way. We lock everyone out." She shook her head and looked at Paul. "Don't you lock Ellen out. Not ever. Let her share the worry and the fear and the failure as well as all the good. Don't let her be lonely. Believe me, I know what loneliness is." She made a gesture of dismissal. "You've been up all night. Go have something to eat."

Scott was sitting over a cup of coffee. "I've been left out. Fill me in." He smiled at George. "Does that surprise you? Let's say that I'm curious to know what is happening." It was not simple curiosity. It was something far deeper, and he would have been at a loss to explain it except by one word—Jenny. He was here in Stanhope, summoned. Jenny remained in Berkeley facing without flinching what he should never have involved her in. There was the word—involvement. "From square one," he said, and settled back to listen.

339

While he talked, George ate—freshly squeezed orange juice, bacon from Stanfield pigs, eggs from Stanfield hens, toasted homemade bread, honey from Stanfield hives, freshly ground coffee.

Paul ate, and listened, and the single word *water* set up a clamor in his mind. He waited until George had finished talking before he mentioned it. "Benjie says they talked about water." He was speaking to Scott. "All Ruben could think of was wells." He hesitated. "That doesn't sound right." He looked at George, but it was Scott who pursued the subject.

"Why doesn't it sound right?" Scott said.

Paul shook his head. "I don't know. It just doesn't." What was he doing here, anyway? He didn't know the answer. At a time like this an outsider's presence was resented, and after last night's performance, going in with Ellen to see the old lady, accepting the diamond ring, putting it on Ellen's finger and then facing George. . . .

George said sharply, "You had some idea. What was it? Why not the wells?"

They both watched him. Put up or shut up, Paul thought. He said slowly, "Why *two* cases of dynamite? And Pete told Benjie they came from different places. Why go to all that trouble if you were only going to blow wells? How many sticks of dynamite does it take to blow a well?"

Scott sipped his coffee, his eyes on George. He lowered his cup slowly. "I should think one stick of powder to a well would make quite a mess."

"It would," George said.

"And we don't have nearly that many wells."

There was silence.

Scott said to Paul, "Then what is your guess?"

"It's—far out, wild."

George snorted. In a rare display of temper, he said, "Goddam it, speak up. If you've got an idea, let's hear it." They were all jumpy, he thought.

"All right," Paul said. He took a deep breath. "All my life I've listened to talk about water. This was a desert once, or near enough, and now it's the richest agricultural area in the country. Because of water. The climate has changed, the humidity had risen. Because of water. I grew up swimming in the

340

canals. So did Pete. We know how much a part of life they are here . . ."

Scott said, "Oh, my God!" He was looking at George. "He's right. Don't you see it? Right now, at the beginning of summer, all those irrigation canals, what would two cases of dynamite spread around in bombs of two or three sticks each do to the whole irrigation system in this part of the Valley?"

George was silent. His face was grim.

"Or worse yet," Scott said, "bombs at the sources, where the canals are fed by natural streams? A burned-down dehydrator or a cannery temporarily out of action are minor compared to that." He paused. "Well?"

Slowly George nodded. He was looking at Paul. "Lucero said you understood Pete's mind better than he did. What would be his point? What would he gain by ruining an entire irrigation system, not just for us, but for this whole part of the Valley?"

"You don't dig it yet, do you?" Paul said. "I guess maybe it isn't your fault. You think there has to be a reason. Well, there does, but the reason doesn't have to make sense except in a special kind of way, and it isn't your way."

Pete had said that trying to explain to George was like talking color to the blind. Was this what he had meant? "Go on," George said.

"All your life," Paul said, "You've built things, put them together on top of what your grandfather built, and mine, and the ones before them, bigger holdings, diversification into bigger conglomerates, bigger banks . . ." He spread his hands. "Name it. Bigger everything."

"And," George said, "that is wrong?"

"I didn't say that," Paul said. "I don't even think it. I think we need a lot of changes, but I think the structures are sound." He paused. "But that's the point, right there. There are people who think the structures are unsound, that they are so unsound and unfair and degrading that the only thing to do is tear them down, period."

"And build what?" George said.

Scott said, "You're still missing the point. Tear down, period. Building something else isn't even thought about. Rebuilding isn't on the agenda."

341

George was silent for a long time. He said at last to Paul, "And you think that is Pete's idea? Destroy, or at least cripple, an entire agricultural complex? Try to turn this area back into semidesert?"

"I told you it was far out, wild."

"But," Scott said, "put two cases of dynamite into a discussion of water, and what other conclusion do you reach?"

George shook his head helplessly. "I don't know. I'm over my depth." At least he was trying, Ellen had said, and had thanked him for it. But trying by itself was not enough. Success was what mattered. He was a stranger to despair, but he was hearing its lament now.

"*Hasta jueves,*" Scott said. "Until Thursday. And Thursday comes in at midnight tonight."

Consuelo appeared in the doorway. She spoke to George. "Telephone for you, Señor. It is Señor Meyer at the bank. He says it is urgent."

Paul watched George nod, throw down his napkin, push back his chair, and rise wearily. "I'll come back," George said.

Paul drank his coffee. Scott's eyes were on him, and he wished they were not. "What's on your mind?" Scott said.

He was an outsider, Paul told himself, remember that. And of all families, this one resented intrusion most. He had said it to Benjie last night at the gates. This was the castle—the rest of the world, and the peasants in that world, shut out. Suddenly he thought of the old lady in the bed upstairs, and of the diamond on Ellen's finger. Maybe he was not as much of an outsider as most, at that. He said slowly, carefully, "How much can he stand?"

"George?" Scott's eyebrows rose in mild surprise. "Why, I suppose as much as you, we, anybody can pile on him." The words were suddenly silly, meaningless.

Nobody's strength was without limit. That was a truism, of course, but he was seeing things, even truisms, in a new light today. How much could George stand? He looked at Paul with new interest. "It is a good question," he said, "and I don't know the answer."

"He has Pete to worry about," Paul said, "and Ellen. He has Ruben Lucero to deal with, and a hatchet man named Lang. After Ben Wilson killed himself, I listened to Ellen

342

calling your brother away from Clara Wilson when that's where he wanted to be. Ellen told me that he was at work in his study at five o'clock yesterday morning, because, I guess, he has to know the facts and make the decisions on all the things that matter in all the directions Stanfield interests go. I heard him dealing with Lewis Mattingly on the telephone . . ."

"The power play," Scott said, and was surprised at Paul's reaction.

"Is that how you see it?" Paul said. "Because what he said to Mattingly was that he'd been caught with his fingers in the till and he was lucky he wasn't facing criminal prosecution, and instead he was trying to turn a profit on what amounted to downright theft."

Scott blinked. "I didn't know that."

"No," Paul said, remembering Julia out in the hall, "he keeps his problems to himself." He was silent then as George walked in and sat down heavily.

Scott said, "Now what?"

George shook his head.

"Karl said it was urgent."

"I'll take care of it," George said. But he would wait a little time before he did, he told himself, because in his present mood he would be too strongly tempted to pick young Cleary Ward up and break him in half for his disloyalty. He looked at Paul. "You seem to have guessed right so far. Now what?" He saw resistance forming in Paul's face, and he met it head on. "You dealt yourself in," George said. "You heard what Benjie said, and you made your decision and brought her here. You're involved."

There was that word again, Scott thought; it grew larger with each repetition. "I'd say the first thing is to try to find Pete," he said.

"And the dynamite," George said. He nodded.

Paul said, "Just Pete." They both looked at him. "Julio," Paul said, "is a mute, but even if he could talk, he can't think. The others are just young punks with black berets and dark glasses trying to make themselves important. By themselves they wouldn't know what to do with dynamite. Pete's doing the thinking for all of them, telling them when, what, where,

343

how." He paused, looking straight at George. "I grew up with him, remember? I know . . ."

"Yes," George said. "I know." His voice was tired. "You know him better than I ever did, just as you know Ellen." His voice sharpened. "I could hate your guts for that, young fellow, because I have to sit and listen while you tell me about my own children." He snapped his fingers with the sound of a whip popping. "All right. Pete it is. Can you find him, you and Lucero? Can you talk some sense into him, or at least sit on him? Can you—?" He stopped, and shook his head slowly. "I'm asking. I don't ask very often. Can you help?"

"I can try," Paul said.

35

All his life he had been alone—he understood that now. Oh sometimes, as during those years when he and Paul were growing up together, inseparable, he had cherished the illusion of belonging, but he knew now how false that concept had been. Benjie, of course, was merely final proof that for him, Pete Stanfield, deep personal attachments were impossible. He felt now that he had recognized truth and finally shucked off the last sense of restraint.

The house where he had holed up like a badger in its den was old. It stood on the outskirts of Stanhope, well away from the *barrio,* isolated in the midst of a forest of giant eucalyptus trees that filled the air with their pungent odor. Pete had long ago chosen the house and rented it against need. You thought ahead. What else was intelligence for?

He had the pickup in the barn, the door closed. He had carried the two cases of dynamite, tape, fuses, and caps into the house, and now, humming softly to himself, he was assembling packages of explosives and setting them carefully in one of the opened boxes. It was monotonous work, but the results would be worth the effort. On the floor beside the boxes lay a black beret and dark glasses.

That scene with Benjie still rankled. Many scenes still rankled—with Paul and Ellen the night of the canal swim, with Scott, with his father, with the senator, with Ruben Lucero, especially with Lucero, who was an unimaginative jerk totally unwilling to take suggestions. And how could a man like that be looked up to by anybody, let alone somebody like Paul Meyer who was not without intelligence? It made no sense.

The pile of explosive packages grew. Once, Pete remembered, the New York newspapers had kept referring to an unknown man as the Mad Bomber, and Pete had resented their automatic assumption that the man was deranged. Maybe he had his reasons, and maybe they were good reasons, as Pete's own were now. Then who was mad, the man or those who were so quick to accuse him falsely? The trouble was that people refused to understand, and so they had to be shown. It was as simple, as logical, as that.

He worked on patiently, taping dynamite sticks into small bundles, attaching fuses and caps, laying the bombs carefully into the opened boxes. He was still humming. It was the Mack the Knife tune from the Beggar's Opera, and like some of his thoughts it tucked its tail in its mouth and rolled endlessly like a hoop. He wished he knew how to end it.

* * *

Jenny Falk's voice on the phone was, like herself, calm, controlled. "I am seeing Judson Brown again this morning, Scotty. What do you want me to tell him?"

He had no idea, and the result was pure frustration. "Damn it," Scott said, and there was that word again, "you haven't any business being involved."

"We settled that, Scotty." Was there a smile in her voice? And then, gently, "How is your father?"

"On his way out." And, he thought with surprise, I am going to miss him. So are a lot of people. When death is imminent, many views are changed. It was a new concept.

"I am sorry," Jenny said. "I liked him. I admired him." Epitaph.

346

Scott said, "Everything's happening at once. Thank God you're not involved in the rest of it."

"If you are, Scotty, I am." Gentle reminder.

Scott stared at the far wall of the study. How often had George sat in this chair and faced up to problems that were almost insoluble? By comparison to what he has dealt with, Scott thought, my life has been serene. Shameful thought. "Will you marry me?" he said.

On the phone there was only silence.

"This," Scott said, "is the hell of a way to propose. I know it. But I am proposing. Will you marry me?"

"Scotty." Protest. "You are involved in a paternity suit, and what the girl is willing to settle for is marriage . . ."

"There is a way," Scott said. He was staring still at the wall. There is always some way. True? False? Unimportant. "What Cathy wants," he said, "is a name for her baby. And she wants that name to be Stanfield." He paused, waiting.

Quietly, "Go on, Scotty."

"Am I being arrogant? I suppose I am. Maybe arrogance is born in me, in all of us. Never mind. Marry me. We will offer to adopt the child at birth. Its name will be Stanfield. In addition . . ." He paused. "What kind of cash settlement will Cathy accept?"

There was a long silence. Then, in a new, different voice, "I have no idea," Jenny said.

"Will you find out?" The private telephone on the desk rang softly. "A moment," Scott said, and picked it up, spoke his name.

"This is Clara Wilson, Scott." The voice paused. "I wanted to speak to George, but maybe this is better." Another pause. "Will you give him a message, please? Right after Ben's funeral I am going away, leaving Stanhope. For good. I think, I hope that George will understand."

"I'll ask him to call you," Scott said.

"I don't want him to call me. Tell him that, too, please." The phone went dead.

Scott hung up slowly. Into the other phone he said, the words automatic, "I'm sorry. Interruption." It was hard to readjust. "Where were we?"

"In the midst of confusion."

The tone of her voice alarmed him. "Look . . ." Scott paused, and took a deep breath. George had blown it with Clara, that was obvious. Was he, Scott, about to blow it with Jenny? Or worse, had he already? "Did I say the wrong thing?"

"That depends, Scotty."

"I guess," Scott said slowly, "I've gone about the whole thing the wrong way. I'm trying to have everything, but mostly you, because you're what I want. No, maybe need is the word. In order to have you, I'll do whatever I must." It was somehow easier now, the balm of confession at work, And the stakes were plain. "I'll go begging to Cathy myself," he said, "if that is what it takes."

There was a long silence. "There is no need," Jenny said at last. "I will plead for you." She paused. "For us," she said.

* * *

Ruben Lucero said, "We have look, and I do not think Pete Stanfield is in the *barrio*." He and Paul were alone in the small office, Lucero at his desk, Paul on one of the straight chairs. "Is possible," Lucero said, "but I think not."

"And Julio?" Paul said.

"Julio we will find. I hope before the police." Lucero shook his head. "But he will be able to tell us nothing." He tapped his head with his forefinger. "He is a *niño,* a child."

Paul was thinking of Benjie and of two men dead. "A dangerous child." He made a sudden, sharp gesture of dismissal. Pete was the important one, not Julio.

Lucero saw it too. "Where to hide?" he said, and he shrugged. "I have say it to you: you know the mind of Pete Stanfield better than me. If you are wanting to stay out of sight, where do you go here in Stanhope, the town you know well? Think of that."

"If I were a cow," Paul said, and could smile faintly, "where would I go? And I went there, and the cow had?" The smile was quickly gone. He nodded. "You make sense, Ruben." As usual. He paused. "About the other, dynamiting canals, what do you think of that?"

Lucero spread his hands. He studied them. Then he

348

looked up. "How many mile of canal? How many control gate? How many hundred of section of land, of crops needing water?" He shook his head and anger sparkled in his eyes. "A man gone mad? That is how you think?" Slowly he nodded. "*Creo que sí.* I believe yes." He paused and drew a deep breath. "Julio . . ." He shook his head again. He opened his hands and closed them with slow relentlessness. "When we find Julio, I would squeeze the truth out of him, but he is a child and he does not talk."

"There are the others," Paul said, "the *chicos* in the black berets."

Lucero was silent, motionless for a little time, thoughtful. Slowly he nodded again. "*Sí,*" he said, and that was all.

Paul walked out into the bright sunlight. He nodded to the two men on guard and felt their eyes following him as he walked out to his pickup. I am Anglo, he thought, therefore suspect. At a time like this all groups close ranks, our own as well. He stopped in surprise at the sight of the white Mercedes waiting, Scott at the wheel. "Get in," Scott said. "I'll be your chauffeur. Just tell me where." His usual lightness and ease were missing.

Pete's little house first. The front door was held closed by the twisted wire one of Walling's men had rigged. Paul undid it, and they went inside. Scott said, "What are we looking for?"

"I don't know." Simple truth. I am trying to put myself in Pete's place, Paul thought; and walked slowly through the few rooms. Nothing. He came back to Scott who watched him quietly. "I'm no good at this," Paul said. "I don't even have an idea."

Always competition brought out the best in him, the refusal to quit. "You were kids here together," Scott said, "just as George and Peter Juan and I were. We walked and rode bicycles, horses. We swam in the canals and stole melons, tomatoes, peaches from farmers' fields and laughed when somebody chased us away." He paused. "Didn't you?"

Paul nodded. "We did."

"We had games, too," Scott said. "Cops and robbers, cowboys and Indians, hide and seek. We had secret places, and places we were afraid to go after dark. George was *serio,*

349

but Peter Juan and I had friends, girls we knew and weren't supposed to know, and we had places where we took them." He paused. "Give you any ideas?"

Paul was silent, contemplative, trying to let memory work. At last slowly, doubtfully, he nodded. "Maybe a couple," he said. "Let's go."

The first stop was Stanhope Lanes, clean and shiny, echoing with the rumble of the bowling balls and the clatter of pins. Scott said, "I didn't know Pete bowled." He shook his head. "I expect there is a lot about Pete I don't know."

The manager was in. "Johnny Velarde," Paul said, and they shook hands.

"Pauley boy," Velarde said. "You going to roll a few frames?" He was a short, square man with heavy hands. "This boy," he said to Scott, "could have been one of the good ones. A beautiful natural hook. He and Pete Stanfield . . ."

Paul said, "Have you seen Pete?" He tried to keep his voice expressionless.

Velarde shook his head. "Last I hear he's off somewhere, maybe over to the coast, maybe down L.A. way." He shrugged. "I see him, I'll tell him you're looking for him, Pauley." His quick ebullience was gone. "No more bowling, huh, kid? Too bad."

Paul smiled. "Maybe someday, Johnny." He and Scott walked out to the parking lot. As they got into the car, "There's a room behind Johnny's office," Paul said. "We used to play poker there." He shook his head. "I don't think Johnny would lie to me. Not about Pete." He paused. "It was a long shot." Another pause. "They all are."

"Until the last one," Scott said. "Where now?"

Out of town, past the vast vineyards under John Silva's care, past a projecting corner of fenced green land where the Stanfield Angus grazed. On the way they passed a solid forest of giant eucalyptus, isolated, incongruous and wasteful in this fertile valley.

Scott gestured at the trees. "We've made mistakes," he said. "There is one of them. My grandfather planted those trees, forty acres of them. Fellow from Grand Rapids was going to use the lumber for fine furniture. He never did, and there just isn't any economical way to get rid of the trees.

350

They've poisoned the soil, and it would cost more than it would be worth to cut them down, blast out the stumps and leach the ground back to use."

Paul nodded. He knew the story well. His mind was on Pete. "You talked with him," he said. "So have I. Did he seem all right to you?"

"I didn't give him a Rorschach test, if that's what you mean."

"He's flipped," Paul said. "What happened to Benjie is the final proof." He paused. "And that means that trying to run him down by logic just isn't in the cards." He looked at Scott. "What do you think?"

"We keep trying," Scott said. "Unless you have a better suggestion?"

"That's the hell of it," Paul said. "I don't."

It was a farm they drove to, a small house and barn surrounded by fields of tomatoes. In the yard chickens scurried out of the way of the white Mercedes, and two dogs set up a clamor as Paul and Scott got out. Scott looked around curiously. "The name," Paul said, "is Baccigalupa. We used to sit in the cellar with Mr. B and drink his grappa." He paused. "Stanfield land," he said. "Did you know that? One tenant your brother has let stay."

Scott shook his head. "I didn't know." There is much about George that I don't know, he thought, and always I have been sure I knew him inside and out. Humbling discovery.

The back door of the little house opened to the dogs' clamor. The woman who came out was tiny and old with white hair in a coil on top of her head. She wiped her hands on her apron as she looked at the automobile and then at the two men. Recognition was slow. "Land sakes alive," she said at last. "Pauley Meyer."

"Mrs. B," Paul said. He bent to kiss her cheek. "This is George Stanfield's brother Scott. We're looking for Pete. Have you seen him?"

The old lady's eyes were shrewd. "What has he done, Pauley?"

"You've seen him?"

"I didn't say that, child. I asked what he had done." She was silent for a moment, watching Paul's face. She said, "He's

351

done something. I always knew he would, and hoped he wouldn't." She shook her head. "Some boys are scamps or worse. Pete was. You weren't. I don't know what the difference is, but some are headed for trouble just as sure as sure." She shook her head again. "I haven't seen him, Pauley." She hesitated. "And don't tell me what he's done. I don't think I want to know."

Paul nodded. "Thank you, Mrs. B."

"Maybe," the old lady said, "you'll come back some day and sit in the cellar again and drink grappa with Papa. He would like that. So would I." She turned away and walked back into the house.

They got into the car and Scott drove carefully out of the yard. "Zero," Paul said. His tone was bitter. "What the little boy shot at—nothing." He glanced at Scott. "Only one more idea," he said. "If she still lives where she did. Pete and I . . ." He shook his head. "Never mind. Her name is Carlotta. She says."

Carlotta lived in the same apartment and she was home, large, blondined, jovial, wearing tight blue toreador pants and a flowered blouse beneath which her large, unbrassiered breasts jounced. "Pauley baby. And who is your friend? Come in."

Scott, smiling, watching, thought of a line from Kipling: "More like a mother she were."

"We're looking for Pete," Paul said.

"He's back in town?" Carlotta looked pleased. "Maybe he'll remember Carlotta and come around some time." She shook her head. "But I haven't seen him yet, Pauley. How about a beer?"

"We can't stay."

Carlotta shrugged. The large breasts bounced. "Too bad." She smiled at Scott. "We could have fun." The smile spread. "Maybe another time?"

At the door way Scott hesitated. He took out his wallet and extended a ten dollar bill. "Even negative information," he said, "has its value."

Carlotta took the bill and folded it carefully. Her smile was apologetic. "If you come back," she said, "I'll remember this. Thanks, mister." The door closed reluctantly.

Paul got into the car and sat quiet, dejected. "I ought to be able to think of a dozen possible places to look," he said, "but I can't think of one." He paused. "And even if I could, Pete wouldn't be there because I'd be thinking one way, and he's thinking another."

"You've been up all night," Scott said.

"I've done that before."

"Maybe not quite the same kind of night."

True. Waiting for Ellen at the gate, the drive to the airport, the sight of the senator and the clash with the doctor, that unreal scene in Marquesa's bedroom and memory still vivid of the great diamond on Ellen's hand, Benjie, George, Walling, Lang—it all ran together in a dull weary stream.

"I think some sleep for you," Scott said.

"There isn't time for sleep. Damn it, man, don't you see what's going to happen if we don't find him?" Paul's voice had risen. He controlled it. "Besides, I promised your brother." Ellen's father.

"You promised to try. You've tried. After some sleep you can try again. We'll go to the ranch." Scott put the car in gear.

"Look," Paul said, "Lucero . . ."

"Lucero can telephone the ranch as well as anyplace else."

True. Logical. And all wrong, because something was nagging, muttering to itself in the back of his mind. He tried to identify it and failed. Like a name forgotten, Paul thought, if you try too hard to remember it, it almost never comes. He relaxed wearily in the seat. "Okay," he said.

Ellen met them in the front hall. She was wearing cut-off jeans and a short-sleeved blouse, barefoot, the diamond flashing on her hand. She was, Paul thought, the loveliest thing he had ever seen, and she kissed him right there as if it were the most natural thing in the world. He wondered if it would ever be. "Daddy's sleeping," she said, "and you should too." She led him off, up the broad stairway, and Scott, smiling, watched them go.

* * *

There were three youths, chicanos, all wearing black berets and dark glasses, and they stood uneasy, attempting

353

bravado, in front of Ruben Lucero's desk. The man with the potting spade stood behind them. Lucero spoke in Spanish. His voice was quiet, but it held an edge.

"I do not like violence," he said. "You know that. You, Jaime, you, Pepe, you, Joe. I do not like this Anglo world we live in either, any more than you do."

The three glanced at one another. The tallest, Jaime, smiled a little. He spoke in English. "We fix it, dad."

"No," Lucero said, In Spanish still, "you will fix nothing. You will not destroy more, ruin crops, waste water, put everyone out of work . . ." He spread those large hands. "Only to show," he said, "what great men you are, *Conquistadores*." He spoke the name with scorn.

Jaime smiled again. "They pay attention to us then."

Lucero stood up. Jaime's smile disappeared. Lucero said gently, "The only attention they will pay is to find you and put you in jail." He paused, watching Jaime steadily. "And then," he said, "they, those Anglos whose world this is, they will say to one another, 'See? What have I told you? These chicanos are like mad dogs. They are no better than animals the way they live, and all they know to do is destroy, destroy. So we will teach them a lesson.' " He paused again. "That is what kind of attention you will get. You, and all the rest of us." A third pause. Then, very quietly, "You will not do what you think to do. Instead, you will tell me where and when and how. You will tell me, Ruben Lucero, everything—is that understood?"

The room was silent. Pepe and Joe looked at Jaime. Jaime took a deep breath. The smile was missing. "Look, dad, we tell you nothing. You dig? Our business. You wait an' see what happen, an' then . . ."

"You will tell me," Lucero said. His quiet voice was like a blow. To the man with the potting spade, "Take those two outside," pointing at Pepe and Joe. "This big one I will—talk to alone."

As the door closed after them, the three heard Jaime's voice, overloud, saying, "I tell you nothing, you got that, dad? Nothing!"

"We will see," said Lucero.

354

Ellen came into the study, closed the door, and stood indecisive. Paul was sleeping, and Daddy, and the big house was quiet, but tension and a sense of waiting were in the air. Ellen stared at the wastebasket where Daddy had thrown the crumpled paper he had been reading when she came to see him—how long before?

"I couldn't wait, Daddy," she had said. "I'm sorry. I know everything is happening, but I had to talk to you." She was very conscious of the diamond on her hand and she was tempted to hide it behind her back, but pride would not allow it.

George's face was tired when he looked up from the paper, and for a moment he seemed almost bewildered. Then he crumpled the paper and tossed it in the basket. His voice was expressionless. "About what, honey?" And then, "That is a silly question, isn't it? You and Paul?"

"Yes, Daddy."

He nodded as if gathering his thoughts and walked slowly around the desk to sink into the big chair. "Sit down."

"I'd—rather stand. If you don't mind."

His gesture was weary. Ellen could not remember ever seeing weariness in him before. Always he had seemed large, indefatigable, indestructible. "Suit yourself," he said. He put his big hands flat on the desk top and stared at them. Then at last he looked up. "You want to marry him." It was a statement, no question, but it required comment.

"I am going to marry him, Daddy."

For the first time George's face lightened a trifle; he almost smiled. "Stanfield women," he said. "Conchita. Marquesa." And then, "Maybe just women. I don't know much about them." He seemed to rouse himself. "What do you want from me?" His eyes went to the hand that wore the diamond ring then lifted again to her face. "The decision seems to have been made." A faint bitter smile appeared. "I am outranked, honey."

"I want your approval," Ellen said.

"If I refused it, would you change your mind?"

"No, Daddy." She paused. "But something would be—

355

spoiled." Her voice rose suddenly. "Can't you see that? Oh, I know, it isn't as important to you as it is to me. You have too many other things to worry about, people, affairs, what's happening all around us now, today, what's going to happen." The words were almost running together. She forced herself to slow down. "All I have is me. And all I want is Paul. And to have you say it's okay, that you'll be happy because I'm going to be happy, because what you think, what you feel is more important to me than you've ever known." She paused. "That's why I want your approval."

The room was still. George's big shoulders stirred gently. His eyes had not left the girl's face. "I didn't know that."

"Maybe," Ellen said slowly, "maybe I should have told you. But how could I? What could I say? 'Daddy. You're very important to me?' Wouldn't that sound dumb?"

"And if you had," George said with a slow solemnity to match her own, "I would probably have said, 'Yes. Of course. I'm busy now.' " He was silent for a time. "My fault, honey. I'm sorry."

"It's okay, Daddy." Compassion stirred. "You're tired. Why don't you get some sleep? We can—talk later."

George hesitated, and then nodded, and heaved himself out of his chair. "I think I will." He walked to her and put his hands gently on her shoulders. "You're going to be very happy with Paul, and that is going to make me very happy too." He kissed her forehead lightly and walked out.

Now, standing in the study, remembering, staring at the wastebasket, Ellen felt off-balance and even vaguely frightened because it had been almost too easy, a single push toppling Daddy into capitulation—marvelous, but unbelievable.

Slowly she crossed the study and looked down at the crumpled paper. Under normal circumstances not for the world would she have pried into Daddy's or anybody else's private business. All her life she had been taught and had lived by that creed. Now she was going to transgress; she had to. She bent and picked up the paper, smoothed it, read:

"George: Clara Wilson called. She asked me to tell you that right after Ben's funeral she is leaving Stanhope for good. She doesn't want you to phone her. Sorry. /s/ Scott."

Ellen heard the door open. She turned and through her

sudden tears could recognize George only because of his bulk. She gestured with the paper. "You and Mrs. Wilson," she said. "Oh, Daddy, I am so sorry!"

"Thank you, honey." He caught her and held her close. "So am I." He kissed the top of her head. "Some mistakes," he said, "you can't do anything but keep paying for."

* * *

Paul was in that precarious state between sleep and full consciousness, drifting free amidst half-thoughts and unreal images. There was sound like the stirring of wind in trees. There was ghostly laughter and footsteps in the dark. No bird sang, but from time to time he could hear small-footed scurrying, and moonlight from a gibbous moon filtered down. He tried to run and could not. His own voice made no sound. Somewhere·a dog howled, speaking clearly of recent death. Shadows writhed. Suddenly a voice was lifted in a single wordless shout, and instantly he was awake, sweating, for the moment not knowing where he was.

He was lying on top of the bed, wearing only his shorts. His shirt and pants lay folded on a chair above his socks and shoes. He was inside the castle, he thought, and smiled at the concept as he got up and began to dress. Through the windows he could see lengthened shadows on the broad lawn. Part dream, part the reality of memory—as he went into the bathroom and sloshed cold water on his face he tried to sort it out. Then he went downstairs to George's study.

George was there, expressionless, and Scott; both men studied him. Scott said, "Ideas? We have no news."

Paul sat down. He ran one hand through his hair in a gesture of uncertainty. "It's far out," he said, "and maybe all wrong. But I dreamed. Something I hadn't dreamed in years. Maybe because we saw it today."

George was scowling. Scott said, "Something rang a bell?"

"That eucalyptus grove," Paul said. "There's a house in it."

"I'm aware of it," George said. "So?"

"Kids thought it was haunted," Paul said. "Chicano kids wouldn't go near it. Pete and I did once. At night. On a dare.

357

We were scared. Somebody yelled at us, and we ran. I dreamed about it for weeks. Pete did too. We used to talk about it."

George, scowling still, shook his head. Scott said, "You think Pete might have gone there just because it's an unlikely place for him to go?"

"I told you it was far out."

Scott stood up. "But worth a try." He looked down at George.

"No," George said. "I'll stay here. Walling has promised to call if he finds anything." He was no longer scowling as he watched Paul stand. "Be careful," he said. "Both of you. If you find him . . . " He paused. "Call for help," he said.

Outside in the dusk a ground mist was gathering. Scott thought back to the drive home from Carmel. It was on that night too, he remembered, that the cannery had been bombed.

"A good night for mischief," Paul said, and it was obvious he was thinking along the same lines. "*Jueves* isn't until midnight, but if I'd planned something and fog came along, I think I'd speed up the timetable." He turned in the seat to look questioningly at Scott.

Scott nodded. Already the mist was heavier. He switched to low beams and concentrated on his driving. "George thinks he's flipped too. He thinks he's dangerous."

"Once a few years ago," Paul said, "at Squaw Valley, I think he tried to kill himself, and if he hadn't lost a ski, I think he might have made it. He was trying to turn into the trees, but his safety binding let go. There was a girl giving him a bad time."

Scott thought of Cathy Strong and said nothing.

"We never skied together again," Paul said. "A lot of things we stopped doing together for various reasons." Epitaph for the past. "He thinks I'm a nut for following Ruben. Ruben thinks I'm some kind of nut for not staying inside the Establishment. He told me the other day that sometime he'd have to negotiate a contract with me and he hoped I'd remember how it looked from below." Paul paused. "That will be a day."

"Maybe," Scott said. In the fog he had once more that

odd feeling of isolation, of speaking as to a stranger casually met and never to be seen again. "When you start out," he said, "you don't know where you'll end. For twenty years I thought I knew. Now I wonder."

The fog was thicker, and they came to the eucalyptus grove almost before Scott was aware of it. Paul said, "There's a road into the house. Over to the right. It winds——Jesus!"

Dimmer lights and the roaring shape of a pickup shaving past them and gone into the fog out toward the highway. Scott had reacted instantly, wrenching the Mercedes out of the way, wrenching it back from the looming tree trunks. Now he slowed and let his breath out in a long sigh. "Could you see who was driving?" he said. "Was it—?"

"Black beret," Paul said, "and dark glasses, one of the *Conquistadores*." He paused, his nerves tightening now. "I think we're getting close."

The great dim shapes of the trees were all around them, and the mist was heavy with their pungent scent. A haunted wood—Paul could not escape the thought—and remembering that night so long ago he felt the tingling of tiny mice feet running up and down his spine. "There's the house," he said. He was almost whispering. "There's a barn over there."

Scott stopped the car and they sat quiet, the engine ticking over with hardly a sound. The house showed no light. In the eerie glow of headlights reflected in the fog, there was no discernible movement. Scott turned off the engine, and the silence was absolute. Paul opened his door and stepped out. Scott opened the glove compartment. "Flashlight," he said, and pressed it into Paul's hand. He got out of the car on his own side.

Together they walked to the barn. The doors were open, and the building was empty. There was a scurrying sound in a far corner, and when Paul turned the flashlight beam toward it two tiny eyes glowed red and then disappeared. He turned the light on the dirt floor. Tire tracks were plain, and dropped oil gleamed wetly, not yet absorbed by the ground. "That pickup that almost hit us was parked here," Paul said. "Let's try the house."

The boards of the front porch squeaked. The front door opened on noisy hinges. Inside, mingled with the eucalyptus scent, was another, sweeter odor, unmistakable. "Pot," Paul said. "Somebody smoking Mary Jane." He played the flashlight beam around the room. In the fireplace lay four smoked-down cigarette stubs. Over near a crude bench lay a partially used roll of friction tape and an opened pocket knife.

Paul picked the knife up. It was small and flat with a red handle inlaid with a shield and cross in steel. He opened a second blade, a nailfile, and by the beam of the flash read the engraving on its smooth side: ABERCROMBIE & FITCH, MADE IN SWITZERLAND. "That was no local chicano," he said. "They don't patronize Abercrombie."

Scott said, "You said the driver of the pickup—"

"Anybody can wear a black beret and dark glasses." Paul's voice was definite. "It was Pete. We were that close." He closed the blades and slipped the knife in his pocket. "We'd better tell George." He paused. "And the police." He paused again. "Wherever he's going with all that powder, he's already on his way."

George was waiting in the front hall when Consuelo opened the door and showed the two men in. The first was a tall young chicano in a black beret and dark glasses with a bruise high on one cheek. He walked slowly and seemed to breathe with effort. Behind him came Ruben Lucero, his face expressionless. "In here," George said, and led the way into the study, held the door, closed it after them. He walked around to his desk chair. "Sit down."

Lucero shook his head. "This is no business meet. Jaime here, he have things to tell you." Lucero's voice was low-pitched, level. He faced George squarely. "Jaime," he said, "is chicano punk. Not all chicano young are punks."

"I am aware of it," George said.

Lucero acknowledged agreement with a faint nod. "Jaime," he said, "is *Conquistador*. If he was Anglo, and if he had the money to buy motorcycle, he would be Hell's Angel, that kind of lousy bum. Your son, Mister Stanfield, have use these punks, these *Conquistadores*. He have also use a man of me, a child, Julio."

"I am aware of that too," George said.

"After midnight tonight . . . "

"*Jueves,*" George said.

360

Lucero nodded. *"Sí, jueves, mañana."* He had automatically switched to Spanish. "Over by the mountains, the dams that store the water for the canals, the locks of the main canals themselves—those are what they are going to destroy, Mister Stanfield." He switched back to English. "Your son have show Jaime and the rest how to do these thing. He have the powder. He make the bombs. That is what Jaime tell me." Lucero paused. "That is what I believe, Mister Stanfield."

"I believe it too." George paused. "Do you know where they are to meet, the *Conquistadores* and Pete?"

Lucero looked at the young man. His voice very gentle, "Tell him, Jaime," he said.

Jaime hesitated. He looked at Lucero and did not like what he saw. He looked at George and found no pity there, either. "There's this road," he said in a voice so low it was scarcely audible. "It's called the Turkey Creek road, you know?"

Echo out of the past. Turkey Creek. "I know," George said.

"There's a bridge," Jaime said. "An', like, after the bridge, there's a road that goes off to the right, a little road. It goes to the first dam."

"I know that, too," George said.

Jaime's voice sank even lower. "That's it," he said. "That's the place. Just after midnight." He looked down at the floor.

Lucero said, "I come to you, Mister Stanfield . . . "

"I understand why." Their eyes met. "For the same reason," George said, "that Paul Meyer came to me last night with the girl and word of the dynamite. To show me that you had nothing to do with it."

"Sí."

"I believe it," George said. "I believe you." He looked up as the door opened and Scott and Paul walked in. "We have the word," George said. "We know where and what. And we know when."

"No." Paul shook his head. "You haven't been outside. Fog. And Pete's already on his way in a pickup. He almost hit us." He dug into his pocket, took out the knife, and laid it on George's desk. "He left this, with a roll of bicycle tape."

361

George looked at the knife in silence. He poked it slowly with his forefinger as if to test its reality. He looked up at Paul and nodded. Then he picked up the telephone and dialed the operator. "I want to speak to Chief of Police Walling," he said. "This is George Stanfield. It is an emergency."

* * *

The fog was thick. From Stockton to the Tehachapi, from the Coast range to the Sierra Nevada it filled the great Valley like a bowl, slowing to a crawl the truck traffic that during the summer growing season never ceased. When the produce was ripe it had to be picked, transported, processed—grapes, melons, lettuce, tomatoes, all of the bounty of this rich irrigated land, on the road.

Pete pushed the pickup as fast as he dared. The fog was a good omen, a propitious sign. "We cut open the sheep." He said it aloud. "And we examined its entrails, and all signs were go, go, go." He was smiling, high, flying, as once he remembered, he had told that silly bitch Benjie and they had flown together.

But always, always, as he knew now, he had really flown alone. "There is only me and thee. And I don't even know thee. Which leaves only me." The rattle of the pickup body and the clatter of its engine were accompaniment to his thoughts.

He was on the Turkey Creek road and he liked that. Of course it had some stupid number these days, and it was no longer dirt and no longer meandering as it made its way across the Valley toward the great mountains, but to anyone bred in the Valley it was still the Turkey Creek road. And this was fitting, because—God knew Pete had been told often enough—Turkey Creek was where it all began, the whole goddam dynasty, Ezra Stanfield meeting Rudi and Lotte Meyer for the first time. Turkey Creek was where the 1849 action was, and what better poetic justice could you have?

Maybe back in 1849 things had not yet come to such a fucking mess. Maybe. Maybe if Turkey Creek had never been, things would have been different. Maybe. But maybe was as silly as what might have been, and the only time was now, now, now. His thoughts were a high fierce chant, and in the

362

fog, thick and fluffy, hiding him as securely as he had been hidden in his mother's womb, he could allow them full play. He turned in the driver's seat and shook his fist out of the cab window back in the general direction of Stanhope. "I'll show you bastards! Every goddam one of you!"

He did not see the approaching truck lights until it was too late.

* * *

Twenty miles away they heard the explosion and even, so it is said, saw the reflected flash in the heavy fog. The sound, they will tell you, was like distant summer thunder but sharper, more concentrated, with no rolling aftersounds. The moment you heard it, they say, you knew what it was, and what it had to mean, although not until daylight and fog burned off by the summer sun, could anyone assess the total destruction.

It was God's hand, they say, that caused the collision to take place in open country, away from houses, farm buildings, people. One truck loaded with what appeared to have been melons and the other, God only knew why, carrying enough explosives to blast that great crater in the Turkey Creek road. Why?

* * *

George heard the news from Walling by telephone. He hung up and leaned back in his chair, suddenly old and tired and wanting respite. Scott was with him, and Paul, and when through the open study door he saw Ellen, he beckoned her and she came to stand beside Paul's chair, her hand on Paul's shoulder. George told them what had happened. He told them straight out—there was no other way. And when he had finished there was only silence.

George stirred himself. "At least partly my fault," he said, and he raised his hand to forestall objection. "I can live with it. I have to because I have no intention of giving up life."

They watched him quietly.

"You two," George said to Paul and the girl, "haven't made the bad mistakes yet. Maybe you never will. I hope not. But you are going to have to walk carefully because the mis-

363

takes are always there, waiting to be made—when you have responsibility."

Scott said quietly, "That means what?"

"Lucero," George said. "He came here to show me that he is an honest man. I believe him. You," he said to Paul, "have believed him all along. Can you deal with him? For me? For us?"

Ellen opened her mouth and closed it again. Her hand tightened on Paul's shoulder and the diamond flashed.

So Ruben had been right, Paul thought, when he said that one day they would negotiate together. Well, he, Paul Meyer, would remember how it looked from below. "Yes, sir," he said. Ellen's hand was warm and strong on his shoulder. He covered it with his own. "I can. I will."

George nodded. "There is another matter." He hesitated. Was it fair to pile on the responsibility right at the start? And the answer, too, was plain. It was. Either you accepted responsibility or you did not, and if you did then the amount you could carry had to be determined. The sooner, the better. How long ago had he found that out. "Talk to your brother," he said. "You and he decide what is to be done about Cleary Ward." It was as if at least a part of his own load had been lifted. "It is time," he said, "to pass the work along."

36

Conchita sat beside the bed. They had rigged an oxygen tent of transparent plastic, and through it the senator's face was clearly visible, shrunken, gray; stubble blotched his cheeks and his chin. His breathing was audible, labored, but his eyes, watching Conchita, were alive.

Conchita said, "Do you want me to send for George and Scott? They're just downstairs."

The head waggled faintly on the pillow. The lips formed two words, "Just you." The eyes tried to speak.

"Almost fifty years," Conchita said. "Not many are that lucky." She was unaware that she was speaking in Spanish. "And few women ever know as good a life as mine has been. Do you remember our first year in Washington? George was two and Peter Juan only one. We didn't have Scott until the next year." She shook her head. "Pregnant in that Washington summer heat, I wished you had chosen another career, Mike."

The lips moved faintly in a ghost of a smile.

"Not really, of course," Conchita said. "I've loved it as

365

much as you have." She had switched unconsciously to English. "Do you think I should write my memoirs, Mike? Describe the pecking order in female Washington?"

The lips moved again with amusement. The breathing was heavy, harsh. The eyes never left Conchita's face.

"Do you remember, Mike," she said, "when that French minister, I forget his name, called on the acting secretary and discovered that his fly was unzipped, and zipped it up but got his necktie caught in it and had to walk out to his car bent double?" It was a favorite anecdote. "So many things to remember," Conchita said, "and laugh about. That favorite saying of yours: 'Take your work seriously, never yourself.' I wish more would do it. Oh, Mike, I'm going to miss you."

The head waggled faintly. The eyes tried to speak.

"I know," Conchita said. "I'll have George and Scott and Ellen and Julia." She shook her head. "But you're the important one. You have always been. Oh, you have been a handful at times, for me, as well as for half of Washington—the important half. You have been a good man, Mike, as well as a great man. There will be letters and telegrams to tell me so, but I've known it longer than they have. Do you know what a paradox you have been in my life? Because I was raised to revere some institutions, never to question them or even examine them. And yet the quality that first attracted me to you was your irreverence, your unwillingness to take anything on faith, your ability to stick pins into pompous balloons and stuffed shirts and to destroy sacred cows that ought to have been slaughtered years ago.

"You can be proud, Mike. You have helped to make a world that is better than the one we grew up in. Oh, there are those who say it isn't, but you and I know that it is. Young people now want to change it. They are changing it. I can't think that is bad, and I know that you agree. It is their world, not ours, and if sometimes I may feel uncomfortable in it, why, that is the price I pay for growing older. We have said all this before, many times. How we have talked, Mike. Do you know that when we were first married, I wondered what we, what any couple, would find to talk about after the first few days?

"Do you remember, Mike, that spring in Scotland? The

hotel at what was the place—Drymen? A lovely place. There have been so many lovely places. But always, always this was the place we wanted to come back to. You always said that chauvinism is buried deep in all of us. It is true. I know that now. I understand why we dropped everything in Washington and came back. California." She smiled. "Home." And then softly, "Goodbye, Mike." She stood up, and walked steadily out into the dressing room of the suite.

Dr. Ross stood up.

"He is gone, doctor," Conchita said. She walked out into the hallway and down the stairs to carry the word.